DECADENCE

THE CRADLE OF DARKNESS BOX SET

ADDISON CAIN

Cover art by Elysium Book Covers

Read on, dear reader. Read on for tales of vampires, of true love, and of things that go bump in the night.

CATACOMBS

CRADLE OF DARKNESS, BOOK ONE

Catacombs is a tale of horror.

1

The whole city of New York stank.

Boulevards, vacant due to poor weather, crusted with a slush of mud and garbage. But it was the living crammed inside tightly packed houses, drinking coffee by their radios, snoring in their beds, that stung Pearl's nostrils.

She could hear them, their scratching and breaths. Worse she could smell them.

Every last one reeked under cheap perfume and lack of washing.

Patchy fur collar hitched up to cover cold ears, cloche hat doing little to keep the snow off her face, she kept her arms tight around her middle and plodded onward through the night streets. Under the threadbare coat, a fringed dress too short for common decency did nothing to keep out the winter chill. Each draft up her hem set her teeth chattering, stronger gusts earning a hiss.

Even with the smell, no matter the icy cold, she wasn't complaining.

So far, life in the big city was grand.

She'd had a busy night in the smoke-filled supper club, *Palace Delight*. Her neck may have been sore from supporting the weight of her cigarette box's strap, but she'd made two dollars. Added to the cash she'd earned the night before, and the night before that, Pearl was set to have a little extra for New Year's.

Maybe she'd get a new dress, or a nice lamp to spruce up her apartment. Better yet, some ruffled lace curtains for the room's single window—something pretty that would frame the view of the street below but keep the sun bright on her body when she slept beneath it.

She'd never had so fine a place to sleep. The walls were papered in fading floral ribbons, linoleum floors showed previous tenants' wear, but the one room abode was all hers. If she was lucky and kept to the night hours, it would be many years before neighbors even noticed she lived there. She might continue to enjoy her view of the busy street, remain sheltered, while decades crept by.

Small town life had been much more complicated. Everyone asked questions, everyone watched. Big cities, no matter how bad the inhabitants inside their borders reeked, were a boon.

If she played her cards right, no one would know that... that there was something deeply wrong with her.

All Pearl had to do was stay out of trouble.

"Hey, girly."

She'd heard him, but she knew better than to so much as raise her chin to a stranger on the street, daylight or midnight.

The Roaring Twenties offered much for a girl... but it had not changed the hardline manner of men. They were as much trouble as they'd ever been.

This one, in his pricy coat and polished wingtips, had no place wandering her working class neighborhood at 3:00 a.m. This one, huddled under the corner drug store's awning, didn't smell of bootleg whiskey; he didn't sway from too much drink. He had not come from one of the speakeasies and just gotten lost. Even from across the street, Pearl could smell that there was no lingering wash of women's perfume telling the tale of a late night dalliance with a mistress to explain his midnight stroll in foul weather.

Cocky by half, he was lurking with a purpose and by the growing beat of his heart, he'd found it: prey.

Poor women made easy targets.

Two more blocks and she'd have a locked door between herself and everyone else in Manhattan. Two more blocks and there would be nothing to worry about.

The would-be Casanova pushed from the building, cutting across the slushy street in a beeline for her. "Isn't it a little late for a stroll?"

Pearl took a sharp left, hoping he'd be wiser than to follow.

He was not.

She'd stolen a sidelong glance at his face, but did not

recognize the man. It wasn't her habit to catalogue each patron she'd served. After all, they came and went night after night. Hell, she rarely spoke more than one word during her shifts unless she had to. *"Cigarette?"* A quick nod and an exchange of funds and Pearl would slip to the next table. *"Cigarette?"*

Her job wasn't to be memorable. It was to be pretty while making correct change. That's what they paid her for.

Pearl could afford her little room on the fifth floor of the Madison Building. She didn't have to make small talk or flirt. Beyond the occasional pat on the rump, patrons left her alone. No one really wanted to gab with a cigarette girl. She was part of the scenery—an ornament that made underground supper clubs like Palace Delight swanky. It was the female patrons who earned all the attention. Pearl's hair wasn't sparkling bottle blonde like theirs, it wasn't finger waved and bedecked with feathers. Hers was sleek and dark, heavy bangs across her brow, bob tight and simple.

Men didn't follow her home...

But then again, it seemed this one had been waiting for her.

"I'm talkin to you!" The stranger grabbed her elbow, yanking Pearl back so hard her heel broke on the ice. A dumpster hit her back... and everything went wrong.

Everything always went wrong.

2

Frantic, Pearl scrubbed her hands together under the tap. She couldn't get the blood off fast enough. Icy water sloshed, her hands shaking so hard little drops of pink water splattered the cracked sink, leaving a macabre mess on the porcelain.

"You've done it this time." Harshly whispered self-chastisement stuttered past chattering teeth. "You should have just let him have his fun."

Acid hit the back of her throat. One gag and her stomach emptied.

Tears running from her eyes, Pearl gripped the side of the sink. Red smeared the bowl but it was nothing to the horrid puddle of bloody vomit the drain could not draw down fast enough.

A little whirlpool grew in the mess. Running water

diluted the crimson from deep red to a light blush. All the while, hot tears ran down cold cheeks.

The man had tasted terrible.

Mottled bruises marked her cheek where the stranger had struck her. The back of her head was a pulped mush from the impact of the sidewalk. One look in the mirror told her there was more blood... in her hair, around her mouth, saturating the black wool of her only coat.

Torn throats made a mess.

Behind a split lip, a pair of delicate fangs remained distended. She'd been unable to retract them, too upset and far too scared.

Bloodshot from weeping, violet eyes stared back at her. "You have to wash off the blood. You have to wash your coat. You have to clean this room before anyone wakes up. Stop crying."

A block and a half away, a corpse was being dusted by snow, the same snow that bore a pair of uneven tracks right to her door.

At her back, the communal bathroom door was locked, but it was only a matter of time before one of the other tenants knocked so they might get ready for work. It took over an hour before water off her coat ran clear, for Pearl to wash her hair in the sink, to clean up the cuts and scrapes.

The sun was rising by the time she huddled in her bed. Outside her only window, the storm raged on, and the world looked white and clean.

Pearl knew what was hidden under that snow, and in a matter of hours, so would the rest of New York.

Black and white photographs of the sprawled corpse filled front page news. He'd been found frozen solid, mild bruising on his arms and legs, throat torn open—bite marks identified on his neck. Beside the horror was the smiling image of a handsome man of quality reputation. Chadwick Parker: entrepreneur, man about town, and son of the powerful Judge Parker. He glowed with life in that photograph, handsome and chirpy—a real heartbreaker.

One conniving lie of a man.

Good Christian men didn't attack seemingly defenseless women in dark alleys. They didn't rape them.

Pearl knew better than to assume she had been the first woman he'd followed home. Over the years, how many others had he hurt?

She wasn't sorry he was dead… but she could still taste his sour blood in her mouth, could feel him shoving his cock inside her, and felt completely unclean.

Though the man who attacked her would never be able to hurt her again, she was the one left terrified.

The police were looking for the killer. For her.

The boroughs had grabbed onto the story, the press sensationalizing every known fact regarding the grotesque murder. Though the body had not been exsanguinated, it didn't matter. The official coroner's report stated that long, sharp teeth had been the weapon—that they had torn through the carotid artery while gnawing a path from left to right.

It did not resemble the bite of any known animal. The bite pattern appeared human, save two fang-like incisors.

The City Daily had been the first paper to use the word *vampire*.

Illustrious Chadwick Parker's death was treated as the most vicious murder New York had seen in ages. *Keep your children inside after dark, your womenfolk safe. Nightmares lurked in the cold dark.* No one mentioned that he'd been found with his fly open, cock out, or asked why he had been on a late night stroll through a shoddy neighborhood during a blizzard.

"Cigarette?"

Every table, every canoodling couple was whispering, boasting, making conjecture on the same thing. Her.

"Cigarette?"

Pearl had never felt physically well a time in her life, but since that man's fetid blood had pooled in her mouth, she could hardly keep anything down.

More bones than curves in her clothes, her paunchy boss was dissatisfied with what he saw. "You look like shit."

It wasn't just her flagging looks. Pearl had been jumping at shadows; she'd knocked over drinks on guests. Her time at the supper club was up, her little room with its window was going to be lost, and once again, any type of life she had tried to imagine for herself had been ruined.

She should have known better than to hope things might be different.

Pearl, her voice low so the other girls wouldn't hear, said, "Just give me one more night, sir."

"You ain't been so bad, Pearl. You show up on time, do your job… but no one wants to look at a skeleton slinging cigs."

"I'll put on more rouge, take the section farthest from the stage lights." Lightheaded, she flat out begged. "One more night, Mr. Weller. Please?"

He was unconvinced, eyeing the dark marks under her eyes, the bony knobs of her shoulders. "You got the consumption?"

That wasn't what was wrong with her. "No, sir. I am just hungry. Winters are hard."

"Well, for Christ's sake, eat something, girl!"

She took his admonishment as approval, and flung the strap of her cigarette box over her head. Once she had it flush to her neck, she offered a close mouthed smile. "Thank you."

Rushing from the dressing rooms, she heard Mr. Weller call at her back, "The first complaint I get, you're gone, kid."

Smile glued on, everything was by the book: drop a curtsey at each table, stay moving, no lounging. Assure guests were happy. The sidelong glances, Pearl could handle, even the occasional look of disgust at her split lip. If they sneered, she smiled even bigger, fangs retracted, all her teeth on display, until they stopped sneering and looked through her.

That was how people worked; that was the world Pearl had always known.

One more night, two more dollars then she would leave her little apartment with its floral papered walls and single overhead light. In a pair of sturdy shoes, she could walk to

Boston or maybe Philadelphia. It would take time, weeks, but there would be no more scary newspapers, no more feeling like the buildings were closing in around her.

She could find a job just like this one, maybe even another apartment with a window.

Or... what if she didn't leave? What if she took some time and ate a great deal? If she could fatten her cheeks up by spring, maybe Palace Delight would want her back. Without funds her room would be lost, but living on the street wasn't so bad. She'd done it before; she could do it again.

Hope, it was a vicious deceiver, but still it came to prick at her heart. It had been two weeks and no soul had knocked on her door. Perhaps New York was big enough to shield her. After all, she'd come here for a reason. The Big Apple, the Golden City she'd dreamed of for decades. Art Deco, shimmering buildings, picture shows.

Everything would be fine.

A deep breath and her smile became genuine.

True to his word, Mr. Weller fired her at the end of the shift, but not without payment. He even tucked an extra dollar in her hand out of charity. By the time she'd pulled on her coat and stepped out into the icy night, her bad turn had begun to feel manageable.

He'd hire her back, Pearl was certain. She just needed to gain some weight first. The long walk home was a good place to start. There were always rats in New York City, and they were easy enough to catch.

She snatched up two, draining each out of sight of the street. When her teeth sunk into the third, her heart stopped racing, her breath became even for the first time in days, and feeling began to come back to her frozen toes.

Starving herself out of fear of the shadows had been unwise. It was a mistake she promised herself not to repeat.

The dead, mangy creature was dropped on dirty snow. A full sigh puffed like smoke in the chilled air, Pearl leaning her head back against the brick wall of a dreary tenement. In the narrow alley, sandwiched between two tall buildings she had a small view of a pretty sky to enjoy.

"I can smell the human's blood on your coat, apostate."

Cutting off her startled shriek, a hand closed over her mouth... a hand attached to an arm that had grown from the wall at her back.

Screaming behind the clamp of rough fingers, Pearl threw a terrified glance side to side in a desperate attempt to see who'd caught her.

Nobody was there, only a wall and a garbage bin.

Fear elongated fangs behind her lips, kohled lashes spiked with cake mascara went so wide, the whites of her eyes shone bright in the dark.

The feeling of jagged mortar grinding against her spine melted away, morphing from ice cold brick to the firm body of a man.

He hoisted her upward, despite her frantically kicking legs, while silent figures materialized to her left and her right.

Brick met her face, cheek split, teeth cracked.

Dazed from the blow, Pearl's mouth gaped and her eyes settled on an angel.

The being, the stranger, gripped her chin, his fingers

distorting her cheeks as he smiled. That grin promised pain, the torments of hell, and was the most terrifying thing Pearl had seen in her long, laborious life.

Begging was not beneath her. "I never meant to hurt anyone."

From the monster's mouth, a milky white pair of razor sharp teeth grew long and menacing.

Two long fangs just like hers.

It could not be…

It couldn't.

Things like her did not exist. She was sick, that was all. She was sick and needed the absolution of God to save her from her deformity and perverse hungers.

Instinct would disagree with her. One look at those fangs and Pearl hissed, began to fight in earnest, and was punished horribly.

The smiling man jammed his fingers into her mouth. Gagging when he hooked her fang, she tried to bite. It took several hard jerks, but with a final twisting wrench, he ripped her tooth straight from her skull.

Gums torn, the socket open and spurting blood, Pearl wailed.

No pain she'd ever known compared to this.

Her second fang was gouged out, her cheek ripped fully apart from corner to ear when the man laughing in her face caught his sharpened nail on the flesh.

The angel had no interest in her words, the question in her eyes, or her gurgled prayers... only her agony.

3

Feet dragging over pavement, a stream of blood poured from her mouth to mark the path. In the time it took to bring her to this place, she had counted them. Three men with angelic faces and evil hearts had hauled her the distance, and not a single soul had seen.

Dangling between them, the best she could do was press a hand to her maimed face, swallow the constant flow of blood collecting in her mouth, and weep. Her attacker had taken more than her fangs, he had taken her misguided hope that there might be answers to her life—that there might be more for her than year upon year of isolation and loneliness.

There were others like her.

How could she have never known?

Even as they'd beat her, Pearl had tried to ask them what they were. But these men, these glowing angels, were so much stronger and possessed no pity for what they'd deemed *an apostate*.

She was going to die, be ravaged. If what he'd done to her face was any example, it would be a painful and brutal end.

Sticky crimson ran down her chin, over her neck, staining her clothes. Trying to keep her jaw together despite torn tendons and shredded skin, she failed at speech. Useless lolling tongue only smeared gore from ear to ear, mixed it with her tears.

Tearing the fabric, her coat was yanked down skinny arms, the girl left in only the supper club's flashy uniform and torn stockings. And that was how they made her walk down the dark, littered alley where she expected they would murder her and leave her to rot.

It was not a good place to die.

Hair in the grip of the one who'd torn out her teeth, head bent back, she saw one last view of the stars.

The man began to chant.

Groaning in protest of the unnatural bend of her spine engorged a bubble of blood on her cheek. It popped, her bones cracked in symphony with her captor's guttural pronunciations, and the world lurched.

Vision distorted, walls leaning toward her as if ready to crumble and crush her to dust, Pearl watched the awful world twist in upon her and turn her inside out.

This must be death.

A moment later, it was over.

The grim reaper had not come. Her heart still banged

against her chest, her blood still poured from her ruined mouth, and pain only grew.

They were no longer standing in the snow, hidden between tight row houses. Now, uneven, time-worn masonry was under her feet, her scream echoing off an arched stone roof, with not a speck of sky to be seen.

The cry died, and all around them the sound of softly traded conversation, the noise of footfalls echoing as if they stood in a great cathedral replaced it.

A church?

But there were no crosses or priests, only a congregation of strangers watching as she was dragged deeper into the sanctum.

Maybe she had died and this was how she was to be judged, bleeding and broken before heaven's shining hosts.

As she was dragged forward, she caught a glimpse of the quiet crowd watching her advance. She found the gazes of curious strangers.

She disgusted them. Some even sniffed her way, sneering.

A sharp kick hit the back of her legs; knees knocked into stone so hard her teeth snapped and the pain in her jaw doubled. Hunched over, Pearl clutched her torn cheek, pathetic, scared, and completely confused.

The angel who'd torn out her teeth and ripped open her face shouted so all might hear, "This apostate is responsible for abandoning the remains of Chadwick Parker where humans would find them. I have brought it before you, my lord, as you ordered." He threw her stolen coat on the ground before them. "And here is the proof. The dead human's blood is matted into her coat."

Tightening his fingers until her scalp burned, the man jerked her head back so all might look upon her ruined face.

The men and women gathered around whispered excitedly, but Pearl saw none of it, heard nothing. From the moment her head had been flung back, her eyes were fixed in horror, glued to the *thing* that waited at the head of the room.

This was not heaven and she was not to be judged by God…

It was dim, the chamber lit only with gas lamps instead of the popular electric bulb, but she saw the visage of the fallen one. Light flickered, drawing the pits and edges of its face into stark relief. More hideous than any imagined devil, it spoke, glowing red eyes engaged upon the man who held her down. "Ten days it took you to find the one responsible, and all you have to show me is one unremarkable, toothless female."

Towering over her, her captor answered his liege. "Weak as it is, it obviously has not fed in days. My lord, it thought to hide from your authority. Once it emerged, the apostate was captured easily, defanged with minimal effort. Its teeth I offer to you."

Like the shabby coat, the bloodied pair of elongated incisors were tossed to bounce like dice toward the feet of the monstrosity.

The *gift* was ignored.

The devil turned his eyes to her instead. The power of

that burning red gaze traveled like a living thing to settle on her bloodied face.

It stared through her, unmoving where it rotted in its seat. Rope-like muscle encased prominent bones—as if the creature's flesh had wilted in the grave. Grotesque as it was, its form remained massive.

It wanted to see the whole of her face, demanded that she lower her hand—Pearl could hear him whispering into her mind, urging absolute obedience. There was no possible question of resisting. Weak, her fingers slipped from where she'd relentlessly tried to hold her jaw together, the damage on display for all to see.

Her captor had called her toothless; Pearl grasped the slander was meant to shame. It did. She was almost as hideous as the demon.

Incapable of forming words, incapable of screaming, she could not move, not a muscle, when an arm stretched impossibly far across the room. Boney fingers slid over the ruined side of her face. He probed, snagging her bloody lip to prod the empty sockets and the bits of exposed bone between torn gums.

Her throbbing, horrible pain faded into nothing.

An unexpected caress of the devil's thumb wiped away her steady trail of tears, the long yellowed nail at the end careful not to scratch.

Just as the pain had vanished, her fear began to drain away until she was empty of all things.

Red, scorching eyes were all she might fathom, her end

and her beginning. Nothing else mattered; nothing existed but that rotting devil and her.

A flicker of satisfaction and his interrogation began. "Child?"

The mummified monstrosity cupped her jaw, holding it in place to facilitate her speech. Tongue thick, Pearl found herself answering without hesitation. "Yes?"

Raspy and horrid, his voice slithered through her ears. "Did you slay the human, Chadwick Parker, and leave his body on the street?"

She blinked once. More tears fell from red-rimmed eyes, her voice vacant. "He was hurting me. It was the only way to make him stop."

The unblinking monster projected his pleasure, looking upon her as if beholding something truly worth devouring. "Tell me what happened."

Still as stone, legs awkward under her, Pearl found herself leaning into the corpse-like touch. "It was dark. I didn't want to talk to him."

"And?"

"He forced me down, tore up my skirt so fast he was inside me before I could scream." No one would have come even had they heard her cry for help. People didn't go down dark alleys in search of damsels in distress.

Humans ignored screams in the night.

The demon answered her unspoken thoughts. "Because they are nothing but animals."

"It hurt."

There was no change in the fierce expression of the creature who commanded the room, only more demands. "Why leave the body?"

What had the devil expected her to do with it? "I had to crawl away before anyone saw."

"And in doing so broke a crucial law." If such a thing were possible, he seemed even more immense, her immediate world nothing but withered lips and glowing eyes full of fire. "Like any vassal under my rule, you must be punished."

Her words came jumbled, as if from a drunken mouth. "I'm scared."

The beast almost seemed to smile. "An apostate should be scared. You'll be lucky to survive what's coming."

"I don't understand." Pearl blinked, a twin trail of tears escaping dazed eyes.

"You entered my city without permission, hid from my authority, and thought to hunt here, leaving a mess humans identified correctly. Is that clear enough for you?"

No. Even with her mind filled by the will of something powerful, Pearl disputed what the monstrosity had said. "Vampires are not real. I'm deformed. I'm sick. If I am faithful, God will have mercy on me."

The monster chuckled, then seemed to catch something in her thoughts that stopped his mirth. "You believe such ridiculousness to be true."

Sniffing, feeling her mind mush as the monster dug deeper, Pearl wept. "I want to go home."

Utter silence grew between them. Glowing eyes burned, the creature's concentration palpable. It clawed its way through her head, scraping through memory, picking apart what she was.

It startled.

At length, words came from the demon's mouth. “You have brought me a daywalker. It doesn’t know what it is.”

A ripple moved around her, strange enough to fractionally distract the girl kneeling on the flagstones. Incessant buzzing murmurs grew, *daywalker* whispered again and again.

“This one is to serve her sentence in solitary confinement.” An announcement came from the throne, the room silenced by their rotting lord. “See that she is fed, Malcolm, and seal the door. Brick it shut.”

The dreamlike quality that had invaded Pearl’s senses came to an abrupt end. When the gnarled hand of the monster receded, her pain roared back to life. Scooped into the crushing arms of the stone-faced angel who offered no pity, she was carried away from the mob and deep into the dark underground.

4

nchored to the floor by spilt wax, the flicker of a single candle offered the damp crypt's solitary illumination.

Pressed against the opposite wall, another sorry soul shared Pearl's gloom—a man, cowering and crying, whom Malcolm had shoved into the cell shortly before he'd locked her away. Together, they both listened to the splat and bang of brick piled up on the other side of the room's only exit.

Their eyes met over that candle, both aware this was their end.

A moldering cot under her, Pearl rocked, arms tight around her knees, as if the pain of her cheek and gums might be soothed by such movement.

Nothing helped.

She was in agony.

"Please... don't hurt me." Like a cornered animal, the man—and unlike the other things she'd seen upstairs, he was a man—stared at her with wide, bloodshot eyes.

He was petrified.

Pearl could hear his heart, the thrum of his blood loud, but she paid him no mind, too wrapped up in her own misery to care.

The panicked stranger watched, bracing, as if she were going to leap up to devour him. "It wasn't my fault... I told them it wasn't my fault. I don't want to die."

Head throbbing, she snapped, words lisped by slack, swollen lips, "No one wants to die. It doesn't change the fact that everyone does."

He sputtered out a list of excuses as if she might exonerate him of whatever crime landed him in the same room as her. "The boy. Yes, I took him... but I didn't mean to kill him. I don't belong here, dame. You gotta believe me. I do not deserve this!"

Pearl wanted silence. "The *thing* upstairs would disagree."

The fretting human was so much larger than her, but he cowered as if a slurring, toothless girl was the greatest threat in existence. "Please don't eat me. I want to go home..."

"Eat you?" She scoffed. The taste of men was foul and this one smelled especially vile. "I am not going to eat you. Find your way out. Go home for all I care."

He took her word to heart, and like a fool, tried to pry open the door. "It won't budge."

Nor would it.

It was bricked shut.

Unless he was set free in a few days, the male would die from lack of water and food. Then she would have his corpse for company and the sweet smelling rot that putrefied the dead. And it would grow quiet—fitting that they'd shoved her into an old tomb.

Pearl had to admit, the candle was an interesting touch... one last moment of light soon to snuff out. The stone walls held no windows, only the notched shelves of a coffin-less crypt, the cot, and the dirt.

When she'd first been dragged into this horrible place, before her interview with the devil, the stone structure looked like a church. Now she was certain it had been before being desecrated. It was the feel to the place: ungodliness, desperation. Bad things had happened in these halls over various, sundry years. How many other old tombs held prisoners bricked away to rot? How many of them had one final candle?

Pearl considered burning her clothing to extend the light, but it seemed pointless. Dark would intercede soon enough, and she'd rather be warm—as warm as one can be in a freezing box—than hold onto false hope.

Knees under her chin, she watched the flame spark on the last fragment of wick, until it was only an ember. The tang of smoke in the air, the space grew stygian. Eyes open or closed, it made no difference. There was nothing to see.

But there was something to fear.

Now that all the light had been snuffed out, she could feel *it* watching from the dark.

Before having her cast down into this pit, *it* had looked at her, the feel of *its* cold hands had caressed her face. She could see the glowing red eyes, the devil peering at her from the lightless abyss. And then he was there, growing from the shadows, seeping up from the floor as if pulling darkness into the form of his desire.

Screwing her eyes shut, Pearl buried her face against her knees.

Standing over her, towering and projecting agitation, the demon hissed, "You were ordered to be fed. Why is this human still living?"

The human started screaming.

Pearl shrieked herself when a cold touch landed on her stinging scalp. "I can't!"

The caress of talon tipped fingers tripped over her skull. The feel of wind moved through her hair, the creature's nails teasing a lock of blood-matted sable. "Have you not learned how to bleed them without using your teeth? It is not difficult to open a vein."

Why was it touching her, lightly following the shell of her ear with a claw?

Petrified, Pearl tried not to breathe, not to move. Still the red-eyed monster explored, dipping his yellowed fingernail lower to explore the curve of her throat before pulling away.

Moments later, across the room there was a wet, squelched squeal from the human.

His screaming stopped.

"There, I have done it. His throat is open. Drink."

Pearl refused to budge.

Another threat was issued. "Do you wish me to force you, child? Obey me at once."

Her disgust was obvious.

"So be it." The *thing* took her by the hair, tilting her head back. Something hot and wet dripped on her cheeks. Papery lips fell on hers, the devil's mouth opening so coppery fluid might pour from him to her.

Gagging, Pearl tried to push him off. It was no use. He was going to drown her if she didn't swallow. Obeying, blood went down her throat like acid all the way to her belly. The instant the demon pulled away, she retched, every last drop spit up on her lap.

"I see..."

It drew away, Pearl curling into a sobbing ball on the cot.

She didn't need to see him to know what the red-eyed monster was doing. Sounds of slurping, of human pain, mixed together until the dying man's stuttering heartbeat told the story.

When it was done, a corpse thudded against the floor, and once again *it* slithered closer. "Shall I offer a female? Can you drink from them?"

In sharp jerks, Pearl shook her head.

A smile altered the monster's growl. "What of children, babies... do they not tempt you?"

She was going to throw up again. "God, help me."

Again he dared to lay his hand atop her head, to finger the spot where chunks of hair had been ripped out by his minion.

A laugh layered the devil's offer. "And what of me, do I entice your attention?"

Pearl vehemently refused, shrinking from the feel of unyielding arms slowly encircling her shoulders. The cot creaked, the weight of the demon settling close enough those glowing red eyes hovered inches from her face.

When instinct moved her to struggle, to kick and scream as if she stood even a chance of forcing the vile thing from her, the devil seeped into her mind. He manipulated her just as he'd done when she'd been dumped before his throne—slipping behind her barrier of fear—taking it away until his prey lay still and calm.

He had her quiet. He had her controlled. "Tell me your name in this life."

Torn lips parted. "...Pearl."

"And you find me so repulsive, Pearl?" The creature did not require a reply. Instead he offered a lesson. "I offered you dark, so you might not gaze upon what you openly recoiled from at first sight, and still you cower. I offered you food, the comfort of my presence, a gentle touch... yet still you dare to refuse my attention"—the red-eyed demon let that horrid gaze go to her ruined mouth—"my Pearl."

Powerless, she unfolded when his body shifted against her, bowing back at the feel of a light grip about her throat. Unable to see beyond the glow of his eyes, she could only feel—the chill of him, the whisper of his breath on her face.

Pinned to the mattress, Pearl lay listless while his fingers both crept and cradled. He moved her at will, laying her head to the crook of his shoulder, her legs entangled in the tattered fabric of his rotting garments.

"So lovely..." He was more enraptured than she, fingertips ghosting over the arch of her brow, teasing the fringe of her lashes.

The icy touch receded, but not before the tatters of her jaw were made to part.

There was a crunch, a sound similar to the snaps of splitting wood, and the thing began to bleed. Having rent its own tongue straight down the middle, it laved it against the roof of Pearl's mouth, over her teeth, until the sweetest flavor she had ever tasted began to trickle down her throat.

Blackberry cordial. Melted ice cream. It was like sipping moonlight laced with wine.

Sluggishly, thick blood flowed, the forked tongue of her tormentor toying with hers. She found herself keening, pants of trapped air puffing from her nostrils as she succumbed to hunger and drank. Sucking his tongue, frustrated when the source of nourishment healed before she'd had her fill, she tried to bite.

Her teeth could not keep his flesh open no matter how she gnawed.

Without her fangs, she could do little more than inspire a rumbling chuckle in the demon's chest.

His invasion of her mind withdrew, the hunger remained. Pearl found it was she who clung to him, she who lapped at his mouth, greedy for more.

That was his trick...

He stole his arms back, left her lying dazed and starving on the cot. "Are you not going to kiss me, Pearl?"

She'd swallowed enough to feel the effects of a sip of darkness. The skin of her cheeks was pulling together, itching as it mended... but her belly was still so hollow.

It wasn't enough.

Daring to admit confusion, repulsion, and delight, Pearl grew drunk. "I'm still hungry."

A sharp nail gently grazing back and forth over her collarbones, the creature smiled. It leaned down, mouth working over her throat, teasing gently at her pulse point. "Shall I slit my throat so you can feed?"

The instant desire for a deeper drink was at odds with clearer thought. What he offered was not what it seemed.

Breathless, eyes open and unblinking in the dark, she felt a sharp nail graze over her nipple and complete revulsion returned. The demon's hand crept lower as if to delve between her legs.

Insidious fear bloomed right back to life, licking through her, ruining any chance Pearl might have had at further reason. She did not beg for mercy, or scream when a talon pierced through her undergarment. She was past that point when a separate flash of claw raked through leathery skin.

The monster sliced himself so deeply, a river spurt over her face.

Perhaps if she had not been so hungry, Pearl might have exercised self-control, but one tiny taste, his offering dripping over her lips, and she latched on despite the dry digit wriggling deeper into her body.

Fixed to his wound, she opened the fissure of flesh, jabbing her tongue into the meat of his neck to force the fountain wider. Greedily she gorged, never having known a meal that fulfilled and warmed as this deep drink did.

While she gorged, it pawed at her clothing, picking it apart with nail and fist until breasts popped free of her dress and cold air moved over bruised thighs. He stripped her naked, the scraps of her clothing left to bunch under their bodies, and then he did the same to his own ancient garments.

She would have drunk him dry, utterly unaware of his actions had his palm not settled like sandpaper over her breast. One scrape of his dry-skinned touch grating her nipple and she whimpered, lips parting from his neck.

It felt... odd.

The pebbled tip of her breast tingled, responded to a pinching roll of the monster's forefinger and thumb. When his thighs purposefully maneuvered to her parted legs, when pressure was placed against her mound, Pearl found she had no focus to resist. Not with that delicious fountain oozing to fill up her mouth.

While she fed, the monster spoke. The things he said, had Pearl been beyond bloodlust, would have set her screaming. "I have waited an eternity for you, *kara sevde*. Your blood will be my blood, your cunt dripping nightly from my attention. Every last part of you will be saturated in me, in your lord. Forget your God, and worship at my feet."

When her belly grew full and her mouth fell from his throat, Pearl was given no absolution.

It was a devious seduction; the red-eyed one having

waited so it might look upon her face when his cock speared straight into her unsuspecting body.

The shock was less from pain and more from astonishment. Pearl's mouth fell open, head thrown back at the intrusion. The deceitful monstrosity had taken raw advantage, leaving her cramped around the dead meat inside her.

Her female parts... the slit he'd called her cunt... felt stretched unmercifully. The burning wash of sensation didn't ease no matter how hard she tried to crawl out from under the unwavering glowing red eyes.

There was no negotiation. He did not try to soothe. Instead the creature roughly jerked his hips, ground against her, and restrained with ease. When his thrust grew more than experimental, when her breasts bounced and friction built, *it* began to groan.

The hissing breaths and pleasure saturated hums were grotesque, the way her body responded sickening.

She was engorged, nerves tingling, tightening, fear and hunger feeding the buildup. If the ruthless pounding did not stop, Pearl was going to split in two.

Tears leaked from her eyes when the ripple of muscle where he invaded began to seize. Unsure what was happening, she called out to her God.

The devil laughed.

Pain crept through nerves, coming to life in her gut, and forming into something obscene.

She wasn't screaming in agony at all, it was something else—something foreign.

Pulling out until only the tip of his instrument was tucked

in her sopping slit. Once she'd found her breath, staring up in horror, it began all over again.

Every time she was on the cusp of abandon, the devil took away what tore her apart. It may have been hours, it may have been days, before Pearl understood his brand of torment.

It was never going to end until she begged for the very thing she found so disgusting.

Sobbing, she asked for mercy. He told her what to say—filthy words worse than any she'd picked up from men in the supper club fell from swollen lips, desperation lacing every last entreaty until the monster reared and redoubled his effort. The instant she discovered her first climax, he put his teeth to her neck, puncturing soft skin.

His cock kicked and he gushed.

He didn't drink much, but exhaustion unlike she'd ever known made Pearl's eyes heavy and her limbs useless. The dusty groan of a beast still filled the air, and it was not until he'd fully savored his pleasure, that the demon laid his lips to the very skin he'd bruised.

Small kisses peppered flesh tender from the scrape of his chest. Gently, he sucked her nipple, tongue teasing, teeth nipping. Warm breath fanned over her flesh as he sighed. "How I wish you would remember the glory of this moment as I will, but alas, that cannot be."

While she lay struck and horrified, it rolled its hips to tease out a cruel reminder that she had enjoyed his blood, his cock, and even his brutality.

The room was once again cold, Pearl aware of the

hideous thing that had fucked her raw and the threat his last words posed. “I don’t want to die.”

If pure evil might be sweet, the demon made an attempt, cooing at her gently. “You are too valuable to break. No, my Pearl, you will be mine forever.”

5

Waking groggy, Pearl turned in her bed and snuggled deeper into soft blankets for warmth. A dull ache irritated her gums, and absently she tongued the spot, only to find two teeth were missing. Not just any teeth, but the sharp teeth she'd tried herself many times in life to wrench out.

The thing that made people afraid of her when she got scared or angry...

Her fangs, were gone.

Throwing back the covers, her hand flew to her mouth, and the shock over the nagging discomfort was replaced with absolute bewilderment.

She had no idea where she was.

There was light, golden and soft around the strangest room she'd ever seen. Not a single window contributed to the glow, only weighty gilded candelabras, ancient in design, strewn about. A small portion of the candles had burned to stubs, beside them fresh tapers with wicks white and untouched waited to be lit.

She was in a bed larger than any she'd ever seen. It gave off the subtle fragrance of teakwood and was foreign in its design and height. Above it draped a canopy, heavy curtains of embroidered gold, tied and gathered by anchors implanted in crumbling stone walls. Layered around her body were red velvet coverlets, the pillows sumptuous and plentiful at her back.

Between the candelabras and bed, there was scant other furniture in the small room. A writing desk took center stage, a thick tome open atop it. Beside the blotter were pens, a brush, a hand mirror. Even a pot of rouge.

There was more, other things littering hoary, somber stone. Strange *fabric* against her skin...

Over her breasts was not the familiar uniform the Palace Delight had charged her three dollars for, but black chiffon. So sheer her nipples were on display, it hung gathered at her shoulders like some tart's version of a nightgown.

Someone had dressed her in this. Someone had put her in this room.

Memories of a man holding her down in the snow, of pain, left her colder than ice. Had he brought her here after he'd finished? Hadn't she killed him?

There had been so much blood…

A sour flavor.

What was going on?

There was no exit save a wooden door straight from a

medieval movie set. Leaning against the portal, half concealing the frame, was a massive mirror. Like the candelabras, it was overly ornate, gaudy, and looked far too heavy for her to move.

Untangling from the covers, Pearl's feet landed on a woven rug of burgundy and cobalt. Under the brightly colored wool lay rushes that crunched the instant she placed weight on her foot. With her every step, the drying grass's scent mingled with the room's must, the smoke from the candles, and the smell of ambergris.

Her wrists had been perfumed.

Nose to her arm, she inhaled, and noticed an ornate ring sparkling on her hand. She had not felt the glimmering collection of stones, but now it held her complete attention. The piece was much larger than the art deco jewelry in fashion; the stones were much grander. In the center was a ruby rounded smooth, as big as an eye, anchored by tarnished gold and surrounded by seed pearls.

Unlike the other objects in the room, something about it was *wrong*. It pinched and felt unwelcome. Yanking the ring from her finger, she cast it off as if it were cursed.

Chest rising and falling in panicked breaths, Pearl tried to make sense of it all—of the stone walls half hidden by pastoral paintings, of the feeling of foreboding—and knew this was a bad place.

Hurtling toward the low, arched exit, she found herself caught by the mirror before her shaking hand might even try the knob.

There was a reason the colossal furnishing had been left

there... the door was only an enticement. The true aim of the object was to get her close enough to the reflective glass to see.

Her hair was no longer clipped into a sleek bob. Wrongly, it hung past her shoulders, tangled from sleep. The shape of her body was foreign as well. Where were her prominent ribs, the dark marks under her eyes?

Yes, she'd always been attractive in her way, but she had never glowed with health. She'd never had soft curves or full breasts.

Blue eyes lacked the makeup she'd painstakingly applied every day. She didn't need the kohl, or the cake mascara. Had she shown up to the Palace Delight looking like *this*, Mr. Weller would have never fired her. He would have promoted her.

Hell, he would have married her.

"Most nights when I come to you, you have yet to look in the mirror. It's the journal that habitually grabs your attention, Pearl."

An unladylike shriek came from the girl, Pearl spinning to find a stranger stepping toward her.

Pinched between long fingernails, he held the ring she'd rejected. He offered it to her, smiling and splendid, but all she could see were his eyes.

They were red as fire and so utterly wrong she thought she might be sick.

Putting the desk between them, she took in the face of what every last woman in Manhattan would deem perfection. He was beautiful, cheeks shaven smooth, dark hair slicked back in the style of Gary Cooper—more handsome than Gary Cooper, if such a thing were possible. But he was not dressed as a gentleman. In nothing more than a long black robe tied with a sash at his waist, he was hardly dressed at all.

Something about him, beyond the blood red of his eyes, set the hairs on the back of her neck to attention.

His gaze lost the crimson glow, growing into an almost soft brown as he smiled. "I am Darius."

Red eyes, cold stone, and the scream of a dying man in the pitch black… fragments of memory echoed until the room with its finery looked like something else.

A tomb full of monsters.

"Where am I?"

His gaze tripped over her breasts, admiration all over his face. "I did not mean to startle you, Pearl. Come closer so I might see that you are well."

Dizzy, Pearl put her fingers to her cheek. It had been torn open last she recalled, held together by a red-eyed demon who'd crept through her mind and asked her his questions.

A single candle in a room colder than death.

A corpse's body moving against and inside her.

Mumbling to herself, caught between the present and the past, Pearl said, "The light went out and you came in."

And now golden light was abundant, the red-eyed demon was back, wrapped up in beautiful skin and walking toward her with a smile.

She dared to counter his advance with a retreat, and a face that was beautiful grew twisted with impatience. "Kneel, my Pearl."

It was as if some unseen force shoved her down. Legs hit the floor, the girl folding downward, her body utterly out of her control at his command.

"Look at me."

In the attitude of prayer, body prostrate and hands clasped before her, Pearl stared up at what had come to tower over her. A manicured hand reached forward as if to bless her.

His fingers were warm, soft, but a ghostly touch of memory came with it. Sandpaper, claws… pain in the dark.

And then memory of something that wasn't pain. The intimate sensation twinging in her belly was profane, as was the urge to reach between her thighs and rub.

The man chuckled. "Your mind goes interesting places, dear girl. You are afraid and aroused all at once. It makes you taste particularly delicious. Are you trying to tempt me? I would hate to neglect my treasure."

A pulsing heart grew between her legs, sweat breaking out over her brow as Pearl's breath grew shallow. "Is this hell?"

The stranger raised her from the floor. "If it was, would it be your hell or mine?"

With no preamble, he cupped her breast, his tongue wetting his lower lip.

Impulse brought her to raise her arm. She struck him.

All her strength, and the slap didn't so much as turn his chin. Instead, it inspired ravenously heated eyes and a growing smile full of unsavory promises

Run.

But there was nowhere to go.

The door met her back, the man pressed indecently to her front. Lips came to her ear, warm breath offering, "You may lie upon the bed, legs obediently parted, and I'll see that you feel the pleasure of my mouth where you itch. Or, you may kiss my hand and beg my forgiveness for such rudeness, and I might find it in my heart to be patient and see to your other needs first." His hand came to her face, taking her jaw with enough strength to be more sinister than sweet. "But never strike me, child, unless you'd like your night to be one of suffering."

She had known enough pain in her life. Seeking mercy from a thing that terrified her very soul, she beseeched, "Please. I didn't mean to kill that man."

Smirking menacingly, the stranger, Darius, captured her fingers. "Darling, kara sevde." He did not break eye contact. The ring she'd thrown slid home, nestled where he desired it to be, and then he lifted her fingertips and kissed them. "You have a weakness for desiring to live in the past. I require you live only in this moment. What came before and what will come after do not matter. They do not exist to you. Nothing but this room and my attention exist to you."

"I don't understand."

His hand came back to her breast, the red-eyed man daring her to slap him again. "What is there to understand? I am your everything, and you are my beloved treasure."

Skin crawling, she knew more than anything that she wanted out of that room—just as much as she wanted the man to stop kneading her breast. "I don't want to be your treasure."

A low growl, demonic in nature preceded, “Where is your gratitude today, Pearl? I do not appreciate when you wake in a temper.”

“I belong to God.”

“And what would God do for my darling one? Where are you safer than here? Where could you be more comfortable? As you are, you’re buried so far under the city no soul could ever find you. No one will take you from me. No others will know the taste of sunshine in your veins. I made them all forget. You exist in my world alone.”

Eyes cast to the ceiling, she offered a prayer. “Jesus, help me.”

“There is no God for you but me. There is no heaven waiting for you. I own your soul and your body. I own your mind, daywalker… your blood.” All of this was spoken gently, lovingly, each word acidic and tainted by evil. His voice burned her. “I am your life and your only reason for existence. Without my care, you would live alone in this tomb for eternity… forgotten by the thing you would pray to.”

Stroking her hair, ignoring her incantations to the Christian Lord, he cooed, “Your affection will earn a reward. Give me a kiss and cease these theatrics at once. I’m giving you one chance to avoid punishment today.”

She shook her head.

He caught her hair with clawed fingers and forced her neck to bend where he willed it. On the straining column of her throat he licked a path all the way to her ear. “I told you to kiss me, Pearl.”

Breath shaking, unable to move from the strength of his grip in her hair, Pearl whimpered, stopped the prayer, and gasped when a little sting set her neck to jumping.

"Delicious. Your fear is almost worth the trouble." A tongue ran over her pulsing vein. "But I have another flavor in mind today."

Stepping back, he released her hair, smirking as she sagged against rough stone.

Twisted in his sweet offer was a much more sinister threat. "Last chance. Kiss me, beg my forgiveness for your rudeness, and let's begin anew."

Pearl didn't want pain, she'd known enough in her life. She didn't want terror, but it was staring her in the face. Swallowing, certain she was going to be ill, she reached for the door handle at her back, and found it frozen.

It would not be moved.

If he was keen to the scrambling of her fingers at her back he said nothing, the gloriously beautiful devil seemingly patient.

Brick it shut, he'd said. She remembered the sounds, the human trying to claw his way out. She remembered what this room truly was.

A crypt to be buried in.

There was no way out.

God did not hear her prayers.

Her tongue tripped, and out of her mouth came the only slice of salvation she could reach. "I'm sorry for my rudeness."

"And?"

He may have been handsome, but she remembered the monster who'd spoken to her from the throne. It was almost impossible to lean forward and press a kiss to the man's cheek, certain he would stink like a rotting corpse.

Instead, he smelled of sandalwood and fresh blood.

Something about it made her mouth water and brought a tingle to empty tooth sockets. The prickling became a sharp pinch, two small teeth descending to burst through the gum-line and end as useless points too short to be of any use.

Chuckling, the demon drove her back until her head hit the impenetrable door and his tongue was deep in her mouth. He licked each smear of blood, toying with her stumped fangs as if she'd performed some cute act.

It was less a kiss and more a scouring, the whole time red glowing eyes staring straight into hers.

With one final tongue curled lick, he pulled away, teasing, "Hungry, are you?"

Yes? No. She wasn't ravenous, not in the ways she remembered. But under the terror, she was hungry for *something*—something sweet and filling that healed the soul and fattened the flesh.

Something that made it all better.

She wanted that delicious succor as one would pine for a drug. Breaking eye contact, she looked to the stranger's neck, whining low in her throat and completely lost in unfamiliar need.

Stretching forward, Pearl caught herself inches from setting her useless teeth to the devil's flesh when it gave a warning tut.

He took her chin, tapping her nose as he counseled. “It is a good thing you stopped yourself this time. Never take what isn’t offered. Though I never allow your mind to cling to the memory, I promise you, it is the worst of punishments I can offer.”

Again her blood went cold. “You make it sound as if I have been here a long time.”

Rolling words full of smoke and brimstone, he asked, “What did I tell you about time? The only time of any worth in your life are the moments you spend with me.”

“How many moments have there been?”

“Not nearly enough.”

What had he done to her in the days she’d lost in this place? What would he do? “And you punish me?”

“When I feel so inclined. But I’m not eager to harm your sweet body tonight.” Turning his back and walking across the room to settle his mass on the edge of the overly large, ornate bed, he said, “This evening I have come to my pet for pleasure. If you please me, I will let you drink your fill. Disappoint my appetites, and I will bring you great pain. For I have no patience for an insolent treasure. Save yourself the torment.” He crooked a finger, calling her forward. “Come here.”

She knew nothing about pleasing men. The men who had used her, had done only that—leaving her sullied and shamed as they’d tucked their cocks away and abandoned her where she’d bled.

It was to be one pain or another.

Pearl could submit now and spare the girl who would

wake tomorrow to some unforeseen horror. Or she could refuse, earn the demon's wrath and know suffering immediately.

She *was* in hell.

Killing Chadwick Parker had landed her here.

One foot in front of the other, ten steps total, and she stood before her tormenter.

Darius took her wrist, brought it to his lips to gently kiss, before yanking her face first into the mattress. Tense and trembling she lay as she fell, cheek to red velvet. He stood and moved behind her, flipping the girl face up.

"It's like the first time every time, isn't it? My Pearl is practically a virgin. Always fresh. Always frightened." Creeping over her body, he took her gauze-draped nipple into his mouth for a sharp suck. Once it popped free, he teased, "But I know how to make the virgin a whore."

Eyes to the bed curtains, fingers fisted in the sleeves of the man's robe, Pearl tried to lay still. Let him do what he may, let him take, knowing the night would end and she would forget all of it.

Tomorrow would be better.

6

There was no tomorrow.

The first time he'd fucked her had been slow, deviously tender. It didn't feel like the same frightening creature who'd taunted, threatened, and mocked.

He took her as one takes a lover, a cherished wife. Long kisses, sweet touches, even the sweeping entry of his engorged cock had been smooth. Long nailed fingers drifted over her body, delving into places that brought unimaginable pleasures. She could have wept knowing love like that might truly exist in the world and that she'd never know it.

This *thing* didn't love her. The proof was there in his violence when he'd grown bored of soft moans and fluttering cunts.

With his semen dripping from her slit, Pearl had panted, satisfied in body from a kind of release she'd never known.

Or had known many times but could not remember.

He'd pulled out, kissed her on the mouth as if she'd behaved perfectly, then abruptly shunted his arm straight inside the place he'd just used—all of his fingers, his fist to the wrist as she bucked, screaming for him to get them out.

Ripped and bleeding, he'd just as brusquely tore them away, leaving her hole gaping, oozing a blend of her pulped flesh, his cum, and a steady flow of blood.

Her womb had been torn, her tunnel ruined, and with his teeth growing long and sinister, he met the screaming girl's eye and watched her try to escape. He licked up the mess, swallowed bits of flesh, and savored her every cry.

Healing under those teeth and tongue, her insides knit back in place, her vaginal passage grew once again tight, and all the damage his nails had done disappeared into new flesh that was pink and engorged from vigorous attention.

The cruel lover concentrated his tongue near the top of her sex. What he did there arched her back in both loathing and unbearable sensation.

Restraining her with ease, he licked and sucked her swollen nub, twisting her nerves until she came, sobbing for mercy.

He stared down at the quivering mouth of her cunt, smirking at the pink fluttering lips that framed a hole empty and aching no matter how hard she'd climaxed. Shelving his chin atop her mound, Darius ran his gaze upward over her wildly heaving ribs to meet frantic eyes. "You wet the bed."

Too far gone in her terror, all she could do was sob and wildly shake her head. She even begged him for help as if he were not the root of all her torment.

"Poor dear." His weight came off of her thighs, Pearl curing into a ball.

It was a short reprieve, for the *contented* devil was eager for more flesh.

She shook like a leaf as he cooed and fussed, kissing healing bruises, whispering words of love against her skin. "Come now, my Pearl. Let me show you my love."

It was almost impossible to speak. "This is not love."

Groaning out a blissfully broken laugh, the man licked her tears. "In my thousands of years ruling our kind, I have never cared for a single female with such devoted attention. Not one of my own flock have I used since you became my possession—no matter how the slavering bitches beg for it. I have filled your home with treasures; drained many humans night after night so my face might please you and my blood might be sweet." A lingering kiss was pressed to her slack mouth. "My entire existence is faithful to my delicate daywalker and the light she shares with me."

Too much had been done in the short hours since she'd woken in the cursed room. Clinging to a pillow as if it could offer salvation, she buried her face and cried, "You promised to be gentle."

"Is this not bliss?" Tangling his fingers through her hair, he forced her head back, drew her body to his chest, and sighed. "When you weep for me, I can taste the sunshine in your tears. When I drain you almost to the point of death, I can even stand in it for a few short minutes before I begin to burn. Whoever raped your mother and left her alive after the feed has my gratitude."

That wasn't love, his words were not soothing, and Pearl was in misery. "I don't have a mother."

"I know." Amused, he nipped at her ear. "The fact you were even conceived, given the odds, is miraculous… almost impossible. She would have died in labor as you fought your way out."

"What?"

"I know all your secrets, Pearl. I know about the Jesuit priest at the Mission Orphanage in California. I know how he hung you by the neck from a tree for three days when you were a little girl because he found you drinking the blood of rats. I know about the exorcisms, the beatings, the rapes. You have told me everything about you. Despite your misgiving at this moment, you adore me. I'm your savior. No soul can hurt you but me, and I always put you back together."

He was insane, absolutely crazy, and she felt the evil in him with every breath they shared. "You said you wouldn't hurt me if I was obedient."

"You enjoy pain, Pearl. You crave the things only I can do to you. How can you fully embrace pleasure otherwise?"

He had just ripped out her insides and swallowed them while she'd screamed for mercy. God might not be real, as he'd never once answered her prayers, but Pearl grasped that the devil existed. He'd found her as the priests said he would, and now he was going to eat up her soul. "I don't want you to hurt me."

"No?" A smile made his voice playful. "What is it that you think you want?"

Sobbing she said, "God's forgiveness."

"For what, being born? There is no creature more evil than this false God you think to worship over me."

She knew her prayers and her sins. "I want to go to heaven."

"I was turned before your Christian God came into being. This religion, like all others, was created by humans so they might rule over other humans. Your Jesus never existed. There was no virgin birth or cantering angels in the skies of Bethlehem. Every last drop of it is a lie." Turning her body into the crook of his, he promised, "What is real is what is before you. Now, tell me you love me before I grow jealous."

He was talking her in circles, and Pearl felt he'd done so thousands of times. Her own tongue could not break from the cycle. "I was obedient and still you hurt me. If I tell you I love you, you will hurt me again."

"True." The monster seemed appeased, even gratified by her statement. "My Pearl, isn't honesty a beautiful thing?"

Before she could answer, Darius had her splayed on her belly with supernatural speed. Face pressed to the blankets, she bit back a scream, the feel of something boiling hot penetrating the cavity he'd torn apart. True, the damage had healed, but unlike the first time he'd taken her that night, she was ill prepared for such brutality.

Clawing at the bed, trying to find purchase, she pitched deeper into the mattress with his every thrust.

Struggles and pained grunts only drove him on. He wanted her to fight back.

He wanted to steal.

Going limp did not save her either.

A muscular forearm flexed around her throat, a fist once again knotted in her hair, and he bent her back until her spine screamed. Roaring like the devil he was, Darius slammed his cock into her body, snapping his hips violently against her backside.

He denied her air. Twisted as she was, there was nothing but him to hold on to. She couldn't even see his eyes, only red velvet bed curtains that blurred as her world tripped between conscious and unconscious. Pain and true suffering.

But in there, under all the malevolence was a twinge and a lesson.

She was only allowed to be limp if he made her limp. She was only allowed to scream if he made her scream.

Pearl was a possession. She was a *treasure*.

One he could control physically or mentally, the point driven home when the tendrils of his dominion invaded her thoughts and tempted her to revel in the violence.

The instant her cracked psyche gave in, flashing fangs tore through his wrist and the spurting wound was pressed to her slack mouth.

Absolution arrived. She swallowed.

As he fucked her, she drank.

Gurgling around a mouthful, Pearl felt herself dragged to a higher state of being. High on his power, she could feel everything: each shredding thrust of a veined cock moving through skin not quite lubricated enough to facilitate smooth passage. She could feel the microscopic tears healing even as they split open anew. Overwrought nerves throbbed from both pleasure and pain, for he had found a place inside her body where, textured skin ached for punishment.

Under her knees, the bedsheets were slimy with blood, with bits of her that had escaped his feast, and with the very fluid he had accused her of spilling earlier.

She had indeed wet the bed, but it was not with piss.

Twisted by the glory of such perfect pain, what was dry became drenched. It ran down her thighs, clung like droplets of rain to the hair on his tight balls.

He abused her, left her aching and bone broken, and drew her greedy cunt through the worst sort of debasement and bliss.

Belly sloshing with his blood, she moved past fear straight into the red fires of the hell he'd designed for her. She came with such power it fractured her crumbling mind into pieces no amount of sweet words or broken promises would ever put back together.

You worship only me. He whispered the words into her mind. *I am your God.*

Darius slid from her twitching insides, cock hard as rock and pulsating as its master rolled his drooling conquest to her back. Thighs straddling her head, glorying in the smears of his blood over her chin, lips, and cheeks, he commanded, "Open your mouth. You are to swallow this too."

She didn't understand, and from his feral grin, it was obvious he took great pleasure in her innocence. Though could it be called innocence? Night after night did he not use his treasure, do unspeakable things to her, and work his evil over her body? After he was done, did he not strip away her thoughts and leave her a shell to wake again in this cold room, startled and scared.

A blank slate he could paint with blood.

A stupid girl he could pin down, where he might relish the pleasure of watching the shock on her face as he forced his cock past her lips and down her throat, choking her and denying her air.

Tongue pressed flat, her blunt teeth scraping the sides of his shaft, he ruthlessly fucked her mouth. When she began to bite, something changed, a look in the fiery red eyes, and Pearl swore that meat down her throat kicked.

The devil roared, pressing forward with such strength he tore out bits of her hair.

Salty tang burned like bile, coating her tongue, stinging her throat, and dripping from the corners of her swollen lips. Mashing his pelvis to her skull, Darius ushered more of that poison down his pulsating shaft and straight into her belly.

He held her that way after the last drop was spilled, watching her suffocate as if the view were magnificent.

Frantic for air, she begged with wide, wet eyes.

He smiled, yet did not move. "Speak of your God again, Pearl. Name him."

Scratching at his thigh, working her throat around his softening tool, she garbled, desperate to form the sounds of his name in a bid for freedom.

A satisfied cock popped from her lips, bloody vomit and tears following.

Much of what he had given her was spilled, cum and

blood pooling on the bed. As she heaved, he patted her head, as if a good dog has performed well.

Arms came around her. Cuddled to her back despite the mess, he pressed his lips to her ear. "There is no reason to be afraid of the demands I make on your body. I would never truly harm you past the point your body might regenerate."

She was sobbing, coughing between gasps. "And tomorrow I will have forgotten, and you will do this again."

"Hush, child." Darius kissed the back of her head, sliding his fingers over her ribs, across a sick belly, and lower still, until he cupped her bruised sex. "You've pleased me. As a reward, I swear to be the sweet lover you wish for tomorrow. I'll fool you into smiles and laughter. When I fuck you, I won't draw blood. You have my word."

His word meant nothing to her. "And you have mine that I will hate you tomorrow as much as I hate you today."

He smiled, and let his finger penetrate where she was slippery with his cum. There they played no matter her sulking or lingering discomfort. "You love me, kara sevde, of that I have no doubt."

7

There were so many pages, unfamiliar entry after entry—all of them in *her* choppy handwriting. Yet, each lacked a date, filling up the tome that sat upon the room's solitary desk with a vague story of her time in this stone room.

I did not sleep last night, and when Darius came to me again, he smiled as if he knew I'd waited for his return. Bone tired, I was poor company, but he was kind to me. He even offered an explanation. My sentence in this room, he claimed, is twice the lifetime of the man I killed.

Chadwick Parker had not been a young man, and I worry I might be trapped here for near a century.

How many times had Pearl read this first entry? It was impossible to know, but the page was growing worn and the book was filled with hundreds if not thousands of similarly pinned memories.

Darius held my hand when I grew sad at this news, claimed he hated to see my anguish. That is why he enforces his gift. My memory each night is wiped away so I might be spared from a monotonous eternity in prison. One day he'll hold my hand as I am set free. One day, I'll be allowed to meet others like me. I'll never be alone again.

Flipping through the journal, Pearl looked for something she couldn't pin. Over and over this Darius character was mentioned, but so far, she'd seen no sign of anyone in the cramped cell. Which was well and good. Yet something about the book was disturbing, obvious in its wrongness, but with no explanation.

Pages were missing, torn out. Gone forever.

Why?

Why remove pages from the journal? What had been written on them that Darius didn't want her to see?

Had she torn them out? And if she had, why do it?

Letting the book thump back on the desktop, Pearl looked over the grotesque grandness of the items piled inside her cell. From the red velvet draping the walls, to the jewels scattered over desk and crevice, everything seemed staged—like an altar.

Like an offering.

What would a girl locked in a room need with jewels? She was hardly even dressed in little more than lace bound by a sash around her middle.

She was also sporting dried blood under her nails and she smelled in need of a bath.

But there was no water, no urn, only a chamber pot of sorts that was uncomfortable to use.

There wasn't even a rat scurrying around for her to catch and eat.

Then again, according to the massive tome on the desk, she drank her meals from the mysterious Darius. In flowery language she even described the taste and how addicting it might be.

Pearl didn't use flowery language. A great many of the entries she scanned didn't sound like her at all.

Had he told her what to write?

More importantly, if she had been the one to tear out a page, where would she have hidden notes in this crypt?

Running her hands under the heavy mattress had led to nothing. Nooks in the wall were explored, the space behind paintings, even the trunk of scandalous clothing at the foot of the bed.

There was nothing but dust.

Dust?

Stamping her foot, Pearl felt the earth under the room's sumptuous rug. Things could be buried in dirt.

Like bodies.

Or trapped women.

Throwing back a corner of the rug, brushing aside dried rushes, damp earth met her fingers. Clawing at it here and there did naught but pit the ground. Fueled by a growing need for answers, Pearl threw handfuls of earth aside, careless of where they fell.

"You won't find what you're looking for there."

Crouched like a spider and panting as if she'd just run a race, Pearl cut a glance over her shoulder and hissed.

The mystery man himself stood like a beautiful beacon. And he was smiling at her, serene and unthreatening.

"Darius?"

A winged eyebrow arched. "Yes, Pearl?"

He obviously knew what she was up to, and seemed unconcerned. Tickled even. "Where are the missing pages?"

Walking toward a fantastical painting of an ancient warlord, the stranger pulled back a bit of torn canvas to display a nook. "Sometimes I find them here." He then changed course, moving to a stone in the wall that came away easily when jiggled. "And often here."

Both cavities were empty. Whatever she'd hidden away had been lost. And he had known to look for them. Nervous despite his kind expression, Pearl asked, "Why do you take them away?"

The handsome man's smile grew charmed. "Take them? I *collect* and keep them for you." He pointed to a small, obvious box on the desk. A place Pearl had ignored in her hunt.

Wiping dirtied hands on the impractical lace gown, Pearl crept forward, untrusting and cautious. It was as he claimed. Inside the jeweled box, the folded notes were haphazardly stacked.

Once she stood before them, he crossed the room. Appearing out of thin air behind her body.

His heat met her back. Lips to her ear, breath warm, he asked, "Do you want to play a game?"

Her fingers hovered over the notes. Buzzing nervously from the intimate way he brushed against her, Pearl whispered, “What kind of game?”

“For every note you choose to read, I earn a kiss from my beloved treasure.”

It was a trick. Men were never forthcoming. But there was something deeper than cautious intuition that warned she needed to see what was on those stolen pages. “One kiss for one note?”

A rich smile in his voice, the man nuzzled closer. “A kiss, my love, nothing more.”

Delving in, a random scrap of paper was chosen, pulled free, and unfolded.

Darius is the devil and you are in hell.

A hearty chuckle shook her body, the man pressed to her back extremely amused. “I do so love the look on your face when you read that one. In those first precious moments, you don’t want to believe it. You’ll turn and look me over from head to toe. Where are the horns? Where is the tail and cloven hooves? What reason might you have to think I am this character from your nightmares? Maybe it was written as a joke. Maybe, we’d argued that day… Perhaps you’d fallen gravid and grown *difficult*.”

Fear crawled up her spine and blood ran cold no matter how warm the body at her back. Turning her head so she might glimpse the one wrapping his arms around her torso, Pearl met his glowing red eyes.

His gaze burned all the brighter, fangs slowly descending behind a positively elated smile. Teasing in the meanest voice she'd ever heard, Darius hummed, "Or, maybe it's absolutely true."

Mortally afraid, she stood there, a hairsbreadth from those teeth, and asked, "What does gravid mean?"

He brought a hand to her cheek, reminding her that there was a price. A kiss for a note. After all, there were rules to this *game*. Fingers pinched her chin, turning her attention back to the box. "I never claimed questions were a part of our fun."

One folded page would not be enough. Snatching up another, she tore it in her haste to read what was waiting.

He raped me over and over until I bled from every hole a man might abuse on a woman. I begged him to stop, and he laughed.

"That's two kisses now, my Pearl."

Fat, silent drops slipped over trembling cheeks. She reached for a third.

He's never going to let you out. Find a way to kill yourself.

A tongue traced the shell of her ear, followed by a low rumble. "But how would you do it? All your wounds heal almost instantly thanks to the strength my blood has given you."

Shivering, Pearl wrapped her arms around her middle, the heat emanating from the man pressed to her back worthless. "I don't want to read anymore."

"Three kisses are owed me then, sweet treasure." With a flourish, he spun her about, the desk cutting off any chance of retreat. Sniffing at her hair, he demanded like a spoiled prince. "I'll claim the first one now."

After only a few moments in his presence, the idea was repugnant no matter how handsome the stranger might be.

"We had a deal, Pearl. Honor it, and see how reasonable I can be. Why be so frightened of words on a page?"

Because unlike the book, those hidden words seemed real. Very real, as if a locked corner of her mind was pounding against a wall, trying to warn her danger was here.

Play his game or resist, what would lead to a more favorable outcome when trapped with the devil?

Standing on tiptoe, Pearl pressed a chaste kiss to sculpted, smirking lips.

It would seem chastity was of no interest to Darius. His tongue slipped into her mouth, delving to undulate inside. Razor sharp teeth nipped, drew blood that he sucked into his mouth with a satisfied groan.

Lips were abandoned for her jaw, his mouth working its way next to her neck.

It was there he sank in those fangs.

The pain was extraordinary.

Legs giving out, it was only the strength of the man that kept her upright as he drained a punctured vein.

He feasted no matter how she fought, until her vision narrowed to a pinpoint. Limp, useless, she hung like a ragdoll.

Pain seemed to fade, her body ready to release the spirit where it could leave this room and go to God.

The sweet silence of death so close, she craved it. Smiled at the coming light.

Until Darius dropped her.

Weak, twisted like a discarded marionette, she could only groan while the man licked his lips and grinned.

He wasn't going to let her go to the light. No, he wanted to keep her in his darkness forever. Isn't that what the missing page claimed?

Trying to get to her knees, to crawl under the desk as if it might offer shelter, earned a barked laugh.

"Kara sevde, there will be none of that." He seized her ankle, and pulled her under his crouching body. "What would you gain by hiding that pretty face from me?"

"Help me." Her plea was not for him; it was said out of sick desperation that God might listen.

"Hush, child. You are not going to die." A rumble of demonic glee, of a thirst for more than blood, moved from sculpted lips to an unwilling ear. "But I will grant you sleep. Enjoy my mercy. But when you wake, two more kisses are owed."

8

Floating in warmth, Pearl was certain this had to be what heaven might offer—weightlessness, intoxication by a sense of perfection.

Nothing could touch her here.

Nothing, until softness brushed her brow, urging lashes to part to the glow of gold.

Candles burned, flickering soft light off a cracked oil painting. It was the image of a woman tending to goats on a rolling hillside, beautiful by any stretch. The sun shone as if real, more real than the dots of light blurring in the periphery of her vision.

"That, my dear, is our favorite painting. Can you not feel the wind in the bent grass as you look upon it? Seeing it now, I almost remember the scent of a field warmed by summer."

Shifting, only just growing aware of her body, led water to slosh and splash against her skin. Blurry vision settled on a man so near her face, she could smell the soap on his skin. Following the line of his arm from neck to hands, she found his sleeves were rolled up, his forearms dripping wet and half submerged.

Pearl felt weightless and warm because she was prone, naked, in a copper tub… a stranger hovering over her.

A strong hand came to her jaw, angling her lolling head back to rest on the waiting towel. “It’s only I, your Darius.”

Certain she was drunk, Pearl sucked her bottom lip. It was smeared with flavor. Wine? Or was that bourbon? Reaching up to gather what dripped from the corner of her mouth, she looked to her fingers and found blood.

A deep, perfect red.

Her throat ached to lick it up, craving that crimson bead as she’d never wanted anything before. “I don’t…”

The man winked. “Know how you got here? We were playing a game, and I’m afraid you grew utterly drained.”

Entranced with that red dot, Pearl brought it back to her lips so it would not be wasted.

The man had other ideas.

Catching her wrist, he brought the finger to his lips and sucked it clean.

When she tried to snatch her finger from the heat of his mouth, he pricked her flesh, laughing when she squealed. Then he gave her a dazzling smile.

Two long fangs, milky white, glimmered in the low light. “There is nothing to fear. Look at your finger, Pearl. It is already mending.”

Mouth agape, she was unsure exactly which topic was

most in need of immediate attention: the fact she was naked, obviously being bathed by a striking stranger. The fact there was another person like her. One who spoke warmly to her, knew her name, and seemed *almost familiar*. Or, the fact that her finger was healing right before her eyes.

Nudity was addressed first, both arms slipping so they might cover where her breasts bobbed in steaming water.

This earned a breathy chuckle. "Your shyness strikes me as particularly charming in this moment."

Knowing her cheeks were a vivid pink, Pearl tried his name. "You said your name was Darius. I don't… I don't know you. I don't know how I got here. Is this the hospital? Have I been ill?"

Red eyes, that's what they were—red as blood and glowing like an ember ready to set the world to flame. "Darius, yes, and I am at your service, my Pearl. And, yes, you do know me. You know your lover very well, you just don't remember me. You see, we meet anew each night in your chamber."

She had to be drugged or ill. Not a word he said made sense.

Neither the painting nor the handsome man held her attention. It was the walls she looked to, the chipped hunks of stone, the lack of windows. She was in a cell, blocked in a corner by a screen that hid the remainder of the room. "Why wouldn't I remember you?"

Her chin was caught, Pearl made to meet the eye of the stranger. "So that you might be happy, always. Time has a way of twisting our kind. You have the gift of constant newness. Your God has blessed you. He dotes on you."

"My God?"

"Every day is fresh. Every time I touch you, it's the first time. Every time I kiss you, you still blush. I am the perpetual bridegroom, and you are my darling treasure. There is much joy to be had in this."

Men did not speak that way to women; they didn't look upon them as if they were going to swallow them whole. She sunk lower in the water as if it might shield her from the weight of his gaze.

Darius tutted. "You wish for privacy so you might dry yourself and dress. That is unnecessary. I know your body inside and out. There is no cause to flinch or try to hide in the tub." He picked up her hand and began to clean dirt from under her nails, no matter how she fought to pull it back. "*I* shall finish bathing you, *I* will dry you, *I* will dress you. Then, *I* will feed you."

He made her sound like some doll, tutting and clucking when he found a broken nail or a hanging bit of cuticle. "Such a mess. Be still."

Be still. The command rang inside her skull, and still she became. She couldn't move, not even to blink or turn her eyes from his scowl.

Next he soaped her shoulder, the remaining length of her arm, Pearl stiff and unable to respond.

Strangers didn't touch this way. They didn't issue unspoken commands that a body was physically incapable of ignoring.

"You may breathe and speak, Pearl."

Throat dry, Pearl sucked in air. "How did you…"

An impish wink, and he kissed the tips of her clean fingers. "I'm your God, remember?"

"And you said… lover." She had never had a *lover*. Men had never touched her for her benefit. They certainly had never buffed her nails. "Have we… umm?"

A subtle twitch came to the corner of the man's mouth. "Have we umm what?"

He was going to make her say it, Pearl blushing all the harder. "Known one another well?"

Moving slow enough to assure he had her total attention, the man dipped his fingers under the bubbling soap scum. His wrist followed, his forearm. "I have known you in every possible way."

Fingers crept between her thighs, separating folds, to tease a place that made her gasp when treated to small circles of friction.

His head hovered lower, Darius observing her parted lips and dazed eyes. "You suffer such attention beautifully, and I think you always will. I dare you to tell me you do not enjoy this."

A noise caught in her throat as he breached her, a single finger wriggling inside that place men liked to damage and use.

Only his attention brought no pain. There were gasps of surprise instead, little sounds coming from lips that spoke of trepidation, confusion, and a drugged hunger for more.

Water began to splash when his exploration grew more

vigorous—what had been slow and meticulous became wild and unbearable. Head back against the lip of the tub, Pearl squeezed her eyes shut and found a rush unlike anything she'd known. Before she might stop herself, she cried out and lurched, spilling water and soaking the man's shirt front.

He pressed a kiss to her slack lips as if she were some sleeping beauty waiting for the prince to wake her. "That is only a taste of what we have shared."

In her wide, dazed eyes sat sluggish relief. This was no monster…

Hovering over her mouth, he smiled again. "Kiss me, my Pearl. Kiss me, and I shall be sweet."

Kissing was not a familiar activity any more than the odd sensations of having a man touch her gently between her legs. All the others had shunted in ugly, hard flesh for their own pleasure. Usually they drew blood.

Certain now that she was drunk, ill, completely mad, she gave in and pressed her lips to his—because all of this had to be a dream, and rare sweet dreams should be savored.

There was an instant reward. His fingers went back to teasing that magical place even as his tongue tangled and teased hers. Moaning under him, unsure why her body moved as it did, Pearl gripped the edges of the tub as if that might anchor her in this wonderful sensation.

As she was about to crest, shatter, and be reborn, he stopped. Pulling his fingers from the fluttering hungry part of her body, his lips followed suit. A string of spittle stretching between them before it snapped. "Stand. I want to look at you all clean and shining in candlelight."

She leveraged her weight against the tub, completely graceless as she fought feeble legs to stand. Without the comfort of the water, she felt like death warmed over.

"Ungh." Unsteady, she swayed, and muttered, "I have been ill."

Seated on his stool, he began to touch the tottering woman, humming approval when she leaned into his hands for support. "Fragile little kitten, you're hungry." He crooked his fingers, commanding her from the tub and to his lap. "Come."

Ravenous, in fact. Swallowing, she looked to the thigh he indicated should serve as her seat, and muttered a dazed, "I'm wet. I'll leave a mark."

"Yes, you are. Now obey me. Come." Flat out chuckling, he gave her hand a yank. She tripped from the tub, caught in his arms, and draped over his knee.

Breathless, she gawked over her shoulder when he set his hand to her rump and explored. As he leered and toyed between her cheeks, she felt more and more the prostitute and less the lover.

Exposed, weak, and growing cold, she sucked her lower lip between her teeth and tried to push away.

"No wriggling!"

She heard the sound of the smack before it registered how hard he'd struck her.

The flesh of her ass jiggled, stung horribly, and would bruise. But it was her pride that was far more damaged. Red faced, mortified and aching, she shook her head but had no words.

"Had you sat as you'd been told, I would have cuddled you dry with sweet kisses and soft words." Drawing up a soft towel from where it rested beside the bath, he began to blot droplets away from her bowed back. He palmed her ass, squeezed that bruised flesh, and grinned when she looked away in shame. "I'm only teasing, Pearl. Who could resist such a view?"

Gently he turned her, sat the shamefaced woman on his knee and pressed a tender kiss to her temple. "We were playing a game before you fell asleep. I think we should play another."

Aching, aroused, unwell, and starving, she sighed. "I'm not very good at games."

Nuzzling her wet hair, he whispered, "But you win so often."

"I'm cold."

"You owe me one more kiss." He was already at her mouth, sucking the trapped lip from her teeth before he added, "One more kiss, then we play a new game."

The pressure, the friction, even the sharp edges of his teeth, all of it was his doing. She was trapped under the onslaught, gasping for air and shocked to feel the stirrings return between her thighs. But as it was, she could not kiss him, not with his tongue already in her mouth. If that was his game, she had no way to win. All she could do was try to make words that were swallowed, ignored, and grunted at.

But she was growing warm again. Every last attention he lavished on her felt… nice.

A rush grew in the place he'd explored under the water, a

plumpness Pearl did not recognize that made her want to press harder to his thigh, and forget the lingering soreness of her ass.

When he gave her a moment of breath, she panted, found herself squirming, and just about fainted when he suddenly took her nipple between his teeth. "Is this the game?"

Grunting a non-answer, those long teeth he'd used to cut her thumb were planted into her breast. Sucking her nipple, tonguing it, a mix of searing pain and unknown pleasure mingled as he drank the scant blood that ran.

Pulling his mouth from her breast, teeth red with her blood, those eyes burned with hellfire. "Bite me."

Gawking at the small trickle of blood that ran from her skin, staring at the man who'd left the mark of his mouth on her, Pearl felt her gums tingle. When she tongued each tip, she found two teeth descended, far too short to even break skin.

Reaching up to touch the useless tips with her finger, shocked she hadn't noticed earlier, she balked. "They're gone."

The fervent stranger didn't care. He took her hair and drew her mouth to his neck.

The smell she found there set her to salivating. The needle-like pain on her scalp from his overly enthusiastic grip forgotten as her tongue traced a pulsating vein.

The man moaned in a way Pearl had only ever heard when men were finished with her.

For once, she liked it.

She bit and gnawed, did everything she could to get that

vein to burst open and spray her mouth with what was hidden inside.

Nothing worked.

Well, something was working. The man's hand had delved into his trousers and between their tangled bodies he was pumping his fist.

Unfed hunger led to sharp frustration. Her teeth were too short to pierce, her jaw too weak to break salty skin. Everything she needed was right there, so close but unattainable.

But then the smell of blood filled her nose.

His warm, perfect blood.

Yet it was not coming from his neck.

She slunk to the floor without thought, hand around an organ that dripped rubies from an even more generously throbbing vein. When she tried to suck just from the side of that thing, strong hands repositioned her skull. It was put between her teeth, forced toward her throat until she gagged and had trouble swallowing the pooling blood.

All she wanted was a rich drink, annoyed with the man bobbing her head up and down.

Swallowing with that thick organ down her throat became necessary. Breath was forgotten, all that mattered was the struggle against what held her down and wasted blood she *needed* in her belly. Just as the vein closed and her meal was cut short, something salty sprayed against her tongue.

Made to swallow it in her quest for the final drops of perfection, Pearl retched.

Flailing, half drowning and unable to breathe, she felt the weight on her skull give in. Falling back in a graceless pile, sucking in air as if she'd been under water, Pearl saw the man, his trousers gaping, his mouth open and head thrown back.

It was then she realized just what she'd so ravenously drunk from.

His cock.

That part of a man they liked to stick like a brand into a woman—the thing that burned and brought pain.

That had been his game.

Something was running from the corner of her lips, a wasted drop both salty and sweet.

Darius caught it with his thumb, pushed it back between her shocked lips before using the tip of his finger to close her gaping mouth. "Did you enjoy your dinner?"

There was no answer. The blood had been overly delicious, the things he'd been doing during her feast unrecognized. It couldn't be normal, a woman's mouth on a man's body that way. Embarrassed, unsure if she could bring herself to stop cringing on the floor, Pearl muttered, "Why would you do that?"

Stroking her cheek, Darius smiled. "Swallow my cum like a good girl. Taste it on your velvet tongue. Next I'll leave it dripping from your tight cunt. After that, there is another place on your body I like to bury my seed. Play nicely, and I'll fill your belly with another mouthful of what makes you swoon before I fuck your ass."

Pearl looked back at the thing she'd just had down her throat, not at all eager for it to be back inside any part of her body. Just as she was no longer eager to pretend this was a pleasant dream.

He was still hard.

Usually, after they had pushed in, thrust about, and told her to stop screaming, those things got smaller.

Taking the meat of his cock in hand, the man crooned, "You still owe me a kiss. Press your lips here, and thank me for all I gave you."

She didn't want it in her throat again; all she had wanted to taste was the blood.

This dream was no longer enticing. In fact, now that she'd had a meal, it didn't feel dream-like at all.

It was real.

Darius was real.

She was in a room with a man who had put his organ in her mouth.

An organ she had licked manically for drops of blood that did not make her retch as human blood did...

Semen did not taste appealing, the belief confirmed a moment later when he fisted her hair, and led her mouth to the tip where a drop of tang remained.

She kissed it as she was told to, felt her stomach rumble and her throat itch.

Mostly, she felt unclean.

"Are you thinking of the mean old priest?"

A flood of terrible memories intruded as if a dam had broken behind her eyes. This interlude had not been the first time she'd done this. How could she have forgotten something so horrible?

A cry caught in her throat, one that turned to a whimper of degradation.

A hand came to her bowed head and stroked her hair. “And that, kara sevde, is why I do not allow you to remember. That is why every night for you starts new and clean.”

Who would want to have such dark things always lurking in their mind? The stranger had given her blood that had not made her sick, he had given her pleasure in the tub, and then he had given her the memory of a terrible past. Falling to his feet, she put her lips to his shoes and begged he take the nightmares away again.

Voice like iron, Darius warned his treasure, “I shall take all he did from your mind, but remember this fractured moment tonight should you question your life in my care, buck my requests, or shy from my attention. There is no suffering in this room but the torment you bring upon yourself. I would give you the bliss of permanent innocence. I would fill you with pleasure. Thank me for it.”

Sobbing, she vigorously held to his leg. “Thank you.”

And then the rancid memories that had broken her heart were gone. Confused why she was even upset, the tears stopped.

Cupping her face, he wiped wet trails from her cheeks. “Your life with me, in this place, can be sunshine or it can be darkness. Every night, the choice is yours.”

9

Over several hours, Darius taught her the meaning of rapture.

And the price…

His attention had been so wondrous that she'd almost forgotten how degrading it was to be used. Yet no matter how he kissed and touched, under her joy she knew all he did was for his own entertainment. He wanted to see her beg like a whore, knew what nerves to manipulate to earn a slattern's response.

Twisted by the expertise of a practiced lecher, she'd cried out, unsure of the exact moment his body had pushed her past sanity. For only a mad woman would have thanked him for fucking her so raw she'd bled.

She'd even tangled her hands in his hair when he'd pulled her cunt to his mouth so he might feast on their shared fluids.

When his cum and her blood were smeared over his chin,

red eyes burned and his long teeth shone in the candlelight. "Turn over. Bow your head to the covers."

She'd obeyed without question.

"Tell me you love me." Glistening cockhead notched between her cleft, he'd raked his nails over her hips.

More of her blood spilled from the gashes, just as the foul words fell from a drunken tongue. "I love you."

"Call me your God!" He spread her cheeks, sluicing forward through all the mess that dripped from her cunt.

It felt as if there was a knock on the door of her skull, a mental caution to refuse such blasphemy. There was only one God. *The* God. The creator of the world who'd promised to deliver her from evil.

Evil shunted in, straight into a hole that was unslick, upstretched, and unprepared. Bawling, flailing while tears fell, she screamed, "You are my God!"

The creature tearing her ass apart roared. It was not the sound of a man in pleasure, but a demon set free from the abyss. Unwilling to turn her head, she imagined great wings had spread behind her tormentor to beat the air as he pulled her down that blood-stained cock.

The damage was extensive, for the devil had been unshackled.

He claimed his due from her flesh.

A single, worthless soul.

One that God had rejected long ago. One that was treasured by a monster who relished perverting love into pain.

Empty of hope, full of cock.

That was how she died inside. Any proselyte knew there would be no forgiveness in the eyes of the Lord for this.

The flesh agreed, twisting up around the pulsating intrusion. Her cunt fluttered, opening up like a little mouth seeking a sweet kiss. The nub at the top of her sex throbbed as if an overripe berry near bursting.

Despite how he ravaged her hips, it was *her* touch that found that pulped flesh and dove in to fill the empty hole. He bellowed a sickening laugh to see little fingers play.

When she came, it was while riding a scream of pain.

He sprayed white globs of stinging grossness so far inside her, it would linger like a stain she could never push out.

What had she done?

On fire, pinned under the weight of a monster lazy with slaked lust, her tears fell hot and free.

At last that organ was shrinking, slowly worming its way out of her ass. But the mark he'd made on her, the blasphemy he'd drawn from foolish lips would never seep out, no matter how many holes she tore in her flesh.

"I am lost…"

Filth crusted nails raked her chin, forcing her to twist her neck at an impossible angle so that one large blue eye might find his devious smile. "I so ador—"

The floor dropped out from under them, and with an earsplitting crash, dust and debris snowed down upon her room. It was as if the earth itself shook, as if it worked its jaws, intent on devouring the vampire whore and the beast panting on her back.

"HE WOULDN'T DARE!" Darius pulled away, careless

of the damage he caused, or the detritus that followed the path of his dick from her anus. Once on his feet, the ground wrenched again, almost upsetting the devil's balance. "You." Turning his fury on the bleeding woman soiling the coverlet. "Stay there! This insurrection will be crushed at once."

Through tears, Pearl saw the air bend, distort, and Darius, the devil she'd named as her God, vanished.

It would be easy to say that the rocking of the earth which sent her candelabras toppling over was a sign of her salvation. It would be easy to claim divinity smiled upon her.

It didn't.

In fact, no one came to smile, threaten, bleed her, or denounce.

Hours she lay under a ceiling that dusted her room in a fog of ancient dirt. In that time her body mended.

Darius did not return.

One by one the candles began to flicker and wane. All the soft golden light of her cell faded, snuffed out to scent the air with a wisp of smoke. It was not until the last three had almost met their end before Pearl found the will to rise from the bed. New tapers were lit, and had she been wiser, she would have rationed her meager supply.

Rocking herself in the shadowy room, surrounding by fine paintings, by jewels, by sumptuous furnishing and a tub grown cold, she saw the cell for what it was.

A tomb.

Her tomb.

Day's passed, Pearl sleeping anywhere but the soiled bed.

Starving, down to her last candle, she read through the

book she'd found on the desk, and knew the gnawing in her gut was more than hunger.

This was a bad place.

A bad place where she had been tempted, and spoken terrible words.

When she opened the filigreed box on the desk, when she found the notes, she didn't weep. After all, didn't the church teach that there was no such thing as victims of the devil? She had come to him of her own accord.

She had killed Chadwick Parker. She had served as the demon's slut.

She had renounced her God under the ecstasies only the prince of darkness might offer.

And every word on those torn notes was true.

She was in Hell.

Damned, Pearl snuffed out the last candle before it might burn away. Pitch black filled her vision. Shuffling through the furniture, she found the stinking bed, and pulled the covers crusted in all things unholy over her body. There she lay, forgotten, abandoned, and without hope.

Just as she deserved.

Starvation drained her flesh over weeks. Shriveled, desiccated, she lay like an age worn corpse unable to blink. Yet, where the body failed the mind *persevered.*

She couldn't scream into that endless night. Eventually, even her chest no longer rose to draw breath. But awareness and desolation never faded.

Hell was a dedicated custodian. It refused to release her stolen soul.

Years, decades, passed trapped on that bed staring up into unyielding dark.

Alone.

Forgotten.

Forsaken.

Another corpse in the catacombs.

Thank you for reading CATACOMBS! Ready for more? Turn the page and indulge in CATHEDRAL.

CATHEDRAL

CRADLE OF DARKNESS, BOOK TWO

1

JADE

I have a taste for fine red wine.

Elusive, decadent. It pours down one's throat with all the richness of desire. It can even be thick on the tongue. But it's nothing to the drenched, pervasive cream that smeared over my lips.

Blue-blooded and smug as smog, Ethan knew this as he stood beside my bed, stroking his cock while I hummed appreciation at my surprise.

He wanted me to taste him… dripping from another.

And that's how I found myself awoken from slumber. The smoothly waxed lower lips of a pretty female, caressing my smile.

The slip and glide as she performed exactly as Ethan must have instructed, teased me to take a lick. Labia puffy from a recent fucking, the tang of female lubrication churned creamy by male ejaculate.

She smelled like life that I was only too happy to let pour down my throat.

Opening my mouth, I dragged the flat of my tongue through the mess. Hooking it so I might catch his cum all in a glob for Ethan's unwavering stare to absorb as he rubbed new life into his recently spent cock.

Salty, an exclusively human bleach-like tang. I knew his taste well.

One might consider me a sexual deviant, the way I rolled his flavor around on my tongue. How I swallowed before grabbing the globes of the offered treat's ass to move her where I would.

Though she enjoyed my exuberance, this act was not about her gratification. It was about mine. Twisting my tongue through her folds as her legs shook from the pleasure, seeking flavor and lingering juices, I devoured.

As if I never need come up for air.

I didn't.

I could hold my breath for hours. Days even.

Which gave me all the time in the world to dig my tongue into her cunt and scoop out the remainder of my prize. Her toned ass, clenched in my hands, bore the sharper edges of my nails, as I took so much more than I gave.

Even so, even though the sensation was too much, rubbing her clit on my nose, she came.

The noises, the squeaks and squawks, *the honesty of them*, excited me.

So I spread my thighs so Ethan might see.

Thinking he was king of the world, he climbed between

them, his heartbeat fast and loud. "God, Jade, you two are fucking hot together!"

It must have been near noon, for I could feel the sun cut through the floor to ceiling windows my penthouse afforded, overlooking the city's most exclusive view. The weight of that direct light danced on my pale skin, the unseen pain I was an expert at concealing bleeding together with the impatient stab of a cockhead through my slit.

I sleeved him, wrapped around his turgid length, and bore down in a way the delicious snack riding my face never could. He fought me to remain seated, jerking his meat through the clamp of a satin-coated cunt.

Knees braced to black silk, a bruising grip on my splayed thighs, I didn't need to see him to know the vision before me. Sweat dampening his blond hair, leaving it to hang in his eyes as his lips parted in a blissed-out groan, Ethan strained. He strained to fuck a hole so tight I'd forced him out before his balls might slap my ass.

"God damn..." Equal parts frustration and awe, he bullied his way back inside. Half-seated, he landed a slap on my clit as if to punish the teasing cunt he did so love to conquer. The sting did its work. My muscles jumped just enough that he gained an inch.

The throaty noise of victory made me smile against the woman too sensitive and no longer interested in my mouth. Not that she would *ever* say so aloud. Whoever might have the fun of playing third to our duet knew that they had a body, and it was here for our use.

Complain, and be easily replaced by the next pretty blonde who caught Ethan's eye.

So she tolerated my nips and licks, how I gasped against her when my lover's thumbs pulled the pretty hood of skin away from my clitoris. Threatening me with excessive pleasure, Ethan hissed, "Let me in, Jade."

I softened just enough for him to sink another inch, rippling around his girth in an ancient tease.

The pad of his pointer finger rubbed my exposed clit with the perfect pressure to trick my body into surrender. Just like that, straining and bucking, manic hips between creamy thighs, I was fucked for breakfast.

When I'd tossed the girl away, forgetting she panted at my side while I made frenzied love to Ethan, I couldn't say. One moment we played with her, the next we did not.

Because it was never about whoever else we brought into our bed. They were a garnish, unmemorable.

That wasn't because we were cruel. Ethan for all his failings, was a nice guy. I, despite my heritage, never hurt them.

"I love you, Jade." Delivered with perfect timing, Ethan, believing his proclamation was true, got what he wanted.

Eye's rolling back, his cock expanding with imminent release, my lover enjoyed his second orgasm of the day. One my own climax drove past the pale as my internal muscles twisted tight, released, cramped, and fought to expel him.

"Oh my god! *Oh my god*!" Face the very image of ruin, Ethan threw back his head. The following animal whine, the way he swayed as if on the brink of a faint, it led me to be merciful.

Again I opened, the seed I'd choked off from bursting down its tube allowed to splash against my womb.

Falling to his hands, forehead to mine, he panted through the following waves of euphoria, while I cooed in his ear and ran a comforting caress down his spine.

"I fucking love you, Jade."

Melting into the mattress, my mind wandered through ecstasy and pain. The sun had climbed higher; soon I'd be forced to move. But for now, the hidden cameras needed to see.

I had done my duty for the day.

Though it was permitted, there was no expectation that I come. My orders were only to be seeded.

Daily.

Which made it doubly lovely that I had gotten this reproductive requirement out of the way so early in my schedule. Perhaps I'd even partake again later instead of leaving Ethan to play with his latest toy, should the mood strike him to get his dick wet.

Warm weight of toned male flesh sliding off my body, Ethan stood with a sheepish smile. After taking my fingers to kiss with adoration, he sauntered off to the bathroom to shower.

Eventually his father would require him to show up at corporate HQ and make an official appearance. Dashing smile, suit immaculate, and model beautiful, he'd be expected to do nothing more than saunter in and fuck around at his computer for an hour or two. I imagine he spent it playing Candy Crush or dallying with the prettier girls in the building.

Entitlement at its polished finest. That was my darling Ethan Parker.

"I'm going to join him." Despite the aneurism-inducing orgasm I'd given her, it seemed the girl at my side had collected herself. Standing on shapely tan legs, she meandered towards the ensuite's steaming shower and the man whistling inside it.

Arms stretched overhead, I enjoyed the zippering pops of my spine. "You do that."

Throwing me a smile over her shoulder, she blew me a kiss.

What was her name? Polly?

Vaguely remembering some *Polly wants a cracker* reference, I couldn't recall if this blonde was Polly or if the last blonde had been Polly. Jenny?

Sam?

No, not Sam. Sam had been the curly-haired Venus from last winter.

They all ran together. They all giggled the same, pouted the same, and sported the large gravity defying breasts Ethan had an eye for.

God bless the surgeons who gave those pretty, carefree girls such perfect tits...

For God sure as fuck never blessed me.

And I'm not talking about breasts. My breasts were lovely.

I was stunning, in fact. Dark hair, porcelain skin, designed to draw adoration and attention.

Wealth? I had more money than any man could spend in a lifetime.

But I was not favored by God, and never would be.

After all, I was the child of Lucifer.

2

Perfume.

The scent of good taste and deep pockets. Specially blended to my precise specifications.

Over the multitude of years, only one distinctive blend has graced my throat. The ritual of application, the slip of cut crystal chilling a scented trail down my skin—I found it comforting, even if I have never enjoyed the smell.

With the inevitable passage of time, everything changes. Trends, styles, freedoms… but this concoction, the way it alters the air around me, *what it signifies*, is as ageless as I am.

In the modern, more sophisticated era, several of the ingredients sloshing within the crystal vial gracing my vanity were extremely illegal. Some so rare, their acquisition cost a greater sum than the annual rent on our metropolis' finest penthouses. Humans of a certain cut, whether it was ingrained in them from high birth, or because they conquered the upper echelon and elbowed their way in, need only take a sniff to know precisely what the cloud of scent signifies.

Affluence. Reverence.

Souls feel me linger in the air long after I've left a room.

Their brains tickled and twitched over a ghost of memory they can't pin down.

As if they'd known me all their lives.

They have. They just can't remember.

"Uncle Randal wants to know if your father will be joining us at his birthday soirée tonight." Attention locked on his phone, Ethan scrolled through his messages, as if what he asked were nothing.

I stopped humming.

No breath entered my lungs; my heart shuddered to a stop. Still as a corpse, no longer musing over frivolous perfume, my eyes rose in the mirror, waiting for Ethan to glance away from his phone.

I cannot imagine what he saw on my face, but I knew it was not the shattered glass panic scratching at my veins.

To him, that flippant remark and the assumption behind it were… innocent.

To me, it felt as if the room was a dead thing rising from the grave.

Speak of the devil and he will appear.

Though Ethan was about as deep as a puddle, even he took note of my brief lapse from flawless composure. "Darling, it's just that—"

Hasty words fell from my lips before he might make this

worse. "Has Papa reached out to the senator?"

Blond brows lifting with ingrained snobbery, Ethan pressed. "*Senator Parker* would really like him to come."

No. He wouldn't. My father likes to play with his food.

Stupid, selfish, silly, happy Ethan whose antics offered me the sensation of *normal*... by the time my father was done with him, he wouldn't even know my name.

He wouldn't remember dancing with me in the moonlight, or laughing as we jumped on the bed like children. There would be no naughty smirks when his prick engorged at thoughts of what I'd willingly do to him.

I'd be nothing but a whiff of familiar perfume when I strolled by, gracing the arm of another prominent man.

Hand shaking, so subtle a betrayal of my feelings that no human eye would catch it, I set the crystal stopper back in the bottle.

And I felt… bereft.

Because I'd grown too attached, and I had known better.

Someday, this game of playing house would all end.

Blue eyes falling to my inlaid Louis the XV vanity, I hated that perfume bottle of revolting honesty glinting in the scorching afternoon sun.

How sad to be reduced to something so fleeting—crafted, expensive stink.

Knowing full well that Ethan could never grasp the fate he tempted, I let spite make pretty words ugly. "Next time I see Papa, I'll mention how much *the senator* is looking forward to the attention of his favorite benefactor."

Waving off my fake smile as if it were real and inconsequential, Ethan rolled his eyes. "When you put it like that, it sounds tasteless, Jade."

Because it was. The Parkers were extravagantly affluent in their own right, but it was nothing to the wealth the father of darkness wielded. And, after all, it was an election year… and campaigns were expensive.

Lifting up a tube of Chanel Shanghai Red lipstick, I ended the topic. "He's not coming tonight." Perhaps it was true, perhaps not. One thing I knew was to never anticipate the moves of the devil. "But I promise I will mention it to Daddy tomorrow."

Another lie.

Tucking his phone in his pocket, Ethan bent down to press a kiss to my shoulder. "You sure you don't want to call him? It's going to be a fun party, you'll see. The president's coming."

And that was disgusting for a very different reason.

Not all of my former companions had been as sweet or as horribly selfish as Ethan.

He was a treat compared to men I was duty-bound to air kiss upon greeting. Aging men who had no memory of our long-ago, fumbling trysts, their tempers rattling my ear, or their slaps to my cheek.

One could write off such behavior as belonging to a different time with different rules, but I'd lived long enough to know better. Some men were just lesser than their gentler peers.

The current leader of this great nation, for example, had been just as disgusting, insecure, and chauvinistic in the

1980s as he was sitting on his fat ass in the oval office scarfing down Big Macs.

In less than an hour I'd float past him; I'd stomach the feel of his paunch pressing against my body as he leaned forward to smear his fleshy lips across my cheek. A shudder would run through him at a whiff of my perfume, and somewhere deep down, ugly, old feelings would stir.

Desire, covetousness… fear.

I looked so young, so fresh, how could shadow memories of my face flicker in the darker corners of his mind? The sensation of someone walking over his grave would be brushed off, ego stepping in to answer with an affable, "I knew your mother," or "I loved you in that film."

Though I'd graciously say *thank you*, I'm not an actress.

Not of the paid variety, anyhow.

And I don't have a mother.

But the human mind had to reconcile; it had to bend.

Weaker intellects made up the best stories.

So I would smile, I would laugh, I would make him feel important. And then I would drift away on the night air.

"It's past five o'clock. You know it's too late for me to call Papa, Ethan. He's very old. He's already in bed, and I can't imagine his night nurse would be willing to poke the viper. *He needs his rest.*" And the sun was still up. Even if my father were awake during daylight hours, he'd be feeding at the trough of captives stored in the Cathedral, not pulling on a tux to mingle with cattle. If I were to even mention such a thing, his laughter would rail down the phone line until my ears bled.

That is not an exaggeration.

Puppy dog eyes in a face that had graced GQ, Ethan begged. "For me?"

Smiling as if I'd fallen for his charm, my freshly-painted red lips replied, "I'm happy to write a check on his behalf. How much would the senator like?"

Before Ethan might do the unthinkable and mention a figure out loud, the pouting spectator who sat naked on the corner of my sex-mussed bed piped in. "I don't understand why I can't go."

Ethan's latest bleached blonde's timing was both perfect and awful.

Adjusting his bowtie, Ethan colored. I sighed—both of us having forgotten she was in the room.

And there was pity to be had for her. It was never pleasant to be excluded—knowing one was lesser than their peers, cut—that I understood intimately. But the three of us going through the paces knew why she couldn't attend Senator Parker's birthday party. Not that I, or Ethan, or even she would say so.

Low class mistresses were condoned only behind closed doors, more of a light joke than treated as living flesh and bone. They were not tolerated, or heaven forbid, acknowledged publicly. Even with MTV and feminism.

It was a mercy when we left her behind.

Where we might give her gifts and pleasure, others would eat her alive.

Speaking of food, my stomach rumbled.

But I refused to dine tonight; habit led me to wait, the need to feed ignored as long as my body might comply.

I still had two days.

Forty-nine hours to be exact.

So, now was the time for perfume, and parties, and stolen moments with old friends who had no true recollection who I'd been in their lives.

Now was the time to mock terrible presidents with artfully applied smiles, and know, *for a fact*, that they had the world's truly smallest, most pathetic penis.

Artfully applying a final sweep of black mascara, eyes currently a shade of blue, unlike my father's glowing red, stared back at me. Lids dusted gold, painted to entice.

From my bed, our blonde wrinkled her nose at our refusal to acknowledge her complaint.

Ignoring her huff, Ethan—exactly how his grandfather Gerard had done decades before—placed his hands on my shoulders, smiling over me while I completed my toilette. In the soft light of the vanity, it seemed a tender moment, the way his thumb caressed the side of my throat sweetly as he chided, "We're going to be late."

"You look very handsome in your tux."

How he fed on praise. That grin, those dimples, I could eat him alive.

Not literally. Humans were vile on the tongue.

And vampires shouldn't be able to walk in the sun.

Those two anomalies in my life were the very reason there were hidden cameras catching every angle of my perfectly applied smoky eye. They caught the facets of metal glinting off extremely expensive Agent Provocateur underthings. Why the gown draped over my massive bed, picked at by our resident pet, was flawless as she pouted and whined that she was not included… again.

Lips painted the perfect shade of red. Eyes blue as the Mediterranean Sea. Skin pale but carrying the undercurrent of a long-ago bronzed people. I was alluring enough to reel any hapless mortal to an early grave.

Yet I knew that no matter this soul-solid reality, beauty never mattered.

Standing so Ethan might help me into my couture dress, I meant the smile I threw his way. The slip of a satin-lined gown, the cold clasp of diamonds circling my throat.

He was perfection at preparing a woman for the slaughter.

And I… I was perfection at leading the room by the nose.

Knowing better than to kiss me once my lips were smeared with rouge, instead, my darling ran his fingers from my shoulder to my wrists, surprising me with a gift.

I loved presents.

The cuff was weighty, immaculate, and worth a small fortune.

His grandfather, before he'd died in World War I, had given me one just the same.

"I love you, Jade." Brushing a stray lock of hair behind my ear, ignoring our huffing blonde, he did something a man of his station never dared. He carefully kissed my red lips.

And was all the cuter for smearing my favorite color on his grin.

3

Sipping a third glass of champagne, my red lips quirked at whatever politician's wife Ethan was buttering up. The charm of a peacock, that one—all bright feathers and squawking.

Spell woven, he'd fully enraptured the woman to his cause with little more than dimples and a practiced swagger.

It was a ploy to aid the Parker family's political agenda. Trying to swing a senate vote in his uncle's favor would determine how far Ethan might take the night's seduction.

"Are you enjoying yourself, Miss King?" Watching the same choreographed dance across the city's chicest hotel's rooftop, Ethan's powerful uncle—the mercenary and corruptible Senator Randal Parker himself—planted his bulk by my side.

I was not there to enjoy myself; I was there to overhear

softly whispered conspiracy. Still, I offered a smile to the man of the hour. "Happy birthday, Senator. It's a lovely party."

View immaculate: the glittering evening skyline of the financial district's skyscrapers, the celebrity guest list, even the pot-bellied, bleating president holding court over the country's greediest misers, was pageantry serving a solitary purpose.

Clout.

It took more than designer garments, a pedigree, fine schools, or even contacts to rule this world. The key was in the small moments of ruthlessness.

Such as watching my lover seduce another woman and encouraging him with a sly wink.

"A pity your father couldn't join us." Pompous, fleshy cheeks reddened by bourbon and the night's chilled air, Senator Parker fisted his lapel.

I gave the unspoken complaint no weight, sipping from a coupe of champagne as I answered, "He sends his regrets."

"I was hoping we might discuss…"

Money. He was hoping he might discuss my father's money and how much Senator Parker might jam into his blood-drenched pockets.

"You should marry that boy."

Now he had my attention. Skating my glance from Ethan's antics to the scheming politician at my side, I quirked a brow.

Once upon a time the senator had been handsome and

charismatic like his nephew. Now aged, and powerful enough to ignore the crutch of vigor, he'd entered his twilight years, morphing more and more into a jowly blobfish. It had been an interesting transformation to behold.

Ugly and terrible as he was, very few men could hold a stare like a cold-blooded Parker.

This offer of marriage… he wasn't flattering me. He was trying to buy my father with the gilded Parker's name. Which meant he knew something I didn't.

Mistakes, oversights, plain fucking up, led to unspeakable punishments I had no interest in enduring. Senators didn't throw their nephews at heiresses, no matter what the movies portrayed. "You anticipate my father will change factions."

"He mentioned—"

Slipping at the mention of my father for the second time that night, I demanded an answer from a man I'd been commanded to flatter. "What did he say?"

My eyes were blue, my dress was green, and my dark hair had been spun into classic elegance. I was everything memorable and forgettable all at once. I smelled of whale vomit and dead wood.

A born vampire who could walk in the sun—the weakest of my kind and also the most valuable.

Daywalker.

The only offspring of our king.

And I was afraid of my daddy.

For good reason.

When the senator went glassy-eyed under my influence, I demanded, "Tell me what he said to you."

"We have not spoken yet. But, immigration… he expects open borders. My platform… my base. I need to sell hate to secure the vote."

I didn't give a shit about politics, and my father didn't give a shit about people. Humans were a food source, nothing more. He demanded open borders because he wanted undocumented targets to harvest.

I did mention that he was the devil…

Angry, hating being caught off guard, I used the slight influence I possessed. Touching my hand to Parker's fluttering fingers, I planted a seed. "You're senate majority leader. Lying to your constituents is your only vocation. Promise them whatever they want, deliver what *he* wants. You don't want to disappoint Darius King, now do you?"

As I lacked the skill to fully enthrall, Senator Parker had already begun shaking off my pathetic mental influence. Ready to put a little miss in her place, he narrowed his eyes. "Well, you see, child. This is all above your pretty head."

I was older than him by decades. Hell, I'd fucked his grandfather! But that was neither here nor there. "Of course, sir. I apologize. It's just that I adore Ethan."

"Then marry him."

And that, a marriage, in this era of internet and images that even my people could not scrub out of existence, would grant me more time with my Ethan. I would not be easy to wash away. "I'll mention the idea to Daddy."

Sauntering away, the old man crowed, "You do that."

Thirty years prior, I might have let the thin glass of my champagne's coupe shatter in my hand. I might have hurt that man. But I already carried enough regrets and grasped that I'd have to pay for America's uglier desires once my father heard this… despite my obedience.

The devil knew how to extract his due no matter how hard I'd tried to obey.

Draining the glass in my grip, I set it on a passing waiter's tray, reaching for another.

Effervescence danced down my throat, everything gulped in a single swallow. Bubbly champagne spun in my belly, warmed me, but did nothing to slake the thirst I had ignored for the past week.

Having worked my pathetic resources on that flabby prick, working to squash the impending sense of doom, I was starving.

And no soul here could feed me.

Often, I'd flung away feeling of any sort that would not keep me breathing. Loneliness, depression, the need to run as far as I might from this horrible place. Engaging, handsome distractions had served. Obedience served.

Alcohol served.

I snatched another glass from another white-coated server, Cristal running down my throat.

Next, I'd marched toward the food. Caviar, candied bacon, delicacies too difficult to pronounce. I picked at the offered fare, smiling and making small talk with anyone and everyone nearby. Because that was my job.

That's what I was.

A showpiece existing only to overhear gossip and have my mind stripped at my father's leisure.

A fallible disappointment.

The devil would see me crucified for the slip I'd made that night. So why not exacerbate it?

Act a fool before the masses.

Pretend I loved it all, that I was friends with everyone. That I mattered.

Most of my act was for the single interloper who'd invaded my stage.

I saw him before he'd dared speak to me. Slurping down an oyster, assuring he had a clear view of how I sucked the shell as if human food were ambrosia, I sneered.

Of course, night had fallen. My kind had arrived.

Undying, gorgeous, and the last thing on earth I desired, he pushed through the crowd to approach. "Your father granted me rights tonight."

"Have we met?" I could never be sure, because I made no effort to engage with my food.

"I'll be careful of your fragile state." Beautiful chocolate eyes in a Nordic face. That man had been a warrior ages ago, bore the years and experience I lacked.

Pointing out my inferiority and documented physical weakness let me know exactly what type of male my father had sent to seed my womb. "How kind."

Leaning closer, the most beautiful male in attendance dared run his nose near my neck. "You smell of sunshine."

And he'd forgotten sunshine centuries ago. No born vampire would notice such a thing. "Let's get this over with."

"I have a fine room prepared." Smiling, thinking he might

seduce by flashing the tips of his fangs, he beckoned me inside.

"I know someplace better." Weaving my arm through his, daughter of the king of evil, I edged him toward the exit.

4

Arm in arm, I led my father's chosen stud through the city's finest five-star hotel, down halls meant for employees, around corners no patron should see. Escorting him out the side exit where the kitchens tossed their garbage.

A stinking alley infested with rats.

Stiffening, the male seemed to catch onto my game. But it was too late. I had already slighted him and shown the stranger exactly what my father meant when he offered me up for the night.

Dumpster to my right, some poor soul's vomit to my left, I hiked up my skirt and placed my forehead against aged brick. "I'm ready."

No panties. Dry as a desert.

Ass up like a cheap whore, I waited for the inevitable complaint.

"I earned this right! There is a room upstairs where you will serve me."

This old speech I'd heard thousands of times. "You were told you had the right to seed me. That you'd been honored with the opportunity to potentially father the next in my bloodline." And that was a fucking fact. "Not that I was to entertain your pleasure or orgasm. Get to it. I have laundry to do."

He wasn't the first to exact violence when I failed to live up to the fantasy.

Sexy daywalker reeking of bad perfume and the heat of sunshine. A poor vampire weakling who failed to thrive within the hive and bedded down with humans.

How lucky I was to be granted their old cocks.

It was the nose that always broke first. Smashed into my chosen wall as they hissed and tore down their flies.

Not once had my father ordered they be gentle with his weakling offspring. After all, I was immortal. It might take my body time to stitch itself back together, but very few things could actually kill me.

A violent lover certainly wouldn't.

And if he truly wanted the honor of fathering my child, no vampire male would take it too far. The womb must remain intact, after all. Otherwise, where would their little spawn implant?

But before my father's chosen might get underway, the air rippled with the chill of magic. Cursing at the interruption, the man dropped fang and hissed.

A portal opened in our *special* space.

Fuck.

At my back, my paramour stiffened, but wisely withheld acting out further once he beheld who walked through the gate.

"She's been summoned. Finish your business and go." Melodic, wondrous. I hated that voice with a passion.

The blunt head of a half-hard cock prodded my entrance. "I slaved for this honor!"

Blasé, cold, the perfect soldier… my despised guardian folded his arms over his chest. "Enter her, seed the womb, and make offerings to our God. Perhaps he will deem you worthy to try her again."

Under the Viking's breath the slander, "Bastard," paired with a forward thrust.

I didn't recognize entry, or pay any attention to the animal rutting. It's not as if this situation were unique. All vampire-kind were consistently ordered to fuck in an effort to keep the bloodlines strong. Even the pretty asshole trying to spend his cum in me must have been forced to mate hundreds of times, considering his age.

But I? Over and over, those who didn't know better assumed my pussy was some prize worth having. It wasn't.

A sleeve to slake lust within. A potential garden for the next life.

Not that I had ever conceived.

Every single day since I'd reached maturity, I had obeyed the order to try.

Miss a turn of the sun and be beaten. My father's creative

concepts for torture were so extreme that I'd only refused to mate once.

More daywalkers were needed to be his perfect spies. Daywalkers he could flaunt when visiting aristocracy graced *the Cathedral.*

And his troublesome embarrassment of a daughter would become instantly disposable the next time I inevitably pissed him off.

I'd often wondered if I'd even be allowed the honor of holding my future child before I was murdered. Would I be granted the honor of choosing their name?

Jade was such a common stone, as unremarkable and easy to find as a pearl.

I'd hated that name long before I'd heard others laughing behind their hands at how little my father cared to choose something so commonplace.

At my back, the man picked up speed.

A grunt, a hiss, a grunt, and a rougher thrust shoved my slack body fully against the wall. Wafting stench of garbage, steam rising from cooling vomit, the scratch of vermin. He came.

No single apology for breaking my nose was offered when he pulled out and cursed.

"Darius will be notified that you received your honor, Calder." Chanting preceded the opening of another portal gate, our observer expending his magic to expedite the Viking's departure. "You've done us all an honor."

Without so much as a farewell, my horrendous lover obeyed.

Moments later, the air stilled, my paramour gone. But my handler remained.

Turning so my sex could be covered by falling silk, I pressed my shoulder blades to the brick and wiped blood from my healing nose. "*I'll be careful of your fragile state*, he'd said. Dick."

Edging closer, close enough that my stomach rumbled at his scent, the inevitable chastising began. "Jade, you wouldn't be so physically weak if you'd feed as you should. More importantly, starvation clouds your judgment. It makes you unreasonable."

"Malcom." I parroted his demeaning tone. "Despite my submission to having cameras all over my home, I do not enjoy having an audience while I'm being fucked." Angry, hating that this man had stood witness to another session of my degradation, I snapped. "You could have at least turned around!"

Faster than I by far, exponentially stronger, one moment Malcom was a comfortable distance away, the next his fingers carded through my fallen hair. "You need to feed."

How I hated that I jumped.

Against the undead, I was a piss-poor fighter. That didn't stop me from instantly shoving him so hard the wall he flew into cracked from the force.

"Don't touch me!"

He'd rebounded to his feet in a blur, completely unharmed by my outburst. Brushing dust from tailored black slacks, he had the audacity to smirk. "Pathetic, really. You can do better."

And then his fingers were playing with my hair again.

I couldn't effectively retaliate, because he was right. I was starving, and weakened, and so fucking tempted to tear into his flesh, that behind my lips, my fangs punched downward.

Embarrassing.

So I turned my head away instead, eyes locking on the dumpster as if failing to acknowledge him would make him disappear.

Lips at my ear, a willing throat far too close to my salivating mouth, Malcom murmured, "Give me your word that you'll feed tonight, and I'll leave you in peace."

Grinding my teeth, refusing to concede to such a blatant taunt, I hissed, "I'll eat."

Oh, I'd eat. I'd eat and I'd disgust the bane of my existence in a single swoop.

With the pitter patter of rats already creaking under the dumpster, as soon as one might skitter by, I'd snap it up and tear in.

Right there where he could see.

I'd suck that vermin dry and then grab another. Who cared that feeding from animals was forbidden, lowly? Agitated as I was, I didn't even care that I would most certainly be punished once my father found a hint of my action staining my memory.

He backed away at my agreement.

Once my eyes darted to where skittering was the loudest, Malcom knew what I was about. Silvery golden hair wafting about his shoulders like he was some goddamn phantom, he barked, “Jade, don’t.”

But I had already reached out. Fur filled my palm, and almost my mouth, before I realized that I held no rat.

A mewling kitten, dropped before I might scream.

Blood drained from my face. Vampire pale, I stared in horror as the feline scampered back to its hiding place, and I felt a thing I was forbidden from feeling.

“Look at me, Jade.” Why did he dare sound so sympathetic? “The cat’s gone. Look at me.”

Gowned in Chanel couture, prettied, and coiffed, with cum running down my thigh, I didn’t even attempt to pretend that we both didn’t know why I trembled.

“It’s gone. It’s okay.”

Before his fingertips might ghost over my shoulder, before I might have embarrassed myself further, I snapped. “I told you not to touch me!”

Hand hovering, still as the corpse he was, Malcom obeyed. He even took two steps back. Only then did I make my eyes track from that sliver of dark under the dumpster to look at his face.

Like a carved marble statue, beautiful in the same unearthly way all undead were beautiful. It was like staring at God's favorite angel. Outranking almost every last withered soul in the hive, he’d never fallen into the habit of outlandish costumes.

Slacks, a fitted sweater. Utilitarian yet impeccably tailored.

And pity.

He was wearing pity on his impossibly attractive face. "It's ten minutes to midnight. I'll count this last mating towards your debt for tomorrow."

I would not let my wet eyes spill. "Fuck off, Malcom. If you think I'm falling for that, you're going to be disappointed."

His face returned to its normal state of smugness. "You're due home at sundown."

Wiping my nose on the back of my hand, I sighed at the ruin this evening had made of my dress. "And you're reminding me of a standing appointment why?"

"It is my duty to inform you when you have been summoned."

The exact thing he'd announced when he'd intruded on the Viking's interlude. "I see."

He'd interrupted on purpose. Technically he had not broken any rules. I hated when he did that.

Eyes like starlight, jaw flexing, Malcom dared another modicum of emotion. "Do you recall the exact reason why you dislike me, because I can't?"

I had no intention of playing this game with him.

But he muttered on, running a hand through his hair. "I remember *that day*. Why you grew upset when you saw a cat. I remember that you were wearing a blue dress with a red bow."

If his reason for existence was to torment me, he was doing a phenomenal job. "Funny that you remember that dress but don't remember why you sicken me."

"Funny that we remember anything…" The anger on his

face washed away into deep consideration. Crossing his arms over his chest, my custodian sighed. "You haven't even reached a century in age, Jade. You're still such a blind, inexperienced child. Acting out without thinking. Refusing to eat. Pouting."

The light in his eyes, it was as if he thought I were cute. There was no reason I had to stand there and bear it. Brushing past, I made to exit the alley.

"I'll throw you a portal, Jade."

The very thought of taking Malcom's magical charity made me want to scream. "I'll walk. Thanks."

Despite my rejection, he cast a gate at the mouth of the alley, leaving me no other option. "If you'd have eaten, you'd have been able to summon your own."

Fucking prick.

5

Disobedient and ego bruised, I broke my promise to Malcom. I didn't feed.

Not on rats, not on cats…

Not on vampires.

Stomach churning with acid, drenched by the spray of a boiling hot shower, I let the magic of indoor plumbing wash away what had happened in the alley.

Malcom most likely watched me via pinhole cameras, waiting for another sign of weakness he'd taunt me with later —his team monitoring Satan's daughter for one slip.

Guarding, he'd claim. Watching over a precious asset other vampire rulers desired to collect to serve in their courts. Or eat in an attempt to feel the sun one last time.

Fuck modern technology and the all-seeing eye. What need was there for it except to pry?

All I need do was stand in the presence of my father and

the devil would see every last contemplation, mistake, exchange, disappointment that crossed my thoughts.

Darius could tear the mind apart looking for a memory so remote and useless he'd done it only for his own amusement.

I know this because he'd done it to me.

Water turned off, I stepped from the steam and caught my reflection in the mirror. Nose healed and perfectly straight, scrapes and bruises long gone, any set of outside eyes would see me as pristine now that the deluge had scrubbed away the blood on my face.

Inside I was uglier than the pile of vomit I'd just been fucked next to.

I couldn't wait for the sun to rise, to burn my skin and promise me in the sting that no other immortal might come near.

The only company I'd have to tolerate was Ethan's plaything. The blonde had been munching a bowl of chips on my $20,000 couch when I'd walked through the door. Without lifting her eyes from the TV, she'd announced, "Ethan said I could stay."

Well, she was going to be disappointed once she realized he wasn't coming home tonight. My phone had already flashed with a message stating he had a rendezvous lined up. Just like me, he was getting fucked for his family.

Unlike me, he enjoyed it.

His blue-blooded prick was balls deep in a sixty-year-old pussy who liked flowered hats.

Ignoring the beautiful blonde, satisfied that she hadn't

seen the state of my dirtied dress, I shuffled down my hall and locked my bedroom door behind me.

Head throbbing, I'd bunched up my discarded clothing and tossed them out of sight.

Out of mind.

Like the kitten.

Had I been wearing a blue dress that day?

It was so many years ago, and that horror had been the ugliest moment of my life. Small details I couldn't recall, but I did remember the sound my skull had made splitting against stone when my father had flung me across the room.

I remembered seeing chunks of my brain spilled out on the floor.

Everything had gone orange, and I could taste grape.

Six years old.

A baby when I'd cuddled my pretty white cat to death.

She'd had a pink bow around her neck. She'd been sweet. And I'd been so hungry. The next thing I knew, the ball of fur wasn't moving.

So I'd carried her from my glass conservatory where I was made to bear the pain of sunlight while I slept, and entered the hall where my daddy kept court. I'd interrupted to show him, so he could fix her.

Standing from his throne, he'd been furious.

It was the first time I'd recognized his anger directed at myself. Young as I was, I hadn't understood that there were esteemed guests greeting our king. On no level did I grasp his embarrassment when the king's daughter walked in with the animal she'd accidentally eaten.

Feline blood must have been all over my face, I probably licked my little pouted lips as I'd pulled on my daddy's hand and asked for help.

"Daddy, I broke my kitty."

When he'd ignored me, I'd settled for putting my fingers in his, hanging on to look over the reason I wasn't being addressed.

A man with shining, long brown hair and a high forehead. He looked like an old oil painting. Distinguished, old-world aristocratic, and dead-eyed.

Too young to grasp his station, I'd offered the stranger a smile.

Completely failing to notice that the retinue behind him and the entire room were staring at me, I'd said, "Hi."

Belly longing for food, I pressed against my father's leg and clung. I probably had even tried to climb him.

"This is your daywalker?" That man, that golden-eyed stranger, smirked. "She's precious."

I'd shimmied my shoulders at the attention and swung harder on Daddy's arm.

The unsmiling guest measured me with unblinking attention. "Does she favor her mother?"

Large hand settling over my hair, Darius, my beloved father, stroked my head. "Vladislov…"

That one word was the only warning offered. That, and the squeak of pain I'd made when my father gripped my fingers too tight in his fist.

"Come now, old friend." Vladislov picked at his sleeve, outwardly serene. "The little one means no harm—"

And that's when I had done it. Staring at waved brunette hair far longer and prettier than mine, still hungry, I'd instinctively sunk my little fangs into my father's tempting wrist.

Airborne before I might flail at weightlessness, my skull met the wall. Shattering. Large parts of what made me *me* spilled all over the floor.

I don't recall if I'd cried before his overflowing court. After all, half my brain was gone. All I remember is orange. A world of orange and the need to move my body away from danger.

No undead dared assist me, though I could hear my human nursemaid screaming.

To this day, I don't know if she screamed for me, or because that was the last day of her life.

Smearing old stone, over many long minutes, I dragged my broken body out of the throne room with my only functioning limb. Across worn, icy stone, down the galleries to my sunroom where day after day I slept in a glass coffin and burned in the light. I have no clue how I managed to get my body up inside that bed, but that's where I went to die.

Like a wounded animal working on the last dregs of instinct.

And I should have died. A long way from full-grown, the damage was that severe.

But with my head pillowed on bloodstained ivory satin, liquid life itself slipped over my tongue.

Careful fingers put parts of my skull back together. Unable to scream, I wriggled as he'd popped my eye back into the socket. Clinging to the stranger's wrist with the scant energy I had left, an orange version of that foreign, brunette man leaned over my bed and stuffed handfuls of pocketed brain matter into my skull.

While I'd fed from him.

Over horrific hours, I'd mended, and I'd cried. And from that night onward I was terrified of my father.

It was never spoken of, not once. The next interlude where my stupid, childish steps had crossed my father's path it was clear he'd been surprised I still lived.

He had not sent his ancient guest Vladislov to save me.

More importantly, my father had never seen in my mind just why I still drew breath. Everyone just assumed it had looked worse than it was.

Pleased that his naughty Jade wasn't shattered after all, King Darius demanded a kiss on the cheek.

I had run away screaming.

6

"Harder!" I could not shriek it loud enough, could not spread my legs wide enough to make that joining satisfy.

Thrusting with all his sleek-muscled strength, his blonde standing by as she watched, a sweating Ethan pounded my cunt.

"Fuck me harder, goddamnit!" For three more thrusts, the poor human did try, until he came at the unrelenting squeeze of my pussy.

We'd been at it for less than five minutes, after I'd gone down on my knees and worshiped his cock with my mouth.

Because I had a *need*.

The third party staring from the corner had not been invited to join, which was for the best. She could watch Ethan pound into my slit and have him later when desperation and duty called me away. Internal organs throbbing in their requisite for actual release, my body sucked in human cum from a spent cock, churning it up at the gate of my womb.

And I furiously rubbed my clit, chasing what had been lost with Ethan's premature ejaculation.

When I did come, it did nothing to chill the boil—thoughts of dumpsters and vomit and violence the only thing that carried me over the edge.

Unfulfilled despite Ethan's somewhat valiant attempt to hold back, I closed my eyes and tried to melt into the mattress. I tried to breathe through the disappointment.

With a slap of my hip and what was most likely a jaunty smile, he took his weight from my body and did his typical post-sex stroll to the bathroom. He always took it first…

"Do you want me to eat you out?"

Cracking a lid, I peered at the blonde.

Technically, I had been seeded. There wasn't any standing rule that someone couldn't slurp it all out. But I knew that was past the pale.

Not that I gave a fuck in that frustrating moment.

Spreading wider, I invited what's-her-name's attention and let a raspy tongue play where I needed so much more than anyone in my penthouse might provide.

It wasn't until she tried to fist me that I'd finally bent my spine and screamed release.

Immediately, I'd asked her to stop. Sitting up, I'd kissed her cunilingus swollen lips as if she'd done well, and went straight for the freshly-abandoned shower.

Ethan would finish her off, I'd caught them tangled in my

sheets more than once upon exiting the bathroom. She'd squealed like a champion porn star, and he'd winked at me, surging with silly male pride.

I liked the show, the fakeness of it. Both were grade-A pretenders.

Both tasted sweet when their fluids hit my tongue.

But she was gone by the time I'd washed and dried my abundant dark hair.

Ethan remained, dressed in a beautiful gray suit for whatever function he was to attend that night.

Smiling, I sat at my vanity and began to style my hair.

"I adore you. You know that." An eager puppy, all big-eyed and cute.

He earned a huge smile, one that grew stunted at his next words.

"Kitty's pregnant." Expression warm in the reflection, adjusting his cufflink like he always did when he was nervous, Ethan softly pled, "Can we keep her?"

Brow arching and like the perfect idiot, my brain failed to put two and two together. "Can we keep her?"

Kissing the exposed nape of my neck, he smiled against my skin before stringing a glittering new necklace around my throat. "Yes. Imagine the three of us and a little baby. Won't that be fun?"

…he was talking about a person, not a pet. "Who's Kitty?"

Ethan's startled chuckle failed to hide unusual agitation under his mirth. "You're kidding, right?"

He couldn't be talking about the blonde. "I thought her name was Polly."

The last bit of his smile dried up. Straightening to loom over my reflection in the vanity's mirror, he frowned. "We haven't played with Polly in over a year, darling. Her name is Kitty."

The necklace, the ambush of compliments and sweetness… it began to sink in. If it wasn't so disappointing, it might have been amusing. "And she's pregnant..."

A locked jaw, sheepish answer. "Yes."

Knowing my extended direct gaze made him uncomfortable, I refused to let him look away. "And you want *us* to keep her."

"I do."

Now this was something... that didn't feel at all good.

Slipping an earring into my left lobe, I stood. Velvet robe gaping just enough to hint at nudity underneath, I moved with the grace my thoughts lacked. "You got your fucktoy pregnant, and what you're really asking is if *I* will keep her. As in, keep her here for you." Knowing what his answer would be, but making him voice it all the same, I purred, "Since you seem awfully enamored with the idea of your *Cat* filling up with cream, why not take her back to your penthouse and play daddy?"

"You know I can't—"

"No. I don't know that. All I know is that you want your girlfriend to house your pregnant fucktoy."

"Stop calling her that."

"I didn't even know her name." Which made this all the

more humiliating considering my unseen audience. "Why you think I'd be invested in hiding your love child from Senator Parker, I cannot begin to understand."

Gritting his teeth, jaw working, Ethan set aside the charade. "She was a stripper, Jade. A nobody. I can't take that home! Imagine the scandal."

Reaching for my phone, going through the motions as if this conversation were a quick chat about the weather, I shrugged. And I felt *angry*.

I'd never been angry with Ethan.

"Look. You have plenty of rooms here and the green guestroom already has a bunch of her clothes in it. You're never home and you won't even notice she's here. We'll get a nanny to keep the baby quiet."

Pinching my brow together, I turned on him, as if such an idea were totally absurd. To say I wish I had not charged from my room like a disgruntled lover to find that my expectations were not reality was an accurate statement. I should have been embarrassed; instead I was totally baffled upon arrival to the *green guestroom*.

Just as Ethan had said, feminine shit was everywhere. The bed had been slept in. Even dirty clothes were on the floor. Most of the scattered couture was mine—borrowed without permission by an interloper.

I'd known she'd hung around. I'd known she'd eaten my food and fucked my lover when I was too busy to do it. But this… carnage. She'd been living here, and I hadn't deigned to notice.

Abashed, when he found the stricken look on my face,

Ethan offered, "I'll have her clean this up. We can set the rules. Manage her allowance."

Why did that hurt so much?

Like the viper I was—a true daughter of the king of deceit—I let anger, hunger, and humiliation wash away reason. "You are extraordinarily out of line. My answer is *no*." I lifted a finger when it looked as if he thought to interrupt. "This relationship has been taken for granted far too long for you to expect my feelings about a stranger living in my house would be blasé. A stranger, it would seem, who already is living in my house… I don't mind sharing you; I like fucking other people. But they are just faces, and pussies, and cocks. We are not a ménage."

And there it was, a flash of shame in his desperation. "I *love* her, Jade."

He couldn't. He was supposed to love me.

"No, you don't." Softening the blow, I put a hand to his arm and gave a gentle squeeze. "You may like her a lot, but she's no different than any of the other blondes we've tangled with. They all look alike. They all laugh the same. Each of them fawn over you. That's what you love. The only reason Kitty, or Polly, or whatever her name is seems special, is that this one got pregnant. Most likely on purpose. Cut her loose. We'll find a new one. A better one."

It was as if someone had told the spoiled boy he couldn't have a new kitten for Christmas. All frowns and hurt feelings, he said, "Kitty and I have gotten to know each other. I mean it when I say I love her."

Lacking my father's skill at making people dance on my

stage, I tried my damnedest to take that lie straight out of his mind. "No. You don't."

If he'd loved her, he would have taken this Kitty home, and not tried to hide away his massive fuckup at his conveniently non-jealous girlfriend's penthouse.

Lifting the cellphone clutched near cracking in my grip, I dialed security before I might do something I would always regret. When the officer answered, my voice didn't waver in the slightest. "I'm going to need my locks changed and codes reprogramed within the hour. Ethan Parker is no longer cleared to enter. He'll need to be escorted off the premises immediately."

The line clicked, Ethan raising his voice to me for the first time ever. "Jade!"

"You need to leave now. I'll have your things sent over in the morning." I'd barely finished the sentence before there was a loud knock on the door. "Be happy with your Kitty. Congratulations on the baby."

Angry, flabbergasted he was not getting his way, he sneered. "Don't make me choose between you!"

He'd have to learn this lesson the hard way. Just like me, he had no choice in this.

He'd be made to marry me. There would be no more blondes. This Kitty, Ethan would keep her as a novelty for a little while, and then he'd start to chafe. He was right; he couldn't take a stripper on his arm to the Met. He couldn't take her to gallery openings, or to the fine restaurants his kind populated. She'd be out on the street with a baby he'd conveniently forget he'd fathered before the year was up.

Then he'd be back at my side, loving and funny, and everything that kept my nightmares away.

Until then… I'd survive.

The door opened, a familiar security detail entering my house.

"Goodbye, Ethan." Padding barefoot over cold marble floors, I made my way through the beautiful penthouse my father made me live in, and left Ethan to Malcom's daylight team.

It took twice as many hours to apply my makeup, my cheeks embarrassingly wet.

7

Sundays, from sundown to sunup, belonged to the Cathedral. Ethan had always believed I'd attended evening Mass, that I escorted my infirm, eccentric father to take the Eucharist and drink the blood of Christ. The boy had found it equally hilarious and appalling that I kept to my family obligations in such a way.

I, the sexual deviant and sinner.

And never questioned why he wasn't invited.

The man would joke that he'd rather be beaten within an inch of his life than attend church—that even his senator uncle had never made such demands.

More than once I'd been beaten within an inch of my life. So faithfully, I arrived on time to my father's seat of power and left thoughts, regrets, agitations, and dissatisfaction at the door.

No savior carried the weight of my sins here.

There was no worship on site, not of God anyway. A great deal of sacrilege took place in its stead.

Ethan would not have survived five minutes under these ancient, hidden spires. Buried at the blackened heart of the city, an entire block wasn't what it appeared. Innocuous row houses, well-kept and quiet. Picket fences and garden pots. Cars parked on the street.

No human soul would be the wiser of just what haunted the shadows here… just what was tucked behind those houses.

I preferred to access the hidden Cathedral through a less conspicuous entrance than a magicked portal into the warded entrance hall. A cab down tree-lined streets, a regular key on a Tiffany's keychain, a modestly decorated façade of a foyer, and a contract bound, recently changed servant waiting with modernity's tablet in hand to greet those granted access through my favored private entrance.

Heels clicking over waxed wood floors, I stripped off my coat, handing it to an unfamiliar fresh-turned, without breaking stride.

Fumbling fox fur and hand-held device, a pretty brunette whom I suspected had been chosen for her particularly stunning eyes, made a noise of impatience at my rudeness.

I never came *home* to make friends with new and very expendable servants. And hungry, I was in no mood to try as I might have decades before. "Is there anyone set for execution? If so, send them to me."

"Excuse me?"

Blowing over her non-question, I tried to shake off the

itchy feeling this place pressed upon me. Impatient, I snapped. "The conservatory. Send me something to eat."

Having made my way through the townhouse, I reached the end of what hid my father's fortress from a city of cattle. Hand to a spike-riddled door more ancient than this country, I pushed the weight no human might shift alone. Hinges groaned, and candlelight waited.

We did things the old way here.

Well, it might better serve to say we blended some human novelties with beeswax, scented lamp oil, slavery, and the distant sounds of screams.

Many of those echoing shouts were of ecstasy. Not all though.

In my father's expansive region, it wasn't considered tasteless to fuck what you fed from. After all, how else was his flock to make new little vampires with pretty eyes and bad manners? It was best to woo them first. Those always made the best contract servants. Forced changes rarely ended well. More to the point, if you're signing away your life to practical slavery for three hundred years, it was best to at least get an orgasm out of it.

Besides, sexual procreation was difficult, and wars that ate up fresh meat were always fought between ancient rivals and their flocks.

This time of dusk, few lurked around the Cathedral halls, the ritual of preparation *to be seen* so deeply ingrained in many of those who ranked highest here, that it might as well have been the court of Versailles. Like the others of my station, I too had spent an inordinate amount of time dressing.

I had to be perfect.

My father expected it.

A princess was a reflection on her king, wasn't she?

Even an outraged one.

Immaculate, coiffed, makeup flawless, and a new a glittering reminder that I'd get my Ethan back clinging around my throat, I looked the part. More care was taken with the choice of sapphire blue cocktail dress than I might spend on the red carpet for the Met's outrageously ostentatious annual costume gala.

Hair gathered back from my forehead, sleek and long, it hung from a ponytail so my throat might be bare. A subtle *fuck you* to my father's people—vampires who went to outrageous lengths to keep their weak points concealed with jewelry, collars, ruffs, turtlenecks.

Yes, I was physically weaker than even the freshly-turned, pretty-eyed female who still stalked behind me asking questions I ignored. Yes, I feed from immortals who could snap me in half on a whim. But none would *ever* dare.

Not unless they wanted to spend an eternity as my father's newest plaything. After all, the devil could think up extraordinary acts of pain, make a symphony from tortured screams.

A dark-haired servant—another freshly-turned contract worker—walked past me as I moved through narrow stone halls. The delicious scent of a well-fed vampire wafted, drawing my eyes for a lingering look.

Mouth watering, I fought the urge to feel the silken slip of my fangs slide down. Gums tingling, I repressed the need. I left the unknown immortal alone.

One, who unlike my yammering shadow sniping about protocol, knew who I was.

No damned soul wanted to be fed upon by a daywalker. It was an embarrassment of sorts every last member of my father's herd avoided at all costs, though none were allowed to deny the king's offspring should I ask for a taste.

All designed to keep them hating me. To keep me from making a home with the only creatures in existence who wouldn't die with each passing year.

To keep me lonely and politically weak, while giving me more power than any creature haunting this hellhole.

The tight smile the male offered, the subtle nod of his head said just as much. *Please, I'm new and already fodder for the ancients who toy with us at will. Please, I might be too weak to survive the things I've heard Satan's daughter likes to do.*

"My lady."

Those two words, and still the young female tracking me kept yammering. "You can't be back here. I don't have you on the list!"

Instead of helping a fellow contract-bound fresh-changed, the male slipped away when I forced my head to turn away from the appetizing temptation his very presence presented.

My hands shook, but my feet continued forward on the well-worn stone. Conservatory before me, head aching from denying the feed, throat parched in a way water might never relieve, I put my hands to the unguarded double doors of a room made of glass.

A room made to harden the soft skin of a baby daywalker to sunlight.

Before I might find sanctuary in my private indoor garden, the freshly-changed vampire female grabbed my wrist. "I told you, you can't—"

To my left, shadow became flesh. And before the youngling might finish her complaint, her head became pulp against the wall. Smell of blood overwhelming, a shudder vibrated from my spine to bloodless fingertips.

There was no preventing the excruciating way my fangs descended, long and deadly, behind my tension thinned lips. Eyes to the door I'd only barely cracked open, I tried not to slur through my teeth as I deadpanned, "She didn't know who I was."

Malcom stood stoic, the embodiment of disapproval. "Nor did you tell her."

Which meant he blamed me for the death he'd doled out.

Abandoning the blood-splattered hall that left my stomach loudly growling. Refusing, even famished as I was, to feed upon the dead, I left stone floors for sumptuous Persian rugs, ivory inlay, and cobalt tile. Victorian architecture made up my beautiful cage, the scent of growing things, and a room that, come daybreak, would be drenched with stinging sunlight.

Home.

The little glass coffin my father had once demanded I sleep in still had its place, untouched by time, yet polished to a sparkling sheen by some unknown slave in my absence. Edwardian couches, ancient wardrobes, tables set for a feast that would never be laid. Branching glass side rooms for sleeping, bathing, reading—every need readied and staged for immortal and mortal alike.

There were even trickling fountains granting the air a pleasantness that the sheer beauty of the room could never accomplish. No amount of sunshine, tended roses, fruit trees, or satin might break up the taint of this place.

Fisting my fingers until knuckles cracked, I grew irritated that the dead servant in the halls had never placed my order. No breathing undead meal waited.

What was the point of having a smart device in these dead halls if the greeter for the Broad Street entrance didn't use it? What had she done with my fox fur coat? If her blood was on it, I'd never be able to wear it again without salivating constantly.

"Jade… your eyes are red."

Malcom's impatience at being left unacknowledged fed my impatience at his lurking. "You were not invited into my rooms."

"I have leave to enter any room you choose to grace with your presence." He dared run his fingertip down an errant drip of blood his little show in the hall had left on my bare arm.

"Not here you don't!" Already I had him by the throat, his shined shoes barely scraping the ground once his back hit the wall. "No soul has leave to enter my rooms without permission. I know that for fact."

What a vision I must have made: lips drawn back, fangs glinting, and eyes as red as the demon who'd sired me. Holding one of the most powerful males in my father's guard pinned by the throat.

And he could have broken my arm, broken my body, at any time in retaliation.

But hunger made me as stupid as Malcom had warned me it would.

I couldn't truly hurt this man if I wanted to, and I did. I wanted it badly.

I wanted to tear into flesh and sinew, gnaw his bones for marrow.

I wanted to feel his last heartbeat while I sucked in the stygian blood that made him immortal.

I wanted to feast.

Reaching out, fingers soft because predators of the night were designed to be tempting in all ways, Malcom gave my earlobe a tweak. "You should have eaten. You promised me, Jade."

Hating how often he used my name, I meant to hiss, but found my head turning toward the subtle *thump, thump, thump* of the pretty arteries in a beautiful wrist drumming by my ear.

Marble white skin, blue capillaries. A lovely delta spreading from a single, juicy vein.

The groan left me before I might rein in the animal inside. Tongue flicking out, I forgot the man I held by the throat, the one suspended over the ground by my sheer strength, and tasted my lower lip instead.

Pleasure waited with just one bite.

Fulfillment.

And I began to ache, *I was so hungry.*

Right there, right before me was a balm to such pain. Right there was everything I'd ever wanted.

Teeth sunk in, raking deep so cool blood might flow so much faster into my mouth.

Pressing that wrist to my lips, I gorged, sucked hard… drained him.

Until a horrifying moment of clarity broke though the frenzy.

He must have noticed when sanity returned, for the bastard dared stroke my hair with his free hand… Or had been the whole time I'd acted the fool?

"Take what you need."

I dropped him. I backed away. I ran the back of my hand over my blood-red lips.

And I could not meet his eye for the shame.

That was nothing to the utter dread that surged into my breast a moment later.

"Daughter," a living nightmare whispered into the room behind me. "How good it is to see you."

8

It had been five months since my Father had last approached me in his Cathedral. Five months in which I'd grown complacent.

Five months since I felt raw fear the way I felt it when his dulcet voice drifted over my ears.

Scrubbing my mouth of all traces of blood, as if that might make any difference, I'd made sure to straighten my dress before turning to curtsy and cast my eyes to the floor. "Father."

Robed, he still dressed as if ruling the ancient Persian empire from which he'd hailed, vivid, gem-encrusted red scraped over the floor. He came nearer.

"My king. Senator Parker has proposed a marriage between your daughter and his nephew. He seeks to keep your favor as he abandons your policies. Jade argued with the boy this afternoon, sent him to his mistress." Just like that, the only report of note I had to deliver was stolen—Malcom taking the credit and leaving me to look petulant, weak, and most importantly, disobedient.

For I had not made note of the situation the previous evening, too busy scrubbing off the stink of garbage and cum. Then I had played at bed sport with the human who'd failed to seed my womb for years.

Unable to resist the scratch of filthy fingers picking though my thoughts, I wobbled on my feet, regained balance, and tried my best not to resist King Darius' mental probe.

"It's unbecoming, daughter." I heard it. I felt it. I knew my daddy's words in every last cell.

My attachment to Ethan: the feelings of comradery. He and I, both servants to great houses. Trying to paint myself as if it were us against an unjust world. My righteous anger that he'd claimed to love a replaceable blonde.

"How many times must we have this discussion? Did you learn nothing from your time with Gerard?" As if loving, as if he wasn't seeking to make me squirm for his own amusement, my father chided, "Did that old corpse leave his wife for you? Did he love you back?"

"No." Yes. Yes, he had. He'd loved me and he'd been sent off to die in the war thanks to Malcom's interference.

And that was entirely the wrong thought to have in the presence of all-seeing evil.

The taste of King Darius' displeasure soured the stolen blood in my belly. It turned my bones to mush. Even so, I looked up, certain my eyes were pleading for mercy I'd never know. "I wish to marry Ethan."

I wished to run away with him and hide where no shadows could ever touch me.

"Hmmmm." A warm sound that chilled my marrow. More beautiful than any ancient contracted to walk the halls of my father's Cathedral, the king of my entire universe sighed. The unbearable weight of glowing red eyes left my body to settle on my guardian. "Tell me, Malcom. Has she been repeatedly disobedient?"

My father's favored guard did not hesitate. "She uses starvation as a means of rebellion, but in no other way has she dissatisfied." Feet planted as if an entire temple were braced on his shoulders, Malcom was the perfect servant. The perfect informant. "I suggest a mandatory feeding schedule and the installation of rotated offerings placed in her building to attend her requirements."

A trough of unwilling and embarrassed immortals for me to nip at when I had a hankering.

Already my cheeks heated from the mockery that would be made behind my back should my father agree.

I'd rather starve, eat once a week, and look strong in the only way I could, than be forced to snack nightly like my brethren did. This *rebellion*, as Malcom called it, was all I had to own my place here.

I hadn't seen him move, but next thing I knew, my father's thumb and forefinger pinched my chin. "You don't look enough like your mother to please me, girl. Keep that in mind when you let your thoughts run wild."

Because I looked just like him. Same high forehead, same lush mouth.

The only thing I had of her was the blue of my eyes… when they didn't go red.

"I apologize." For being born the way I was.

Next I knew, my hands were taken, arms spread so my father might peruse my clothing. "I like this color. Next thing you know, black will no longer be the staple at court."

Black had not been in vogue for years, but my father had not sat his throne or paid attention to such trivialities for longer than that.

My thoughts made him smirk.

Pressing a fatherly kiss to my cheek, I heard my sentence for whatever list of failings he'd compiled. "Malcom, you've done well. Tonight she's yours."

"Sir," Malcom said with perfect reverence.

"Well, go ahead. She's failed with everyone else. Enjoy your reward and give me a grandchild."

To protest in any other way than the hysterical quickening of my heart and shallow breaths was unthinkable. I hated Malcom more than I hated life itself, yet still I turned, bending over the nearest table to present.

With my father as witness, my short skirt was lifted, lace thong pulled down my buttocks to stretch across my spread thighs. And then the blunt end of an extremely hard cock met the dry lips of my sex.

Quickly working himself in, Malcom took my hips and began a slow, steady pace. All the while I stared at the wall, unblinking, even when my father's red robes slipped from my door.

The snap of the latch, two more thrusts, and Malcom ceased the rock of his hips. "Do you wish for me to stop?"

Nodding my head, I was already sobbing before he drew completely out. Slipping from the table to the floor, too overwrought to be ashamed of such a display, I curled in on myself and cried harder than I had in years.

I wept at the feet of a man I'd never forgive, and let him pet my hair because I lacked the strength to show him just how much I desired his death.

Broken by something so commonplace as penetration, I was every bit the child Malcom endlessly accused me of being.

Crouching so that his weight rested on the balls of his feet, he set his lips to my ear, whispering things I could not hear over the sound of my sobbing. Not one utterance made sense, just catches of meaningless sound.

But somewhere, somewhere between my gasps and choking, a single string of coherent, unlikely words broke their way through the gibberish muddling my thoughts. "This does not change how much I love you, my darling Jade."

9

MALCOM

And yes, I loved her. I loved her with my entire being. For a century I'd watched her every breath and counted the beats of her heart. I'd broken her, I'd hurt her, and I'd done every evil thing possible to keep her alive.

Because my Jade was so young and so foolish. So goddamn blind.

If she only knew what I'd sacrificed, what I still gave, to keep her safe. What do I care if she hates me? Jade doesn't need to love me back. I love her enough for both of us.

"You will eat now."

"Get out, Malcom!" Crouched down at my feet, she tore at her hair as if to erase my touch, ruining the sleek ponytail she'd worn to mock those she secretly wished would accept her. And, again, I loved her enough to make up for every last immortal's loathing of their princess.

"Your father, *your king*, decreed that you are mine tonight. A specific period of time, Jade. The sun won't rise for many hours yet. You will eat. You will bathe. You will converse with me."

It was as if I had said something utterly inconceivable. Blue eyes ringed in red, bloodshot from crying, and unbearably beautiful, turned up. She looked at me. Right at me. And could not see what stood before her.

And I knew why. I knew what tricks Darius played. How many times he'd written and rewritten what memories this female possessed, how many times he'd altered her and coerced the ugliest parts of her psyche to come forth.

And even those parts were beautiful.

She was a creature of his twisted design, as selfish and proud and cruel as he could make her. But even he could only push so far. In the wreckage of his mental machinations, under all of it, Jade was still Jade.

My Jade.

Who for the first time in almost a century, I got to have for the night. *To have*, not to guard. Mine until sunrise. All because I understood the games and she did not.

"You may feed from me." I straightened, imperious and imposing as those wet eyes measured my stature. "Or I can summon another."

Without thinking, without understanding the true reason why she picked cruelty, why she chose exactly as I knew she would, Jade named, "The fresh-changed male from the hall. I want him."

What she wanted, deep down, was to irritate me. Because

no matter what her father stripped from her memories, *she knew*. Somewhere in that mess, she knew she was mine, and desired a display of my regard.

Spying from the shadows, I'd seen the way she'd salivated for the male. And yes, I was envious—black blood boiling jealousy I'd never expose. Not where the Devil might see.

Here minds must be kept blank. Here one never lied.

After all, the truth could conceal far more than any subterfuge. Jade was too free with her feelings, those fleeting childlike things.

Even that I loved about her.

My blind little mistress still had her panties caught around her thighs, I could almost see a sliver of her beautiful cunt. I certainly could smell it.

"Don't look at me like that." Her whip-like snap, her embarrassment and anger… even after all her lovers, she was still so *innocent*.

"You're beautiful, Jade." Especially when she blushed.

Finding her outrage and pulling it about the sad, frightened, and cracked parts of herself, she filled weakness with rage. Glue settled into a damaged spirit, my princess lashing out. "I hate you."

"That can't be helped."

She hated when my voice remained even in the face of her anger. *Hated it*. But what was I supposed to do, quote sonnets to her? Sing? I was forbidden from courting her. I was forbidden from wooing her.

Darius knew.

He'd seen it when I'd first set eyes on the infant, and he'd laughed. A pealing, cackle of evil mirth I could still hear echo between my ears. The honor of guarding his offspring, the demotion from favored assassin, assured I'd know torment every waking hour. Forced to watch her fall in love, forced to see her fucked by multitudes. Forced to watch her father use her in the most horrendous of ways.

I had made mistakes over the last century, and she had paid for them. But I am also the only reason she still breathed.

My aching cock had been in her for two minutes, forty-seven seconds. I could have come on that first thrust… but it would have only made her sad.

My *starving* cock had been in her after a century of longing, and it had been done to punish us both.

I wouldn't fail her again, but I was also not giving up my night of her company. "Come now, Jade." Helping her stand, I dared much. Lace in my fingers, I pulled up her panties, my features perfectly controlled.

Hers… were not.

Batting my hands away, she pulled down her skirt and put as much distance between us as she could. Straight to a side table bearing a decanter of her favorite wine she went—difficult to acquire wine I had procured for her and ordered to be available in her rooms. It was difficult to acquire because I had bought every last bottle I could find the very night I'd first seen her try it. Three cellars in this city were packed with cases of the rare vintage, doled out by me for her without her knowledge.

Red fluid hit her tongue, that moment of recognition, the flicker of appreciation when the flavor profile worked its magic. It calmed her, just enough.

These little things. These small moments I gave her…

“Repair your appearance before Lawrence arrives. Should you let him live, you don’t want there to be talk.”

Exasperated, she kept her back to me yet snarled over her shoulder. “I’m not going to kill him.”

That remained to be seen.

She fed like the demon who’d bred her. Not always, and the lad had a greater chance of survival considering she’d already had a taste of me. But when she starved, as she was wont to do, she was as messy as a freshly-turned babe.

Pride, alluring and adorable, Jade reeked of it as she smoothed her hair. Silver handled brush *I had obtained* from a long-dead Russian noble in her hand, ran through jet locks. All that raven glory was caught up again, tied back, beautiful, vulnerable throat on display. Almost every trinket in this room, every last treasure, an unknown gift from me.

A knock came to the door.

Jade poured herself another glass of wine. She made the nervous male wait.

Cruel.

Maybe she would let him live…

On that note, I was wrong. Detached from the scene, unmoving from the same spot where I’d penetrated her thirty-eight minutes fifty-four seconds ago, I stood by as she unleashed what she really was on the boy.

His first mistake was trying to fight back when she'd drained him just a little too much. It was the only time Jade was stronger than the rest of us, and whatever deeply set inferiority her father had fostered made a bully of the starved girl.

The harder they fought, the more violent she grew, the deeper she drank. Someone should have warned the child. Daywalkers couldn't help but kill.

When it was done, when her dress was ruined with immortal blood and the life had gone out of the rival male's eyes, the flash of regret in hers came. As it always did.

I would have killed him outside of these rooms, my jealousy in that moment was so acute. I longed to wrench his head from his shoulders, to tear off the cock she'd ridden as she'd feasted. She'd made him cum in his frenzy to survive her.

Sexual quota met for the night, but there wouldn't be a child.

Jade would carry no male's child but mine. We had eternity to assure it.

Disengaging from the corpse, its sorry, flaccid cock falling from her body, Jade failed to disguise her self-loathing.

My feet began to move, carrying me toward her because I could never resist. "Bathe yourself. I shall choose what you will wear."

Voice small, she stared down at what she'd done. "Please leave me alone, Malcom."

Never. Never for a single instant was she ever free of me. "No."

"You've made your point!" The nearest treasure went flying, shattering against the conservatory's bullet proof glass.

A Fabergé egg. Irreplaceable. I'd acquired it for her tenth birthday.

Ignoring her common outburst, I refilled her abandoned glass of wine, wondering what it was about that vintage that pleased her so profoundly. I'd never had it on my tongue, not when it was for her.

Someday I'd taste Jade's after she'd consumed this drink. Maybe it would perfume her flavor. Maybe it would calm her when I drank from that perfect vein between her creamy thighs.

She took the offered glass, vibrant eyes weighing the temptation to throw it in my face. Instead she sipped, rinsing the taste of that lesser male from her mouth.

"Take a bath." Wash the stink of another off your skin. "You've had a *complicated* day. You'll feel better if you allow your body to relax."

I love you. I love you so much that I broke an almost century-long pact and whispered it in your ear while you wept.

"I'll clean this up." Already I was dragging the corpse by the ankle toward her door. Servants would be called and the blood removed. Ours was an efficient hell.

Frustrated, tired, my darling said, "Malcom. You don't have to stay…"

"Your father ordered me to give him a grandchild." And these rooms were made of glass, the moon was high, and very little was more interesting for my people to watch, to hate, and to gossip about. Should I leave, it would cause her more harm than good.

"But I…" Blue eyes darting toward the door I'd flung the corpse of her feast through, all the color drained from her face. "I already…"

She would not be getting away from this. I'd watched every breath of her life and knew every last trick she'd used to humiliate the others. Not a single one would work on me. "There are ways to assure you enjoy it."

I knew exactly where to touch her, what pressure she preferred, the order of strokes that would make her scream my name. There was not a single act of coitus she'd participated in that I had not viewed. With modern technology, I even had recordings of the best, so that I might study them and prepare.

Fresh tears, real tears began to gather in her gaze, and then she pled, she pled beautifully. "My father promised me he'd never let you have me."

What was there to say? Only the truth. I'd literally just penetrated her before him. "He is the king of lies."

And the things she'd done to earn that promise, the humans she'd allowed sully her skin. Another fragment of her pride crumbled, another flash of the real Jade shining through from underneath.

"I've ordered lamb for your dinner. It will be waiting when you've completed your bath." Her favorite, prepared by a brilliant chef I'd personally turned in 1936 for this express purpose, because daywalkers need more than the blood of their brethren. "You will eat. Afterward we shall play a game of Risk. Beat me, and I'll allow you to choose a film."

A sculpted brow arched, Jade's hands coming to her hips. "You want to play board games and watch a movie?"

Is that not what humans did? Yes. Yes, it was. Jade loved human things, human toys, human bodies. Modern human customs…

It was adorable, reminded me of my long-lost youth.

I drove the point home. "If you'd rather, there is a hunt planned throughout the premises for tonight's entertainment. The humans are to be set free from the pens, led to believe they might escape, and chased for sport. A great prize is being offered to the vampire who gathers the most ears."

Like me, she knew what the prize would be "A night with me…"

"There is no greater prize than you, Jade."

Shifting her weight, my love took a step toward her bathing chamber. "I don't want to terrorize humans and cut off their ears."

Exactly my point. "Then we'll stay in and avoid unpleasantness."

As she soaked in a tub crafted of solid gold, as she washed off the other male and her disgusting perfume, I chose her clothing for the night. Modest silk pajamas and a blue robe to adorn her limbs.

Hair wet, face devoid of paint. Purely herself with the artifice scrubbed off, she took a seat, drank her wine, and faced me over the game board.

Of course, I let her win.

The film of her choosing was *Seven Samurai*, a movie so long it assured the sun would chase me away before the story concluded. Smirking, I allowed her this rebellion, horrifying her a moment later when I drew her feet to my lap and began to carefully paint her toenails a soft pink.

I didn't need to read her thoughts to know she grasped it was *this* or be fucked by a creature she hated even more than herself.

I'm not a doll, her eyes screamed. *You can't just dress me up and paint me!*

Blowing on her toes, I ignored the silent protest, too caught up in the fact that I was touching her, that the arch of her foot rested on my palm… that it might be centuries before I'd be permitted to do something so intimate again.

Before dangerous thoughts might follow on that wave of realization, I switched off feeling. I became blank. Then I met her eyes and stated, "The new feeding schedule will be enforced starting tomorrow—every evening, under my supervision, until you can learn to feed without killing your prey."

Lips curling, a hint of undescended fang catching the light, Jade threatened me like a kitten poking a tiger. "I thought you wanted me to feed from you."

"The option stands." Chest puffing out, arms flexing as if I'd already had her pinned, I smiled right back. Unlike my timid kitten, I let the full length of my fangs slip down. "But even at your worst, you don't stand a chance of overpowering me."

"We'll see."

So I offered my wrist, knowing she'd reject potent blood half the females in this flock would kill to taste.

Nose in the air, she turned her head. Predictable. Adorable. And mine for another two hours.

10

When the sun's approaching rays began to pinken the sky, I felt the burn itch and scratch anywhere flesh was exposed. Still I sat beside my Jade, her film nearing an end, and her easy snores divine.

She'd fallen asleep in my near presence, a thing that had not happened since she was a child.

What a human thing to do. After all, vampires didn't sleep; not in this way.

We became dead, we even rotted. Another reason immortal vanity was an endless cycle. Wake, bathe and deny the rotting truth with paint, and silk, and rare jewels.

Coffins were not entirely out of fashion, they kept the smell at bay. Until our eyes opened, until that heart began to beat again, whatever damage done in our rest immediately mended so long as we fed. Death reversed. Beautiful under the pus, tempting once the worms worked free… I don't miss the days of digging a hole underground when moved to slumber.

In those foundling years, sleep could last for months. But with age came freedom from the grave.

With the passage of time came extravagance.

A windowless room where I might lay naked so expensive clothing would not smell of decay. Solitary and hidden in the hive while death took what it felt it was owed. After waking, bathing was a chore and a luxury in this era. I recall going years at a time, stinking putrefaction stuck to my furs. Not that it would be noticed under the foul odors unwashed humans emitted.

Even when circumstance required I'd lived in the mud, I'd always had a penchant for cleanliness. Typically, when I'd dined, I'd devour a family person by person, leaving the most industrious to wash, stitch, weave, or prepare whatever I might require.

Often enough, that person was female.

Had they performed to my standards, I'd even turn them so their service might continue. Well, unless they refused to stop weeping over their dead husbands, brothers, fathers, children. A lesson all vampires learned young. Don't waste eternal life on those who might bear an endless grudge.

However, more often than not, the females were relieved to be free of their yokes. Half in love with the beautiful stranger who whispered in their ear that the world could serve their every desire.

Hundreds of women I gifted with the night. To this day,

perhaps a dozen still walked the earth. For immortal beings, vampire's lives were miraculously short.

War. Feuds. Humans. Earth too hard to carve out a hole in which to sleep before the sun might strike.

Boredom…

Centuries passed. True cities began to spring up, to offer hunting grounds and a haven for immortal delights.

Vampires became myth—desirable, eternally young, untouched by the troubles of the human world.

Glorified, yet every last one of us in this age was beholden to a master.

Those who lived ages, lived in even a way I—after century upon century—could hardly grasp. King Darius was not the only ancient.

If rumor stood, neither was he the most cruel. All of them were rotted souls on the inside, whether their bodies be beautiful or hideous. But they were also necessary to the survival of us all.

We were not a gentle species, and with such long memories, we rarely forgot even the smallest of slights, eager to exact our petty revenges. Kings were required to control the flock. Queens were required to enforce laws. Those who could not be cold and cruel and do what needed to be done became dust.

Jade was a terrible vampire, a terrible human, but for a daywalker… she was everything.

Could be anything.

So pretty with her lips parted and her chest rising and falling in rest beside me on the couch. Dark hair, thick and smooth as satin. I preferred her unpainted, unpolished, just like this.

With pink toes.

Had I met her when I was still human. Had I pillaged her village. At first glance, I would have taken her for my own, hefted over my shoulder after spilling my seed in her womb. Claiming her for my tribe to see.

She'd have born me a dozen sons, half dark as her, half fair as their father.

My mother and sisters would have taught her our language and marked her with lashes until she loved me as she should. No matter what modern history books say, women didn't get traded for goats. They were stolen, branded, and claimed.

I would have fucked her day and night until her belly swelled with my offspring. As my father did my mother, I would have tamed her until she accepted that she belonged in my hut. In these modern times, males drew their women with food, drink, entertainment, gifts.

It was exceedingly unnatural.

Had I found her ages past, she would have earned gifts from me as she nursed our young. Stolen trinkets from the Romans, fine furs from my kills. We could have grown old together. Whichever of us had survived the other having been burnt alive with their spouse's body so united souls might never be parted.

I'd burn with her now in this horrible rising sun if it would assure she'd be with me for eternity.

She and I in the fire, ready to face the Gods of the afterlife. Finding the children we'd lost to fevers waiting—and her brothers, slain by my sword, would smile to find her joined to such a powerful warrior. Even there I'd care for her.

It felt like eons since I'd seen my mourning mother burned with my father, since I'd heard the songs sung.

Jade would have been happy in my hut after I'd filled her with a child or two, after she'd surrendered. And what a glorious surrender. Those who fought the hardest made the best wives.

Modern humans had no idea what they'd lost with each *advancement*.

Had her King Darius not prevented my rightful claim, Jade would have done well to be locked in my vault for a few decades, where I could take care of her, and she could grow to know me in the old ways.

Hate could be broken with a hard cock and a practiced tongue, and my sleeping beauty was a glutton for physical pleasure I was only too happy to dole out.

Hidden underground, with no sun to set me to sleep, I could fuck her for years straight, feed her from my very veins as I pumped her full of seed. Instead, I watched her traipse around a window-filled penthouse. Instead, I rejected sleep so I could lurk in the darkest shadows of her life.

Instead, I bought up entire vintages of wine, created undead to serve her, left trinkets in her room she never noticed… and painted her pretty toes pink while she watched a movie.

Our night together ended.

With unearthly grace, I slipped my arms under her body,

moving so slowly that not a hair was disturbed on her head. Lifted to my chest, I took her to bed, making sure she was covered by a blanket that would offer some respite from the rising sun.

Daylight's rays might not kill her, but they still gave her pain.

Jade should never know pain unless it was to make her better. Had she been mine in that long-ago time, I would have only beaten her to guide her to prosperity.

Now I tucked her into bed, the vulnerable daywalker none the wiser. And I waited with her until my skin began to blister and the stink of burning flesh tickled her nose.

Casting a magical gate, I retreated from the cursed sun, straight to the pens to feed. I ate ten men in the twenty-two minutes since I'd been forced to be parted from her.

And then I went to my private rooms, to my monitors, to guard her sleep. I'd rest another day, perhaps in a year or two. Old as I was, I no longer required much time in the coffin.

I'd refused sleep since I'd first set eyes on her.

The very woman who turned over, settling into the pillows, and slept as if the thousands of undead in the Cathedral didn't want to see her dead.

Watching her, I pulled down my fly.

11

JADE

I hated waking up in my father's Cathedral, baked and aching from so much direct sun. I swear, the conservatory was designed to amplify discomfort, the glass panes gathering daylight to dump on my head and burn me senseless. To make me stronger, my father claimed.

What it made me was irritable. Head pounding, I sat up to find a fresh glass of water had been left at my bedside. Parched, lips cracked, skin taking on a stinging pink burn, I drained the whole thing with no care for who had left it.

Or what poisons might be inside.

Instant relief, but only a temporary one. I could walk in the sun naked the whole day through and survive it, but to do so would leave me weak, horribly sunburned. Fortunately, I had fed well last night.

Which was the last thing I wanted to think about.

In the main room, breakfast waited under a silver dome.

Fluffy omelet with ham and… a teacup of *blood.* Fresh, so fresh it must have only just been milked from a vein.

"What the fuck…"

Beside it sat a note, folded over and written on fine paper.

Finish your breakfast. All of it. Afterward, your weekly commitment to the Cathedral will be considered complete, and you may return to your apartment.

Malcom's feeding schedule. I wanted to roll my eyes, but it was impossible to remove them from the black liquid, warm and smelling of everything I'd ever wanted. Rim of the cup at my lips, I sipped before my mind might warn me of the trick. One taste, and both my hands pressed the china closer so I might gorge.

In a frenzy to swallow every last drop, I'd begun to moan, to use my fingers to scoop out any lingering smear. And then I split the porcelain in half so I might lick the inside completely clean.

My skin no longer burned, my throat was soothed, and my eyes cleared.

As did my thoughts when not a single scented molecule of a disturbingly familiar flavor remained.

Malcom.

The fresh vampire blood had come from him. Which meant he was watching this, most likely grinning. That he'd mock me mercilessly later.

Fingers fluttering, I dropped the split halves of the teacup, checking the corners of the room for laughing immortals. I was alone. Of course I was. The sun was up. None of them could touch me here. But it still felt as if he were in the room with me.

He *had been* inside me.

The room still held traces of his scent from all the hours he'd haunted my space last night. Eyes back to a note written in his vicious penmanship, I found the arrogant scrawl such an obvious taunt that my cheeks burned.

Had I not been groggy, uncomfortable in so much light, and eager for breakfast, I'd never have fallen for his trick… like a true idiot.

Feeding schedule.

Jesus, was I doomed to drink my food from a teacup? Was I to be denied the throats of my prey?

He wouldn't dare! Such a thing was unnatural; even as a daywalker, I cringed at the thought.

Finish your breakfast. All of it. I could hear his voice in my head, his snide tone sinister. I could even feel his goddamn smirk.

I didn't even want the human food, just as I had not wanted so much as a bite of the lamb from last night. I was *full* enough. And I hated when he treated me like a human. Especially here.

There was no higher insult in the Cathedral.

Golden fork to my dish, I shoveled in eggs yet tasted nothing. All I got for my trouble was a sour stomach, a sinking feeling, and growing resentment. But I cleaned that plate. I drank the juice. Swallowed each crumb, and then I fled the Cathedral to find sanctuary in my home.

I found no such thing upon arrival.

My apartment waited, devoid of life when the door snapped shut at my back. Ethan was gone, his blonde was gone.

Blaring sports didn't come from the den, the smell the astringent greasy lingering of takeout stink didn't add to the room's flavor.

The house was dead.

My heart beat three times, slowing, slowing… slowing… until I was dead too.

And then that godforsaken thing beat again.

No messages waited for me on my phone. No notes taped to the door.

Ethan had not even sent a text, because he was holed up with his blonde bunny. And I could see it. I could fucking see his warm palm circling her belly while he cooed nonsense to a fetus he'd abandon with the first dirty diaper.

This was loneliness. That horrible, worming feeling right there. The hole in my heart that ate me alive and turned my mouth to ashes.

Sniffing, I glanced around the elegant foyer, and found I didn't want to go deeper into what had once been my sanctuary. Not when I'd have to see with my own eyes how hollow it was.

But I didn't have a choice.

With Ethan or without Ethan by my side, I had *obligations* to fulfil. Charity events to attend. Important men and women to sup with and manipulate.

Yet hours passed while I stood like a corpse in my foyer,

staring forward, unblinking. And in all that time, still no messages, not a single apology from my lover.

It wasn't until it began to grow dark that I moved, walking through the tomb-like house to find my bedsheets still rumpled, Ethan's clothes haphazardly thrown around our room.

He'd taken nothing with him.

Not that I'd really offered him the chance.

And even that had not earned me a spiteful text demanding I let him gather his things. Nothing. I'd earned nothing.

Fine. Let him sulk a day or two, but he would come back. His collection of fine watches was here, his heirloom cuff-links, *his future wife*. His uncle or his father would make him come to me. And then there would be no more blondes.

Unless they came with a dick.

Perhaps I should even ensconce a lover under the roof, so Ethan might understand just how fucking lenient I had been. A lover whom I'd allow to wear Ethan's clothing, wear his watches, and claim my affection while Ethan was out fucking old women for the glory of his family.

"He's not worth crying over, Jade. He's only a human."

"Goddamnit, Malcom!" The sun wasn't even full down, yet my babysitter dared stand in the room's darkest corner. A quick wipe of my cheek with the back of my hand removed embarrassing evidence before he might see more. "Why can't you leave me a moment's peace?"

As my back was to the man so I might repair any smeared mascara, I heard him take a step toward me. Instinctually, I countered, stepping more into the light. But the light was fading, even then I could see only the last sliver of sun sinking away from the skyline… and this male… this male braved the sun in reckless and dangerous ways.

"There are going to be changes, Jade. Alterations to the status quo." His voice was even nearer than it should have been, so close I knew his skin must be burning to a crisp. "It would be best if you chose not to resist, and instead put faith in my ability to know what's best."

A scoff, a tired, worn, and unhappy laugh.

"You were raised by a human nursemaid. After she was killed, you were left to your own devices, sent to human schools, and rarely mixing with your own kind.

He could not be more wrong. "I don't have a kind. I'm the only known living daywalker."

"You lack the basic fundamentals of being vampire. You fail to feed until you're weak physically and mentally. And when you do feed, you devour without restraint, and leave a mess. More importantly, you enjoy your infamy within the flock. You enjoy that they fear you since they have been forbidden to love you."

I didn't need this right now. Not while I was stung. Not while the sun continued to disappear and stretching shadows brought my tormentor closer. "You get such sick joy out of this, don't you?"

"It has been discussed, moving you permanently into the Cathedral while reassignment is organized."

The blood drained from my face, Malcom earning my full attention. "What? No!"

I was going to marry Ethan and secure that family to my father's bidding. If all went well, I'd have at least ten years enjoying the role of being his wife. Ten years with a partner who made me happy. For Christ's sake, I had spent fifteen with the last husband and he was awful in every imaginable way. Ten years was not asking much. And at the end of it, I'd bribe one of my father's flock to change him, to make him as much like me as they could. We could have eternity.

As if he could read my thoughts, pity crossed Malcom's angelic features. "Your father would never condone it."

"My father disappears for months at a time. I don't even think he knows what decade it is. One new fledgling would be nothing to him."

Cold, dismissive, my guardian said, "The answer is no."

Fists clenched, my heart racing and my color high, I marched straight for the blockade to my only happiness. Close enough to physically challenge him, I hissed, "That is not your decision to make, Malcom."

"It is forbidden from changing humans from a certain class."

"Bullshit! Marie was the queen of France before that ogre Gustavo snatched her away. I can fake Ethan's death."

"And spoiled Ethan would run right back to his family. Don't you think a man of his cut would want to rub immortality in their faces?"

"...Then I keep him from them for a few decades until all his living relatives are dead. This is not novel. Many fledglings have to be locked away until they're ready to accept their new role in life."

Fire lit behind an ethereal gaze. "I'm glad you agree on that score."

What had been shrill dropped to an animal growl. "You wouldn't dare…"

"Locked you up?" Dressed in his typical spy-on-Jade black slacks and sweater, Malcom crossed his arms over his broad chest and smirked. "I would have buried you so deep underground that no soul but I would have known you existed. Hunted for you, fed you, taught you our ways… *properly*. Eons might have passed before I felt like sharing."

Now he was goading me, and for once I was not falling for it. "You want to talk about infamy? You've changed hundreds of females and left them all to scatter and stumble through immortality. How many of your children still live? Ten?"

The fastidious man didn't know the exact number, and I could see in his expression that it irked him.

Trailing a finger between the flexed pectorals of an agitated male, I dug my nail in right over his heart. "And I wasn't changed, Malcom. I was *born*. You've never sired a pureblood, though not for lack of trying."

Miniscule, the movement was so subtle. A slight cock of his head. "Is that what you believe?"

It was impossible to read that expression, leaving me without the proper dagger to make my next stab at such an ego.

In typical Malcom fashion, he spun the argument out of my comfort zone. "I know you were born. I held you as an infant. The first time, you nipped my finger and drew blood. You had a taste for me from that day forward."

Shuddering, I pulled my claw from his chest, and moved myself far away. The room went ice cold, my skin bumping, more shivers following. And now it was full dark.

"I… I have to get ready for tonight."

Why did he have to pursue every time I retreated? Why couldn't this man just leave me alone? While I shrank into myself, while I tried to rub heat into my arms, the bastard toyed with my hair. Just like he always did when he really wanted to piss me off. "You're not attending the fundraiser this evening. The excuses have already been sent. I don't trust you not to approach Senator Parker."

Screw that. Defiance stole my chill. "I'm going to marry Ethan."

It was hardly a whisper. "We'll see."

"If you try to take him from me like you took Gerard, I'll kill you." Slapping the fingers away he thought might trace my jaw, I dropped fang and made sure he heard every word. "Do you hear me, Malcom? I'll see you dead no matter the consequences. And then I will hunt your children, and their children, and their children. I'll see your entire line demolished."

There was a look in his eyes, something utterly unsetting when he purred, "Then you better start feeding so you might gain the strength you'll need. Not a single challenger in seven hundred years has been able to take me down, child."

And we were back where we'd begun. A feeding schedule.

"Let's get this over with." That's when I noticed the cut of his sweater exposed his neck, and my panic returned. "Not from you!"

"Yes, from me. And then from another where you will practice restraint. There will be penalties if you kill your dinner."

This had to be a joke. A barb because of my embarrassing slip last night. "Last night was an accident…"

Rolling up his sleeves to expose strong forearms, Malcom ignored my complaint. "And starting tonight you'll learn how to prevent them. Starting tonight, you'll learn restraint."

12

MALCOM

She argued with me for an hour, just as I knew she would. Jade argued, she threw things, she went through the stages of denial, even begging so prettily it took a sheer force of will not to grow hard and frighten her.

I believe she sensed my arousal anyway, where tearful begs were abandoned in favor of her making a break for the door.

Never run from a predator.

My speed could not be beaten by one so young or weak, and the violence her act inspired caused me to be rougher with her than I'd intended. Which in hindsight, might not have been so bad a mistake. Jade's pride was legendary; crushing it was nothing but good for her.

It also solved the dilemma of how to inspire her to bite. This hissing, scrappy monster salivated for a chance to harm the male who pinned her in place and held her by the hair.

Snapping a quick bite into my own wrist, I assured she'd latch with proper placement, and rubbed my taste on her mouth.

The sound she made, the half-scream, half-moan, and I was fully hard. Cock weeping. Just how I wanted this first enforced experience to proceed, I pulled her back to my chest, sat us both upon the bed, and wrapped the snarling kitten in a tangle of my limbs.

With her distracted by the feed, with both her hands gripping my arm so she might gorge, I was free to begin.

It started with a featherlight kiss to her neck, over her jugular, so soft it was only a whisper. Every night I would do this until my touch was no longer associated with whatever horrid thing her father had planted in her mind. Until King Darius undid this work, my attention she'd slowly learn to abide. Another kiss, and another, trailing down her vulnerable throat. Innocent as it appeared, this very kind of affection did not exist between vampires. Not at the throat. Never at the throat.

Unless they were *extremely* intimate.

Cautious with her, finding she was far deeper into a feeding haze than I might hope for, I set her hair free, and let my other hand wander. I dared stroke the daughter of the king under the pretense of comfort, and then I took advantage of a cruel man's poor word choice.

"Give me a grandchild."

Sitting beside my love in her conservatory I had focused on those words. Trapped behind stone while Jade slept in the sun, I'd broken down and rebuilt my thoughts until the only concept that might be pieced from my brain was that of obedience.

I was doing the king's will in this.

My touch ghosted between her legs. Soft, creamy thigh, satin panties. I didn't dare intrude past that soft fabric, not yet, but so thin a barrier made it easy to still tease. I circled her clitoris, so delicately that the flood of wetness that instantly soaked the gusset of her panties astonished me.

The girl redoubled her efforts to gnaw my wrist in half, leaving me to smile against her neck. This was what I had been waiting an eternity for. And this was what I would take.

Skimming my lips to the shell of her ear, I murmured warmly, "Jade. You've had enough."

Just as I knew she would, she growled.

It took every ounce of my self-control not to tease her ear with a lick. "This is your final warning, Jade. Disengage."

Have I mentioned that she's greedy? My greedy, little terror dared draw a deeper pull of my blood.

The delicious ache of fang dropping inspired my cock to jump where it was nestled between her cheeks, the urge to tear at that soaked satin shielding her cunt and fuck her through the rest of her feed so overpowering I groaned in delighted anguish. But this was a lesson on restraint.

For both of us.

So I acted.

Driving razor sharp canines straight into her throat, I hit a vein with practiced precision, and made sure it was not a bite of pleasure. Jade squealed, knocked straight from her stupor into horror, when I took a taste of *my* female.

She screamed all the harder once my wrist was free to twist us both into the perfect posture for feeding. Like this I could use her as I wished. She could not break free, yet her blood freely filled my mouth and warmed a dead heart until it raced.

I swallowed a single, perfect gulp. I drank of my love straight from the source. Not stolen licks of spilled blood left behind from one of her punishments. Not the desperate gathering of her tears on my tongue when I moved so fast she hadn't fathomed what I'd done.

"Malcom?"

By the Gods, she was so afraid. And I wasn't sure if it was because her life was in the grip of my teeth, or if it was the way her legs had spread and her panties had soaked. I cupped her there, warmed her before I retracted my fangs from her bleeding throat and let out a guttural growl at her ear. "You were told to disengage."

Her only answer was a whimper.

Last night's feedings, this morning's cup of blood, and her most recent binge on my wrist had already strengthened her, the wounds on her neck closing while I took all the damn time I desired, licking them clean.

Poor, trembling thing wasn't accustomed to her food being so much stronger, not after her beautiful fangs had found their prize. Not when I stood over every feeding she'd ever had, threatening even elder vampires to remain still or I would see them ended when it was over.

Ancients tolerated her brazen feasts. Younglings died.

She sounded like the little girl she had not been in so

many decades. “My father will see you punished for hurting me.”

I could not help my smile, or the touch of conceit warming my voice. “A master’s bite is a common reprimand in training. If you don’t wish to feel its sting, learn.”

She squirmed, as if only just noticing my hand over her sex. “This is—”

“Tell me now, before I escort you into the other room. Have you had enough of my blood to keep your wits through a proper feeding?” Strengthening my grip on her just enough to give a hint of discomfort, I drove my point home. “If you lie, and if you kill our guest, your punishment will be worse than a gentle nip on the neck. So think on your answer, Jade. Do you need more of me before you attempt to feed?”

More fight went out of her. “What are you going to do to me?”

“Why? Are you expecting to fail?”

Yes. We both knew she had zero restraint or self-control. “If you fail, I’m going to make you stronger.”

Jade hated when I spoke this way. *She hated it.* Already I could feel her tensing even further, and considering the punishments I’ve doled out over the years, I grasped why. But I am gentle compared to her father… and oh so careful.

The fact that she wasn’t fighting harder to extricate herself from my grapple, the fact she hadn’t fallen into a full-fledged panic, demonstrated that my less than idle threats were working. However, there is still a great deal of bite to her question. “Are you going to let me up?”

Smiling into her hair, I consider how much longer I might

get away with holding her so close. King Darius placed very specific rules to prevent me from ever earning her love: I'm forbidden from courting her. He will always unravel any progress I've made circumventing that decree, leaving the girl with nothing left but hate for me as he walks away laughing. It's with a delicate touch that I seek to upend and take what I can between his *visits* with his child. Considering I broke a vow by confessing that I loved her, knowing what that will cost me should my transgression be uncovered, I'm willing to bend the rules a great deal this round.

But even I can't break them.

Not yet, at least

"Answer the question, Jade. Do you need more of my blood before you attempt to feed?"

"I… no."

And right there I knew I'd won. She would kill the vampire waiting to serve as supper, and I would gain another inch in this eternal battlefield.

13

JADE

"I won't do it."

"You will."

The way he murmured his easy retort, the way I could feel it against the flesh at my throat… I didn't need to see Malcom's eyes to know they glowed. If my father were Satan, this infuriating male was Lucifer. A fallen, devious angel. God's lost Morning Star.

Again, and with every fiber of denial I might muster, I spat my refusal. "I will not do it, Malcom."

"At what time did you think you were being given an option?" Pushing my hair behind my ear, tucking it back despite its crusted, unwashed state, he allowed his touch to trail over the delicate shell.

Practically naked, hardly a scrap of silk could hide my shiver. No, all I had to hide behind was old, dried blood and dirt.

I wanted to cry.

I had cried, in front of this man.

Seven nights of punishment, each progressively worse, because I couldn't… I couldn't *not* kill my prey. And this one was already sobbing.

A pure-born vampire child, no older than twelve. A terrified, blood-fat babe dragged into the same pit I'd been thrown in when I'd made a genuine endeavor to kill my guardian four days past.

It was the first real violence I'd attempted in all the decades of my life, outside of the feed. Every last cell, each singular thought, had been focused to a point. I'd sprung, used every pathetic trick I knew, and he'd… toyed with me.

Laughed.

Mocked each swipe of my arm as he waltzed under the best assault I could muster. Faster than a human's eyes might catch, our bodies had danced. I'd even drawn his blood. One single slice across his cheek, and then I'd been forced to watch his tongue dart out to catch the black rivulet I'd earned.

Mesmerized by the movement, I'd ceased flailing. I'd stared. *Hungry*. So many meals I'd made of this male in the last waxing of the moon, that I *craved*. And when I hesitated, eyes stuck on that tongue, he acted. My cheek hit the wall. Old, musty brick and mortar leaving the taste of old dust and pain on my lips. My fangs ached, fully extended and throbbing.

My body, crushed, bent, manipulated, went slack from pain as if it were pleasure. I'd then done something unspeakable. I'd turned in his arms, eyes locked to his blood smeared lips, the thief tongue who'd stolen what was mine, and I'd put my mouth to his to get it back.

Devouring what he'd gathered, sucking his tongue, scraping it with my aching teeth. Licking at his mouth, even as his cheek healed. I'd bitten his lower lip, wrapping my legs around his waist. It wasn't a kiss. I was wet and he was erect, but it wasn't sex.

It was devastation.

Senseless, starved for more, I went straight to the nearest pulsating source. I'd raked my teeth over a black-hearted pulse. When my fangs punctured, I'd come. And… so had he. Because I'd jammed my hand down his slacks, and it was only his greater strength preventing it that kept his cock out of the hungry cunt that wept over his crown like a dribbling poison fountain.

I'd fought to put him inside me, as I did with most of my male food. Habit. Survival. The quota.

"Disengage."

My cunt was still milking nothingness in that ill-spent orgasm. Sucking upward as if his spattered, warm spend on my lower lips might be dragged inside. Within my fist, the shape of his member, I felt it all. Each pulsation. Each spurt I aimed. Malcom's seed drenched my labia, saturated my swollen clitoris… his blood running down my throat.

I ground down, fought, and lost, more focused on receiving, of being breached, that my locked jaw unhinged.

"Good girl."

And though he'd already come, though my climax had

begun to abate, he punched forward to penetrate me in that moment—pushed his spend as deep as it might go, and held me there, spread against him, full of cock, startled, and silent.

He didn't fuck me. He didn't move. Instead he made me feel him, twitching inside me, flexing his meat so it might jump, so I'd have to meet his eyes, know what I'd done, and feel every last inch of him.

"Jade. It doesn't have to be all violence or games." His voice was velvet, those glowing eyes warm as molten gold. "When you're ready, I'll show you."

What the fuck was there to say to that? I'd tried to fuck my food, lost my senses and my temper as he batted around my feeble attempts to end him.

I hated this male, and *I* had done this.

"You don't need to be scared. I've always kept you safe, even from yourself. I always will." His cock jumped again, as if he'd willed it to spill a second burst of seed against my womb despite a lack of friction.

This was a level of intimacy even Ethan didn't press. No, he'd always spurt and then jumped up to shower. He certainly hadn't plugged my body, held me open, and tried to talk to me. Not unless it was sweet platitudes and praise for the glorious things I'd just done for his pleasure.

Out of my element was an understatement. I had just tried to kill this man. I wanted this man dead more than I wanted anything… except perhaps my father's love. The strangest sensation crept over my heart, one I'd never had and couldn't place.

An unnerving desire for my mommy.

Whom I'd never met and was long since dead.

"Whatever you're feeling, allow it. But do not speak it out loud. You must learn to be more cautious with the opinions you voice. *Thoughts* can be arranged, words spoken can't be retracted."

Under everything was the very thing he'd cautioned me not to acknowledge. Because saying it out loud, giving life to it, meant that Darius would pick it from my thoughts and toy with it. Still my lips moved. "My father is never going to love me."

"No, he won't."

Spread wide, back to old brick, spine scraped, and pussy still full, I forgot my body, the mess I had made, and was too buried in thoughts to care. "And for eternity, I'm going to be alone."

"Jade…" Malcom spoke my name with such weight, as if he actually cared and *knew* what it was I carried.

In that moment, what was there to do? I'd lost the battle, I'd shamed myself beyond repair. Even still I had his cock in my body—one he didn't thrust or use to give me pleasure. It was just there, forcing me to recognize the incursion… so I did the only thing that made any sense. I notched my head back, and smashed it into his so hard I felt the bones of my face break.

The pain was excruciating, beautiful, even as nothingness stole in.

And I woke in this pit. No doors, no windows, no way in or out. Just a round room of dust and darkness. My shredded clothing from the fight was gone, no pallet was on the floor for my comfort. Empty, naked, cold, utterly alone, I took my punishment without complaint.

Left with nothing but my thoughts, without the luxury to which I was accustomed, without human background noise and social media and farce. A well-fed daywalker with a mind full of ugliness that was chilling to be alone with. What I would have given for Ethan's stupid jokes or irresponsible smile: any distraction from the mental racket.

Before my father had flung me against the wall and spilled my brains on the Cathedral floor, I'd had a wet-nurse. A human who lived in a state of terror that I assumed was normal because it was all I had ever known. She did care for me, and not just out of a sense of duty… or slavery. Her lap was warm when she'd read me stories. Her voice, when she sang, was sweet. I remember the taste of her milk in my mouth. But I cannot remember her name. Maybe that segment of my brain matter was left back on the stones, and I wondered in those lonely hours what else hadn't been put back in my skull.

Had I loved ponies once? Was my favorite color purple?

Because of my father's wrath, there were pieces of me left to be trampled into the floor by careless feet all over the Cathedral. There were pieces of me missing.

"Are you hungry?" Malcom. I couldn't see him in the dark, I didn't know if he'd been there all along, or if he moved through the shadows and magicked himself outside of the pit.

"No." For once I wasn't responding to be difficult. I really wasn't hungry, in any way. Not after the amount of blood I'd been coerced to swallow since the feeding schedule had been inflexibly enforced.

Light blazed, a single small candle that was over-bright in such a dark place. Dressed in his impeccably tailored and pressed slacks, a fitted sweater highlighting the physique of a natural predator, his typical expression, Malcom held the flame and looked me over. "Stand up. Come to me and drink."

It felt like the same conversation we'd had for decades. His demands, my pointless, irritated responses of denial. "Fuck off, Malcom."

"You could have cast a gate and left this place at any time. Why are you still here?"

"This is where you put me, isn't it?" After I'd attacked then molested him. After he'd penetrated me to make a solid and twitching point that I really was the world's greatest fool.

Malcom minutely tilted his head. "Answer the question, Jade."

Irritated he was going to make me admit it aloud, I snarled, "For the same reason I take taxis everywhere. I don't know how to cast a gate!"

"I have watched you cast gates since you could walk. You used to laugh and lead me on a chase through the Cathedral that I found quite… frustrating." But the way he'd shared that memory sounded anything but frustrated.

"And then my brains splattered the floor, and I forgot how to do it."

"You cast a gate last month, after a feed so that you might

leave the Cathedral and return to your apartment before Ethan left for his business trip to Paris."

Absurd. "I traveled by cab."

Another fractional tick to his head. "And here I thought you were smarter than to trust every memory in your head. Consider where you are, Jade. Consider why."

Bare ass to the dirt, back to the wall, I let my head loll back. Lazy in my perusal of him, admittedly forlorn and equally apathetic, I measured all I knew. Like how this man had been responsible for the death of Gerard ages ago, and how I swore I'd never forgive him.

As if my thoughts were bared, he nodded. Squatting down, as if to exist on my level, Malcom waited.

He who spoke first lost. Wasn't that the common saying?

The perpetual loser, I broke the silence on a sigh. "How much longer are you going to keep me in here?"

He set the candle atop the dirt, red wax dripping, and began to roll up the sleeve of his sweater so his wrist might glow on display. "Forever, perhaps… it seems it's doing the spoiled princess some good. A quiet time-out until you feel like trying."

"I'm not in the mood to play with you anymore, Malcom." And that was it. I was tired, disgusted, empty, and too full of blood to consider the wrist he held out.

Soft as a breeze, his fingers danced over my hair. "Were you playing when you tried to tear off my head?"

I could hardly remember the rage that had set me feral. "Yes, my favorite game."

"Were you playing when you tried to fuck me?"

Head in my hands, dirty hair covering my face, I couldn't even try to defend such an unspeakable thing. "I have a quota…"

"Ahhh, but one you have failed to meet for the last three days." But this disapproval he so thickly poured on me was not about required sex. It was about the rotting bits of torn apart immortals that decorated my circular cell and perfumed the air. I'd failed to restrain myself even a little, and it wasn't for lack of trying.

As if I might explain myself, I muttered, "You've only brought me females."

"But you could have cast a gate…"

There was no keeping the cracking weakness from my voice. "What is it you want from me?"

There was no answer, just a long incomprehensible look that was hard to read by the light of a single candle.

Hating pregnant pauses, having lived a life of filling them up with false laughter or banal jokes, I didn't know what to do. What would ease the monumental itch that vibrated in my veins when he looked at me in such a way?

Unfurling from his crouch, he stalked closer, wrist out so I might drink.

The now familiar taste of him so near, the smell, and my mouth began to water. "I'm not hungry, Malcom."

"Good." Bumping my lips with the cool flesh of his inner wrist, he added, "Then perhaps tonight you might show mercy."

My teeth sunk in, as if my mouth were separate from my psyche. And I looked up at him like a dirty, starving waif as I fed. The entire time he held my eyes. The entire time he praised me, petting my hair as if I were some puppy.

And then I heard the crying.

The child had been dumped in my oubliette. A clean little vampire girl in a blue dress. A replica of the one I'd worn that day. Red satin bow, hair in curls. All that was missing was a fluffy white kitten.

14

"It's simple enough. Don't kill her."

But the sobbing, begging, traumatized kid was so frail one bite—even from a weakling daywalker—would probably rip her neck in half.

Thick, black, male immortal blood coated my tongue, mixed with the dirt on my face after I'd spat out his wrist to pace. Bare feet crunched over rotting limbs, squishing old meat into fetid dirt. Bone parting from bloated flesh squelched. I kicked a skull, half the face flying one direction, the bone smashing into the wall just as mine had long ago burst like an over-ripe fruit before my people.

The child screamed, clawing at the walls as if she might get out.

I ignored her, tearing at my hair, looking every bit the monster that I was. Clumps of black came away in my fists, bare feet still slapping through the remains of my last meals.

Like some demon from Grimm's fairy tales, I hunched and hissed, aware I was so ridiculous that even I had to scoff.

"Whenever you're ready, Jade."

Assurance, positive reinforcement? Why the hell did he use that tone as if instructing me on how to play the flute? Just lift the instrument to your mouth, purse your lips, and blow. It's that simple, silly rabbit.

Under my breath, scattered, I muttered, "I think I'd rather play the harp…"

"What?" Real confusion was in his abrupt reply.

I was going completely insane, that's what. "Malcom, I will drink from you every day, from any vein you want. I'll do it on my knees before you. Bow to you as if you were my king. Do not make me kill a child!"

He spread his arms as if to call me to him, and I flew like a bird to his fist. Soft cashmere hit my cheek, molding myself to the creature however I thought it would best please him if that's what it took to get that little girl to stop screaming. Lifted, cradled, maneuvered so my lips neared the juiciest of arteries in his neck, I sunk in the bite he silently ordered. And I drank until I thought I might be sick.

No hint of weakness came with loss of blood. Malcom didn't stagger. The arms around my body didn't twitch or sag. I swallowed far more of him than I ever had before, past the point of my discomfort, and then swallowed more.

A never-ending fountain of black, primeval blood.

Full vampires could eat dozens of humans a night, one after the next like popping grapes between their lips.

Malcom, I suspected, fed a great deal, though I'd never once seen him do so before me.

"You've had enough, Jade."

Truer words, even with my lips to his neck, my fangs in his veins, each swallow had a backwash of equal size. A vomit of blood that waved from my belly to splash against his skin for me to fight to swallow again.

I was shaking from the effort to keep the sick down. Overfed, for days… and still I'd torn the bodies apart.

And I'd do it to that little girl too.

Cuddling me to him, petting my hair like his prize kitten, he hummed at my ear. "Take her throat. One sip. Just one. And that will be the end of it."

But I'd run to him, I'd let him hold me. I'd drunk more and more and more. Hadn't we agreed?

I couldn't think straight with her screaming. Another wave of blood purged from my belly, falling over my lips to dribble down my chin like a cheesy zombie horror flick. I must have looked like the worst kind of demon.

I certainly felt like it.

Maybe it wasn't so bad in my pit filled with splintered bones and rotting organs.

"Oh, and Jade…" My hair was gathered in a fist, toes set to the floor so I was made to look up at the menace I'd smeared in filth. "If you kill the child, Ethan will die in the most diabolical of ways. I'll toy with him. I'll make him suffer, maybe for years, until his mind is nothing but a waste of human mush. And then I'll make you eat him too."

Fucking asshole.

Threats and mind games and blue dresses and pain. Cock and fucking and quotas and eons of slavery.

Child's brains scattered on the floor, the half dead carcass dragging itself to its glass coffin to die.

No more nursemaids, or cuddles, or milk.

My virginity had been sold when I'd bled as humans do. The man had left money on the table, laughing when it was over, and I asked for him to keep me.

"Didn't think your kind existed anymore." Because his cum had been tainted a soft pink from the breaking of my hymen. And he'd checked before tossing cash to the night-stand the brothel's madam would collect after he'd done up his pants.

His name had been Gerard.

He'd died in the war despite his family's attempts to keep him from the draft. Malcom had assured it. Somewhere on a beach in Normandy.

And in my mouth was a little girl's neck, and on my tongue was the pure-born thing that gave her eternity. She tasted of heaven.

And it made me sick.

Still I swallowed.

I always swallowed, every last thing my father made me do.

Staggering, I dropped the doll in the blue dress, half-dead atop my pile of rot. Her heart beat on.

Mine raced, raced so fast I was sure it would burst. Blood came from my nose, and my eyes, and my ears. It came from my womb just as it had that first time.

"Jade?"

Was that fear in Malcom's voice?

Bits of someone's rib cage jabbed into my spine, the whole of my body seizing. Pupils blown, I stared into the dark, whispering, "I loved Gerard."

Lips to my ear, hard body pressing mine to stillness in the gore, Malcom whispered, "There never was a Gerard."

15

When I woke, he was there. When I slept, he was there. I ordered Chinese takeout, he was there, beside me and silent at the table as I saturated fried wontons in mustard sauce and stared into space.

Malcom no longer relied on the cameras to track my every move. Not even the sun kept him from the darker corners of my apartment. He thought to *converse* with me.

As if sitting in Ethan's chair, moving out Ethan's things and putting *his* things in their place made him a fixture in my world!

Refusing to look at him, trying my damndest for days to ignore him, I finally met the startling clarity of his eyes, and said, "I don't love you in return."

"I know you don't." Reaching for an eggroll, Malcom made a show of joining my dinner. He even took a bite, chewed, and spit it out in a napkin so quickly it was almost unseen. "These are disgusting."

It had been two weeks. No texts from Ethan. His clothing, his collection of designer watches, all packed up and shipped out before I'd been released from the pit. He had not come to grovel, to say he'd like to keep me.

His uncle had not emailed with demands for wedding dates. And instead of mourning like I wanted to, I was saddled with a lurking houseguest who'd dared hang his trousers and sweaters in my closet.

The male used my ironing board.

Made me coffee in the morning and brought me fresh croissants.

And he touched me almost constantly unless sunlight kept him at bay.

Even now, under the table, his foot pressed against mine. And if I moved, he followed. My routine was so programed in his brain that he handed me cosmetics as I painted my face.

He'd stolen my perfume. My credit cards. Every last bit of jewelry Ethan had ever given me.

When I'd demanded my necklace back, Malcom had deeply frightened me. I was pinned and his fangs were in my throat so quickly, I wasn't even sure how we'd gone from the walk-in closet to my bedroom. He drank without permission while I fumbled beneath him and gasped for air. It wasn't until I was weak and limp that he pulled away, wiping red blood from his mouth.

A new necklace lay around my neck. One bearing a ruby

the size of Manhattan. A weighty choker crafted in the old world by artisans and jewelers long dead. It was nothing like the sleek, modern pieces Ethan's assistant would choose for me. It was a treasure long kept, hoarded, and draped over my throat as if he'd waited millennia to put it there.

A quick flick of his nail and black blood dripped down his neck. Warmth splashed my lips, the salt of ever-living flesh followed. Drained, addicted, I drank. Far, far more than I should have.

It was the orgasm that snapped me out of the feed.

The bastard had *dared* to put his fingers inside me, my skirt bunched and my panties stretched by his fist. When our eyes met, mine full of accusation, his thumb brushed my clit, and I shuddered.

"This time I want to watch you." And he moved his hand again.

It wasn't just the shock of it all, it was the hunger. There had been no suitors arriving demanding their chance to seed the vampire king's daughter. There had been no human males seduced in seedy bars or dragged into dark corners before the clock struck midnight. There had been no playful touch from a selfish lover or his blonde toy waiting to lick my pussy when said lover was done.

Starved for touch… that's what I was as I lay under Malcom's weight and felt my hips rock of their own accord to the pressure of him strumming my clit, riding the fingers that hooked and beckoned my insides to run with lubricant.

I came so quickly, my eyes on his, that I didn't understand what was happening until a cry broke from parted, swollen lips. Lips he kissed when dumbstruck incredulity took the fight from me.

His stilled hand parked inside my pussy, a cunt that tremored and twitched despite my horror, refused to budge. Even when I muttered a sad, "My father…"

"Isn't here.

Was that anger in the unflappable Malcom's voice? Anger toward his king?

"I'll be punished." Horribly punished, Malcom's house arrest having forced me to break several of the rules I survived by.

Fingers squelching from my fluids, the male teased every last nerve below. "Let me make love to you. If there is a child, there will be no reprimand."

"Jesus." Was that my breathless voice, my head tossed back as if I might close myself off to all of him if I just refused to look. "No." I was going to die of pleasure in a blood-drunk haze of agonizing and instant lust. "Malcom, stop."

And he did, rearing back to sit over where I was spread and ready. Licking his fingers of my juices as he studied all that lay before him. "What do you want in return for letting me have my way in this?"

Was he out of his mind? I couldn't even stop the laugh that jiggled my breasts and drew his eye to the neckline of my rumpled dress. "The centuries have set you mad."

There was no moving him, by strength or by power. A point proven when his finger came to trace the swell of my breast and no grip on his wrist might stop him. "I'd rather not force you, Jade. Name your price."

"Did you think playing house with me would warm me up?" Anger set my heart pounding, narrowed my eyes, and layered a hiss in my voice. "You make me sick."

No amount of spite seemed to affect the man. In fact, he began to rub himself over me as if he were a cat in heat, soaking the front of his trousers with the tell-tale lubrication that drenched my panties. A full body massage with just a few carefully maneuvered limbs.

His weight on me. The smell of a delicious, available blood source that left my insides fluttering.

Tongue flicking my ear, pelvis grinding against where I'd begun to ache for more, Malcom whispered, "Jade?"

I would never be able to live with myself, the shame would kill me. "No."

Knowing how best to disassemble me, the constant demon in my life offered a greater temptation than I could resist. "Not even for Ethan?"

My nails dug into Malcom's back. Lashes flaring, I drew in a breath but found no ready reply.

"Did it not cross your mind to ask me to change him? You wanted to keep him forever, didn't you?"

And then my heart raced for another reason. "But you said…"

"Give yourself over; let me make love to you, and I will see your human turned. A member of my household, protected by my name. An eternal Ethan to do with as you will. I'll even see his centuries of service are cut in half."

"My father..." Why did all my statements always circle back to Satan?

"Will enjoy the irony more than you can imagine." Smirking, Malcom leaned back so I might see his face. "Do we have a deal?"

"Yes!" I didn't even need to think about prostituting myself for such a cause. I'd fuck the entire city to have my way in this.

Unhooking my claws from Malcom's back, I reached between our bodies so I might undo his fly, but my wrists were caught so quickly I yelped. Pinned over my head, I was trapped again. Next thing I knew, I was being kissed until I grew delirious. And I gave, I gave all of myself to that kiss because I wanted Ethan more than anything in the world. A tongue tasting of my blood, of my pussy juices, of cloves and honey and shadows richer than the rarest Bordeaux danced with mine. Nicked on my fangs, he dripped heaven onto my tongue to mingle with a droplet of blood his quick nip had drawn forth from my lower lip.

I came.

From a kiss alone, sensation washing all the way down to my fingertips as his groin rubbed, and rubbed, and rubbed between my legs.

A curse—I don't know what language it was—crossed Malcom's lips. His grip on my wrists grew almost too hard, but the pain had the opposite effect. It left me wanting more, force and pressure delivered in a way Ethan's human frame could never supply.

"I love you." The words were breathed into my mouth, the softest of confessions. Malcom's ruination.

He was so hard. Even with the fabric of his trousers and my panties between us, I could feel the pulsating outline of him. I could *smell* him—the tang of cum yet to be spilled. His sack was so full, swollen with what he'd usher between my legs so I might have my wish. Thinking of it in that way, of his cock, of his seed, had me making noises the man greedily swallowed.

Provoked, encouraging him with my arching body and digging heels, a space inside me shifted. I felt it like a physical thing, an opening door I was forbidden to look through. Desire unraveled, it possessed me with terror. Unsure how to equate the two, or why I suddenly began to tremble, to weep.

To beg. "I need you to hurt me."

"Never." Soft kisses trailed down my throat, my shoulder, the careful drag of fang leaving just enough sting to soothe.

Ethan. I thought of Ethan and why I needed to stop hyperventilating and control irrational fear. I'd been fucked by hundreds of men: violent men who took pleasure in my misery. Shy men with fumbling hands and sloppy mouths. Generous men who coaxed climaxes from my body. Terrible men I'd been attracted to. Vagrant men. Drunken men. Men of God. Women.

A virgin's fear had me pressing my thighs closed, had me stretching away from an expert mouth and the weight of oblivion.

Fully clothed, cashmere sweater, pressed, pussy-soaked trousers, even socks, this male was more threatening to me than all the others combined. And I'd once lost a limb when my father's champion was far too rough.

I was going to come again. From nothing. From just soft touches and rocking hips.

"Help me!" God help me. Save me. Deliver me. End this!

"I swear to you I will." How earnest this fallen angel sounded as he spun me into greater torment. Wet, hot, his mouth closed over my fabric-covered breast. Nipple aching, it was undulated, worked. Suckled.

Tears were in my hair, sobs wracking my ribs. "I'm dying."

This had to be how the sun felt to pure-bloods. A blistering, searing incursion that turned a body to dust. But I held form, even when couture split on the claws of a vicious warrior. My panties, ripped by the flick of his finger. My thighs gripped and spread until my knees hit my shoulders.

Malcom, ruthless Malcom, twisted his demon's tongue through my folds, penetrated where his fingers had planted their uninvited touch earlier. And I screamed, deformed, and scattered.

One moment I was having my pussy eaten by a starved man, the next I was in hell.

The Cathedral.

16

One moment the world was up, the next it was down, travel through an unanticipated magical portal leaving me to cough up a bubble of blood. One immediately swallowed down before a drop might pass my lips and mark the ground. I knew where I was by rote. The cracked, worn stones, the stink of agelessness, rotting flesh, and everlasting life.

Evil, unseen and gelatin, weighed down all things in the throne room. Even the air refused to stir despite the masses gathered to watch a rare occasion where my father sat the throne.

A sight even I had not seen in decades. Not when I avoided him at all costs.

Yet there I was on my knees, the straps of my slip dress having fallen down one arm, panties sodden and sticking to skin swollen from friction. And I had garnered attention.

There was no need to glance up to confirm that those vampires nearest where I had appeared out of thin air stepped back from my panting, bent, and objectified frame.

It wasn't before the dais I'd landed. It was amidst the crowds. Hidden by the grandeur of court dress and the press of many bodies.

Terrified.

I was terrified, and almost screamed like the little girl I had been when a hand twisted into my hair. Pulling black tangles by the root, subjugating me before curious glances, the very bane of my existence put his lips to my ear and snarled, "Think of nothing but the hate you bear me."

And I did hate Malcom.

How could he drag me here, like this, after what he'd just done to me?

Only seconds ago his tongue had delved demon-deep into my cunt. The bastard had made me come. Arousal, a single bead of hideous, naked, and plain truth, dripped down my thigh for any behind me to view.

I hated.

I hated thoroughly.

To be seen this way. To have my head held in a bow by strength I'd never match. Left kneeling in a crowd where all others stood over me, where they laughed behind their hands at me. Where they hated me. That's what the Cathedral was. That was the revolting malevolence fostered here and worshiped by all my father collected in his flock.

Pressing against the stone with all my strength, shaking from the strain as hairs tore free from my scalp, I gave over.

Daughter of the Devil.

Unimportant. Completely forgotten once evil incarnate broke the chambers echoless silence. "Vladislov, welcome."

Straining to catch a glimpse between the knees of those separating me from my father's gaze, my full attention was caught up in that name. I even felt an echo of my brains busting against the far wall as if reliving *that day*.

Waved brown hair, long as a woman's. High forehead, pointed nose, an ugly sort of eternal beauty. An immortal potentially as old as my own sire stood before the throne and didn't so much as dip his chin in deference.

I knew his eyes, I'd dreamed about them puzzling me back together. I'd drank of that man when he'd come to where I'd gone to die all those years ago. I'd swallowed blood thicker than tar as he'd stuffed handfuls of brain matter back in my skull.

The guest more important than my little life when I'd made the mistake of biting my father before him.

The reason I still lived.

Perhaps I hated him as much as I hated Malcom. He should have let me die.

Corner of thin lips twitching upward, it was as if my mind were as open to the immortal as my skull had been decades before. I think he laughed at me. Not that his face was turned my direction, or that I had been in any way acknowledged

My gaze was forced lower, Malcom still as marble, if marble might vibrate with a threatening decibel too low for even vampire hearing.

Denied another glance of my long-ago secret savior, driven to bend in ways that left joints screaming, I found my nails uneven, dirty, and chipped.

Which troubled me in the oddest way.

That I was not dressed for court—lacquered, scented, draped in jewels for this ancient to see. Because I knew he would. Despite the crowd, *he could see me.* Under all of it. Just how ugly I was. And maybe he'd give me that last fragment of myself that had been left to rot on the ground when I'd been a silly child who'd thought her daddy adored her.

His voice, like his features, was unattractive in an entrancing way. Making something lackluster pleasing. "My faction accepts these new terms with open arms, Darius. The alliance between our flocks grows stronger with each tithe gathering."

How long could he have been alive to have learned such a trick? To manipulate so many with so little effort.

"And just what have you brought me, old friend?" I didn't need to see the throne to know how my father's immensity sat upon it. There was no more chilling sight to behold.

"We are beyond the age of chests of gold and favored bloodlines. Dreadfully boring as they were. Yet, as you requested, one hundred of my healthiest stock shall be transferred to your pens, for breeding whatever blood vintage you prefer."

"And one hundred of my human cattle shall be placed in yours." My father was a greedy man for blood. My own eyes had seen him fell thirty in a single feeding. One hundred was a snack.

All of this was politics, even though I had no idea what took place, it was clear the back and forth were practiced, unimportant yet required.

Father didn't want Vladislov in his realm.

And that I had never heard of a tithe gathering though I had lived for many years.

Though by the way his fist refused me so much as an inch, Malcom had. Everyone in the chamber understood what this was.

"Where is that precious daughter of yours?" My flesh chilled, the fine hairs on the back of my neck rising. "I have a stud who wishes to woo her. Of course, any offspring would belong to my house should he succeed."

"Which daughter?"

No hesitation came with the answer. "The sweet one."

Slander nailed those words to my back. Physically bowing, I felt the drill of *sweet* and knew the joke they made of me. There were no other daughters.

None living, at least. Had King Darius fathered others, they were long from this world. Or had escaped him through the ages, no longer counted and free.

Which was impossible when every immortal mind was open to him like a book.

Once, long ago, I'd tried to run.

Malcom had found me in minutes. Literally minutes. He'd brought me to the throne bloodied to dump at my father's feet.

He'd beaten me so badly that my father had not so much as lifted a finger to crack another bone. Knowing him now, I imagine Malcom thought he'd done me a mercy. My father could *do things* even to an immortal that could not be undone.

"Where is the little girl?" How strange it was to hear a hint of teasing in Vladislov's voice. One did not mince words with the devil and survive it. One did not poke the bear.

A coarse, bored, devious, and light reply. "I will allow your stud to attempt to breed her, but there will be no talk of my daywalker."

"But I like her." Again, I knew the foreigner was aware of my presence, and had the sinking sense that through some strange turn, my father was not. "Why be so greedy? She was a taste of heaven when she sat on your knee. I'd offer you a legion, an army, any member of my court in exchange for the precious child."

"Denied."

The guest grew openly agitated. "Ten years."

I moved, fought to look up. Malcom twisted my hair tighter, clawing my scalp until skin punctured, simultaneously grinding my knees harder into the stone.

"Think on it, old friend." Though I couldn't see him, I imagined Vladislov smoothing his embroidered sleeve, careless that the man on the throne could see his head rent from his shoulders with little effort. "No need to make a rash decision. I can offer your kingdom much. And what is one, unwanted, burdensome half-breed? It would do her some good to go to the old country and learn of her heritage. I have a particularly vicious warlord in mind for her to tend. Instability on the continent affects even your Americas. And, of course, I'd watch over her as if she were my own daughter…"

"You'd find her lacking, weak, and insubordinate. Ungracious in bed. The complaints I've heard…" Was this really how my father spoke of me to strangers? To ancients? My mouth went sour with the shame of it, thighs quivering to close despite my painful posture.

"Sad news for my stud, I suppose."

"I have no interest in your stud's complaints." And the meeting was over. A shuffle of silks, the king of all undead this side of the ocean rising to leave as if bored of all he saw, all he'd lived. As if he had somewhere to go.

And go he did. The force of his presence lifting from the room. Those within sucking in a breath as if they had been denied air for an eternity. I found it funny, the immortal, *breathing* in relief.

The crowd began to jostle and migrate, careless feet stepping upon splayed fingers. Caught up in the tide, Malcom kept me still, like a dog on a leash by the hair. Tethered to be stepped on.

Until the room was vacant, as if all inside acted on some unseen order to wander away.

My father's throne empty, until it wasn't. Until the brunette foreigner in his surcoat and cravat, his thin fingers heavy with rings placed himself upon it.

And my heart stopped beating. Arteries stopped pumping. Ghostly white, I felt dread to see something so horrific.

"Child." He smiled at me. One perfected with age and practice. "Is it true you are disobedient?"

Eyes darting around, looking for the trick, the lingering vampire who would have me existing in a room where another dared sit my father's throne. "How is it that you have done this?"

Proud, arrogant, ugly-beautiful, in completely different ways from my sire. Vladislov offered a shrug. My father would never shrug. "We all have our tricks. What's yours?"

I don't know why this banter drew my anger, but it did. There were enough problems piled on my plate, and pieces of my brains had once been in that man's pockets. "I can walk in the sun."

Without taking his eyes from my face, Vladislov flicked his wrist. A kingly, courtly gesture, both demeaning and silly. "Get out, Malcom. You're not required at present."

And my hair was set free. Just like that.

And just like that, I reached back for my guardian because I knew to remain in that room would see me ended. I even turned, eyes wide as I pled, "We had a deal."

"But you see." Stretching his legs out from my father's throne, Vladislov murmured, "He and I had one first."

There was no soldier more loyal to King Darius than Malcom. Not a one. Which made this foreigner a liar.

As Malcom backed away, Vladislov mused, "She is young, isn't she? An unopened bloom."

The one fixture in my life—the lingering, annoying presence of my custodian—walked away without answering.

The question had, after all, been rhetorical.

And I was still on my knees, reddened by the stone. I was dirty, disheveled, unable to look away from the figure in the chair.

“Stand up and let me take a look at you, little one.”

Like a child, dusting my hands on my dusty dress, a look of shame about me, I did.

17

There was a hand on my face, turning it to and fro, but no one touched me. A compulsion to move that felt so real I gasped, even as I obeyed.

"I know what you're thinking." He murmured from my father's throne. "I could make you rip out your heart and eat it."

Those weren't my thoughts exactly, but near enough that I shivered.

Vladislov's voice became more beautiful. "You cried that night, the innocent tears of a hurting babe. I found it moved me. Old as I am, very little does."

"I'm not supposed to be here." In this room for this meeting. My father wouldn't want me near the Cathedral or this man. The power of that latent thought was so insidious, so all-consuming that my eyelid twitched.

A frown, the expression insincere when his eyes shone so bright. "Then why did you open a portal and come to me?"

"I don't… know." I couldn't cast portals! I didn't know how I'd come to be here or why Malcom had vibrated with *apprehension*. Why he'd told me to think of hate, and how easy it had been to fall into the habit.

My father had not noticed me. Because my thoughts were ugly and unremarkable in the sea of ugly unremarkable minds.

Hypnotic, a voice I could love moved through my spirit, my flesh, and made all the little aches go away. "Tell me of your father. Spill every secret you know."

And I laughed, loudly. "I know none."

"Ahhhh, child." The caress of that endearment, of Vladislov's complete attention, warmed me despite the chill of the room. "Start at the beginning, and let's peel back some of these layers, shall we?"

My story began with my head cracking against the wall, the sensation of my brain matter spilling out. The smells of the floor and taste of grape as I'd dragged my carcass to my casket. How a stranger had come with handfuls of me to put back in the crater. One who sewed me up with tar-black blood and careful attention. Freely, I told that man these things.

I spoke of beatings and sex. I unfurled every bit of personal shame, all the words spilling from my mouth like a corruption. Decades of my life purged, belched, made the air grotesque, but not once did Vladislov lose interest. He *listened* without speaking.

Uninterrupted hours.

Until I felt unburdened, changed.

Chin resting in his palm, soaking me in attentiveness, the man sitting the throne said, "And you thought you knew no secrets. What a vault he's made of you. Can you even recall half of what you told me?"

I felt so young then, nothing but a little girl in a blue dress. "I'm tired. I want to go home."

"Child, tell me one more secret, and I'll send you on your way." I'd tell him anything. Anything he'd ever wish to know. "What would you do to this Cathedral had you the power to act as you pleased?"

No hesitation, I wasn't even afraid to say something so hideous. "Burn it to the ground."

"With or without your father's flock inside?"

That was the question that stumped me, because I had no answer.

Hands to the armrests, Vladislov stood, moving like a cool breeze. Whispering past me he said, "Think on it. I'm interested in knowing you better."

And then he was gone.

Alone, barefoot and underdressed. I stood like an urchin before a vacant throne, unsure what to do with myself or where to go.

I never even heard his steps before a coat was wrapped around shivering shoulders. "Of all the places you could have traveled through portal to…" Malcom pulled me to him, wrapped me in strength and a niggling, itchy comfort. "Time to return home."

Portals could not be cast within the warded Cathedral. Antechambers existed that allowed the magic to work, but I had somehow, without chanting and without meaning to, landed in the middle of an audience.

I had done that. Not Malcom.

It was to myself I muttered, “I don’t know how I did it.”

But I thought of home and how badly I needed to be anywhere but where I currently stood. And then I was. My kitchen was a mess of takeout containers and empty ice cream bins. It smelled like human laziness and petulance. It smelled of several days gone.

And Malcom was there, having followed me through whatever magic I had unknowingly used, ushering us toward my room. Toward a bath.

It was dark outside, leaving me no sunlight to soak in or the ability to wriggle out of Malcom’s never-ending touch.

Tub full and steaming, bubbles added in, it waited for me. And I stood there like a simpleton while Malcom removed my dirtied dress, my panties, another layer of me. I stood there staring forward, trying to navigate a mind that made no sense.

“I told him things.” Horrible things that I should not have known, that even now flickered in and out of my memory as if imaginings.

“Of course you did.” No censure was in Malcom’s response, nothing but doting attention as he helped me step into the bath.

Knees to my chin I stared forward while he ran a length of expensive Egyptian cotton across my shoulder blades.

Tracing the length of my spine, the shape of my ribs, dips and curves, taking his time.

He washed my hair, an intimacy even Ethan never participated in. Dipped me back to rinse it. Carefully combed through conditioner. Cleaned my nails of chipped polish, shaped them. While I soaked in heat as if I'd been frozen inside and needed to thaw.

I was incapable of considering Malcom's attention as anything unclean. It was impossible when my mind was spinning—full of the face of an ancient who'd opened me up like an unripe bloom. Too early, petals not yet fully formed, but free nonetheless. A forced bloom that looked the most striking in a vase and failed the soonest.

It took unimaginable effort to shift my eyes to catch the devoted gaze of my guardian. It was even harder to ask. "What deal did you make with him?"

Cupping my cheek, gentle, Malcom said, "In exchange for fealty, I begged him to save the thing I loved most."

A little girl in a blue dress whose mind had been tampered with by her father and was in such a riotous mess that I wasn't sure I'd be able to climb back out of it. "You committed treason."

"I couldn't let you die, cast off like… not when I've always known how precious you are." His grip on my jaw grew firm, as did Malcom's fiery expression. Even his fangs elongated to a startling degree. "I stood there the whole time he pieced you back together. Paid an eternal debt in exchange so that one day I could keep you. The little girl in the blue dress all grown up and mine."

And that sank deeper than any bite. "I've been everyone else's but yours."

I'd never seen this side of him, passion enraged, so beyond collected I hardly recognized him. "You've always been mine. From the moment I held you bloody and fresh from the womb. He hadn't even swaddled you, just dumped you cold and naked, cord still attached, in my hands. I quitted your cries. Found you milk; nursed you blood from my fingertips. I hid you from the court except when your father wanted to prance his prize pony about. I've murdered almost every human you slept with, hundreds. I didn't even drink them. I just left them to rot."

This fairytale sounded so untrue I began to wake from my stupor. "My father would have never allowed any of this."

Not out of love for me, but out of control. He dictated every breath I took.

"Your father is an absentee king so obsessed with his treasures he forgets you exist for months at a time. And when the bastard is coherent enough to serve his duty, he orders you whored out—as if you were not the offspring of an ancient bloodline and precious. He had you lay with *humans*." The last word was said with such disgust, I felt it like a living thing in the room.

Malcom was not finished. "Do you not think he would do the same to our children? That he would not toy with them in his sick-minded fascinations with suffering. Darius has lived too long!"

This was some trick, some new game my father played. Sloshing back, water waving in the monstrous tub, I put space between myself and this stranger who spoke of *our children* as if it were some given. And I looked at him. I really looked at Malcom and found a stranger in his skin.

As if he might read my thoughts, he swore, “You don’t need to be afraid of me.”

At that I laughed, choking on bile, and I backed into the farthest corner my tub might allow. “You are insane. No one can challenge Darius and live. I’ve seen it. You’ve seen it! We’d all be a puff of ash with a mere snap of his fingers.”

“I paid the price for you. And I will keep paying it. That’s all you need to know.” Fully clothed, he followed me straight into the tub, burning with all he had to say. Shouting. “Hate me! Hate me with your every last thought so your father remains blind to the beautiful workings of your mind. And when it’s over, I’ll teach you to love me.”

Practically speechless, I shook my head, water droplets falling from my hair. “It doesn’t work that way. I love Ethan...”

“And we have a deal, remember that.” Pressing me tight to the tiled wall, my legs slipping at odd angles due to the tub, Malcom promised, “You will have your Ethan as you submit to me. Your vow was already given. And I’ll take the rest now.” Mouth on mine before I might grasp the need to flee, a tangling tongue drove in.

If a kiss were life, if it were death and rebirth. If it were ownership. That was what was poured past my lips. Into me like blood. So this must be what the change felt like when a mortal was turned, the power flowing from one to another. Swelling empty veins, undoing the rot of a dead heart.

This was how a man in love kissed his bride before riding off to war.

How demons fornicated in the dark.

The very last kiss I'd survive.

I wore Malcom's ruby locked around my neck. I felt his trousers wet with suds pressed into my skin, his fingers already working between my legs. It wasn't even a question of friction or skill, it was a moment of being. One instance I was Jade, the next I was nothing.

Because I came so hard, bones broke.

The pain was unbearable, left me sobbing as I rode pure magic and disassembled.

Agony.

A zipper was torn, fingers pulled from my cunt so a ready cock might replace them. Against the wall, soaking wet and slippery. Malcom fully dressed with his slacks hanging around his thighs, he fucked me so hard the tile at my back cracked. And I came again, clawing at his back through his sweater. Shearing the fabric when another wave of toe-curling torment broke from my center to my fingertips.

It was as if his cock were too big, the way I burned and stretched. Which was unthinkable considering the myriad lovers I'd fucked. The ways in which I'd been fucked. The amounts of cocks that had fucked me at one time.

And yet, I was overly full. When his spend began to shoot down his shaft, when even that fluid added to the corked well inside me, I burst.

Split right down the middle and shed my skin like a

snake. At least that's how it felt when he cried out that he loved me.

Swallowing back screams, I found my voice didn't beg him to stop this madness. I was guilty of the opposite, I begged for more. Harder. To break me. And though he'd emptied his sack, still hard, he ravaged.

Tore at me with his teeth, drank from my breast.

Tiny flutters, minuscule pulsations came from my cunt, feathery light against the intrusion. Edging my enemy past sanity so I might know more of this pain.

"Never stop!" If he did, I'd go mad from want of it.

A world of white and blood where, for the first time in my pointless existence, I felt the truth. There was no pain in this.

Malcom only gave bliss.

18

MALCOM

She was flawless in my arms. And after the hours and myriad ways I had pleasured her, it almost seemed her blue eyes were even enthralled when they ran over the man who ruthlessly pumped his hips to fill her cunt with cock. Never had Jade looked at me in such a way. Not even when she was young, before her father poisoned her mind against me.

She had never looked at me as the females of my kind did. They begged for my body. I had been called beautiful in hundreds of languages. I had driven women to despair when I denied them.

Until that night, Jade had only seen hideousness.

For brief flickers within our joining, she saw *me*.

Inside her, moving our bodies into artistry that would make angels weep.

There was some roughness in my bed-sport. Necessary when handling a female saturated in entitlement. But should she whisper a desire, I gave.

And gave.

And took decades of yearning out upon her weaker form.

So many bites and bruises, kissed with loving lips. Healed when I put her mouth to my veins and offered power.

We drank as we fucked, her lips to the crook of my neck, mine to hers. Like husband and wife while I was cradled in her thighs. Which is what we always had been. Fate had made her mine from the day she was born.

Nipples pink, peaked, and waiting, I'd pinch, pulling them from her body until her back arched and she came… again. Full of my cock. My seed. My blood. When I moved within her, felt her velvet slickness, *I found home*. The words that fell from my lips would have shamed the long-forgotten warlord I'd been.

An eternity I'd waited for this. For slender limbs and guttural moans. For acknowledgment. For Jade to cling to me, arch her hips for what I might give. For me to show her the study I'd made of her body in all the decades I'd observed her whims.

Each nerve was attended, sometimes with pain. Just enough to cull any thoughts she might have of retreat. The notion had crossed her mind, more than once in the hours I'd rode her hard. Small moments of conceptual duress, mental pockets still poisoned that required purging.

She'd retched once. Just the once. When I'd made her say

my name. Panting from the exertion to unwork another buried layer of ugliness her father had tucked in her psyche. Fighting back, claws in my ribs, she bucked to remove me from *my home*.

My cock held fast, drilled all the harder so I might undulate my pubic bone against her sensitive and exposed clit.

"My name is Maelchon of the Picts. I've conquered and decimated tribes, countries, destroyed peoples—salted their earth while mortal. I took no wife in pillage, waiting to find you. Immortal, I waited still—slain for you, sold my soul to have and keep what's mine. The treasures I've collected, finery I've provided, your food, your drink"—pressing my lips to her gaping mouth, I breathed into her lungs—"your very air comes from me, wife."

Twisting our bodies, upending our play so my female might straddle my muscular thighs, I lifted her, lowered her, filled her up as her head lolled and her body fought through a faint. "And you will speak my old name, my true name, until I am satisfied."

But she couldn't, not with her eyes rolling back and her pussy clamping down as if to beg my sack to fill her again.

I obliged.

Convulsions moved her as if she were possessed by the devil, made all the more extravagant when my thumb mashed her clit and my hand left a bruising grip on her ass. Seated, she would stay. Forever, if I had my way.

Seated upon me. Full of me. Who loved her best and would cherish even the most horrible parts of her.

Slick with sweat, she fell forward to my chest, her hand

to my heart. Little claws digging into my ribs. Like this, she slept.

Vulnerable, womb sticky with my fluids, hair matted from how I'd tangled my grip in it to hold her still when she thought to tell me how to fuck.

I had never been more in love.

Right then I made my vows, in the ancient language, inundating each word with magic. I took the vows from her as well, wove them into her being as she foolishly snored over my beating black heart.

Just as I would have stolen her from her people ages ago, taken her to my hut, and made her my wife.

Force was a powerful motivator to eternal bliss.

Vladislov kept his word to me. None interrupted.

Satan himself could be no worse than that one. But he'd been strong enough to hide portions of my memory from Darius, who never once understood how his child had lived.

In sleep, Jade's cunt tried to push me out, spilling some of my liquid gift. I'd give her more, make her fat with babies. But now my dear one needed rest. So I explored the bones of her spine, dipped my finger under her shoulder blades to work out knots. Forming her musculature into soft, pliant, comfort that made her hum in sleep.

Ethan had never done this for her. The mortal pig had never tended her.

Or given her the pleasure I had, dozens of times in the span of one night, I might add.

No male—and I had witnessed every last act of fornication my woman had endured—had made her scream as I had.

While feeding, she'd only tried to kill me twice. A marked improvement and playful tussle.

Wine, food. No bath. A point had to be made when she woke. Already the sun was rising, I could feel the snapping whip of its spark upon my skin. But so full of her, I did not char. I tolerated. For as long as I might.

I sang her to deeper sleep, the old songs my mother had warbled over fires. I spoke to her what my people considered the duties of a wife. How I'd be gentle with her when I laid her in my furs. That she'd drink from none but me, growing stronger daily until she remembered all the gifts she'd been born with.

We'd have dozens of children. Mighty warriors and elegant lasses. Pureblood to glorify our house. We'd change whomever we desired, building an army of servants to tend our brood and to cook my daywalker's fine meals.

Ethan would scrub her toilet, not that I'd speak that slave's name aloud. Why disturb a perfect moment? The sun was already doing that.

My skin began to smoke, to crisp down to the bone, but I had held her in it for at least an hour. And were I not certain it would kill me and leave her without a protector, I would have lain in that misery until moonrise.

Careful with my prize, I rolled my wife from my chest, not so much as twitching when sunlight found new skin to burn. The finest sheets, wet from our lovemaking, were pulled to cover her, down-filled duvet bearing blue blossoms on a white background fell like snow over her body.

She smiled in sleep.

A thing I had never witnessed.

Warmth spread from my heart, bringing with it a horrible certainty that should I lose her, I would cease to be.

My Jade. Named for a common stone but more remarkable than a diamond.

19

I saw it, the look on her face when she woke to find her sheets smeared with char. The outline of my body where I'd burned caressing her as long as I possibly might. Fully healed and well-fed, I stood in the shadows and reveled.

Those beautiful eyes had flashed with concern. *For me*.

For a brief flicker, she'd believed I'd gone to ash in the sun. And she'd *felt*.

Sitting up, linens falling from her perfect breasts, she'd traced her fingertips over a soiled soot mark that smelled a bit of burnt flesh. Jade moved as if aching, groaning and sinking down into her sheets even as she gathered them about herself. Covering the subtle, lingering bruising I'd purposefully left behind.

I wanted her thighs to ache, her sex to throb, her joints to remember what we'd done. It was nothing that a single feed wouldn't erase. But these teachable moments were precious and never to be wasted.

"Coffee first… or a feed?" What a pushover I was. One grimace from her and I was already tripping over myself to lavish my princess with whatever she desired.

Hand to her forehead, eyes anywhere but where I lingered in the dark, she grew shy. So sweet a thing my blood-fat heartbeat. My necklace was still around her throat, had been for days, and it was there her fingers trailed next. Testing the collar, she found it was solid and not designed to be easily removed.

The fact she had not tried sooner, intriguing, though much had happened since I'd locked it around her throat.

"I've taken the liberty of filling your chests with more treasures, but that necklace will remain in place until I see fit to replace it with another." It was not about the childish way Jade enjoyed flaunting her throat before our kind, it was about ownership.

I owned her, and now she knew. Vampires did not trade flimsy rings.

She tried all the harder to remove it, but the clasp was ancient and the workings beyond her ken. "Jade, take a deep breath. Look at me."

It wasn't instant, obedience never was with her, but after a few more pants, a pouty warble, and a long sigh, she did. "Our agreement never involved this."

"You offered me your body. There was no stipulation on how often or for how long I might enjoy it. I have decided on eternity. Take better care when making deals in the future."

"Are you insane?" There it was. Her fire, her anger, her spirit. "I think you really have finally cracked. Get this damn thing off my neck."

Time wasn't wasted sauntering to her. I flashed from the dark corner to our bedside, took her wrist in hand. Her fingers flailed for a moment, the widening of her eyes betraying surprise before she tried to hide all she was feeling behind a cold mask of indifference.

"My gift to my wife stays around her pretty throat." I pressed a kiss, one that would have been considered chaste had it not lingered, to her temple. "And more gifts shall be put upon you and *inside* you."

I lowered her hand to cup my erection, Jade failing miserably at pulling away until I'd made her feel the throbbing, hard line of me. I set her free, she scooted back, the headboard containing her when I crept like a wolf over prey.

I had bathed, though I'd despised rinsing her scent from my skin. But too much had been burnt for the perfume to remain without the stink. I had dressed: pressed slacks, cashmere sweater. Both dark and perfectly fit to my powerful form.

She'd tear at them, I was sure, when I captured her parted lips and pressed her deep into the bed where I'd finally claimed her. Patience I had in spades, but I could also be playful. I knew she secretly loved playful.

And forceful.

She loved me, she just didn't grasp it fully.

Around my tongue she garbled her complaint. "Would you stop!"

Yes. No.

Set her mouth free? Yes. Remove it from her body? No.

I tested the soft flesh above the choker, nipped hard enough she gasped. The gasp of pleasure. Unbidden, unexpected despite a full night of lessons.

"I asked you a question, wife." There was no resisting trailing my tongue over her ear. "Coffee or blood? Which would you have first?"

Petulant, fighting her response even as her nipple whorled into tight buds, my Jade said, "I don't need to feed."

"If I fuck you like this, it might hurt." She'd only get the one warning.

Though she could walk in the sun, compared to me she was fragile, and I'd left my marks in aches and pains enough. Brushing her folds, I found them wet, but she hissed. It wasn't the hiss of disgust, it was one of discomfort.

"No more."

Because I loved her, I pulled my fingers away, hovering over her to take in her routed expression. Endearingly trounced in less than five minutes. Excellent progress.

"I love you. I always have." And I'd already abstained for decades upon decades.

Her lip curled, abject perplexity smearing away her usual haughty sneer. "You say that as if it's a living thing."

Tapping my finger to my breastbone, I stated. "It is. It's here." I tapped her next. "And here." Then I looked over her skull, gave it a long stretch of contemplation. "It might take some time to undo your father's work. I'll give you patience and refrain from my stronger impulses. But I will still fuck you, and feed you, and layer you with jewels. I'll also punish and be rough with you, but I swear on all that ever is or was, that it shall only be for your own good."

"So you'll beat me when I disobey?" A fair enough question, as I'd done it before. And always to save her from her father's hand.

But there was so much more at stake than broken bones and hurt feelings. "Don't try to run. You're only safe where I can see you right now."

Sardonic, as if she'd already forgotten she was naked and I was hard, Jade said, "Going to keep me prisoner in this room?"

"No." I kissed the tip of her nose. "We're going out tonight."

She could not have been more confused when I pulled my weight away and offered her a hand to rise. "What?"

"Ethan." What magic there was in that ugly name. Her entire demeanor shifted from pliant to wary in a blink of a vampire's eye. "I thought you might want to see him."

Distrust, dislike, all the things I didn't deserve from my wife.

"We made a deal, Jade. I'll keep my end. Until it's appropriate to change him, you'll have access to see what you traded your eternity for." Catching a tangle to tuck behind her ear, I gave her the softest smile a warrior might offer.

After all, my intention was never to frighten her.

~

Jade

Malcom smiled… and it was the most chilling thing I'd ever beheld. This one had lived too long, his brains warping. He smiled at me as I fed from his wrist; me trying to keep our bodies as separated as possible before he got any ideas and began pawing between my legs again.

Scratches, gouges, throbbing bruises, and aching joins cleared up as if I'd never known pain a day in my life. Until I was sated and full and like a cat ready to nap, fat and happy.

A glass of wine was pushed between my pliant fingers, a chilled white I had not seen him procure nor smelled waiting on my nightstand. Mineral, crisp, it cleansed my palate and set me leaning back onto fluffed, char-smeared pillows. Aware I was being managed and manhandled expertly by a creature who knew me better than any other, I was at a loss.

I asked for a bath.

Immediately he denied me, Malcom looking over my healed body with a thoughtful eye. Stinking of body odor, sex, and burnt meat. Gritty and sticky and uncomfortable, I pushed past and made three steps toward my bathroom before I was flung back to the bed.

"I need to pee!"

Eyes narrowed, he hissed. "You're lying."

Yes, hissed. The same man who'd just spat all his crazy at me in the tender voice of a lover. And yes, I was lying. But I was also intensely uncomfortable with this *attention*.

A thought openly crossed his face as if something so

common had never occurred to him that I was covered in soot and uncomfortable. “I’ll bathe you.”

I rolled my eyes.

“And after, I get to choose your clothing for our sojourn. No complaints.”

This strange journey to see Ethan? Fine. Arms over my chest, I nodded.

And should have known better. Hours Malcom spent showering my body, his wet, slippery and very naked form pressed to me at all times. My hair was dried, the male working a round brush like a fucking pro. And then right there at my priceless vanity, he bent me forward and thrust in with not so much as a warning.

My cosmetics spilled, the startled scream from my lips hushed when he pressed his fingers into my mouth.

Hard, but not fast. Every thrust an exclamation point to an unspoken promise. All the while he held my eyes in the mirror, mangling my noises as fingers stroked my tongue. Massive ruby bouncing at my throat, tits vulgar in how they jiggled, all of me jerked in the tempo set upon me.

I came from penetration alone. Hard. Far too hard for so little effort on his end. My sleek, styled hair was set in disarray when he pulled out and spun me about. Jerking his fist up and down an ivory white cock that spilled pearls all over my breasts.

Belly.

My hairless mound.

I gaped when open palms rubbed it into my skin like lotion.

"Lick me clean." The statement was not a command. It was a test of the waters.

I wasn't ready for whatever it was he sought. So I shook my head no. Not even a hint of disappointment took the glow from his eyes when he praised me anyway, Malcom pumping his fist from base to tip, gathering the last drops of his cum and smearing them over the flesh of my hip.

Bodily turned around, sat back upon my vanity's seat, Malcom went back to brushing my hair, leaning down, that smile intact as he whispered, "You were wet."

20

I was dressed in white lace… the gown almost bridal. And certainly not one that came from my wardrobe. The man had shopped for me. Everything new, including the underpinnings—my preferred Agent Provocateur encasing breasts and whispering over my pussy. The shoes were blood red, glinting with stones that set off the ruby collar he'd locked around my throat. With the skirt long and clinging, there was only the vaguest flash of a glittering crimson toe when I moved, subtle and considered. This was something Malcom had spent endless hours preparing.

Bearing in mind he nightly wore the same thing in various shades of black and dark gray, I would not have expected he had it in him to adorn a woman in more than cum.

My thoughts were crude. *I was crude*. Malcom was collected to an unnatural level. None of this made sense.

"Remember, do as you will, but always where I can see you. If you cast a gate, I'll have to hurt you." He took my chin before the mirrored elevator taking us to the rooftop restaurant of the prestigious Rothschild building dinged our floor. "And I don't want to do that."

"Your threats, Malcom, are as old as you are." Eyes to my lips, a strange shiver leaving my flesh to bump, I muttered, "If there is a bridal arch and a priest on the other side of those doors, I'll set this whole building on fire."

"Very funny, Jade." His hand went to the small of my back, possessive and just a touch too low to state anything but ownership.

Doors parted, a scene so common I was already bored waiting on the other side. Humans, my humans I'd sheep-dogged over the decades having their boring political conversations, scrounging up millions, begging for scraps while wearing Armani. And into an apparent fundraiser for Senator Parker we strolled.

Noticed.

Immediately noticed.

For I had been away for over a week, no Ethan on my arm, arriving with a stranger far more beautiful than any living creature. One who made it very clear that he was not there with me, but that I was there with him.

He might as well have pissed all over me the way he glared around the room. *Mine. Do not touch.*

It didn't move the humans as it should have. Already the senator descended down upon me, frown fixed above his sagging chin. "You'll arrange a private chat between me and your father. Technicalities are to be ironed out."

I'm not sure why it came over me then, but I was so utterly weary of all of this—these people, their politics, the human idea of wealth. "Let me guess, no check arrived. Short of funds?"

Never had I spoken with such rudeness to this man. I'd always groveled, and bantered, and submitted to grotesque jokes and a *woman's place*.

The senator's face went purple, his voice dropping low as if to prevent a further scene. "If this is due to my nephew's liaison, I can assure you she'll be kept out of sight."

Not removed from the equation, but tucked away so as to save me further embarrassment. "And the baby?"

I don't know why I said it, why I dug that dagger in specifically to cause Ethan harm. Because there was no way either the senator or Ethan's illustrious father knew of the fetus. A child I had just done harm by making it real with words.

Calculations, considerations of the most unconservative kind worked the wheels in the old republican's skull. Was it too late for abortion? Could the baby be given away? How much was this going to cost to hide from the tabloids? "Will be sent abroad to school, of course."

I really was evil… "Of course."

Before the strangest wave of self-reproach might mingle with the unhealed ache in my heart, I heard my name called. With joy. As if the world once again turned because I'd been found. "Jade!"

Ethan was there, as promised, sauntering over in a ten-thousand-dollar suit. No pregnant blonde beauty at his side. Careful of my red lipstick, he kissed my cheeks in the European style, took my fingers and asked me if I'd care for a drink, already pulling me toward the bar.

Leaving the senator alone with Malcom, who was infinitely dangerous and smiling again.

"Listen, I know I should have called." Running a hand through his golden hair, mussing it perfectly, Ethan gave a self-deprecating grin. "You just threw me out… and I… I you know."

"Left me for another woman."

"Well"—he stood a bit taller, slightly put out—"I didn't leave. You had me removed from our house."

"*My house*, where your girlfriend had been living without my knowledge." And one thing bothered me above all others. "She wore my things."

That brought out a grin. "You're the same size."

I didn't even know how to respond to this, it was like speaking to a happy monkey that had no concept of right or wrong. And considering who I was, all the atrocious things I'd done, I was a bit shaken. "Ethan, apologize this instant."

And he did, with great big, wide, shining eyes. "I'm sorry, Jade."

"Do you love me?"

"Of course I do!" This exclamation came with an enthusiastic kiss that felt more for show than real. Because Ethan knew never to kiss lips painted blood red. Not unless he had a chance to repair his appearance or was giving me a gift draped in diamonds. "These situations, they're nothing to people like us. I'll tuck her away, you'll never need to see her again. Split my time between you. Of course, she'll never be" —he waved his hands around the grandeur and elite gathered sipping their martinis—"a part of this."

Oh, the foolish boy. Malcom was going to give this to me. He was going to give me this bumbling, stupid, sweet idiot. And there would be no need for mistresses or hidden families. We weren't the fucking Kennedys, and I had no need to tolerate a Marilyn. He'd be changed and mine forever, and all I had to do was let Malcom fuck me.

Like he had already done a dozen times.

My cheeks grew flushed, my breath uneven, and without intent my eyes sought him across the crowd. Watching me. One glance, and I knew he knew.

I was thinking of him fucking me right now.

Which was so beyond disturbing that I blanked completely. Ignoring Ethan sputtering on about our future, his less than subtle hints that I better get those funds to his uncle before he addressed my father directly.

Wait.

Had Ethan just threatened me?

Had *my* Ethan dared, considering his sins? I knew my eyes went red as disgusting human blood, redder than the ruby at my throat. And all the anger that I hadn't had a chance to purge because I'd been too busy mourning left me looking much less than human.

A thing witnessed by a powerful family's golden child and black sheep.

It was utterly cliché, laughable, but undeniably right in that moment. "Do you have any idea who my father is? Can you grasp what he would fucking do to your entire family for disturbing him for even a moment? He'd see you all slaughtered and walk away laughing."

Ethan went white. The pallor worn by all humans trapped as livestock in the Cathedral.

"You want money, power, things I have assured for your family for an age? The sacrifices I've made to guarantee a Parker holds the Senate? The bailouts for your father's empire? Tell me again that I'd be wise to make my expected donation to a political campaign that goes against your family's direct orders."

"Jade?" I was scaring him.

It felt wickedly good and equally awful. "Open borders, Parker. I don't give a fuck how the senator sells it. Your family works for your bread like everyone else."

A cool hand came to my back, instantly smoothing raised hackles. "I think it might be time to leave, my love."

A blink. Just one, and red went to blue; fangs retracting. I had not even realized I'd gone so far.

"Idiot human"—Malcom stood between us, only inches left between my Ethan and my guardian—"you will remember nothing of this except that you're sorry for rudely asking your ex-girlfriend for a political donation. Which she denied. Bad form."

And off I was swept, through the party, and into the elevator, not twenty minutes after I had arrived.

In a daze, I confessed, "I don't know what came over me…"

All I could see was my smeared red lipstick reflected back to me from the polished elevator doors, and I was annoyed. Annoyed Ethan had ruined it.

He'd ruined everything.

21

Maybe I was young, inexperienced in real feeling. Maybe Gerard wasn't real. Try as I might in those awful moments in the elevator, I couldn't remember how much I'd love Ethan's grandfather.

Or… I remembered someone. But it wasn't the long-lost previous version of Ethan I still pined for.

And my father had most likely done this to me. For sport maybe. To keep me complacent and sad, and hating the world for taking what I'd loved. But I was starting to think that I had never loved. That I was a pretty shell, a puppet, and a dupe so unworthy even Ethan Parker chose another over me.

Silent tears smeared my smoky eye and mascara, though my expression hardened as I considered.

What if nothing about me was real? What if everything, every part of what made me *me* was all made up by dear old dad?

"It won't be easy." Warm palm still resting at the dip of my back, Malcom thought to soothe me with a simple gesture.

Blue eyes, then red, then blue. Red again. I could not control what was churning in my scarred and broken brain. "I think I died that day, when my brain fell on the floor. Whatever I am now, I'm not that girl in the blue dress who ate her cat on accident."

Reaching forward, Malcom pressed the hold button, stopping our descent. In a mirror-lined box where I could see myself from every angle, where I saw infinite facsimiles of myself and this male, he took my hand. Played with my fingers as if touching me in such a way were novel, exciting, that it *soothed* him. "You are capable of overcoming and thinking for yourself. Of growing up, of choosing to resist what you think you know and what you are afraid you know."

Because I needed to hear Malcom say it again, I looked him dead in the eye. "Gerard was never real?"

"Not the version of him you cling to. And yes, I did have him shipped out to fight in the war despite his family's attempts to keep him out of battle."

"So my father didn't lie when he told me Gerard never loved me…"

Malcom shook his head.

"What's real? What isn't real?" Breaking our stare, I looked at myself in those mirrors, at the long line of my face and back, over and over into infinity. "How many times have I figured this out?"

"You've come close, but never this close."

Because Darius would have caught wind that his wind-up toy needed a tune up. What he'd do to me after this. What he'd tear and replace and rework… "I won't go back to the Cathedral."

"Listen to me, Jade." Pulled forward into a cool embrace, touched in a way I think I'd been manipulated into seeing only with disgust, I tolerated and tested the waters as Malcom spoke. "Help me place Vladislov on the throne and all of us will be free."

"And what makes you think he'd be any better than the devil we know?"

"Does it matter?" A hand cupped my cheek, pressing my face to his chest. An act so intimate and uncomfortable that I knew it was my father's exploitation in my mind that made me cringe so. "He has his own agenda that has little to do with you."

"Which would be?"

Strict as he'd always been with me, Malcom pulled back enough so that I might see his smirk. "None of your business."

"Would I still have to"—I gesture upward to where the fundraiser continued—"do this? Let them fuck me? The quota?"

"No." The resonance of his denial, of the rage I glimpsed in that simple answer. It made me nervous that it was all too good to be true.

So I tested Malcom, because nothing in my world, it seemed, could be real or trusted. "You'll still give me Ethan."

Glittering eyes flashed, more agitation of a different kind. "That was our agreement."

I cocked an eyebrow. "Can you make him love me?"

"Yes."

And I wanted that, I wanted that love I'd thought I'd had. That playful sort and laughter, the days in bed where he took pleasure of himself in my body. Like a drug. An impulse I couldn't trust but needed to feed. "When?"

"And you can do as you wish with him, sweet Jade. That fool mortal or immortal is of no consequence to me. Our housecat, one you can fuck if you feel the need to purge that desire."

And right there I grasped that Malcom understood exactly what was wrong with me. That after a lifetime of witnessing my rewrites, he knew me in a way I'd never possibly know myself.

The feeling, like most feelings these days, was unsettling. But it was also sanctuary.

"Who would I have been if…" Darius had not been my father.

Gentle, he tucked my hair behind my ear, massaging the lobe as he smiled. "A spoiled, rotten brat. Too beautiful for her own good and impossibly stubborn."

I smirked and Malcom's response was instant, brighter than any sun, and overwhelming. He kissed me.

Tongue tracing my lips so I might part them, fingers delving into my hair, Malcom took of that small smile, feasted on it, groaning into my open mouth. "Tell me, Jade, that you understand what this is."

A collar around my neck, a white dress, a pet, the touch of a starved man already bunching my skirt up and unzipping his fly. Right there in the elevator. He'd already had me before the soiree, he'd had me dozens of times the evening prior. Insatiable. A word I'd never have considered applying to Malcom. But one second I was breathing out a response, the next he was inside me.

Full.

I don't know why out of all the cocks I'd ever choked with my cunt, his felt so very different. Breath stolen, jerking from the frantic way he worked to bury himself deeper, and clung. It was either that or fall spiraling backward into the abyss.

"Tell me!" He panted at my ear.

He hit a spot inside me that was tender yet eager to know friction. When I squealed and hiked my leg higher, Malcom was not appeased. Not when he wanted words.

"Tell me, or I'll take it, and I won't even give you the ghost of a choice." Why was he doing this to me, here, where I could not control the pitch of my moans and was ashamed? This wasn't like fucking Ethan in all the dirty ways and silly places. Here, I wasn't in ultimate control.

In fact, I had none.

At all.

Not over my own body's reactions to a throbbing, glorious shaft. Not to my mental state, which grew more precarious by the minute. Not over my future.

This man had taken it regardless of what I might be underneath my father's influence. He'd called me wife, borne my teasing because it was nothing to him. Because there was no undoing it no matter if I agreed, disagreed, desired another, or wanted none at all.

And I was coming, and rabid, head thrown back to cry out like a beast.

"It's the end of me." I'd said, breath lost in the waves of saturating, perfect pleasure that was so far beyond sex I didn't understand up from down.

Filled, fluttering and clenching with every bit of unnatural strength my pussy possessed, I milked his cum, sucked it from him. Felt each burst run from the grinding base of his cock to the uncut head.

My body seemed hungry for him, for a chance to be what it was without holding back for fear of breaking a fragile human. And I'd never climaxed with a vampire before Malcom—unless I'd been in the feed and too consumed to consider something as inconsequential as sperm.

It was over almost as quickly as it had begun, but no less earth-shattering.

With so many mirrors, it was impossible to miss that I looked truly fucked… and not just physically.

After smoothing down my skirt, pocketing panties I didn't even know he'd torn, Malcom took my chin and made a clear, concise demand. "Lick me clean."

This was no test.

Mascara having run down my cheeks, hair mussed, dress half here and half there, I looked every bit the prostitute I'd played for years. But I knelt, holding his eyes, lost utterly, and took him in my mouth as a wife.

THE ELEVATOR MOVED, the door opened, and I strolled into the lobby on the arm of a well-satisfied male. With the flavor of his cum on my tongue, I followed along, a bit dazed, my thoughts stuck on the fact he tasted different than a human.

Less bleachy. Salty, but also almost radiant like blood. Which had drawn down my fangs once he'd popped from my mouth, because I'd wanted more. Tempted to reach under my skirt and gather what ran down my thighs, but somewhat humiliated over the thought.

Because it wasn't a sex game where I'd lick my fingers to entice him, it was *hunger*. Groaning I'd forced my eyes from his swollen member, already having sucked the entire thing down my throat, to 'lick clean' until it was only my spit that shined the fat head peeking from his foreskin. I'd wanted to nibble there, to play and rub at him. To see what made his knees weak and what made him hiss frustration.

Cocks could be such fun things.

I also wanted to sink my teeth into that perfect vein running down his turgid length and drain him until he'd be too weak to fight me. At that thought, I'd known Malcom would have allowed it, because we both knew he'd overpower me no matter how I might gorge.

And I found the idea somewhat exciting, my cheeks going pink. Still on my knees before him, but looking to the floor.

No mirrors, no male. Only his leg and a polished shoe that I could ignore. Until he'd put his hand to my hair, told me he loved me, and that I'd earned a great reward. That he was proud of me. That he'd never witnessed in all his years of endless life such a survivor. That I would give him fine sons and deadly daughters.

Slouched and mixed up, I listened, fought back my outrageous hunger, and thought I might have found a piece of myself there on the floor of that elevator.

Malcom helped me rise before the door might open and I'd be seen in such a state. He smoothed my dress and wiped the black tearstains from my cheeks, his fingertip tracing the line of my lips to tidy smeared crimson gloss.

With the practiced grace of a gentleman, the ancient warlord led me through the building's foyer and out into the night. But I knew Malcom. He was no gentleman. Gentlemen didn't gain the rank he had in my father's court. They didn't fuck like he did.

They didn't plan to betray their king and steal the princess for themselves.

22

MALCOM

She could not resist cutting glances at me. Or working her throat. I could see her swallowing, knew her tongue toyed with the tips of her fangs the way freshly-changed vampires marveled at their new weapons.

It was a tick, something again to remind me of just how young my bride was. How much she needed me.

There was a reason all freshly-turned served three hundred years of service in this new world. And Jade, as royalty, had only ever been served. Not that she had not been a slave the whole time… but she'd had no master to guide her. To teach her beyond what I might *suggest* as her guardian, custodian, and chaperon. But those days were over. I'd take my hand to her backside if that's what it took to help her bloom.

I was her husband in all ways that mattered. My sperm swam through her belly even now, and would nightly for the rest of eternity. I'd lavish her with much more than jewels. She'd know the true attention of a powerful being. One who truly loved her.

One who would continue to keep her in line.

An adorable grumble came from her stomach, Jade pretending as if nothing had happened.

"Already hungry?" I teased, warmth spreading through my gaze in equal measure with gentle mockery.

She was. Her cold-eyed glance could never lie, not to me. Embarrassed, she chose her typical silence. But like a true fresh-turned, accidently eyed my throat. So much for the daywalker who'd starved herself and only dined once a week.

Had I the power to break her of that habit fifty years ago…

But her fucking father. As much as I loved Jade, I hated him. And I would see him cut asunder, scorched, his limbs spread across the world to never reunite. I'd see his dust, swallow it in my wine.

"Tonight we return to the Cathedral. You will feed, rest, and be unmolested."

"I've never left this city." Jade thought she was clever, evasive with such a comment. She was cute, extremely ruffled and ready to run.

Tightening my arm where hers was looped with mine, I made it so not only could she not pull away, she could not accidentally cast a gate without taking me with her.

She noted the aggression, digging in her heels and looking every last bit betrayed. "I'm not going back there."

"Soon I'll take you to Paris, to Dubrovnik, to all the

wonders of Europe so you might play and leave this city for the first time in your life. I'll spoil you with feasts crafted by master chefs, with rare wine and rarer jewels."

"You listen to me, Malcom." The hissing, the biting, and the scratching were soon to begin—as if her sweet fangs or tiny claws could possibly do me any damage. "I will not go back."

"And where would you run? Our apartment? Another country? Into enemy territory as a physically weak but highly desired daywalker? I'd find you in minutes. I can feel where you are with every pulse of my heart. And if another beat me to you, an ancient older than your father, what then? Would you rather be devoured so an old corpse might feel the sun one last time? Or will you trust me?"

Her eyes, makeup already smeared, watered. Her beautiful bitten lip shook. "Is this some kind of game to you? Is that what you do? You and my father? Do you toy with my memories until I unravel then take me back home for a proper whipping and a purged mind?"

Out in the open, where we could be heard and might be, I cupped her cheek and asked her to be braver. I reminded her that she was the daughter of a veritable demon and capable of so much more than either of us might imagine.

And I made her a promise. "Vladislov."

"What?" Impatient, her heart beating fast enough to send a human into a stroke, Jade's chest rose and fell. All of her looked ill. "That means nothing to me."

"Do as he asks, when he asks it. It could be that easy."

"And he'll kill my father?" I'd pushed her too far, Jade

throwing up the hand that wasn't trapped by my arm. "You're all insane. No one can best him. You've seen what he can do. The entirety of his body can spread out to all corners of a room. All corners of your mind. He is the devil, and you are a fool for thinking your foreigner might actually take his throne. I'm going to run!"

With a sigh, and a heavy heart, I caught her flailing arm and kissed her knuckles despite how she fought. "Then I'm going to have to chain you."

"You wouldn't dare!"

But we were already falling through a gate. One expertly crafted to deliver us outside Jade's preferred entrance to the Cathedral.

My hand over her shrieking mouth, I dragged her through a foyer with a new, head-shaking, eye-rolling vampire who must have heard how difficult and obstinate the king's daughter could be. Not a soul stopped me. No matter how she kicked, tore at my palm, and tried to scream for freedom.

Spectators, witnesses, smirking lips and the old dame's style of waving hand. They had seen this before: they found it boring; they found it titillating; they found it nothing. In this dead kingdom of lost souls and the damned.

I wasted no time dragging my cargo to the conservatory, even less parting the doors and forcing her inside. Then they were dragged closed despite her attempts to pull them back open. Barred, with steel.

To the guards, I said. "No one enters. Ignore her raving and lies. The princess is in one of her moods."

And I left her there.

Already aware a fine dinner of extremely rare Kobe beef, properly prepared as it would have been in the Land of the Rising Sun, waited under a dome. Two bottles of fragrant wine also sat atop her table. One red, decanted and perfect. The second white, chilled yet uncorked.

She'd had blood enough from me earlier to tolerate a day or two while I did the work deserving of our house.

Though I couldn't hear her while I went about my night, I knew she cried. I suffered with her, and took out my frustration on my food. Not that I killed any of the well-fed and well-bred humans from my personal stock. I just took a bit more, a touch roughly, and didn't give a shit that they begged for mercy.

Of all immortals in this kingdom, there were few more merciful than I.

Then a hunt began, the dregs in the lowest pens released for sport. In that game I was savage, collecting the most ears with ease. Vladislov, still the guest of King Darius, found the whole thing hilarious.

Jade

Days before, I'd accidentally cast a gate while in the throes of unwanted orgasm, I'd dropped my sad self into the throne room before my personal Jesus Christ. But now, stuck in my conservatory I could do nothing. Try as I might.

Blood ran down my nose, an aneurysm to be sure, I'd tried so hard.

And when I could not find my exit from hell, I made hell my plaything. Everything I might reach I destroyed. The glass coffin of my childhood, trinkets, baubles, priceless art, bedding, the rug. I even pulled every last settee and couch asunder. Raging like a demon.

Red eyes, sharp fangs.

Powerless.

Malcom would pay for this. Trickery, mockery, *lies*. He would pay when I tore his cock off with my teeth and shoved it so far up his ass a creature incapable of shitting would never be able to get it out.

Of course, he'd grow a new dick. Leaving me more than happy to repeat the procedure.

The pain I would bring down upon that man. The *hate* I felt. Like a warm blanket, reassuring and normal. Wrapped in the cocoon of loathing, covered in down feathers from torn blankets, I made a nest in shattered glass and pulled my knees to my chin.

I slept through the worst of the sun, waking at dusk.

There was no water waiting when I woke.

I, the princess of this kingdom, was made to stand, burned as I was, and walk to my bathroom to drink from the tap.

Scooping water into my palm, sucking it down a dry throat, I died a little more. Until I stood straight and saw myself in the cracked remains of the mirror. A horror.

A demon's spawn.

In great need of a shower, a new life, a rebirth.

Poisoned by this place and the horrible creatures gathered in it.

Envy at a memory, one my father would tear from my mind the second he sensed it, lanced my being. Vladislov sitting daddy's throne. How I would have loved, even in play to have sat that throne.

To have the immortals here look upon me with veneration. Instead, I'd been dragged inside screaming, not for the first time, and laughed at. The tittle-tattle most likely carrying on would leave me shamed for years.

I'd sucked that bastard's cock down my throat, choked on it—gagging and drooling the way men preferred.

"Jade."

Hands to my marble bathroom vanity, burning as if the fires of hell had been born in my womb, I refused to look toward the one who had reduced me so low. "Get out."

But Vladislov was not moved by something as pathetic as I. "Come, love. We'll find a place in your *palace* to talk."

It was then I realized sunlight drenched us both, the remainder of the day. A pink sky. Death to any vampiric immortal.

"Come, child," he murmured to me. Beautifully ugly. That long, waved brown hair shining and glorious. "You've had your tantrum. Let it be done."

My clothing was shambles, my skin left with marks of broken things and self-harm. Still I turned to face my savior. "Can you really steal the throne from Satan?"

"Let's talk of the River Seine. And beautiful things."

The melody of his song, the very look he laid upon me. My own father had never looked at me in such a way. "I would have been a good daughter…"

How he dug in so deep with so little effort. "I know, child."

"You asked before if I would burn the Cathedral with everyone inside."

"And?"

"I like Marie. She's always been kinder to me than the others." My forehead softened, my lips growing lax. "Perhaps it is her Hapsburg jaw and lack of 'immortal' beauty. Or the fact she lost so many babies when her kingdom fell. She was the first to ever offer me cake. Did you know that?" Brushing rooted glass from my forearm, I continued. "I don't think anyone does. Something so inconsequential wouldn't even have interested my father."

Footstep cracking more broken glass under his heel, Vladislov dared come nearer. "And did you care for the cake?"

"I devoured the attention. Sitting on her lap like a prized poodle."

"You're lonely."

"Yes." None could be more lonely than I.

With a wink, something evil professed. "No fire then. The only friends you've ever known are here, terrible as they are."

Enough. I'd had enough of being toyed with on all fronts. "You said we were going to talk of the Seine."

He moved with the same speed as my daddy. There one

instant, in another before one might see. Picking a feather from my hair, Vladislov blew on it to make it fly away. Together we watched the bit of down tumble and float, to land in the chaos. And then silence.

Which fed me.

This man, this thing who could tolerate just a touch of dying light, grasped me by the soul.

Glancing up from the wreckage on the ground, I caught his eyes, daring much in my request. "I'm hungry."

He grinned. "Don't be greedy."

Yet still he offered me his wrist.

It was like drinking ebony. Glassy warm and blacker than pitch.

23

Telling someone as spoiled and rotten and twisted as I not to be greedy, was, in itself, silly. Even at my age, I was incapable of being anything but. Lips to skin that felt like dry paper, cautious in how I punctured, and feeling the strangest itch upon the parts of my skull that had been put back together, I sank in my fangs.

Delicately.

Like a lady sipping port, pinky up.

Rapture hit me harder than my brains had hit that wall years ago. It took me by the throat, stole my soul from right out of my body, and had me tearing my lips away before more than a few drops of infinite darkness smeared my tongue.

I could not have been greedy if I'd wanted to! To drink of that man would kill me.

"Sure you've had enough, child?" He made a show of

rolling up his sleeve, exposing the veins in his strong forearms and tan skin.

He stood in the last of the day's dredge of sun, had entered my pretty prison without effort, had offered me the taste of infinity. Did my father's blood hold eons like this? How had I survived drinking from this man as a child? "What are you?"

"I am whatever I want to be." He cut me a secretive smirk, teasing, playful even. "Old, to be sure."

Wiping my lips as if some of that dreadful perfection might still linger there, I spoke plainly. Because there was absolutely no point in prevaricating with this one. "The older they get, the more their minds warp. What's to make you any different than him should you take his throne?"

He cocked a brow. "Nothing at all."

"I'm less than one hundred but I feel ten thousand." I felt older than any river he might want to discuss.

"Yet you act like you're five."

True. I was aware of my faults. More aware by the minute, blockages in my mind easing until the overspill of ugliness behind them left me reeling. "I think I might *need* another drink."

If just a few drops of him had untangled hints of what was hidden in me, a mouthful might give me back what I lost that day my brains hit the floor.

"By all means." The same wrist was offered, the greedy girl I was nervous to so much as scratch his skin.

My lips hovered there, amidst the wreckage of my

tantrum, and mental scar tissue snapped apart and made me hate myself more.

I remembered so many disgusting things I'd done. And considering what I'd recalled before, felt so dirty in my flesh that I wished the fading sun would literally burn it all away. Breathing over his skin, over that wrist filled with truths and punishment, I fell to my knees.

They were cut apart on shards of glass, the pain welcome and not nearly enough. "I've destroyed families. I've rewritten histories, done terrible things… because I loved my father and craved his love in return."

As if he were some ancient saint and I a supplicant, he put a hand to my head. "Do you not want your mother's love?"

No. "My mother is dead. I doubt she had much love for me when I ripped my way out of her body."

"What a sad tale…" Said with what felt like real remorse. Ancients couldn't feel *real* anything. He pressed his wrist closer to my hovering mouth. Offering another taste.

And I was too young to know better. "The more of me you undo, the uglier my life will be. You should have just left me alone." Yet still I sunk my teeth in.

And unlike that first sip, I drank.

Remembering rapes, sodomy, prostitution, the ways in which my father had sold me for whatever gain he might. Tears when it hurt, until it didn't hurt. Until it didn't feel like anything. Until I was fucked like a robot, or bent over and took it like a cow might take a bull—chewing cud and bored in my field.

I don't know why it was the sex that broke through first. Perhaps because under my father's influence, it bothered me the most. I was a dishtowel, a tissue used and discarded. Nothing more than a thing to wipe fluids on and cast to the floor.

What search was there for a grandchild in this? This lazy approach of bending my body to every immortal male's whims.

Two thrusts had come from Malcom as I'd bent over that table while my father had watched. I'd been physically ill afterward. Two thrusts after my sire had left the room and Malcom, the first ever, asked me if I wanted him to stop.

And he had. Just like that. No complaints. No violence.

Instead, he'd tried to comfort me as I cursed his cock and threatened his life.

For the life of me, I couldn't understand why the idiot might think he loved me. I was not worth loving. Perhaps age had made him as mad as the man whose black blood trickled like sludge down my throat. This man who had physically pieced my skull back together ages ago, who now mentally ripped through so much damage I'd never be the same.

Never.

The scar tissue was still there, I was just aware of it now. And in many cases could see exactly what was hidden within its knots and gnarls.

And the lies… the untruths planted to make me compliant. Losing those stopped my heart.

Because I knew the answer the rest of the flock would give, I broke suction from that vein of death, and looked up at the smiling figure before me. "Do you find this all amusing?"

"When I made your father, I knew he'd do great things. Build empires. Slaughter enemies." Soft, manicured fingers ran through my hair. "But you might be his greatest accomplishment."

It was just the type of lie that fed me more deeply than any blood might. How I craved acceptance. How it had made me tolerate hell for another taste.

"You won't be a good king. Not if you created Darius and let him run wild for thousands of years." It had to be said. "You don't care."

"Can a father not love his son despite his… shortcomings?" The tip of a finger tapped my nose. "Can he not love his granddaughter?"

I was not falling for it. Not again. "You only saved me because Malcom traded eternal fealty. Otherwise I would have dragged myself to my death, alone, scared, and missing half my brain!"

"We could debate why I was where I was when your lover found me and fell to his knees. I could spin tales more beautiful than any your father planted in your mind. But to be true, I can't recall exactly why I walked where I walked that day. There is something else here that draws my thoughts. Something I want but can't find."

Negotiation, politics, and plain demands. This was my safe space. This was comfortable. So I rose from the ground, bloody knees ignored, and asked pointblank what the sire of my father could possibly lack.

All I received for an answer was a kiss on the cheek. And then he was gone, right as the sun vanished and night broke in.

For two more days I was kept locked in my rooms, living in a new mind that felt alien and too large. For two days I tidied my mess. Piling up broken, glittering things. Sweeping them with the remains of my ruined wardrobe.

There was more chaos than clean. But some parts of my tiled floors did sparkle as if freshly polished. The rest were cracked, broken, and in need of replacing. I slept, and I dreamed, and I drank more water from the tap. And as the hours crept on, as the sun rose and set, I found that tap water tasted better than any blood I'd ever known.

Malcom came on the third night bearing food. I refused his wrist, eating chicken wings off the bone and chugging a local, frothy beer, and found I liked both things.

Heaven help him, he tried to talk to me, but I wasn't ready. It wasn't stubbornness, not at its heart. It was something unnamable. I had almost a century to process and only a handful of hours in which I'd been able to do it.

I thought of the Seine. A river I'd only seen in pictures and how Vladislov had tempted me with the idea of it. I thought of Paris, and art, and modern women, and food.

I thought of what real love might feel like, staring at the male who believed in his heart he felt that emotion for me.

Puzzling over this concept as I sucked the marrow from the bones. *Staring* at Malcom, at a man beautiful beyond description and devious as my devil of a father, I thought long and hard over the mechanics of it.

And wasn't sure our kind was capable of such a human thing.

"You have permission to fuck me, if you want to." That was all I said to him over that dinner of peasant food and beer.

It earned a sad smile, one from a man who just might know the exact torture of a broken heart. "Not tonight, my love."

24

MALCOM

The state of her rooms was a reflection of the state of her mind. Piles of shattered things, spots she'd cleared, everything sharp and ready to harm her—her glass cage where my beautiful bird could never sing.

In all my centuries, I'd never seen a being look so sad. Not even the humans kept by the worst vampire houses. Not even the cattle who'd lost everything only to live out their remaining days drained of the last drop of blood in their veins. Until withered and unwanted, burned where thousands of others just as unwanted as they had been sent to burn.

Ash that floated over a polluted city, forgotten, mourned… nothing.

"You're thinking to yourself right now how anyone could love you." And I didn't understand how it was possible, but I loved her even more in that moment. To the point I thought my heart might burst and the soul I'd sold was returned to me.

She didn't answer or shrug, just watched me. Waiting for some trick, that little girl in a blue dress all grown up. There was no minute flinch when I took her hand. A first. Rubbing warmth into her fingers, I relished this intimacy. I took things slowly with my virgin.

That's what she was now, reborn. Jaded, and aptly named.

Paying strict attention, I smoothed each of her fingers from base to tip, gently attended the webbing between them, before turning her palm up, to spread that flesh with my thumbs. My flower melted, just a little of that ice she'd been encased in from birth seeping away from simple kindness.

"You are not what he made you to do, or the traits he coerced you to embrace. I have always seen the real you. I see it now. And someday, you will too." I pressed a kiss to that palm, and felt a tear fall from my cheek to drip down her wrist. I, the old, tried warrior, wept for this damaged thing that was beyond dear to me.

And by her sudden, violent retreat, I think it might have frightened her more than any torment her father might bring down upon us should he discover we even shared such a conversation. Hand to her heart, fingers fluttering, lips thin, cheeks white, eyes wide. She gave an inch, even as she took another step away.

Rising so she'd be forced to see all of me—my stature, my strength, my prowess, and my superiority to other males, I declared, "I do love you. Every single thing about you. I always have."

"I'm grotesque." This she said, looking down at her body as if all she saw was rotting flesh and bloated limbs.

I flashed to her side, took her fingers again, and kissed the tips. "But there you're wrong. You're clean. Brand new. Mine to treasure."

Challenging, because she was born royal and would never easily cede, Jade sneered. "How do you know that you don't just love me because Darius made you? How do you know it's real? I've had my thoughts ripped apart for the last few days, and let me tell you, most of what is trapped in my skull is utter bullshit. It's no different for anyone else in this place."

This was the question I had been pining for. "Because your bastard of a father tried repeatedly to take it away from me. *And every single time he failed.* I'm far older than you, I know how to maneuver in ways you're too impatient to grasp. I know my love is real because he forbade me from ever telling you how much I cared. Forbade me to woo you, to be kind to you, to even touch you unless it was to draw your ire." I pinched a strand of her hair, the way I had for ages. The way that always pissed her off. Only this time, she looked down at my fingers and saw what they were about. "All he could do was forbid. Take small moments from my memory… but they always grew back. They grew back because since I held you in my arms, all I've ever thought of was how to love you best."

Narrowing her eyes, it looked as if she'd react as she had thousands of times in the past to my touch. Shove me away and hiss that I was beneath her notice.

But that wounded bird resisted, fighting the urge so hard her eyes closed from the effort. Brow tight, several deep breaths expanded her chest. More of my fingers stroking her hair, pushing her to try.

She whispered, "Vladislov is far worse than my father. Do you grasp that?"

"I think you misunderstand him."

"*I drank from him.* I saw what he was." Eyes opening, she gave me a look. A look that spoke more than the words that followed it. "He stood with me in the sun."

Ancients were different than other immortals. God-like, and necessary to keep our numbers in check. To rule hordes of bloodthirsty beasts. And one day both Jade and I would stand amongst them. We too would be changed by time, altered, blood black as death. But we would do it together, whole of mind, and sound of heart. The same soul, in two separate bodies, reunited.

Fated.

The reason I never took another wife. No female flesh as spoils of war.

I had recognized her from the moment she'd been delivered into my arms. And should I die, I would be reborn to find her again. For eternity. Over, and over.

Because there was no such thing as heaven or hell. This I knew. There was only with or without one's soulmate.

But she was too stuck on other issues for me to breach such a weighty subject. "It doesn't matter what he is. What matters is what we have." I needed her to understand that the trivialities, the cost to be together, was nothing. I'd destroy entire countries, burn them and all living things in their borders, laughing, if that's what I had to do so I might claim this female. "Your father envies me for what I achieved in finding you. Vladislov envies just the same. All those doomed to endless life who have not discovered their other half covet this, whether they know it or not. Recognize what is before you and forget the rest. It could be so easy, Jade."

So easy to just sweep her into my arms and carry her off to the place I had prepared. Lock her away from all things dangerous, where she would be only mine until she grew stronger. Until she understood and accepted what this was.

"You're not listening to me!" A sigh, one heavy with frustration, and she swatted my hand from her hair. "Talk of love, if you want to. Talk of"—she gestured between us before she began to pace—"all of this. But you're ignoring my point because you know I'm right. That creature will eat us on a whim."

Her panic was… unfortunate. I'd hoped these days might have cleared her head. "He and I have an arrangement."

"He created my father." The confession spoken with awe and terror.

That I had not known, though such knowledge only gave me faith that soon all I had sacrificed and all my darling had suffered would reap us the ultimate reward. So I got to my knees before this woman, and startled her all the more.

Before she might dart back, I took her hips in my hand. Held her before me as I groveled for her love—for more effort from my lady, even though I know she suffered. "And your father made you. Once a toddler who could cast gates without chanting, so powerful in magic that he fractured her mind so she might never move against him. Darius wants you to think as little of yourself as possible. Degraded you into dust. I did all I could to shield you; though it might not have always appeared that way, I did. And I have gathered such splendors to please you. Every desire that's truly *yours*, I can fulfill."

"You're a little bit insane. You know that right?" Wiping her eyes with the back of her hands, she gave me a look of pity. "Neither of us will survive whatever game Vladislov plays."

From across the room came an overly gentle, "You may call me Grandfather."

She screamed, jumped right out of my hands, portal and all. To appear twenty feet away. Tottering on her feet, unsure how she did it, Jade fell flat on her ass into one of her piles of my broken gifts.

And there she cried like a baby. Mind a ruin, body abused for so long she couldn't differentiate what was her choice from what wasn't, and in pain. When I stepped forward to go to her, to try again to explain, Vladislov appeared from the shadows and held up his hand.

Eternal fealty. I had to obey.

So that entity—that creator of great, evil things—went to her instead. Crouching down, wiping her tears, and whispering things I'd never know.

I'd never know them because part of our arrangement was that I could never ask. And Jade, she never offered information. What I'd pulled from her over the years, was taken by force.

But my lady calmed: the type of forced calm minutes away from violence. A kind of violence that came from desperation should the beast who had cornered her make one wrong move. The kind of violence that would see her ended. Wounded rabbit, rabid wolf.

For this woman, I was not above begging. "Please, don't hurt her."

"She…" The man's long, thin fingers, stroked her wet cheek. "She is my family. Are you not, child? If I let your daddy run wild for eons, why would I tarnish this precious flower?"

"Please," I said again. Darius knew sweet words too. Darius had learned them from him.

And I had bet our entire futures on the whims of a God.

"I cannot recall the last time I offered someone succor." And how chilling such a phrase could be from something so powerful.

For he had not offered it to little Jade. I had paid for it. But now he looked amused, long hair draped over his shoulder and waved, impeccably combed, just like the rest of him. A fancy man for all his less desirable features.

The being came to a decision. "If she'll drink once more, I'll leave her be. Comfort your wife and tell her to open her jaw."

It was there I saw how he'd already tried to tempt her, a wrist offered, the same wrist he'd fed her from the night she'd been left in pieces. And Jade shook her head.

So I obeyed.

I went to her side, knelt, pulled her head to my shoulder as I whispered whatever sweet things an old warrior might think of into her hair. I promised her the River Seine. A life of joy free of corruption. Pretty things.

So many pretty things I had found and hoarded for her to smile at.

Freedom. Even from me should she wish it.

And with those words, she parted her lips and drank of death.

For a third time. For yes, I had watched this woman's every breath for the last agonizing days.

Two painful gulps, and her eyes would never be blue again.

Red as fire, mind deconstructed, she met my gaze, and she saw me for what I was.

Her slave.

25

JADE

I cannot even imagine what my father's body must have gone through when he'd been changed from man to immortal. Once upon a time, a proud Persian king, then the creation of something powerful beyond measure. Did my father even recognize what gifts were given to him in his early state of ignorance? Did he think all vampires were like the man who'd offered him eternity? Had he any idea what Vladislov was?

For I was certain, *Grandfather* was as powerful then as he was now.

Yet in the two interactions I'd witnessed between the men, I had seen no familial conversation. Vladislov had received no more formal a greeting than other emissaries or visiting ancients. There was no closeness, no endearment.

No sense of shared history.

At least none that I understood. Maybe because they were

so old. Maybe because my father had no heart. He certainly didn't love his people, neglecting the throne for months at a time, hidden away and secretive.

One day you'd turn around, and Satan would be in the room. Smiling, dressed in glittering robes. Beautiful, devious, and ready to rend. Like clockwork twice a year or so.

Twice a year to mangle my mind, send his hive into a manic uproar, and then leave after ripping apart enough of our numbers to keep the flock in line. I expected little more from my grandfather.

In fact, I expected less.

Considering what he'd just unleashed within me.

I knew what his blood was, and I knew how insignificant this flock was in comparison. Not even an afterthought. But he was drawn to this place, so for that reason alone, he was going to take it. And when he was bored—and he would grow bored—he'd wander on to walk the River Seine, philosophizing about concepts beyond my understanding with God only knew who.

Because really, in comparison to the years I'd just swallowed with a few mouthfuls of his blood, I was still nothing but a fetus.

One that felt extremely strange and very, very angry now that I felt power for the first time in my horrible life.

So angry, in fact, that it ate up the rest of me, my insecurities and failures burned to ash with the flood of vengeful intention. As if I could shine with the blazing heat of the sun and burn all undead who dared stand so close to something so full of wrath.

From the way Malcom shielded his eyes with a curse, and how the ground shook as he reeled back—how I steamed and rattled, and heard the conservatory's unbreakable, bullet-proof glass crack and fall all around me, it must be so.

Vladislov had once asked me what I would do to the Cathedral had I the power to act as I pleased. And that old wish was taking place without any effort on my part. In fact, I wasn't sure I could stop myself from razing it to the ground.

I lacked any kind of self-control to contain such unimaginable power.

"Remember, young one." Grandfather put his hand to my shoulder, careless of the bright light that had sent Malcom to vanish into the shadows or fry. "No flames. Give half of them a chance to survive, your Marie Antoinette included. Just exorcise the ghosts of this decrepit old place and leave the bones behind."

As if what he commanded were so easy. As if I could stop myself when I felt out the weaknesses of stone and exploited them. Overcharged, inexperienced, and burning from the inside out, I found my body moving from place to place. As if I'd willed it. One moment in the boudoir of one of the cruelest males I'd been forced to take within my body.

All it took was my presence to see his flailing form turned to ash. He'd never even had the chance to scream.

I was the sun. I was death, eating through my people in a very different way than I was infamous for. All the while, those who haunted the Cathedral screamed, scrambling into the night to find cover as stone cracked and entire sections of this ancient, cursed church collapsed into rubble.

How many I killed? I cannot say. And not all were intentional, too many just got in the way as I popped in and out of existence. Ending my massacre in the throne room where my father waited, bloodied from I know not what, and burning with his own power—that was far more immense than mine.

"You ungrateful, useless child!"

There was just enough to his demeanor to see that my sire was rattled, all the more apparent for he'd missed the most important feature of the room.

Immaculate, dressed in a black suit somehow untouched by the dust falling from a building that still shook, Vladislov sat my father's throne. Witnessed by the many factions who'd fled to this very spot in search of rescue. There was the foreign contingent, stolid and unmoved by the carnage. There were my father's sentinels, others transformed for their beauty or gifts in the arts, the rabble, even the fresh-changed. So many, all who would witness my end.

Already I felt the hand of death, cold, comforting, offering me rest. So I faced it as the daughter of a royal, with my head held high and my words vicious. "You are an unworthy king and a disgrace as a father. I am ashamed to have known you, Darius. And before I die, I will bring this Cathedral down to crush you into dust!"

From me. Those words had come from me. And they were sick with all the things he'd done, the mistakes I'd made, the world that was a worse place because we both existed in it.

"You wouldn't dare!"

"Enough." Vladislov broke through the creak of stone and the roar of my father's anger. "Enough, child."

The valve of unrelenting power the ancient had opened in me closed, stolen away, just as easily as it had been given—simple words from his mouth more powerful than any vendetta I might possess. Just like that, I was the little girl in the blue dress, swinging from her father's arm, recalling child-like joy and the sensation of completeness before my head had been split in half.

That was the perfect way to feel when my father tore my heart out. Whole.

I closed my eyes and braced for it.

Whatever parts of me that had been left in my grandfather's pocket were mine again. I didn't even feel the pain when a red-eyed demon whose features I carried reached forward faster than even the undead could see. The sound of a ribcage cracking, the gagging noise of blood shooting up both windpipe and esophagus, yet it felt like nothing more than a scratch.

This rebirth would be painless.

Or so I thought… until a body slumped against me, taller, larger, and had me tripping over my feet to catch him as he fell. An angel's face contorted in pain, *my angel*, with a gaping hole in his chest and his beating heart in the harsh grip of my father.

Malcom.

"No!" Throwing my body over his, my banshee scream shook the crumbling rafters. Our eyes met, my heart refusing to beat if his wasn't going to exist. And I realized, as his blood bubbled over my fingers, what love felt like.

How I'd felt it for this man from the moment I'd looked up at him as a babe.

How it was terrifying, and fresh, and the most beautiful thing that might ever exist. And that there was no life worth living if he wasn't in it, bossing me about and challenging me to be better.

I truly was dying, even if my body was whole. "Malcom… no."

In my arms, his glowing eyes were losing their luster. Yet still he tried to smile through the blood, mouthing that he loved me and begging me cast a gate and run.

That would never happen. I'd die here, with him, seeing him as he was: the glowing light of my life in a world that was nothing but dark. And I swore this to him as I kissed his mouth and tasted heaven.

"Poorly done, son." The lightness of the decree from the throne, made my loss seem insignificant.

So it was to him, I begged for Malcom's life. "Eternal fealty if you save him."

With a smile, the ancient turned me down. "No."

Standing, finding my father held the heart of the man meant to me mine, watching him prepare to crush it into jelly and laugh, I struck.

Vladislov barked with the voice of a God, "I said enough!"

Shaken to my soul, caught in midair and dropped to the ground by an unseen power. I gasped for breath and found that Vladislov didn't require eternal fealty from one as puny as me. He only need speak and I was his thrall.

And from where I struggled for breath, when I fought every muscle in my body that refused to move so I might reach the dying heart of my beloved, it seemed my father suffered the same.

The devil himself was frozen solid, clearly fighting the enthrallment and unable to break free.

As my people observed in absolute silence.

With a heavy sigh, Vladislov stood from the throne. Buttoning his suit jacket, an expression of immense disappointment aging his face by eons, he walked down the dais to where his offspring and his grandchild thought to end one another. "Why make her weak when she could be such an asset to our race? Those, Darius, are the actions of an insubstantial man. There is a difference between wielding power and ruling by fear. I have told you this time and time again. The world has no room for creatures like you in these modern times. My child, you have refused to adapt, created a kingdom so flawed that a mere child tore it asunder in one night. I taught you better than that."

My father, vibrating with the power held by a stronger beast, hissed, "You wouldn't dare steal what's mine. Not after all I've given you!"

"The illusion that any of this was ever really yours baffles me the most." Hand to his chest, dignified in a way I'd never witnessed from this changeable man, I fought with every bit of power Vladislov had poured into me to break the compulsion so I might reach that black heart in my father's blood-drenched grip before it ceased to beat.

Inch by inch, my hand stretched forward. But God, the pain, what I had to sacrifice to raise my arm and brush my fingers over my only love's stolen heart. And still I fought the will of an ancient, one who could see me ended with but a thought… prying that heart from my father's fingers.

Because it was mine, and always had been.

Bones broke as I struggled to take a step toward the fallen Malcom. To piece him back together as he had once done for me. Tears streaming down my face, I made it those three agonizing paces, to fall over his body, and find that his eyes were already closed.

"She's very impressive," Grandfather said as he edged nearer to watch.

The heart I put back, pumping it with my hand as veins and arteries reached for their necessary muscle. Slicing my wrist with little claws, I bled for him straight into that gaping hole in his chest. Red blood that had gone several shades closer to black. And I begged Malcom to come back to me.

But he didn't wake up, and that fluttering heart in my hands skipped beats, failing before my eyes.

My sobbing witnessed by so many, the sound of my own heart breaking louder than the crush of tumbling stone, I somehow found the power to stand. Crumpled, as if held together by overstretched tendon and misaligned bones, I crept back to my father, to my grandfather, and I shoved my hand straight into the chest of my lifelong devil, ripping out what lay inside. Because I was owed—so much more than my father's heart—but this was all I'd ever be able to claim from him.

Falling to my knees, I tore out Malcom's ruined organ and put the black heart of pure evil in its place.

It pumped steadily, weaving with tissues and fascia, bring life back to the dead. The man I loved began to mend, lashes parting as if he'd woken from a deep slumber. To hear me say the truest words that had ever passed my lips, "I love you."

26

"Do you hear that, son?" It was gentle, approving, and unnaturally creepy. "She *loves* him."

Shielding Malcom's rapidly healing body with mine, I watched a dance between a wounded cobra and a slinking mongoose. The cobra capable only of waving his head back and forth, the mongoose circling for the kill.

Darius, heartless as he was, wasn't dead.

As our fallen king stood before his kingdom, his maker rent him limb from limb. Only to gently place those severed bits in multiple satin lined, disturbingly-sized caskets, carried forward by Vladislov's contingent.

And I'm sure I was not the only soul in that wreckage of a room who worried that one such as Darius might never be able to know a true death. Still, I witnessed what would pass for his end. Shivering to see the level of preparation Vladislov had aspired to.

All of this would have taken place no matter my part in it.

They gathered an arm or a leg, quarters of torso, spilled guts. Each container the proper size to hold the piece of the immortal whose heart would beat on forever in the body of another.

In a man who was worthy.

My grandfather's dissection of his son wasn't messy work, considering. Concise, organized, pre-planned and ultimately... sad. Darius was dismembered, brought down from greatness as if nothing more than a dandelion puff blown apart by a passing breeze.

And then the boxes holding what had once made up my father were silently carted off by strangers from strange lands with their own unknown agendas. All the while I imagined those bits would be hidden in various parts of the world, burned, buried, maybe left to rot.

Sold to voodoo queens.

But our fallen king's head remained, cupped in the arms of his creator. A head still blinking, a mouth still moving. Alive.

A long span passed, an hour, maybe more, as my grandfather considered his child. And though his expression failed to alter, I wondered if he felt remorse. But I feared he felt nothing, and that the nothing inside him had somewhat left the ancient surprised.

Imagine growing to such an age where one questioned feeling *anything* at all. Such an existence would be worse than even the life I had lived.

"You don't need to cry for him, Jade." My Malcom,

already sitting up as if his ruined heart didn't lie on the floor at his side, stroked my cheek, offering me comfort.

That shriveled heart dead on the ground called to me, that piece of my angel. So I took it. I held it, finding the flesh had gone white as all the blood had drained out.

A shriveled white heart that I would not give up for anything.

Arms came around me, an entirely new sensation. This was a feeling I would grow addicted to. Melting against the greater strength of a man who had given his worthy life for my disgraceful one. Warm tears on a bloodstained face, holding the dead heart of my lover, I found that I did feel enough sorrow for both myself and my grandfather.

There were so many lost moments to mourn.

Had I the true strength, I would have killed Darius. He deserved to be broken apart, locked in caskets, scattered and forgotten. He deserved hell.

But God didn't work that way. Not for my kind. And watching it happen felt far too real.

"What now?" I wasn't even sure who I'd asked.

Vladislov eyes dragged from the face of his son, finding mine. A moment later he held out his prize. "I believe it's been an age since Darius has seen the sunrise. Be a dear, and take your father for one last look."

Startling us all, he dropped the head, just like that, to crack and bounce on the floor. Fate leaving it to roll my way. And then as if all were forgotten, Vladislov climbed the dais, unbuttoned his jacket, smiling at the chaos of the room as he sat the throne.

Whatever speech he gave my people, whatever was worked, designed, and arranged, I missed. With shaking fingers, I collected Darius by hair as dark as mine. With shaking legs, I did as I was bade.

Malcom did not follow.

After all, he'd pledged eternal fealty and a simple shake of the head from his new king was enough to trap my angel with the rest of the flock.

So off I went. Dazed, drained, wounded, and victorious. I went through the wreckage I'd made with little more than a whim.

At the edge of the fallen debris, I found a crack in an exterior wall wide enough so I might drag my body from darkness into budding life.

The gardens.

The same gardens I had played in as a child. The gardens I'd looked through from my glass cage. And came to stand before what had once been my conservatory. Now, nothing more than bent metal and razor-sharp shards of glass

Taking this all in, holding dear Daddy's living head by the hair, I had no clue what to do with myself… what to do with him.

I know what he deserved, I grasped what was intended here, but enacting it was…

How?

Perhaps grandfather had felt grief dismantling his child. Perhaps this last step he found he could not do himself. Maybe that's why he stared so long into the pain-filled, fluttering eyes of his creation.

Standing in the field of everything I'd broken, I glanced down at what hung from my arm. What couldn't even look up to see the expression on my face. "I think he did love you, however creatures like him know how to love."

And now there was work to do.

I took a step toward a twisted bit of metal that had once been banked by panes of glass—a piece of my prison—and found it suiting. Like a pike, it rose from the cracked ground, sharp, tall, appropriate for a view of such a lovely garden.

"I loved you too," I said, lifting the head without meeting Daddy's blood-red eyes.

Shoving it upon the spike made the exact sound one might expect a head crammed onto a pike might make. And there Darius would stay, unable to scream, facing the east to take in the sunrise. I'm not sure if it was out of kindness—so that he would not be alone in those final minutes—or if it was out of an unbroken sense of obligation, but I remained at his side as the first rays peeked over the horizon.

He burned at first light, smelling of sulfur and evil, melting onto that metal rod until nothing but a mass of charred flesh and blinding bone showed through the fiery mass. Yet, inside that ruined shell, I was uncertain if he still lived. If day by day he'd suffer over and over in the blazing beauty of sunlight. If that were his punishment for whatever true sin he'd committed against a creature so impossibly more powerful than him, it was laughable.

I didn't know if he'd heal without blood, or for how long he'd be left on display. I didn't know if he'd be stolen by a zealot, or if the birds might eat him. All I knew was that I was reborn in the wafting stink from his smoking flesh.

And that I wasn't going to cry anymore.

~

That night, I fell asleep in Malcom's arms. I awoke in Malcom's arms. I took sustenance from his body and pleasure from his attention. And as the evenings stretched by, there were no more political events or human maneuverings. No parties or fundraisers or bending over in back alleys for my father's chosen stud.

Instead, there was a world to see, and a loving warrior to guide me through it. Though I'd lived in that city from birth, I knew nothing of it but what I'd been required to experience. So, he took me to restaurants, he took me dancing, played with me, taught me to smile.

Malcom gave me opulent gifts, and poetry in languages I couldn't decipher. He took me out to films. We walked in parks. I learned about him: the names of his mother and sisters, the battles he'd fought and triumphs he still recalled with pride. His favorite color and the blood type he preferred above all others.

And though I was still uncomfortable with the change, the man took great pride in the fact that my eyes were now the same shade as the ruby he'd locked around my throat. A trait that made it a touch harder for me to fit in with humans, but was easily concealed with contacts or chic sunglasses.

Malcom taught me how to hunt, just as he would have taught any freshly-turned. He gave me access to his herd, and I found their existence not near as dreary as I'd imagined. The blood of happy humans was so much sweeter than that of those who despaired, he'd said. Not that my angel was a saint. He was a carnivore, the ultimate predator, and I found watching him feed to be exceedingly erotic.

And though I had no desire to mingle with them, I began to understand my people. A people vastly reduced in this part of the world. Less than half of what had been left within the throne room when I'd left survived that night. Vladislov had scores to settle. I'd even heard a rumor that he'd approached the former queen of France, smiling as he'd told her that sharing that cake with me decades ago was the only reason any had been left alive at all. Marie Antoinette had not found the 'let them eat cake' reference anything but terrifying. Which Vladislov, no doubt, found hilarious.

I wished never to go back there. Should those survivors wish to see me, they would come to my building, my kingdom, my sanctuary where Malcom saw to my every last need… almost.

"When?" I demanded, impatient in every way.

Smiling, nuzzling my neck, Malcom murmured, "Soon."

Through those days and those nights and those moments with my lover, I had known deep gratification and a lightness of spirit, but I had also known deprivation. Though he would give me endless physical pleasure, he had denied me his cock.

And made me a beggar.

For weeks. Months. Seasons.

Don't get me wrong, his fingers and tongue were magic. The tricks he knew beyond imagining. The man was capable of getting me worked up into such a state I sang out his name like a hymn. But that cock, unless I was feeding from one of its veins, it was not in my mouth or my pussy.

He called me his virgin.

I found I relished the endearment far more than I should.

"Define soon!" Because this was torture, this endless waiting with no real answer. I was so wet, always wet, and I had not forgotten the feel of him. Which is why I primarily chose to dine from the prominent vein twisting up the side of a glorious erection. It was the only way to tempt him to spill. To let his seed mingle with his blood and leave me boneless yet sadly empty.

"No."

"Am I being punished?"

Another of his grins, freely given and so beautiful I sometimes forgot what I meant to say. "You are being adored."

Diving between my legs, he licked my clit with abandon, rough with a flick of his tongue at the end of each swipe until my legs shook, and I found I'd lost the words to beg for more. Replete and breathless, I'd lain like a bit of flotsam on the waves, and felt him snuggle me.

"When I claim you—savagely fuck you, as you so

elegantly demand—you'll never doubt what you are to me. I'll know when you're ready, and that day is not today."

Bastard! He didn't get to dictate or deny me something I'd had practically every single day of my existence. Something it would seem I could hardly think straight without.

A single time I'd threatened to find another who would ride me until I was satisfied.

I saw real anger that night. I felt it in the sting on my skin when I'd been pulled over his knee.

That same night he'd given me Ethan, freshly-changed and ridiculous. Arrogant, and unaware that he was trapped in servitude for a century or more. Though this had been explained to him repeatedly before Malcom found him ready to enter our home.

Which Ethan still considered *his* home.

He went straight to the fridge to grab a beer, popping off the cap and taking a swig, only to immediately spit it back up. There would be no more craft brews in his future, a concept that had still failed to sink in.

That entitlement alone made him unattractive to me, though vampirism had done nothing but add to his beauty. He'd kissed me. The taste of his mouth on mine when he'd rushed forward with all the enthusiasm of a puppy, was unwelcome.

Malcom had given me his word. My body for this creature. Our agreement was that I could fuck Ethan to handle my urges. And Ethan was hard, very hard, as he rubbed against me and rambled on about all the clubs we'd be seen at together. How as immortals we'd control Wall Street, the White House, rule the city like king and queen.

"And what of your blonde and your child?"

Did he not realize he'd never see either of them again? That he'd not be permitted in public for at least two generations?

He acted as if nothing had been mentioned.

After all, he'd learned I was a princess. I could pull strings and there was no need for him to serve. Maybe I'd give him a sip of my blood so he could go into the sun too! Oh, we'd go to Belize, soak up the rays and play in the waves.

This man was an idiot.

And though I was practically starving for cock, his was the last I'd consider.

Malcom had taken him away. I think he might have killed him afterward, to be honest. I didn't care; I just never wanted to see him again.

The whole event had left me in a mood for a night or two, one lifted by a trip to the opera with a beautiful man on my arm. And a sea of familiar faces unsure why I ignored their invitations and waved them away from my box.

I wore white. I always wore white for Malcom, and I suspected that had I placed a veil on my head, it would have done nothing but given my vampire pleasure.

And it hit me, leaving me smiling during intermission as if I were in on his trick. "You're waiting for me to call you my husband."

Malcom kissed my fingers and said nothing.

The lights flickered, and the second act began.

27

MALCOM

It took her a year. Pouting, arguments. Four seasons, timed almost to the day that she'd brought down the Cathedral to begin truly accepting her place in my world. One year for her to be ready, to experience a healthy relationship and life the way a *modern* immortal might crave.

We had all the time in the world for her to capitulate. But she would not be truly happy without that one last, small concession. Patience I could and would afford her. Not that she wasn't regularly corrected. Over my knee, with orgasm denial, with timeouts and physical restraint. Still so young, so impetuous, so *mine*.

I didn't ask when I'd thrown out all the clothing she'd owned before she'd become my wife. My female—my pure, clean, worthy female—would wear white, and only white. Let her believe it was she who chose such things to please me. Let her scoff when a true wedding gown, carefully selected of course, came to hang in a position of obvious importance in her closet.

The minx refused to call me husband.

Were I introduced to humans at all, it was only as Malcom. Even if I pawed her before other interested men. Even if I kissed her dizzy and smeared all that red lipstick she loved to paint on her mouth.

She found my silent insistence on the term irrelevant. Thought to punish me for refusing her my cock, though she was blood and cum drunk on me several times a day. Absolutely addicted. Those glowing red eyes of hers never even glanced in the direction of another male or female. Quite a feat, considering her appetites and former temperament.

The collar locked around her throat, she could not get it off. This bothered her greatly. But the statement it made was far more important than her frustration. We were *forever*. A concept for one so young that had to feel weighty and intimidating.

I might never remove that collar from her throat, what care had I if it clashed with her fashion choices or *chafed* her skin. One day as a God, she'd still wear it.

"You don't wear a collar! You don't wear a ring!" This she'd spat at me when I'd caught her at her vanity picking at the mechanism with some tool. A tool she'd thrown with such precision it had pierced me right through the shoulder. Which was fucking hot as hell. My princess was learning.

An hour later there was a ring on my finger. I'd been keeping it on hand for just this occasion.

At first glance of the hammered band of steel, she

blushed, frustrated to be thwarted, then settled into my side so I might read to her in old languages. So she might know she was safe, loved, and would endure through her tricky transition.

Jade healed.

Considering the amounts of blood she'd swallowed straight from a demon's veins, it still took a remarkable amount of time. I'd catch her in the kitchen, talking to herself as she made a sandwich, piecing out old memories and not sure which was real and which was fake. She'd get stuck in circular arguments with her reflection, grow frustrated to the point of tears, drain me, as if the answers might lie at the center of my steadily beating heart… if only she could get to it.

What mattered most was that *she* had made herself the sandwich. It sounded like so small a thing, but was so epic in a world where she had hardly wiped her own ass.

So we would talk and I would tell her what I knew, fact from fiction. What I could not confirm, we'd consider together. And I found in doing this, I too began remembering things. Things that had Darius still ruled, he would have crushed me on the spot for holding in memory.

Devious Darius had a great secret.

One he'd gone to remarkable lengths to conceal.

With part of him alive in me, there was just enough to recall *her* face. I'd torn out *her* fangs and delivered *her* to a rotting, bored, and unkind king who had not moved from his throne in a century—not even to feed.

One who from that day forward no longer sat his throne.

One who abandoned us all for… a Pearl.

~

Jade

The evil had not been exorcised, but it had been *shifted* just enough to make it tolerable. Unsure if that was the proper description, I ignored the sounds of construction, ignored that simply approaching the passageway to such a place made me sick to my stomach. And I entered the Cathedral, though I'd sworn to myself I'd never do so again.

A new freshly-turned servant waited, and unlike the previous history of flagging, stupid, rude, and wasted baby vamps, this one knew me by sight. "My lady."

To the pretty girl I turned over a snow-white coat, my pair of crystal-encrusted Louboutins clicking over fresh marble floors when I walked past. Marveling. The whole vestibule for my favored entrance had been redone, the center table boasting a massive spray of fresh flowers highlighted by *electric light*.

Unnerving.

The massive, spiked wooden door between this false façade and the altar to the undead throne had somehow survived my onslaught, rehung and waiting, should I dare push it open.

It wouldn't do to be seen hesitating before a servant, yet still my hand met the wood and I failed to push.

"He's expecting you." Kindly offered, extremely nervous, she tapped a message into her tablet.

The *he* in question had not been told I'd been coming. Not even Malcom knew I was here. But Vladislov was a veritable God. And only Gods knew what Gods could see.

Hinges sang, well-oiled as I bore my weight against something it would take ten mortal men to move. And then I was home.

The Cathedral.

I might have thought I was Alice stepping through the looking glass, this world so different, far removed from the one I'd known.

Yet almost the same.

Stone, candelabras, the scent of beeswax and incense and oil. But bright with electric light. Under my radically expensive shoes some cracked stones remained, highlighted by new, fresh blocks of rock. As if the building itself was testament to what had happened here. And what could happen again. The walls were… changed? They were the same? Mirrors and paintings—a painting of me wearing white—and tapestries and literal cave drawings all brought in to highlight a throne that my father had sat.

Had ruined.

That had been taken from him on a whim.

And that sat empty.

He was waiting for me, the girl had said. But he was not here.

How I had suffered in this room once upon a time. Not just the day my brains had been dashed against a wall, but for decades afterward when I had been brought low and shamed. And that throne sat empty.

And *he* failed to appear.

So I dared.

Much.

I dared my life to climb the steps of the dais as I had as a child, to put my hands to the armrests I'd swung from all those ages ago. And I sat my ass in that seat.

Head steeped in my hands, exhausted from the work of it, I found a minuscule slice of rest in my exploit. This wasn't play. I wasn't queen. I'd never rule, and I hated most of the survivors who'd been forced to rebuild what I'd demolished.

"It suits you."

I didn't look up, not with my head spinning as it was, but I did answer my grandfather. "Coming here was a mistake."

Footfalls I heard as he climbed the steps. "One of many you will make, and learn from. Mistakes define what we are. Each worth so much more than any victory."

Was that so? Well then, I was rich in experience and saccharine in the smile I offered. I couldn't put my finger on why, but I was angry with this man. *This thing* who'd hung my picture on the wall. This force that had upset my life and left me with glowing red eyes. "I don't know what to do."

"Well… I'm so unaccustomed to honesty when it comes to our kind where do I even begin to answer?" The teasing, it was so Vladislov.

Sagging back, boneless and finding the seat infinitely

uncomfortable, I snarked, "My guess would be that you demand I stand from your throne. Perhaps you tear off a limb or two, drive home the point that this was no place for Darius's whore daughter to rest."

It was always that waved brown hair I noticed first. Perfect in the unison of its movement. Then it was the ugliness of his beautiful voice. "But you currently sit the throne. Should it not be you who command me?"

I'd play this game. "I command you to release Malcom from his vow."

"Done! See how easy it is to rule as queen?"

He had to be joking! Had to be. For if he wasn't, I might bring down this entire new building and piss on the ashes. But the bastard was adjusting his cufflinks and so goddamn full of himself he may as well have burst from his seams.

I had a life to spend with Malcom and it did not include listening to the bitching of immortals. "No."

And all playfulness was lost in that instant, a demon spreading proverbial wings, that had they existed would span the room in pure flame. Towering over me as I sat his throne, to correct one who dared disagree. It didn't affect me as it would have a year prior. Instead it drew me to my feet to face this thing. This true immortal monster.

"I don't want to be queen."

"At no time did I ask you. Consider that, granddaughter." He pushed a lock of hair behind my ear, reverent in the way he touched my face. "I never ask. Remember that should we banter as the eons pass."

"You promised me the Seine…" And with that latent

conversation I should not have held so close to my heart, I'd thought I'd been offered freedom.

"The Seine you shall have, and your husband I shall make free, if..." He, the most powerful vampire that might exist rolled up his sleeve to show me a wrist marked with black veins. "If you drink all your belly can hold."

Just because I was tired of being quashed, because I felt like being a dick and was bored of politics, games, and a life I had no control over, I took my grandfather's wrist. But only to pull him closer so I might go for the throat. Suit jacket pulled aside, I sank in my fangs so the wool might remain unblemished. The same could not be said for the crisp, white undershirt he wore like a Fortune 500 executive. It would be stained. Others would see that someone had fed from Vladislov as if he were food and not ambrosia.

I'd expected my brains to be dashed against the wall for such gall. I'd anticipated pain. *I'd known better!*

But he was far more clever than I. One mouthful and I saw eternity. A single gulp and I was forever changed. Horrified. Blessed. Unworthy. Pure.

As I drank, a God whispered in my ear, "You don't have to live your life without love. Have your Pict. Take him from me. But you can only keep him if you take this throne. Otherwise, I'll exercise my right to send him where you'll never find him no matter how long you search."

I couldn't imagine surviving a single night without Malcom. So I took the ugly deal, already feeling the building shake around me from my growing temper.

And then Malcom was there, hand to my shoulder, sweet

words at my ear. Foundations stopped their rumbling. My heart beat again… full of ichor and swampy darkness that left my eyes an even brighter crimson.

Drawing my teeth from the throat of an eternal, terrible thing, I buried my face in the shirt of my husband.

And married him that night beside the River Seine.

The gown fit to perfection.

The veil made me feel new.

Our bloodthirsty kiss after vows spun by some random priest sent the terrified mortal running back to his church.

Few were invited, yet many arrived. With little notice, the new Queen of the Americas' wedding became an event for those with rank enough to dare show their face. But there was one there who troubled me. A woman, overwhelmed in appearance, who clung to my grandfather like a tick.

She had dark hair. Blue eyes an exceedingly familiar shade that had once been mine. And stared at me with a mix of awe and horror.

She refused the passed goblets of the finest vintage of human blood. And my grandfather cooed over her, her awkwardness, her impropriety. Her total lack of manners.

My dress was lace, it was white. But my feelings toward that creature were black.

Though I was given no time to explore them. One moment we were before a crowd of undead playing at ceremony, the next I was with my husband in a room so laden with rose petals it was cliché.

Cliché and adorable.

"Tell me you love me." There would be no absolution should I answer incorrectly.

God, how I adored when he commanded me so. "I love you, Maelchon of the Pict."

"You might be queen, but know that I am your king."

He was, so much so that just to hear him speak in that tone had my pussy dripping with need. "I have no king, no husband as yet. Not until you give me what you've denied my body for so long."

And I was speared with such recklessness, that it broke our bed on a single thrust. In that moment, I think I died.

He fucked me raw, over days and nights in a windowless room. Took more than I might give until he filled me with child.

And I came so hard, I swore allegiance to my slave. Gave him my very soul. Felt each thrust of his cock so deeply that I swear it changed my spirit into something new.

A virgin. A husband.

Too rough, biting and vicious, and everything I might ever want.

Utterly in love, ruined by it, I took that throne as Malcom directed the rebuilding of my Cathedral, belly swollen with our firstborn. Who kicked like a fiend.

I was not a biddable queen. I was not amenable. I reordered with violence yet could be gentle as a lamb. Marie brought me cake. To her, I offered grace.

Eventually friendship, even with her despicable mate, Gustavo.

Hating that throne, I kept to my husband, his council, and

his attention. He lavished me with far more than wisdom and pleasure.

Malcom made me new. Made all of it bearable.

Until it began to fit. And the Cathedral began to glow with more than electric light.

Internal peace, a thing my people had been starved for.

I gave birth on a Sunday, in the beautiful room Malcom had designed for me. We named our daughter Eithne—Pict for princess. Our ruby. Her eyes a far brighter red than mine.

And as her father slept, I took her out to see the sun.

Thank you for reading CATHEDRAL! Ready to #FreePearl? Turn the page and indulge in THE RELIC.

THE RELIC

CRADLE OF DARKNESS, BOOK THREE

1

VLADISLOV

All thrones, all palaces, all places in this world where creatures of the night lingered—every corner of every continent where hunting grounds might exist—all of it bored me. I couldn't even recall what state the world had been in, the borders of countries, the wars fought, when I last sat as king. Others were placed to carry out that work in my stead. To lord over the night's denizens and keep our kind in line.

Keep my children thriving, learning, adapting, bringing pride to our race.

Darius had been my favorite son, hand-plucked from the Persian court. So much potential… and the ultimate disappointment. Thousands of years were no excuse to forget one's duty and where one came from. Namely from me, who'd chosen him, raised him, taught him, granted him power far beyond what others of our kind possessed.

Power that was abused.

How soon they forget.

So there I sat, on my dismembered son's throne, aghast to be reorganizing a disrupted hive full of Darius' more evil creations. Their minds were… fascinating. Their inability to answer my questions, clever. My son truly believed his gifts set him on equal footing with his creator. Yet all he did was make a mess. What I was seeing was little more than extreme selfishness, even for our kind.

There were secrets buried here, in tunnels that spanned the entirety of this city. Thousands of humans trafficked and kenneled, disposed of with none the wiser.

That, I would give my boy, was clever.

Vampires weren't even a myth in the new world. They were fodder for television shows and movies. Yet thousands lived in this city, hunting, breeding, bickering, and surviving right under the noses of millions of humans.

The evolution of my kind had been curious to observe. From vicious predators who'd ransack entire towns in one moonlit night, to subtle and stealthy, *wiser*, monsters.

Yet, still a bother. Even with all their new rules and new technology and endless opportunities, some just didn't deserve the gifts they were given. And some were not given enough.

Such as my descendent, Jade. Daughter of my dismembered son Darius with so many remarkable talents for our kind, all stripped from her by dear old dad until she was weaker than the lowliest servant. Until her mind was broken, scarred, and required more blood from my veins than—in my long, long history—I had ever given another.

A soft spot I had for my grandchild, though I imagined in ten thousand years, I'd be dismembering her too.

The beautiful imp looked every bit her father's daughter, no denying the resemblance. But only the fates could say what time and power would make of her. Darius was not the first of my creations I'd been forced to *handle*.

He would not be the last.

A flutter. A single unusual heartbeat at that thought.

I'd rather not see Jade fragmented physically. Not after she'd already been so fragmented mentally. I'd see her rise.

Yet now she played house with her strict lover. Now she recovered, her people recovered, the throne recovered, because I sat the throne for the first time since humans traveled over oceans.

Listening to petty squabbles, culling an overripe herd. Being gracious to my grandchild while simultaneously contemplating war—a mass extinction across all vampire civilizations. The rapture.

Kings and queens all over the world were failing in their rule, chasing pleasure and forgetting to parent. Tithes became poorer, greed on the rise.

Which could be partially blamed on modern times and the infection of selfishness that reigned in all society, human and vampire.

Perhaps a World War was just the thing? Set back this mania, remind all life that death hovered and whispered in their ear.

Without great loss and suffering, what was there to remember to treasure?

Shiny objects? Bitcoin? Art?

The only art I admired these days was the portrait of my granddaughter. Painted myself, and perfect. Life-size, dominating the throne room. A testament of millennia of practice with a brush and the old style of mixing oil paints.

A reminder to the few I had let live of just where their allegiance best rest. The first who had scoffed at it, I ripped in half. Careful that none of their blood might mark the canvas. Purposefully drenching all in the room with bits of dead vampire juice.

Baptized in the blood of a fool. Their one and only warning that she was held in my esteem.

I would have preferred to start fresh with this entire court. Donate some of my own dear flock, augment it with new blood. Find young prodigies with modern tendencies and acumen. But darling Jade had been given the option to choose the fate of this collection of errant idiots. So, I left her a few hundred. Though, to be true, in a year or two, I might return and kill them all if I found myself displeased with how things progressed. Once I deemed her recovery sufficient and forced her to take the throne, that is.

And I would come back. I always came back to this Cathedral, and had every year for near a century. I thought it was my son who drew me, that his inevitable end whispered in my ear. But now he was gone from this place in all the ways that mattered.

Yet still I heard the call.

Which made sitting a throne a bit more bearable.

"My lord."

Ah yes, the one who loved my grandchild. Shining head bowed, manners impeccable, I found I liked Malcom… a very little. "What has she done now?"

These tales were always amusing, his weekly reports while she slept something I looked forward to in this endless slog on the chair.

"She is… perfect." Rushing through his speech on her recent accomplishments, shaking his head, the man changed topics. Clearly nervous. "I didn't come here to discuss Jade. There is something… I remembered."

It was unlike this one to trip on his words. Which widened my eyes in anticipation and left me leaning forward, fingers steepled, a smirk on my mouth.

"Something"—glowing eyes met mine, concern, a touch of fear as if he might not leave this conversation with the borrowed heart in his chest—"that I must show you."

I smiled broadly, standing from the throne, amused by something different. *Anything* different. "By all means. Lead the way."

Long ago blocked off and forgotten, this area of the Cathedral should not have existed. Not on any schematics, not in the memories of those left alive here or stumbled upon in their excavations. But there it was, hidden behind so many layers of random, unused rooms, barred doors, spiraling ancient stairways so tight one had to bend in half just to navigate the descent.

Any recollection of this place had been ripped as violently as Darius might from every last mind who had ever known of it. There weren't even rats, so tightly it had been sealed. Only damp, and cobwebs, and an utter lack of light.

Even eyes like mine could hardly see in this type of dark.

And I found I loved it. The vibration of the walls, the desolation.

It was a prison, once the burial chambers of the clergy this ground had been stolen from. Cells with iron bars where the dead inside had long ago gone to bone, or desiccated to the point a strong wind would blow them apart like paper.

Other cells had been fully bricked over, whoever was left inside trapped for eternity. And I had a strong suspicion I might've known a few missing vampires of a certain age who, by chance, might grace a cell or two.

And had no interest in relieving them from their box.

Not when I heard something I might only describe as singing, not when I felt drawn forward through that nightmare. Following the siren song, I became impatient of the debris, crushing what I might, tossing it haphazardly behind me for Malcom to dodge.

I moved without his direction straight to a wall where the bricks didn't match and the mortar was sloppy and thick.

And knocked three times for good measure.

At my back, Malcom confessed, "I put her in here.

Ordered the masons to brick it shut… and forgot that very night I'd ever laid eyes on the waif. *Everyone forgot*. This whole area just… disappeared."

Ah. Perhaps dear Malcom was worthy of my granddaughter after all.

As if to soften what he thought to be a disappointing blow, the male muttered, "There is no guarantee she's still inside. He could have taken her anywhere."

Oh, but Darius had not. Not if he'd gone to such trouble to have something so unusual right under my nose. "I can hear her, singing an old tune. Not asleep and not awake."

And ready to be uncovered. Brick… something as inconsequential as brick was all he'd needed to cage a true daywalker. Breaking through the mortar with black extended claws, pulling apart a wall that whined with the removal of each stone, the whole slab having settled and grown accustomed to its missing support, I found a door like any other prison door. Unremarkable and built to make the prisoner know they were there to suffer.

Moments later, that wood was dust, fragments crumbling with little more than a swipe of my hand. And on the other side? The back of a massive gilded, gaudy, ornate, and hideous mirror. A huge monstrosity of a mirror that completely covered where the door had been.

Tempted to break it, so eager was I to enter, I held back the urge and slid it gently to the side.

To feast my eyes upon a prison cell transformed.

Darius… so predictable. So petty.

To keep this from me! Here.

Underground with the rot. To know what he had wasn't his. To have dared lie about the origin of his child!

He and I would have words about this. Most especially to think that all his golden candelabras and expensive furnishings were good enough for what had been trapped inside. The crypt still stank of blood and sex and tears and longing. Priceless paintings gone to mold in the dank, Persian rug half eaten by fungus and mildew.

Four poster bed, dressed in tatters. Red rags splattered black from old dried blood that still smelled of sunlight, even down here.

Jewels, treasures, secrets.

A room for pleasure derived from pain.

This was a place in which Malcom was entirely unwelcome, and I cast him back before he might set his eyes to the lovely corpse on the bed. "Leave us. Return to your bride, for her time of rest is almost at an end."

"My lord." Retreating into the dark, he moved with superhuman speed, as if aware how utterly possessive I was of this uncovered treasure. And how tempted I was to kill him just for standing too near.

Pity I had not chosen finer garments for this moment. That I had not brought gifts. My beloved had always loved flowers. Beautiful horses. The scent of pine.

"Here you are, as gorgeous as I remember," I murmured to her withered skull, gently placing my hip to the bed so her remains might not be disturbed. "How long I've waited. Countless centuries searching."

Smoothing back hair that fell from her skull, I leaned

over my darling one. "What it means to me to know you kept your promise..." Overfull with a sensation I'd almost completely forgotten, my voice shook. "You swore to me you'd be reborn. And here you are. Sleeping, waiting for me to find you."

Under my nose for a century. Here where she could have been crushed and lost again while I'd let Jade wreak havoc on the building.

My own displeasure was shaking the foundations as it was. Setting a rainfall of dust motes to cloud the room. Leaning over to kiss her mouth—or where her lips would have been had they not shriveled back over her teeth, I tried so very hard to be gentle. "Tell me you knew I'd come?"

The corpse, eyes long ago withered, said nothing. Failed to move. Failed to do anything but lie on a bed stained with her blood. My poor beloved had been alone since Darius had been dismembered, and from the state of the room, alone and suffering. Perhaps I would go into the garden later and have more than a talk with the head on a pike.

Perhaps if the smells under the rot of this place were any sign of what he'd done to her, I'd crush that skull to jelly and eat it.

Blind, my love was blind. Her hearing, the eardrums, I suspected might be intact enough that she at least heard the cadence of my song to her. That she knew I was here, would never allow her from my sight again.

The nubs of her fangs far too short for the work of slicing through my flesh were inconsequential. My true worry was that any attempt to part her jaw might break it, desiccated as it was.

Problem easily solved. I kissed her mouth again then sliced my wrist with a quick flick of a black claw. “Drink and wake. Come back to me.”

My blood was poison, laced with nature’s contempt for our kind. Yet it contained eternal, monotonous, never-changing life. Pouring it down a throat that could not swallow, I sat with her for the endless hours it took to reinvigorate her, cell by cell.

Nothing was more glorious than seeing my gifts reconstitute lovely blue eyes.

They had been blue in her last life too.

Her daughter’s had been that very shade before I changed her into something more. A clue I should have recognized had I paid more attention to the fact that Darius kept my grandchild from my sight.

She took a breath that rattled her half-reformed ribcage. There was pain in those sky-blue eyes.

A flush to cheeks that were fair and high. Dark hair, long and luxurious.

She drank every drop I might squeeze from my veins, swallowed as I gathered her close.

And was so very afraid of me.

That wouldn’t do. So, ever the charmer, I spun our tale. Starting at the beginning—this new beginning. “Your name in this life is Pearl. Mine these days is Vladislov. And I have been waiting for you for an eternity.”

2

VLADISLOV

Brittle in my arms—half corpse, half goddess—I carried my soul's new form from dust-laden catacombs. As I was in a bit of a mood, any who happened upon me during our jaunt had the unfortunate luck of finding out what they too might one day become should they truly embrace what they were… what human nightmares were born from.

Leathery wings dragged upon the floor at my back, arched over my shoulders, protectively encasing what blindly fought to be free of my care.

It was not just the potency of my blood that had driven her mad. A great deal had been done to my bride. Horrors that were creative—*that might have impressed me*—had they been unleashed on another.

The lack of effort required to see just how mangled the

mind, how traumatized the body, how wrecked the spirit… it was difficult to control my anger.

My gift of blood had left me with a thirst that had not burned the back of my throat in centuries. My veins were bone-dry, and still she was broken.

But I sought no meal. Such irrelevant urges could wait an eternity.

Those curious vampires peeking from their rooms saw what should not exist, and then they saw no more. It took less than a thought to pop their little skulls and leave a mess for another to clean once my path was happened upon. For my darling was too fragile—hundreds if not thousands of years away from learning how to mist through space. More fragile even than the rags on her body flaking away with every writhe as Pearl fought my hold.

She might as well have tried to fight a titan.

There would be explanations and apologies later. I would tend every wound that marked the flesh of her new body, be gentler with her than I had been with any creature since before time. Or at least time by history's reckoning.

Screaming a great deal, despite how I pat. A mewling, toothless kitten, at once pushing the cracked inferno of my flesh and drawing away from the inhuman texture. *Pitch-black* flesh, my eyes a glow of red in my temper, in my elation, in suffering through a mix of emotion I'd forgotten existed.

All I had been over all the ages, all the battles, all the children, all the optimization of a species, had always been *something to fill the time*.

Grief? That, on occasion, teased the outskirts of my thoughts. Dedication? I was nothing if not decided. Boredom? It consumed me utterly.

The world, with all its modern marvels, was really no more exciting today than it had been when my armies swept entire civilizations under my feet. And I suppose, in a way, I was also a touch… probably, yes… *irritated* my love had left me waiting so long.

She'd always been particular. She'd always been beautifully difficult.

Formidable.

Yet I was so beyond in love it stole my breath. So very piqued that rage almost eclipsed joy. The ground shook again under my feet. Sending my children fleeing in the opposite direction of my march.

Seemed not all of Darius' flock was as stupid as they appeared.

Yes, I'd be the first to admit it wasn't princely to lose one's temper in such a fashion. But I wasn't a prince. I was no longer a king. I was a God!

A God who'd found his Goddess trapped in a tomb, withered in mind and body.

Did she just try to bite me again?

What joy! Kissing her crown, I'd never felt more in love.

So cute. Just like the first time she tried to slit my throat all those ages ago.

Our wedding night.

How fond that memory. So fond that I felt the need to cuddle my hissing, screamed-herself-hoarse darling closer.

I might've been old, but I was not senseless to female tendencies. I understood Pearl's terror. It was more than just the current state of my body that brought on this paroxysm. More than my strength, my size, my *altered nature*.

My bride's only interaction with others of our kind had been....

Maybe I would just kill them all. Five or six handpicked old guard would be enough to see to a Goddess' needs. Tens of thousands? Excessive. Yes. That was what I would do. Flock by flock, I'd cull the herd.

Malcolm would have to die for ripping out her fangs. Which would upset Jade.

Who I supposed I had some sentiment for.

There were too many humans these days as well. Easy enough to turn them on one another and let them do the work for me.

Hmmm. But nuclear weapons. My bride would not like a sky full of fire and a world full of death.

A Goddess required subjects to rule. Beauty to enjoy.

Revisiting such a thought later would be best. Genocide was such time-consuming work, and no other creature would have a moment of my time save the one screaming memorized Latin prayers from under the membrane of my wing.

Claws, black as the darkest human heart, clicked. Impulsively seeking out the soft thing that continued to beg for the mercy of Jesus. One smell of her divine blood and I checked myself.

Be gentle. Excruciatingly careful.

Taloned feet ceased their march, and I threw back my head in an uncharacteristic roar of frustration, only to realize that my skin was burning her flesh. Powerful wings tightened around my prize as if they might protect her from the very creature obsessed with helping her, and in doing so caused her further pain.

Such irony deserved a laugh.

A madman's cackle that rang out against the stone walls of the vacant throne room.

Fate was such a bitch. Which was why I fucked fate raw and would do so again.

Fate brought me into life mortal. Fate stole my soul. Fate was denied when I tied that soul to me with an unbreakable oath. And fate would be denied again when I conquered my bride's fears and strengthened her body. She who had fucked fate herself by being born half immortal.

Which was endlessly amusing, considering her past.

But the religious babble, those maddening prayers—they were not good for my beloved one. So I offered honest truth, rubbing my chin atop her head, careful not to inadvertently crush her skull. "I met your Jesus. A decent enough fellow, I suppose."

Adjusting my arms to aid in Pearl's comfort, trying to hold a fragile body as cautiously as I might, I added, "Completely wasted the gift of immortality, if you ask me. He spoke and spoke and spoke, and who listened? Who remembered any of it correctly? Not a soul… except maybe myself. Our time in the desert was interesting, though thoroughly misquoted."

Tiny, her reply was. Tiny and meant only for her ears, her lips pressed to my chest as she sobbed. "Blasphemy."

She was so utterly cute that I could not resist running the back of a razor-sharp claw over her cheek. Success achieved, not a single drop of blood spilled. "Oh, sweet one, how I adore you. You're just… delicious."

All fangs and cracked black skin, all flames and searing heat, wings, and bulging muscle… every last molecule of me was completely enamored with my soul's new face. *All of her was delicious*, down to her toes.

I wanted to eat them. Not really. Well, really. But I wouldn't unless she gave me permission.

What had I done to deserve this? This elation!

The loving sigh that billowed, brought tendrils of steam from my lips, was both lengthy and the right amount of dramatic.

In time, she'd look back upon our reunion fondly. And we had time, a universe's endless expansion and contraction of time.

With care, with feeding, with love and attention, my soul would find that it indeed recognized me. That it sang its song so I might be drawn closer.

That deep down she always knew I'd find her and bring her home.

Oh so carefully, I set the shaky thing on her bare, mostly reconstituted feet to spare her skin from further unintentional searing. Perhaps a little too exuberant in the way I slid her down my body as if she might ice the flames. And I was left with a shiver like an untried boy. "Shall we use this moment"

—what was the best way to phrase it?—"to outline expectations?"

Blood drunk, healing at a rapid rate, yet still bearing gnarled corpse's fingertips and reforming organs. Driven utterly mad, for reasons that spread my wingspan and left her cowering, Pearl hid behind her tangled, dark hair.

An improvement. She wasn't trying to run… potentially because I held her slender wrist in my very large, very dangerous fist. And her pretty, filthy skin only smoked a little.

Beating the air with one relaxing flex of my wings, I gave myself the luxury of a deep breath. And contemplated.

She started screaming again.

The bridge of my nose between forefinger and thumb—a habit from my mortal years I'd never quite set free—I even groaned in mirror to her terror, somewhat tempted to let her wrist go. Yet concerned that chasing her through the maze of the Cathedral would only heighten her confusion.

Instead, I tried to explain. "You died in childbirth. Our seventh son." Bitterness welled from a place I had forgotten, lacing a demonic growl into my litany. "Not in some great war, not from a rival's poison… in duty and fealty to your husband." My free hand, tipped with razor-sharp claws, knocked against my breastbone, a loud bang fitting the mood. "The universe dared take you from *me*, and I have squeezed payment from its bones. As you are my soul, there is a chance you spent our time apart in some version of hell you keep referring to." I rolled my eyes toward the heavens, aware of the pun. "If there even is such a realm."

At the widening of her bloodshot, tear-stained, and beautiful eyes, I amended, “Though I greatly doubt you’d have been condemned. My bride is a creature of light. Even in immortality.”

Which was, in many ways, hilarious.

More importantly, the creature who suffered through hell had been I. “And now you are reborn and delivered. You are home. With me.” Adding, so it could not be said, that despite the form I might bear, I still possessed charm, “And I will love you until time itself ceases to be.”

An already fragile mind unraveling before me, my naked, filthy bride screamed, “Satan, has your demon not shown me suffering enough?”

Never having enjoyed that title, I corrected, calm as the precious dead of night, “Call me Vladislov. Or Steven. Do you like the name Steven?”

If Satan got her hackles up, the name she’d known me by in her past life would cause this hissing kitten further distress. Come to think of it, any of the monikers I’d borne over the centuries would. Therefore, Vladislov it would be. Just as she would remain Pearl.

Wouldn’t that be nice?

A fresh start that I could improve upon in all ways from our last union.

With a reverence I felt down to my unbreakable bones, I said her new name. “My Pearl.” Adding, “And I agree, Steven is too bland. You could just call me ‘darling.’ ‘Sweetheart.’ Oh, I’m partial to ‘honey.’ Bees are such fascinating creatures.”

I said it with love—my eyes, though glowing red, my skin, though black, cracked, and fiery, all of it softened with an adoration more eternal than the stars.

In this, she found me hideous and screamed.

How ashamed she was to be naked before her husband.

How brittle her mind after so much damage had been wrought.

And even as she was now, pathetic and weak, I was moved by the very being of her. I always had been a bit obsessive when it came to my soul.

Just as enticing as the original, her form was a song. And though she tried to cover her breasts and pubis, I did look my fill.

I drank her in.

As *she* had drank me so she might live again. As *my* blood fortified her body and would strengthen her beyond measure.

As *my* care would heal her.

This little hiccup of fear… it would be forgotten once she had more time to learn how wondrous her bridegroom was.

And despite fate's fuckery, one day, Pearl would find me beautiful. For it was not our features that defined what we were, but our shared godhood. And I had spent mine as rationally—as purposefully—as any holy man might. Monitoring legions of vampires while *trying* to leave them free will, an impossible feat I really did not receive enough praise for.

She would appreciate that.

Perhaps that was reason enough not to kill them all? Let them sing my praises and scrape at my feet for her to see.

And once I calmed, fed, and tended to this mess, I would choose a form to please her. One known by vampirekind the world over. One not so beautiful as to stun, but approachable, *real*.

Despite my hold on her wrist, the woman I adored, coveted, and craved above all things fell to her knees before me.

So unlike the queen she had been.

"Queens do not kneel, even to kings." But I wasn't a king. I was a God. And she was not a queen. She was a defanged Daywalker.

Where was my possessive, violent vixen under all this meek ineptitude?

Where was the impulsive, warlike beastie—the mirror of our great father?

Where was the warrior, who the first night I'd taken her to bed had tried to cut my throat? Not that I'd ever faulted her for it. From the day she'd been born, I'd watched her, coveted, peered through the garden walls in which the female offspring of the king were kept, knowing one day I'd be the first man, the only man to have her.

Not even the eunuchs had been allowed to touch, look upon, or pleasure my Jewel.

The Jewel of our kingdom—one of dozens of offspring from hundreds of wives, concubines, slaves, and fodder. But she was the daughter of the Queen. Pure-blooded. A prize no intact male, save our father, was allowed to look upon.

It was even forbidden to me, his favored son. Yet I looked, and I looked often.

She was my soul, and I was her shadow. As she'd breathed softly in sleep, I'd smelled her hair. When she raged against captivity, I'd witnessed her tempers. As she plotted her violence against a fate she did not crave, I'd unraveled her every attempt to be free.

And when I spilled my seed—as was my duty—within the conquered women our empire gathered, it was only her face I saw. Only her body I imagined.

That body that haunted me for millennia.

Her new form, despite the decay and filth, still smelled the same. Like sunshine and the very garden she'd despised. Which had always amused me, as she'd loved flowers, but only so long as they'd been cut, vased, and set out to die.

She smelled like life itself. Uncompromising life.

Troublesome, wondrous princess she'd been.

Dangerous, passionate, wife stolen from me by death.

Pure-blooded sister of a bloodline worshiped by the entire known world.

I'd always admired the incessant and clever attempts to be free of her garden prison before I might claim her and raise her to Queen. That was to be expected, and despite her severe punishments, her every act of insubordination pleased our father greatly. Only a true-hearted Goddess would fight the shackles of luxury for freedom. My docile sisters were left to breed with foreigners and courtiers, their offspring impure. No, only the most determined deserved the role of Queen. Of Goddess.

My Queen. My Goddess.

She dared break her maidenhead on an ivory dagger

handle. An attempt to diminish her worth and unravel her destiny.

The knife was delivered to me, blood still drying as a report was made. Though it was long before this world was born, I still remember that first taste of her when I licked it clean. A memory worthy of a smile.

She had dropped the weapon, one that had been stolen from our father—the king of the known world—and smuggled into the harem. Clattering right at the feet of the head eunuch. Blood was said to still be running down her thighs.

And right there, she had lain upon her back, spread her legs, and shown the damage with a grin of triumph… to a guardian forbidden to so much as look, a half-man who could not tear his eyes away.

As if it would not make me love her all the more.

As if I was not to have the eunuch blinded for seeing the precious cunt of my bride.

Naughty vixen. We would have fun with that dagger. I couldn't even recall the amount of times I fucked her with the handle once she'd learned of the physical pleasure she would only ever know under my touch.

That is, once I turned her body into the woman she was born to be.

It was the very reason I left that dagger on her pillow the first night I dragged my new, hissing bride to our chambers.

The first time she had ever left the seclusion and safety of the gardens to learn the truth of men.

The first time I poured seed into her womb. As our father had poured his seed into our mother. And his before him, and his before him, in a line of kings and queens long forgotten by history—vaguely evoked as old gods by *modern* man, who lived and died long before the pyramids.

They were not gods. I was the only God.

"Please stop looking at me that way." Blushing, her cheeks as rosy as her nipples, she meekly tried and failed to remove her wrist from my grip.

As if I might be capable of turning away from such beauty. Though perhaps the rather large erection pointing her way was a bit insensitive… considering.

I'd never hurt her, but I would transform her. Through tears, gasps, frantic kicking, and ultimate release.

But not today. Not like this.

Not when even after all these years I still remember that… it had taken her some time to love me eons ago.

In that, I was prepared to reevaluate my approach.

These days, I was nothing if not a gentleman.

In my formative years, my father had taught me the ways of our people, of our Queens, of their power and frustrations. How to cow them as a man must a woman, how to physically please in the process, so they might be safe in their furious release and bear strong sons. The strongest sons were always made in battle. Their bodies growing under the changing heart of resentful yet passion-drugged wife.

Until resentment bloomed into respect upon seeing that first bloody baby.

Until it became more than passion shared between a lusty warrior and a strong-willed woman.

Until it became love.

But such was the world long lost.

Such *savageries* were no longer considered romantic or rightful in this time.

I would not rape her.

This time, I would woo instead.

3

PEARL

Three weeks. I knew it had been three weeks, not only by the rise and fall of the sun outside my windows—*windows*, as in more than one—but because something called a digital clock also confirmed the hours and date. Three weeks and I had not left that room, despite the fact that the door was unlocked.

A cozy room, with simple furnishings and warm cream walls.

A room with a feature, a luxury I could hardly describe—a private bathroom.

A private bathroom, where no line for the entire floor collected. Where the warm water never ran out.

Though when I locked myself in the bathing space—who enjoyed such luxuries?—upon leaving, freshly cleaned, covered from neck to toes, I found one wall had been papered. Little flowers, exactly like the paper from my apartment.

Which I now understood had been demolished and something called a mall had been put up in its place.

The exactness of that wallpaper, even the way it was faded and dingy, frightened me.

The exactness of all the things left for me, as if the demon who kept me knew my every secret, was precisely why I knew I was still in hell. This was all a trick of Lucifer.

Even the priest, as he heard my confession, looked at me as if my ravings of demons, of the black abyss, were only a trick of my mind.

I wept when I told him why I was here, that I had killed a man who had followed me home from work and left his body in the snow. That I was damned. His eyes grew sad. "Chadwick Parker died in 1923. That was practically one hundred years ago. What you blame yourself for... it isn't possible."

"You're not listening to me!" And that had to be part of the torment. Those kind eyes so full of pity as I paced and told my story day in and day out. "I've been locked away. There was this book full of entries written in my hand. A box full of notes about demons and hell."

"You were released from the sanitarium, into the care of your husband and his staff. He loves you, and he's concerned, which is why I was called upon. You're very much alive, and though not many may find Manhattan to be heaven, it is a far cry from hell. At least for most."

Pointing—the glass of my windows bright with morning sun, where people walked in multitudes, where I watched them in utter confusion for days—I cried, "This is not the right world!"

Where were the slender cracked roads and cable cars? Everything from my view was paved and shiny. My eyes took it in with such precision, despite the fact that this room loomed high over the city. Women wore trousers! Men failed to make way for them. Nothing, at least the room that was slowly turning into an odd amalgamation of this new world and my former apartment, smelled like cheap cologne or piss.

"You have the influence to change the world. Wealth beyond measure. The donation made to the diocese will go far to rebuild crumbling churches, extend community outreach. This world is *not right*, I agree. Change it."

"You don't understand what I'm saying…" Because he would not listen. According to him, Vampires weren't real; there was no desecrated church at the heart of the city filled with evil.

And I was falling for kind, brown eyes. The soft tenor of a patient holy man. One who had offered absolution, the Eucharist, the blood of Christ. I was falling for the trickery.

Because *this was hell.*

"Father Patrick, I think it's time for you to leave."

I knew he used the door, as I could see him holding it for *our guest*, but I had been so frustrated, so distracted, that I failed to notice just who had come into my room. Rocking back in my chair, out of it so quickly it toppled, I was at the window, wringing my hands, desperately trying not to look directly at the father of evil.

"Ahh, Vlad. Good morning to you." The older clergyman

stood, shuffling toward the door. Pausing to add, "We've read through more of the book of John. She had questions I've yet to address. Considering your theology expertise, perhaps you can enjoy a discussion together on John's finer points."

"Noted." Vladislov gestured toward the door, polite yet brooking no refusal. "Leave."

Not once had the priest questioned such rudeness. It seemed much more than daily prayer could be bought for whatever sum the diocese enjoyed at Vladislov's expense.

Rebuilding churches.

When the door clicked shut and it was just the two of us, he offered a smile. One I could feel, for I still only showed him half my face and tried my best not to look.

He spoke aloud to my private thoughts. "The catholic faiths do love their glitter. I agree the fortune should be spent on the message, not the architecture where limp men try not to ogle the patrons."

Dry lips parting, I dared to defend. "Celibacy keeps the heart close to God."

"But my heart is here." Fingers carded through my hair, the length cut as short as it had been my last night at the Super Club selling cigarettes. Bobbed and angled to land with a sweep at my cheek. A comforting familiar thing in a world of absolute strangeness.

Such as how the man could cross a room so quickly I had not seen him move.

I used to scramble, in those first days when he'd touch me. Cower and cry. I used to feel a heartbeat of pain between my legs, recalling what a demon had done to me in a room

Father Patrick had sworn never existed. A room I would understand if only I would keep taking my medication.

Now, I just froze and waited for torment.

In its place, I got a kiss. One on the top of my head. A kiss and a soliloquy. “The book of John was actually written by a woman. When the Christian biblical canon was compiled—the various known gospels sorted through—only four were chosen to tell the message and story that best suited a clear agenda. Her name was stricken, and John was given credit in her place. Isn’t that fascinating? The account of the disciple who loved your Jesus the most was written by his wife. Which brings me back to the topic of celibacy. He was not celibate.”

I could feel myself splitting down the middle already. “Please.”

He took my hand in his, the hand of a man. Veins upon the back, large and warm. Not burning-hot, coal-black inferno.

In place of talons were trimmed nails.

But I knew what he was underneath.

“Would you prefer I came to you that way?” The whisper at my ear was intimate, unwelcome, and sent a shiver down my spine.

Quick to answer, breath left my lips. “No.”

“Why won’t you look upon me then?”

The father of lies could manipulate his voice in such a way that it stirred me to act. That I felt his longing as if it were honest.

Up went my gaze.

He wore his hair long, in ordered waves any woman would covet. Though handsome, his face was also not. A strange combination of desirable and forgettable. His eyes….

Hooking a finger under my chin, gently encouraging, he murmured, "There's my daring queen."

I burned, thoroughly, inside and out. Felt it so much deeper than just the flush that ran from my chest to my roots. Those eyes….

"You are safe with me. Safe enough to muster the courage to step outside that door and eat your breakfast at the table… in my presence."

And somehow we were already moving, my sandaled feet walking over the rug, though it felt I left my mind behind me. Still lingering at the window, staring down at a world one hundred years past anything I knew.

Until I was at that window. As if I had always been there.

And Vladislov stood at my door, looking down at his empty hand with an open blend of delight and disappointment playing across his brow. "Utterly remarkable."

Grinning, his attention dragged from his hand straight to where I stood. "Well then, this changes a great deal. So, I apologize in advance."

Before I might shriek or rally, before I could even begin to understand how I had gone from one place to another in the blink of an eye, he bore down on me. A wave of indescribable power that scorched all it touched, stole my air, and then retreated.

Prickles of ice stole over what had been burnt. What I

imagined had been the stink of sulfur teasing my nose with a distinctive crispness.

Pine.

Snow.

Mountains at my feet and a dimming sky overhead setting a distant lake to glitter.

“How?” My breath steamed, a puff that dissipated on a breeze.

“Easy now.” Arms came around my middle, steadying a body too cold and too stunned. Warming me with brimstone fire. “Why eat breakfast there, when we can enjoy ourselves here?” Lips came to my ear. “And just so we’re clear. If you try to mist away from me, I will follow. Can’t have my sweet darling wondering the world all alone. You never know just what might try to gobble you up.”

There was a very clear threat in his growl, the beast closer to the surface than the skin of a man he wore to fool the world.

What was there to say when the air was so cold breathing was growing difficult.

To the sound of rending cloth, the size of what stood at my back transformed. Moments later, wings enfolded.

Shivering ceased. A cocoon of vileness tightening as if to deepen the embrace.

“Maya was to serve as your breakfast, followed with some fresh coffee and a scone. She was overjoyed at the opportunity, has feasted upon female virgins for days so her blood would bear a fruity roundness.” The beast at my back chuckled. “I know, excessive for a breakfast. I can’t imagine what she'll plan should I ever ask her to provide your dinner."

Nuzzling into my neck, the feel of his cracked, searing skin somehow velvet soft with artic air to cool him, he purred, "But I will always be your dinner. And maybe tonight, you'll be brave enough to do more than sip me from a crystal goblet?"

Under those membranous wings, massive hands of fire moved up and down my arms. "Maybe you'll sip from a fingertip, my wrist. When you're truly daring, I'll give you free rein of my throat."

After each private morning mass, a priest told me my ravings were due to a condition. That no sin lay on my soul, that my confessions were delusions soon to be rectified by my faith in God's goodness, mercy, and medication. He left, and *medication* was delivered. Blood. Served on a silver platter in an ornate goblet.

Utterly irresistible, I swallowed it down in great gulps. And felt full, healthy, confused at my inability to fight so deep a craving once my eyes or nose were tickled with what waited on that gleaming platter.

Then I spent my day with a talkative devil in the guise of a man. Who I tried to ignore, since pleading had gotten me nothing but a lemon cake topped with raspberries covered in black blood.

An odd combination I had practically torn from his hands in my physical inability to refrain.

Thinking of that cake now…

Gums tingling, I felt the part of me that brought the most

shame try and fail to lengthen. The thoughts of blood, of blood that didn't come from rats or make me vomit, left my mouth to water.

Laughter moved from the beast into me, more of those stroking hands, my body rigid and famished.

"The cake was brilliant on my part. You've thought of it so often I was concerned it might be some time before I'd be able to impress you so greatly again. But now… my sweet soul has developed a new talent much more quickly than I anticipated, leaving me with endless ideas."

Heaven, help me.

"Would you like to stay, enjoy the view… *with a drizzle of black blood on top*?" He was ever the tempter, and I smelled a drop of blood bloom in that icy air, unsure which part of him had been pricked. But certain I was being toyed with. "Or would you prefer to dine on Marquita, back home, at the table?"

The option of remaining sequestered in my room was not offered.

Yet before I might choose, a thumb dragged over my lips. Chilled cheek cupped in the palm of a monster, I tasted eternity. And opened my mouth for more.

The devil always won in hell. I was learning that daily.

Sucking his fingers because there was no resisting such flavor, his groan weakened my knees.

By the time I was full, sleepy, and drawn into unnatural serenity, I found my legs hooked over his arm, my ear to a chest of cracked pitch. *Cradled.* Like the heroes did in films once the actress swooned.

Warmed by wings that ended in hooked talons so sharp there was no denying they could tear through flesh.

And I began to burn, engulfed in flame for the split second it took for the mountains and ice to vanish and for my room to form around us. There hadn't even been time to scream, and already my skin had mended.

But my clothes were badly scorched. And Vladislov's? His were hanging from his human form in tatters.

"How would you feel about a party?" All smiles, he clapped his hands as if he struck upon the perfect idea. "Tonight! Yes, rest now. I'll handle everything. And I promise you, no corny shopping montage will be included."

And he poofed away, like a puff of smoke, leaving the scent of pine and firewood.

Falling flat on my rump, I stared at that spot that moments before held the shape of a man, certain I was completely insane… or he was.

4

PEARL

It looked like some movie prop dagger. Curved, the ivory handle etched with figures worn down by ages of handling. Old.

Brandishing the weapon like a dinner knife, a blade gently tapped the goblet of a chilled glass of white wine. Which, considering I'd been told to expect the toast, startled me to the point I twitched.

And then blushed in embarrassment when every pair of eyes in the room darted to and from me so quickly it almost seemed imagined.

The *party's* host, Vladislov, greeted his—or as he continued to remind me, *our*—collected guests with a smile. "Welcome to our little soiree. As each of you has been given explicit instructions addressing the theme of tonight's fun, I will not insult you with a repetition of the rules. Only to say this. If anyone touches or so much as brushes up against my bride, I will end you and your entire bloodline." Jolly, completely unconcerned with the level of violence just threatened, his smile grew. "Are we clear?"

Cheers came as if such an insane declaration only enhanced the drama and pleasure of the handful of vampires in attendance.

"To Pearl!" A man bearing silvered hair and a thin moustache raised his glass—one filled with a far more viscous red liquid.

And cheers arose, my plain name sung as if in praise.

These creatures were as crazy as their king, holding up crystal goblets full of pungent blood. As the only person in the room who ate or drank food, as a Daywalker, what they drank would make me ill. And what I drank was done in private.

Servants in black-tie, tails, each bearing a platter with a single hors d'oeuvre, entered, leaving Vladislov to amend his singular warning with another. "If any of you try to eat any of the special treats for my Pearl, you won't care for those consequences either. They are not for you, no matter how tempted you may be."

How often did this man threaten to kill his friends?

Again, no open animosity on the faces of the twenty or so gathered in the apartment's grand room. Only attentiveness as they looked me over, as they lightly chatted and touched one another a great deal. A brush of the arm, a peck on the cheek.

A staged production where every last player was dressed

as if they were patrons of the finest club from the 1920s. The ladies: beaded gowns. The gentlemen: starched waistcoats, white bowties, satin lapels in perfectly tailored tuxedos. The music, coming from a source I could not find, was no record. Instead, it was clear as if the singer sat at the empty piano seat across the room to entertain us all.

"Ahh, live music would have been a nice touch. I'm sure someone here has some talent at something." He handed me the stemmed glass of white wine, brushing his fingertips over mine as I took it, *because I needed a drink.* The host, just as spectacularly dressed as the room, eased ever closer. "Olivia, the one in the red dress, dear. She was some kind of performer a decade here or there, though I have no idea if she was even awake during the 1920s."

"The music is fine." This whole charade was already too much.

I was even wearing a dress so exquisite I'd been nervous just to put it on. Nervous of leaving my strange room. Or standing next to Lucifer—

"My name, darling, was never Lucifer. And as much as I am trying not to be insulted, considering the situation, I really…" He paused, rubbed his thin lips together, and chose his next words as if they were foreign on his tongue. "I really *beg* that you think of me as Vladislov. Or anything kinder than comparing me to that prick." For good measure, and while tucking a strand of hair behind my ear, he added—as if infinitely proud of himself, "Please."

And the room was enraptured.

"I, um." I put the glass of wine to my lips and drank, fortified by cool, crisp *nectar of the gods*. "I um, don't know how you…"

How he kept reading my thoughts as if such a thing were natural.

And in my distraction between wine, embarrassment, nerves, and general sense of being completely overwhelmed, I allowed him to grasp my fingers and bring my knuckles to his lips for a kiss.

"I have many talents, as do you. As do my guests this evening. Normal talents you'll navigate beautifully with a little practice." Flicking his fingers, he summoned a servant bearing a beautiful tray with a single treat on top. "Canape?"

"Vladislov." I'm not sure if I had ever spoken his name before.

I couldn't do this. Be here with demons playing dress-up, who I had been told would be dining in their usual style when humans were brought in for sampling later.

"Deep breath. Drink your wine. Look at me." The orders were effortless. The way he subtly squeezed my fingers, familiar.

Those eyes….

Lifting the snack from the tray, he held it to my lips. "So long as I am with you, my soul, there is nothing ever to fear."

I ate, unsure what a canape was. I ate from the hands of Luci—

"Vladislov." With a wink, he smirked. "We'll work on it."

Acidic tomatoes, something savory I couldn't place. The flavors on my tongue paired with the wine and left gooseflesh on my arms, because a drop or two of the host's blood brought all the culinary glory together. Almost as delicious as the various immortal blood *vintages* I had been served over the weeks.

Probably from the very donors in this room.

"You look lovely, Pearl. The most beautiful woman ever to walk the earth. And I would know," he added with a chuckle. "I've walked it for ages. Never thought I'd be quite so pleased to be robbing the cradle."

Men only gave compliments when they wanted something, most likely to lure a girl into sex.

"As much as I would love to lure you into bed, that was not my goal in the praise. I love you and simply cannot help myself."

Bed? The last memory I had of a man taking me to bed was so utterly awful the canape was about to come up.

Like a snap of fingers in my mind, what was in one instant horrible and so real I could smell the damp of the cell and feel the burn between my legs, was gone. Just gone.

"Now that, I will stop. I'd rather not fiddle where too much has already been done, but no thoughts of that nature will ruin your party."

The book. The journal. All the entries and explanations of a mind wiped clean each day.

Another mental snap.

"Not tonight, Pearl. All of this can be discussed tomorrow. Tonight, be in the present. Get to know your kind. *Feel safe*."

And instantly, I did.

Contrition was in his voice, in his countenance. "I apologize. Really, I'd prefer not to, but you require a bit more than handholding to progress into our future."

A servant appeared to pour more perfectly chilled wine in my glass. Wine I drank staring over the rim at my host… Vladislov.

Who smiled an extremely beautiful expression on an interesting face. "Well done, brave queen."

"She really is a vision." A female interloper. One who approached so regally I felt the need to call her ma'am. And would have had Vladislov not clearly *unh-uh*'d me under his breath.

"Maya, might I introduce my bride? This is Pearl." He kissed my fingertips, met my eyes, and finished, "Pearl, she was meant to be your breakfast."

The statement was so utterly ridiculous that I snorted a quick laugh. Mortified an instant later. Cheeks flaming, I faced the insanely beautiful woman, and said, "Hello."

Insane had to be the perfect word for all of this. All of me. The fact that my hand was still caught in the clutches of the name I would not think.

To which he laughed, full-bellied and thoroughly amused. When glittering eyes left mine, after an improperly long stare, he addressed the patiently waiting woman. "She's shy."

"Weren't we all when life was new? Now come, Pearl, I promised the other ladies I would tempt you from your lover's side so they might meet you."

My fingers were freed, and a hand came to my lower

back, propelling me gently toward the woman who countered the space to assure no physical contact was made. Yet still smiled and waved me nearer.

This too made the host chortle, the same host urging me to follow her. “Go on now. Everyone here will be lovely. Just don’t touch any of them.” At my back, his voice darkened. “I wouldn’t like it. And they wouldn’t like what I’d do.”

Maya chuckled yet still stepped back, assuring, “He won’t always be so obsessive. It’s not in our nature to deny physical touch. You’ll be hungry for it soon enough. Besides, he’ll give you whatever you ask for, including mercy on our poor souls.” I followed as she continued. “Besotted, utterly. A fool in love.”

Though Vladislov must have heard her, there was no waspish reprimand. Instead, I heard his tenor picking up a conversation about livestock with another, leaving me to the women who crowded as near as they might without the risk of physical touch.

“This is Eloisa, Kami, Fhulendu…” Each lady introduced by dark-skinned, glowing Maya—most of their names beyond my ability to pronounce. Features and hair, histories, body shapes, and style all so foreign, so out of place in the world I knew. Each beautiful to the point it might leave a person breathless.

All patient as I drank more wine and chose silence over conversation with demons. So they spoke to one another for my benefit, of pleasant things, of trysts, of jokes, of modern luxuries I’d never heard of. Of travel and far-off wonders. Of lost wonders. Of their children, their children's children. A few bragging about the pure bloods they had produced, causing others to narrow their gaze as if in envy. Yet all had dozens—if not hundreds of offspring—chosen from the finest quality of humans to enhance Vladislov's vision of Vampirekind.

As if this was normal, they were normal, and the broken piece of this puzzle was me.

I was a Daywalker. I walked in the sunlight, lived with humans, ate their food....

A kiss fell atop my head, a strong arm circling my middle. More tipsy than I realized, I leaned back into the support of something solid when the ground was sand and the world was… strange.

"What a vision the pair of you make!" A round of feminine giggles, then, "I should snap a photo to show my hive. Smile!"

A rectangular device was produced. A flash.

And the ladies laughed, the joke utterly lost on me.

Warm lips at my ear breathed, "Because of the myth that vampires cannot be photographed."

"Oh, like how people think we don't have reflections?" Had I just said we?

I wasn't like these *things*.

Embracing me, another kiss to my hair, Vladislov spoke over the fading laughter. "My bride means no offense. Not that any of you have permission to peek, but her experiences with her kind have been unpleasant. Pearl doesn't know what great company we can be."

"Pearl," Fhulendu, dark-skinned, heavy braid, beautiful to the point I wanted to cry, said, "sometime, I'll tell you about my early years. They too had been unpleasant, so believe me when I say I understand. We all do—well, maybe not those purebloods born to this life. But for many who were changed, especially in the old world, it was a challenging period of our existence."

"Well said." Maya smiled, running a hand down the arm of the woman at her side.

And they seemed so nice I didn't know what to make of it.

They felt real. So real I wished I might see what they looked like under their pretty skins. Were they pitch like Vladislov? Did they crackle with fire? Wings? Claws? Fangs dripping venom?

Did their touch burn?

"Only mine will burn you, my soul."

Shivering from the feel of cool lips brushing my ear, I failed to resist when he took the hand dangling limp at my side, lifting my arm so I might cup the cheek of the creature at my back.

I felt a face freshly shaved, the sharp angles of high cheekbones.

I felt my eyes grow wide when he turned his head to press a hot kiss to my palm.

And then I began to cry, because I would not be fooled. Not by Lucifer, or Vladislov, or Darius, bright lights, crystal, beauty that was little more than a husk to conceal real monsters from a world that made no sense.

Breaking down into hiccupping sobs, unreasonably mortified, I was turned, my painted face pressed to the white, starched shirt of my keeper. Ruined by cake mascara and lips painted with rouge.

I sobbed, I clung, and knew I had drank far too much wine too quickly.

My teeth ached; the part of me that had always brought me shame tried to elongate. The part of me, I'd been told, that would not regenerate like any other bit of my horrible body. But would grow back over centuries.

My stomach rumbled obnoxiously loud. I was enfolded, yet there were no bat-like wings. My hair was gathered into a fist, my mouth turned up, and a throat slit with a dagger I knew had an ivory handle poured a fountain of perfection on my face.

I drank.

Climbing the figure who bled in my gaping mouth like a monkey. I burrowed my fingers into bronze waves.

Gulping, rocking my hips despite how my mind screamed to stop such things, agelessness poured down my throat.

When I was done crying, nose stuffed and sniveling, I broke suction on skin that had already mended, smeared in black fluid from nose to breast—rivulets from that once gaping wound having run down my throat, staining the modest collar of the priceless gown.

Looking every bit the horrific vampire.

"Did you see that?" Hushed murmurs so soft no human might hear moved like a breeze through the enrapt room. *"She drank from his throat."*

"She really is his soul."

My hair still fisted in the grip of the man I'd just feasted upon with wild abandon, he made me meet his burning eye as he loudly proclaimed, "And she is perfect."

Before pressing a bloodthirsty kiss to my mouth.

5

PEARL

If one could be devoured, have their very soul sucked from their being, the kiss conquering my mouth accomplished such a feat. I was consumed.

Legs already wrapped around his waist, nails already digging into his scalp so I might hold my prey still while I gorged, I was tangled up with no escape.

Prey became predator.

The tongue twisting about mine was anything but gentle. The palm under my rear had grown claws I knew were black as sin and sharp as the nails driven into Christ.

Yet despite razor-sharp fangs, despite talons, despite ferocity and thirst and monstrous passion, I did not bleed. The demon was careful in his assault.

Hard where I was liquid fire.

Dangerous, snarling, savage, and so strong I never stood a whisper of a chance.

He fed on me as I had fed on him. Uncontrolled. Unabashed.

With a mad mind and unquenched hunger.

Was this how lovers kissed?

Did it always destroy one so completely?

Pain would come next. Rending. Penetration that would kill another part of my tattered soul.

Probably here before the room. Probably over and over until I screamed for mercy while the audience laughed, only to wake up in the crypt to find that book and the horrible notes again.

Yet… as savagely as it had begun, it ended.

The force in which he'd pulled his swollen mouth away left mine searching out missing sensation. An action obstructed by his grip on my hair. "I apologize for being so forward."

What? What nonsense was this?

Men never apologized! They followed women through blizzards and raped them on the street. They locked girls in rooms and caused reckless, horrible harm.

My pupils dilated, the oddest sensation coming over me. Blood drunk and wine saturated, I whispered between pants, "I killed a man when he pushed me down in the snow and tried to shove inside. He might have, I was never sure. But I remember his blood all over my coat. I vomited and scrubbed, but the smell would not go away. So, an angel came to deliver judgment. I was dragged from life into death to be thrown at the feet of the Devil." A living corpse dressed in tatters who poked around every last part of me for a century. "I… I am lost. God no longer loves me."

"The God you speak of never did, Daywalker. Not from the moment your mother birthed you, not from the sad rejection of the screaming child she dumped on the mission doorsteps. Not when you were brutalized. Bewildered. Starved. Or left hanging from that tree as a child."

He took my chin. "*I loved you.* No other."

"You are evil." Of that, I had no doubt.

"Then be my goodness." A peck on kiss-stung lips. "Be my sun."

Yet he could walk in the sun… a thought that left a few startled gasps in a roomful of glittering nightmares.

He could walk in the sun where they could not.

But in that instant, I knew why he burned with fire. He *could* walk in the sun, but he could not feel it. He couldn't feel anything but where my mouth had just been joined with his.

The stroke from buttocks up my spine as he unwound and slid me down his body was a screaming declaration that I was correct. The hands that came to steady me when my shoes hit the parquet floors were black, fire licking from between the cracks in the skin, singeing my dress.

But his face, that forgettable, interesting face, was so human it made my heart ache.

"Let me see." *Show me the night winged demon lurking behind that gaze.*

And he did, to the sound of screams.

Screams that didn't come from my throat.

"They didn't know?" How could those creatures not have? The centuries they'd spoken of. The epochs in which they had known this being.

The room was empty, those who could vanish without a trace gone. Those who could not having fled through the door.

"They didn't know." Fanged and hideous, a monstrosity smiled, preening, wingspan stretching to knock items from carefully arranged tables and crash against crystal chandeliers. Making a right mess. "Only you have seen what becomes of a man whose soul is stolen. Who will make any sacrifice to see it returned. Who has been trapped in endless monotony waiting for his lost love to be reborn as she swore she would be."

But others had seen him when I'd been pulled from the tomb.

Chuckling, running strands of my dark hair through his claws, Vladislov said, "Not any who lived."

My next words died on my tongue, what he'd implied sinking deep into my belly. "So, you're going to kill all of your friends who came tonight?"

His response was so simple. "Yes."

"And if I asked you not to?"

"Not to slaughter the monsters you feared?" A shrug. More crystal shattered against the floor when those terrible wings flexed and bent. "I suppose I could restrain myself. But… it's going to cost you for the terrible mess your request will create."

Of course. The devil and his deals.

"Ah, ah." That thing clucked its tongue, bending over me so I need not crane my head so high. "There is no need to always think the worst of me. I can't help but love you, and I am trying rather hard. Be kind."

Kind?

Maya had let it slip in might conversation that I held their lives in my hands. Had they been as terrified as I to be there?

"Some of them, yes." The beast slouched and took a knee. Like a knight—like a villain. "It seemed only fair you not be the only frightened person in the room. Please note how I called them *people*. Your train of thought tends to be a bit less gracious. And mayhap you'll consider that none of us had a choice in what we became. Not really. Not when the orchestrations of the universe are so… unavoidable."

Braced, knowing exactly what men wanted in trade, my fists bunched in my skirt.

This creature was very male. I had already seen what the tatters of his clothing could not conceal on more than one occasion. An organ massive, inhuman, and pulsating.

Yet, as I was already condemned, already made the whore in that god-forsaken pit. What did it matter if I did this for strangers? "Do you want me to lay down here?"

A great sigh sent heat to ripple in the air, Vladislov answering, "I want you to go for nightly walks with me, *outside*. Once every three nights, we'll take dinner in a restaurant. Where you can order anything you want and I can spoil you with compliments."

Why such a simple thing seemed more terrifying than spreading my thighs, I couldn't say. A cold sweat on my brow, dryness on my tongue, I nodded. Because there was no agreement to be made that wasn't even more ridiculous than this party.

"Well, that settles that. They can live. They will adore you for such mercy, clever queen!" How it smiled with that face, I couldn't comprehend. Not that I wanted to, or even stood a chance.

And just like that, he was gone. One moment there, the next not.

I was alone, in a roomful of broken things and scattered glasses. Of immortal blood spilt on the floor and smeared into my skin. What was there to do but seek out the trays of food that had been dropped by the staff and snack? What was there to do but walk over all that shattered crystal and feel my dress catch on the shards?

What was there to do but drink every bottle of wine left to chill until I was thoroughly intoxicated.

Passed out sprawled across a settee.

To hardly wake when strong arms lifted me up and put me to bed.

Cool sheets below, the mattress dipped and a warm body joined me.

And I slept like the dead.

6

VLADISLOV

"Ha! I knew this experience would be something. Just look at your face." She was adorable with her eyes squinted and her cheeks sucked in. "I used the Yelp."

Mouth still full of overcooked oyster, my soul asked, "Yelp? Like a howl?"

As if this were some new Vampire power she'd yet to see. How hard it was to restrain the laughter, but I did.

Heroic as ever, I brandished my smart phone and pulled up the app so she might see. "Newspaper editorials are a thing of the past. Now, anyone can blab an opinion for the world to see. As humans so love to complain—especially where they think they might be heard the loudest—a clever monkey designed a platform where people might review a business and then all glory in their opinions."

Baffled, she stared down at the platter. "So humans like this dish?"

"No. They hated it. And now you are part of that experience! Welcome to the twenty-first century." Passing her my phone, a device it had taken three days to convince her to touch in the first place, I grinned. "Want to leave a review?"

Missing the concept, but so cute I could literally eat her, Pearl leaned closer to my outstretched hand and told the phone. "The seafood platter isn't good."

"Ah." We'd work on how to use the keyboard later. Tucking my phone away, I pushed back the wobbly chair, in full agreement with how it groaned over uneven wood floors, and offered my queen a hand. "Now, let's see if humans are correct about the bistro next door."

Sipping water, still somewhat grimacing, she gave me such a pathetic look. "Does the Yelp say the food there is also bad?"

"No. The chef is a hidden treasure, and she has prepared a feast specially tailored to your tastes tonight." Which I had assured by sending Fhulendu with her favorite human pet to scout out the location. The human sampled every last dish on the menu, required to fully report each sensation. A twenty-five-page essay waiting for me to indulge in, mostly glorifying the merits of the braised lamb shank. "If you like it, I'll buy the location. If you're extremely happy, I'll kidnap the chef and have her changed. She can prepare your meals for eternity!"

Considering freshly changed humans were such a

massive pain, the generous offer most assuredly would impress her.

Except it didn't.

Though I knew Pearl required sustenance of the mortal variety, the snip dared lie to me, placing her napkin on the table. "I'm full. Thank you though."

This wouldn't do. "Someday, you'll see a human *you just have to have*. You'll know your offspring at first glance, or maybe first smell. We, like any species, reproduce."

"I won't turn a human into"—she gestured at herself, so full of self-loathing it made the air taste rancid—"this."

"No. You won't. Daywalkers can't. I will have it done for you." This lesson was far more imperative than the Yelp, honestly. Or even her discomfort when I pinched her chin and raised her eyes to mine. "Mark my words. It is natural and normal. As is reproduction of the more erotic variety. We are a very physical species."

What power a bit of fresh air and bad food had on my darling. She brushed off my hand and even had the tenacity to glare as she sneered. "I don't want children of any kind."

"Your daughter might be hurt to hear you say so."

Check and mate.

Color draining from her cheeks, Pearl bit her ripe lip. Tugging it between her teeth in a gesture so disconcerted, so dumbfounded, that when her eyes went side to side as if taking in the room—as if the truth might be found on the sticky floors or on the mismatched furnishings—I twisted the dagger, so to speak.

"Her name is Jade. She has… had... your eyes and the

temperament of a lonely kitten. I like her quite a bit." Tucking Pearl's arm through mine, I pulled her resistant self from the restaurant. "She has your gift of sunlight. Appreciates fine cuisine. One day—when you are ready—a dinner would suit."

"I have a little girl?"

"She's in her seventies. Woefully neglected by her now decapitated father. Bitter, and absolutely in love with a warrior named Malcom. They are to be married soon. I expect a pureblood child will follow shortly after. Daywalkers are extraordinarily fertile."

"I have a child who's the same age as I was when—"

"When Malcom—the one you described as an angel—ripped out your fangs and brought you before Darius for crimes unknowingly committed."

Shame, horror, there was even a catch in her voice. "She must hate me."

"Oh yes, she does. But she also doesn't know you exist. We all assumed her mother was a human Darius made a meal of. Even I, her grandfather." Bloodlines were complicated, but my next statement was plain as night and proffered with a charming wink. "Or should I say stepfather, now that we are one? Either way, she's a proper combination of our lineage and will therefore be on equal footing with all our fat-cheeked future babies."

Before us, the door of the bistro opened, one of the multitude of servants who prepared this corner of the city for our walk playing their part admirably—assuring everything was as smooth as the dark, silken hair of my bride.

I deserved a medal!

Maybe a kiss.

Instead, and it was so unexpected that despite her miniscule strength, Pearl threw off my arm. She threw it off, shook herself as if to remove something disgusting, and turned on the sidewalk I had scrubbed clean only the night before.

And she stomped away.

"Darling, the food will get cold!" She wasn't listening, prancing off as if I might actually allow her out of my sight. Trotting after her, I tried to smooth extremely ruffled feathers by calling out, "Come now. How could you think such things of your own children? Of course they won't have batwings. You're not spawning imps!"

Tearing at her hair, my soul screamed, "Stay away from me!"

This would not do. Nor would my budding temper serve. Unfortunately, a note of the demonic snarled through my voice. "*We had an agreement.*"

Hackles up, she spun. "For a walk and a dinner. I walked, and I ate whatever that foul thing was."

"An oyster, breaded, and coated in mayonnaise. Worst in the city, according to the Yelp."

Her little filaments of rationality were snapping. I could hear it her thoughts were so loud. Not only that, she was actually angry. Not scared or horrified. *Pissed off*, as the youth liked to say.

So angry she dared point a finger and yell. "You are absolutely insane!"

Pot meet kettle.

Yes, I rolled my eyes, somewhat giddy that we were having our first lover's quarrel.

"Did you just—"

Smoothing my navy dinner jacket, I adjusted the cuff, inspecting the tailoring. "Yes, I did. I rolled my eyes at you, because you are acting like the baby you imagine flying around and snatching up tourists. My feelings are getting hurt. I do have those, you know. Just as I have infinite patience and will follow you, *humming a jaunty tune*, no matter how far you walk. And, yes, I know you walked from California to New York City. I know everything about you, Pearl, in this life and your last. Why not try to get to know me? Have I been so terrible?"

Guilt… there it was. The weakness of all good souls. And my soul was pristine. Pristine with high color and a trembling lip. Regretting yelling at Satan himself, how cute.

Tucking her hair behind an ear, she muttered, "What am I to do with you?"

"Tolerate me." Smile back in place, I strode closer and offered my arm. "Eventually, I'll grow on you. You didn't love me at first when I took you for wife in your last life either."

"Why not?"

A valid question I would never fully answer. "It was a different time, and you didn't want to be Queen. Unlike this incarnation, you had lived a life of pleasure. Like this life, you had been denied fulfilment. Back then, I swore to you you'd find it in our children, just as our mother had—"

Aghast, she tripped on an uneven bit of pavement. "Did you say *our* mother?"

I'd have the sidewalks repaved to be even in this part of the city. No stubbed toes for my bride. "As I said, it was a different time. Earlier than even the Egyptian pharaohs western culture so obsesses over. So ancient that everything about our people was absorbed into new people. Into budding cultures, kingdoms, *religions*. But I digress…."

And she'd had enough. "I've never had a gentleman caller, but from couples I'd observed at the Super Club, umm..." Toying with her fingertips as she mustered the courage to explain whatever this was, Pearl took a deep breath. "These would not be considered appropriate topics for courtship. Especially unchaperoned courtship."

Canting my head to the side, I puckered my lips, considering. Then I stole a peek—a little one. The fantasy sweet Pearl had daydreamed was of a man who wanted to talk to her, to introduce her to his parents, who didn't care that she was half-starved, disgusting, and poor. Where she could pretend she was human and wouldn't have to watch him slowly age and die.

How sad to have lived a life never knowing she had a whole family waiting for her. A family who would never age. Who would love her.

Uncharacteristically pensive, I murmured, "I see that I was right."

It would be that first baby that would make her love me. A beautiful, perfect cherub that would nurse at her breast and drink of my flock.

But this I could not say, because it would just *stir the pot.* Pearl was already half-mad, and it would be centuries before that damage might mend.

Fuck you very much, Darius.

Oh, was I going to have another long talk with my son. The nightmares I would inflict on his mind. And I knew exactly what his next torment would be. Poetic justice.

I would make him relive every single night Pearl suffered in the crypt as if he were she. The perfect sentence. One I could carry out over and over and over until the sun ate this planet and my people repopulated a new one.

Tapping her foot in a feminine gesture passed down through the ages, I came back to the present to see Pearl's arms crossed under her breasts. Her lovely lips turned down.

"I was right." I amended, "In saying I'd follow where you walked. But I was wrong on other counts. Screw the Yelp. I should have asked you where you'd like to be treated on our first date."

That threw her for quite a loop. Shoulders relaxing, my darling one lowered her arms. "I don't even know what street we're on, what year it is, or what I would have liked."

"Quite right. Furthermore, no more talk of Jade, or *ancient history*. It was uncouth to assume you'd be thrilled about children as if you'd waited an eternity as I had." I was salvaging this beautifully, despite the way she unconsciously clawed at her forearm.

So beautifully, in fact, that she said, "Well… we shouldn't let the food get cold."

Offering my hand like a proper gentleman, I said,

"Despite my failure to ask, which I won't repeat, I do think you'll be pleased. The Yelp is a hilarious mishmash of human snark and assholery. But, it has its uses. If you like, I'll teach you how it works so you might live dangerously and pick where we eat next."

"I want to try fast food. Like from the commercials." What a lovely glow came to her eyes before she announced, "Tacos!"

My love was completely insane, but even I was aware of humans' delight and the necessity of tacos. "Done. And then I will introduce you to something so popular I don't even know how to describe the human reaction to it. A taco truck."

Our dinner was lovely. Pearl drank wine and ate her fill. So content that she let me feed her from a vein when we returned to our temporary home. Albeit the vein was in my wrist. And, unfortunately, she closed the door to her room on me when I tried to follow her in.

I was only going to hold her, and maybe steal a kiss.

Between her legs….

So instead, like a mongrel without a world begging to fuck him, I took my member in hand and stroked out a release. My thoughts full of Pearl, listening in on her dreams and lightly inserting the arousal I felt as my seed sprayed my chest.

Her mind responded in kind. In sleep, she orgasmed.

7

PEARL

Back bowed, I woke to a symphony of sensation that left my gasp punctuated with a shameless cry. Pulsating from my pelvis, another wave of feeling broke. Leaving my mouth gaping on another relentless, unstoppable moan.

Sweaty, panting as the dream faded and reality stole in, I sat up. Staring down where my nethers were covered by sleeping gown and blankets. Completely confounded.

What on earth?

"I heard a cry! Are you okay?"

Clutching the sheets to my breast, my head shot up to find Vladislov shirtless, wearing drawstring pajama bottoms, wiping his chest with a towel. One he then dropped on the floor as if it had never been in his hand. All the while stepping closer to my bed.

And still, I tingled, turning my eyes from his half-nakedness and trying to piece together some semblance of an answer. Because what could I have said?

Mortified, unnaturally hot, all I wanted was to fan my face or hide under the covers. But I had cried out rather loudly, and of course someone would have heard.

"A dream." Not that I could remember it now, or even recall my name in that moment. "I'm fine. Sorry if I worried you."

The bed dipped, and a male wearing *no shirt* sat next to me. He did this despite my discomposure, even resting a hand on my blanketed knee.

Leaning closer as I stiffened, shivered, and blushed, he said, "You look rather flushed, Pearl. Do you need anything? Water? A cuddle?"

My nipples were hard, poking against the simple cotton of my nightgown, covered by the sheets I clutched to my breast. And my breasts themselves… ached.

Water would be perfect. An entire frigid bath of it.

Instead, I was given heat. Heat in the voice of velvet offering solace. "You're shivering, Pearl. Shall I warm you up?"

Before I might think of something coherent that might drive him off, my bare arm was stroked, a wake of pure fire left where I had been touched.

And it burned so beautifully in places it should not that I groaned in frustration.

"This won't do, my dear." Gathering me to him, Vladislov somehow already under the covers, I was pulled to that naked chest. "Let me hold you."

Finally, my tongue unhinged. "You're not dressed!"

Words waving off my valid complaint, he embraced me all the tighter. "In this era, men do not sleep with an upper covering. I like to keep my costume fitting with the times. Wait until you meet Vampires who still wear powdered wigs or mud for clothes. Ridiculous."

There was a heart beating under my ear. There was warmth further invading the thin cotton of my nightclothes. The smell of smoke, spice, a cedar forest at night.

The body of a man intimately touching me in a way that wasn't carnal but extremely intimate. Even tangling his legs with mine.

A man so strong I wouldn't be able to stop him when—

"I didn't come in here to have sex with you, Pearl." That big, warm hand moved up and down my spine. "You cried out, and you need comfort."

Which sounded reasonable.

But half-naked? Touching me? Another, last, impossible series of twitches left the place between my legs clenching at emptiness, when his leg shifted just so.

Gulping air, I succumbed to the tail end of a shiver and… finally, mercifully… whatever had possessed me abated.

My wits returned, and though I appreciated that the flaming blush of my cheek was hidden, tucked as I was under Vladislov's chin, the entirety of this situation was wholly improper.

Shushing me, rocking my body as one might comfort a child, he said, "It's late. The sun is going to be up soon. Close your pretty blue eyes. I'll be here, always."

Arms somewhat awkwardly caught between us, I debated on trying to move. Unsure how to accomplish the feat without touching hard muscle. How to position my head so the hair on his chest would not tickle my lips.

"You're still shivering. Here." Out of the darkness, a membranous weight landed over my body. A wing attached to a very human body. One Vladislov tucked around us as if to shield out the rising sun, the world.

Leaving the pair of us in a vacuum.

The only two creatures wrapped in night.

Twisted together in limbs, in flesh. Opposing forces completely and utterly intermeshed.

To the music of his heartbeat and my breath.

"This isn't seemly." My complaint was halfhearted, as such heat made me drowsy.

Self-satisfied, a grin in his voice, he replied, "What could be more natural?"

Is that what married couples did? Did they embrace this way?

No creature had ever held me in such a fashion. Not that I could remember… though the journal had mentioned nights I had been happy in my cell.

So this had to be a trick by the infamous trickster kissing my crown and mumbling to me in some unknown language.

"It takes *practice* to learn the role of wife. To be plucked from the garden and placed in the bed of a king. To discover the power you wield. How at the crook of your finger I would topple worlds. How at a kiss from my lips you'll know pleasures that will make my name sing from your spirit."

One man's pleasures had forced blasphemy from my mouth.

"I would never hurt you that way. What Darius did to you was a perversion of coupling. Your experiences prior to the crypt were against your will. You have never been made love to, and have good reasons for your fear."

In that winged cocoon, in the infinite intimacy of the moment, I grew angry.

Not just about the things that had happened to me over the entity of my pathetic life. But about what I had seen in the weeks since I'd come out of the dark. Couples walking hand in hand on the street. Kind glances and loving strokes. Laughter.

The films I'd been shown on that strange flat screen with their adventure and happy endings. Respect and jokes and fun.

I was never going to know those things.

How he did it—perhaps he grew a third arm—but suddenly my awkward arm was gathered, fingers trailing to mine, where they interlocked. "But you're knowing them now."

"You say that as if this is real," I confessed. "But I'll wake up back in that tomb."

"Even if you should, it's just a room. And there is no room on this entire planet that could hold you should you wish to leave it now. I can teach you why you never need to be afraid of that room. How you can move through space with a thought—to anywhere you desire. Or always to me, where my arms will be open. Where you will never feel pain."

Bitter and suddenly sad, I muttered, "Is that how you tempted Jesus in the desert?"

"Tempted?" Dry laughter filled our secluded space, shook the chest under my ear. "I've never understood how the various versions of that story all got it so wrong. If you want to know what happened for those forty days and forty nights, you're going to have to ask Jesus himself. Though his name is pronounced *Yeshua*."

"What you are saying is sacrilegious. Jesus ascended from his tomb to return to his father."

"He walked out of that tomb after the stone barring him in had been removed. And he's a stuffy, cantankerous bore. Constantly whining about the ways of the world yet refusing to appear and explain himself." With a derisive snort, Vladislov added, "The second coming. What a joke.

"And let's not forget the other figures before him, just as determined to educate the cattle. Mani, Krishna, Romulus, Glycon, Zoroaster, Buddha, Heracles… need I go on?"

The term cattle was not one I enjoyed. Reminding the nightmare wrapped around me, I said, "I'm half human. And I drink from you. Does that make you cattle?"

The beast dared reach down and give my rear a quick grasp, chuckling. "I would gladly be your bull."

Unable to shake off the fingers entwined with mine, I couldn't give him the swat he deserved. "That is not what I meant."

"But you wouldn't blush if I didn't tease. And I adore the way you blush."

Wriggling to get away only got me more encumbered. "Are you an octopus? Where did all these arms come from?"

"Can't a man give his wife an extra hand or two?"

He was impossible. "For the love of all that is holy. Can you be serious for five seconds?"

"I am the embodiment of seriousness." Lips brushed over mine the instant he spoke those words. Which was impossible, as I was still resting on his chest and nowhere near that mouth. "Drab as he is, Yeshua, is the only person, outside of myself, who can tell you of our time in the desert. Since we both know you won't believe a word out of my mouth, I'll arrange for you to spend time together. Though sometimes it's better to hold on to our delusions than face the truth of the world. Consider that should you really want to speak with him."

"Jesus is in heaven!" My snarl earned me another phantom peck.

"Many people do consider Brazil heaven."

"I will not lose my faith." By God, I would not.

"Your faith?" Playfulness drained from the monster, fingers that had been tickling ceased movement. Form curling even more around me, like a centipede eating a bug, razor-sharp fangs found my throat. Scraping *oh so softly* over that tender place. They dragged from neck to my earlobe. Where he nipped, yet drew no blood. Where he whispered, "Your faith, you say? Was it your choice to be abandoned on the doorstep of a mission? Did you have a say in the education those monks graced you with? The beatings, the labor, the abuses of a particular priest? Did they not tell you to fear God and obey? Did they not take advantage of a dependent child with nowhere to go in a world that was savage and dirty, crawling with prospectors looking for gold? At no time was it *your faith*. It was and is your shackles, imposed upon you by a world that use religion as means of control. And if there is this God you imagine, she would agree with me."

"God is *not* a woman." Women were creatures born of sin. The reason humanity fell from grace.

Wing lifting, all touch retreated. Brightness broke through our private circle, causing me to squint at the unwelcome intrusion. Leaving me with the face of a man who looked disturbed, a bit angry, and even sad.

A man with his outstretched wing folding at his back as if he were an angel, even though the wing was that of a creature from the pit. One propped up on an elbow, watching me in silence, bathed in sunlight.

Minutes passed, with each tick of the clock my shame growing, though I was unsure what sin I had committed. Endless hanging silence that left me fidgeting and unable to hold his gaze.

Unable to beat it another second, I muttered, "God cannot be a woman."

"And the world cannot be round. And humans cannot land on the moon. And evolution is not factually based because the most popular creation myth of this era had everything burst into life in seven days. But you don't know that word, because you were raised as a practical slave under starvation conditions. It took you decades to learn how to write, picking up snatches here and there while you wandered from city to city. Famished for education, but female, weak, poor, and frightened. There is nothing evil about you. But there is evil in ignorance. Ask me how many verses of that bible I could quote to support my argument?" He reared back, haughty and grim. "Actually don't. I have no interest in wasting my breath. You can't hear, because you are broken. And I am gravely insulted by all you have said."

Why was I crying? Why were hot tears falling down flushed cheeks? "But you don't understand. God cannot be a woman. He filled Mary with child."

"The immaculate conception? Winged angels in the sky at the birth of Christ?" Unfolding the wings at his back, Vladislov beat them against the air, raising himself from the bed as if to take flight. "Gift from kings who'd traveled far. Gold, frankincense, myrrh. All priceless items left at the feet of a peasant woman and her swaddled baby."

My mouth opened, but I was cut off by another beating of his wings and a louder riposte. "Just to make it clear in case you are not picking up on the subtle hints I've layered through this chat. Mary enjoyed my cock when we lay together. For birthing my offspring, she was rewarded with riches. And to many, I am a God. But the only God I worship has a cunny. And I know this, because I have seen you gloriously naked. Wordplay or no, I will not have you insult my Goddess, my love, or my tireless devotion. You will be educated, starting tonight. And you will meet with Yeshua in time and find yourself in a world so far beyond what you allow your mind to comprehend that you will hate me for it."

Crying all the harder, I put my head to my knees. This only angered the pacing tiger, who grabbed something and threw it to shatter against a far wall.

On a roar, he demanded, "Tell me how to make this stop!"

And I snapped. "Just hurt me already! I'm worn sick from waiting!"

Lifting up an entire chifforobe in rage, Vladislov ripped it apart. No longer man in form, no longer rational. He broke the simple things in that creepy room, bellowing smoke and braying like a wolf.

"Hear me, woman!" Demonic in person, in voice, on every level, that winged monster turned on me. "I will not. You don't need a devil. You torment yourself enough to put the entirety of hell out of a job."

8

PEARL

What a mess…

Not just the room, but my insides. Guilt I could not explain weighed on me. More than that, the things he said, about how long it had taken me to learn how to read. How I had drawn letters on brick with rocks. The decades of practice so I might have *one* redeeming quality.

I too could quote scripture… verbatim.

Misspeak and receive a strike with a cane across the shoulders.

As a child, I'd memorized every part of the bible that made it clear to be female was to be evil. I could recite prayer with a rosary until my fingers bled.

I could kneel on rice, be beaten with a stick, and be hung from a tree.

I could be raped.

But I could not navigate this world. Not that I had ever navigated my own well. Always hungry. Always ashamed. Always last in line and first under fire.

Stick-thin, starving, lonely, waiting to be delivered.

Waiting for exactly what now sat before me in ruins. A room with a window. Companionship.

Food.

As embarrassing as it was to admit to myself, I was tired of starving. Rats, stray dogs, bugs when I was especially desperate. Vomiting after a meal. Hearing the priests screaming the first time my fangs elongated.

I had prayed for my entire life to be cleansed of my urges. I felt less.

Because there was a whole world of things so beyond my scope that I just stuttered and drooled like the idiot I was.

A demon had torn every last bit of furniture in my room to shreds. All save myself and the bed. I bore no scratch or bruise.

That was a lie.

My pride was heavily bruised.

I worked hard. I loved to work hard. It was the only thing I'd ever been appreciated for. Never late, did the job without complaint. The model cigarette girl, or waitress, or cleaning lady.

The very priest that came to offer me the Eucharist each day believed I was mad. I certainly felt it. But I could not forget the feeling of that weighted paper between my fingers, the script in my own hand. Penmanship I had copied from a discarded letter I had found in the streets.

Penmanship of a lady of worth.

Why did all the things in this house always get broken?

Powdered wigs and mud, he said. Yet my costume was from my last years I could remember. Even the nightgown with its ruffled collar and plain cotton. I was the very joke he'd made. Cloche hats, sack dresses, a party in theme to the Roaring '20s.

Ridiculous in every way.

Cold now that the inferno had left. After he had broken sad copies of my former cheap furniture.

The whole room was so at odds with the rest of this *penthouse*. And yes, that was the proper word, as I had been corrected like the idiot I was, more than once.

A veritable castle in a city I remembered but didn't know.

"Cigarette?" My calling card, my trade. A word that came easily to my lips.

A thing that was out of fashion and deadly, not that anyone knew such things back then.

Tobacco caused cancer. Which I would never have. Just like I would never age, and even starvation had not killed me. I was *this* forever.

On a planet that was round.

And apparently humans had walked on the moon. THE MOON!

Staring at the wrinkled cotton of my nightgown, at exposed arms that were no longer barely bone and flesh… I didn't know myself.

And I should have.

All I could think of for those three days I had hung from a

tree as a child was how I was born of evil and deserved to die. But never did. The branch broke before I did.

Darius raped me in body and mind, in so many ways I knew I could not remember. And I endured.

Stupid, ignorant, a pointless decoration in the room.

"Please forgive me." Out of nowhere, he arrived, on his knees, his head in my lap as he sobbed. Those wings of his twitching with each massive inhale that stretched his ribs.

Who asks the forgiveness of an idiot?

And what idiot rests their hands on the shoulder of a weeping devil?

I wasn't afraid of the truth, even if I didn't care for it, admitting, "I am as stupid as you say. I always have been. Stupid and sickly and starving."

Those eyes turned up, cracked black cheeks sparking with flame turning his tears to steam. "I was wrong… and foolish. As much as I hate your evil thoughts about yourself, I should have held my temper. But no soul has challenged me in ages, and I'm out of practice. This entire behavior was so beneath me and so unworthy of what you deserve."

What I deserved was that tomb, the journal, the notes, the rotting things within.

The dark.

"No, my love." Monstrous paw to my cheek, a thumb tipped in a curling claw wiped my tears. "You deserve the sun. I don't care what God you think granted it to you. In fact, I should thank *him*, if it is indeed a man you see in God. For if you had been born human or Vampire, either way, once I had brought you back to my embrace, you would have lost the daylight. And now you can walk in both worlds, holding my hand."

A hand that dwarfed mine as he took it and brought it to his black lips.

"And you can look the angel while I look your devil." Another fervent kiss to my knuckles. "Lead me about by my nose."

Why was this breaking my heart? "But you *are* the devil."

"One who will learn to be good if only you'd love me."

Those eyes. Beast or man, no matter the shade or glow. I knew those eyes. "I do not want to talk to your Jesus, or sit with him, or know these things you know. I'm too tired."

"Lie down, my soul. Rest yourself under my wing. Sleep through the day, knowing I'm here." Beseeching tears fell from his unwavering, weighty gaze. "Forgive me my temper."

There was only one answer for all of this. "I will sleep under your wing, if you take me back to my tomb."

And leave me there to rot.

"No."

"Yes."

"Your soul would sing in sleep, and I'd hear and be driven mad by it." The monstrosity began to rise. "Even eternity entombed beside your corpse would not be enough to sate the beast. I need *you*. I need my soul. Order me about. Make demands. *Hurt me*. But thrive as you do so."

"You sound so—"

"In love?"

"Insane." Yet I said it with a teary laugh.

"Please. Let me beg. Let me grovel. Touch my face. See me."

And it should not have moved me as it did, but his pleading stirred my belly enough to remind me to breathe. "I do see you. The serpent in the garden. And I have been waiting for the apple."

"It was a quince in the first telling of that tale. And there also was no garden nor Adam nor Eve, but I will pretend there was if it will appease you. Tell me to lie, and I will do so."

"Your truths are unbearable." And overwhelming, like walking over shards of glass.

"You are tired, my love. You are overwrought." It crept into the bed, the very bed I slinked toward the middle of to make room for the monster. "Sleep under my wing. Let me serve you."

He already stretched the massive appendage over the two of us, and I found myself having lain back upon the pillows. I accepted the dark. Because the rest of him did not touch me.

I dreamed of Coney Island.

I woke to smiles and joy. His joy.

Grit in my eyes, dog-tired as if I had not slept a wink, I wanted to turn my face into the pillow and hibernate for a year. Or a thousand.

"I think a long sleep would do you well." It had crept closer as I slumbered, flush to my frame and having pulled me to his chest. "Which I will grant you. But considering the mistakes I have already made, I would be remiss in failing to offer you the chance to see your daughter marry her love. I cannot let you regret it later."

The same daughter I had learned of only hours before. On my first date. Where all the actions I had always fantasized about had been delivered… along with many so out of my scope I had neglected to enjoy a moment of it.

"Seeing you—" Talons carded through my hair. "—it's hard to restrain my enthusiasm to have you home. To have you so close and so untouchable. *To crave*. Show me pity."

His pleadings had gone from forlorn to wide-eyed and silly, as had the expression on the face of the hideous thing. And I found that I had fallen for it, smirking no matter how I fought my lips.

"Three days? Three days, sleep. Three days, rest." The beast melted into the form of a man yet kept those wings. Though it had not kept the tatters of its clothing. "And on the third day, rise."

Yawning, the thought of a three-day-long sleep divine, my taunt came out a tease, "You really are Satan."

Wind settling over me, shutting out intrusive daylight, he hummed. "And you do so love to call me names."

Already half asleep, I turned my face into the pillow. "I never liked my own, so it's only fair."

This made him laugh. "I'm not surprised. You were always extremely difficult to please."

Which was utterly incorrect. "All I ever wanted was kindness."

"And you were so starved you fail to see it when it's right

before you. Even if the form offering it is hideous in your eyes."

When he sounded sad, it stirred me in a way I thoroughly disliked. But I was too tired to consider, already dreaming of evergreen forests when his awful lips scraped over my cheek.

"Three days, Pearl. Then I shall wake you with a feast."

On the third day, I rose.

In an entirely different room.

To the sound of church bells.

9

PEARL

The clothing hanging in a room called a *walk-in closet* was enviable. Gowns and blouses any working girl from my era would have spent their hard-earned pennies on. Out of date, yet still so beautiful I didn't want to touch in case I snagged the fabric.

A time capsule of the best years of my long life.

The 1920s had passed a century ago. Yet I'd clung to them and been indulged.

There was no mistaking that truth. Having been beaten, hung, drowned, shot, tortured, I still lived. And I was going to live forever. The more I imagined those immortals, those vampires, who wore mud or powdered wigs—how they failed to move forward out of insanity—the more I saw a reflection in myself.

I saw it in the walk-in closet. In the cosmetics provided for me that were nothing like the advertisements on television. Cake mascara and rouge had not been used in decades, it seemed.

I saw it in my unwillingness to wear a bra, opting for an "old-fashioned" step-in.

I saw it each night when I dressed and looked in the mirror, my reflection, wearing clothes so beyond my means, so pretty, that any cigarette girl would have envied me.

Yet there were no cigarette girls anymore.

No one dressed this way save for themed parties.

And I was doing it by choice.

I—the hard worker, the adaptive employee—was stuck, stubborn, and willfully pouting about a world I had never been able to change. An ultimately pointless pursuit God would not approve of.

"I need *modern* clothing so I can get a job." Daring one last time, I touched one dress, a pale-pink number I admired and longed to deserve. "That restaurant with the terrible seafood platter had a sign in the window. They were looking for help. I could work there to pay for the clothes."

"I mean…" Vladislov sighed at my back, as if I had mentioned a topic he anticipated and loathed. "If you wish to work, it can be arranged. But the question of money? I have more wealth than the entire United States and continent of Europe combined."

"I like to work."

I felt the shrug in his words, imagined wings elongated in a careless flutter, though I knew he was in human form. "Many immortals do. I'd be the first to admit it's a great way to immerse oneself. But, may I counter your suggestion with one of my own?"

Turning so I might look at the person who'd woken me with a gentle kiss, to sacred bells of a church specially rung for me, to a priest speaking in French and a breakfast of *pain au chocolat*, I felt a bit beholden.

No.

I felt a sensation I'd never known outside of desperation. I felt grateful.

Gratitude had always come from begging just so I might survive. With this monster, gratitude came like it was a normal emotion.

"What do women wear? I've seen trousers. I'm not comfortable with that." Considering the final decade I remembered was all about women breaking free, my sentiment was silly. Women had already thrown off corsets, shortened their skirts, cut their hair.

Hell, I had cut mine!

Hell?

I began to laugh. As did my host.

"Husband." A smooth voice paired with a smooth hand down my arm. "I am your husband, not your host."

Something in me bantered easily, was playful in a way I had never been with a man. "But we're not married."

"My sweet soul, if a ceremony would please you, I'll have us 'wed' in the grandest of fashions. A virginal white gown, veil trailing to be held by one hundred attendants."

Chilling as quickly as I had warmed, I thought of only one word. The one that stung. "I'm not virginal."

He pulled down the outdated dress I liked most, turning me to hold it before my frame. “In every possible way, you are a pure virgin deserving the crown of a queen… even if you want to hostess at a restaurant or wash dishes in a kitchen.”

When he talked in such a way, I would blush. Felt it creeping up my cheek as I pretended to admire the upheld, beautiful dress instead of meeting his eye. “You mentioned a suggestion?”

“University.” The tip of his human finger tapped my nose. “Join a sorority, eat pizza, and drink beer, go to parties and make friends. Take classes and expand the mind I already recognize as brilliant. Any subject can be at your fingertips. Work if you wish, but consider that study will be time-consuming. And I must be fair in stating that you will need tutelage before you might be admitted. I have a collection of wise minds ready to teach you, which might eat up years until you can quote Plato as well as you quote Psalms.”

“You are teasing me.” He had to be. I was dumber than a rock. At least fifteen of my former employers had said so.

“Uh, they are so lucky they are already dead.” A peck landed on my lips between his complaints. “Wear this pink number tonight. We can stay in and watch a modern movie if you want to leap forward into what's trending now. If you're feeling daring, we can watch *the movie* that has an entire planet of women overjoyed and salivating.”

“But we're only at 1959.” Jumping ahead seemed forbidden! Yet at the same time… was there really any point in postponing the inevitable. What did women these days watch? I would see their mannerisms and clothes. Hairstyles, cosmetic trends. Perhaps this was the best first step. "I would like to see this movie."

Gathering up the underthings to match the 1920s costume, Vladislov said, "It will be very modern. I think the word might be risqué."

"Women in the 1920s were very modern. They could vote!" And indeed that had made me very worried in that age. For so much violence was brought down upon those females who wanted a voice. And I had not agreed, as women were God's flawed creation. But then I'd seen a cultural renaissance… a phrase I overheard from a guest at the Supper Club and had looked up at the library.

So why not watch this movie? Why not wear the clothes?

But no trousers!

Even in my era, those looked improper.

"How brave you are, my soul!" Laughing, Vladislov wrapped an arm around me. "All of this will be removed and replaced. No need to look at me that way. It will be saved for parties or your whim. Yet I will contradict one fashion statement from the years you're considering. Bras are overrated. I'll cover you in lace, in satin, in silk, but please, I beg you, my darling, do not confine such perfect breasts in a bra."

Nipples tightening at their mere mention, I pulled the house coat tighter around my chest. "What do women sleep in?"

His eyebrows bounced. "In the nude, of course."

"You're lying…"

"Fine…" He sighed as if I were extremely troublesome

for failing to take the bait. “Nightgowns, teddies, lingerie, pajamas. And yes, some do prefer to sleep naked. If I have a vote, I vote naked. You’d glow wearing nothing but moonlight.”

“You’re too forward.” I would have never said that to a patron as I sold cigarettes. I would have let him slather me with innuendo and grab my breast or rump. But I said it now, because I was no longer a cigarette girl. I was to be a modern woman of a new century. “It makes me uncomfortable.”

Grinning, he leaned close enough to take a deep breath of me. “Uncomfortable is not the right word. It makes you nervous, because it excites you.”

Heart pounding, strange fluttery feelings in my belly, I closed my eyes and collected my thoughts. Warmed where his heat poured into me. Oddly breathless when he ran his nose over my hair.

Full-on shivering when he whispered at my ear, “I would be very gentle, immensely careful, if you would only let me kiss you.”

A kiss? Was there really any harm? My lips already felt plump, tingled with the thought of it.

It was all I could do not to touch them.

Yet he pulled away, eyes warm and smile soft. “But not yet. First, let's watch this film and see just what makes the modern woman tick.”

Hand going to the tie of my robe, he pulled the knot before I might react. Off went my robe, followed with a flourish of my cotton nightgown until I was naked, gaping, and reaching out for anything to cover myself.

Chin in his hand, he cocked his head and considered. "Perfect breasts. Perfect sex. Please don't have your pubic hair ripped out the way women do these days. I love those beautifully scented, soft curls just as they are."

Already stepping into my underthings, red up to my ears, I tripped once I grasped what he said. "Women remove… that hair? Why?"

"Cunnilingus. Though the fashion fluctuates decade to decade, in these times, many men complain when their partner likes to be licked between her thighs and the lady's sex is in the natural state. Call me old fashioned, but I disagree. I want to smell and feel all of you."

My breasts were covered in thin satin, and after I snatched the pink dress from my tormentor, my body was reasonably concealed. But I felt the oddest pulsating warmth between my legs. And by the way Vladislov winked and took another deep breath, I realized he could smell it.

"I can, and your arousal smells divine. I bet you taste like honey."

And I was growing offended to be so outmatched. "Such talk is for husbands and wives!"

"As we are married, I knew you'd like it." Hooking my arm through his, he led me stumbling from the closet. "But enough verbal foreplay. Let's go watch this film the female population is aflutter over."

"I don't trust you one bit. I've changed my mind about the movie."

"Too late!" As if playfully offended, he mimicked a wound to his heart. "Besides, I do not decide what women like. Look on social media and see the unrelenting posts about this film. You want to immerse yourself in the modern woman's psyche, there is no better jumping off point."

Waltzed through the rooms, spun until my legs caught the sofa, I plopped down on the cushion. Vladislov stretching out at my side, remote in hand.

His fingers moved faster than the program might load, which I could sense annoyed him, as he was trying so hard to play cool and not pin me in place.

The film began, looking *so real* compared to films from the 50s—like standing right there with the actors. The sound of waves crashing was so fresh that I was enraptured with this *magic*.

A girl taken captive by a handsome, evil man. One who swears she will fall in love with him.

I don't think my jaw closed the entire rest of the film. Every moral part of me knew I needed to look away, but they were naked! How could I have known the brazen filth that women relished in these days?

So beyond what I had anticipated… the beautiful woman seduced the man who caught her in his web. She took his member into her mouth!

Oh lord! He licked her between her legs!

Cunnilingus Vladislov had teased me about, though she was hairless—as he had also mentioned.

And when they made love—if the violence in which they took one another's body could be called that—she enjoyed it.

Women enjoyed sex?

"Very much so, Pearl. Modern women have taken sexual

control of their bodies and enjoy the act even more than the man in many instances."

"I don't understand this."

How the villain showered the wanton captive with praise.

How she adored him, despite the fact that he kidnapped… stolen her away.

I'd been stolen and locked in a crypt.

I'd felt a cock thrust in me, known the tearing of delicate tissues. Hated all of it.

I had climaxed with a scream just as the actress continued to do.

But her cries were of joy.

I had never been sated in such a way.

And seeing this…

It made me sad.

Frustrated.

Angry.

Disgustingly eager.

Did women really like these things?

On a couch, in a room I had never seen, I sat beside a character from all human nightmares and grew confused at the pulse growing between my legs each time the actors coupled.

"I don't understand." But I understood enough to grasp why Vladislov moved to kneel before me. Why he was gently pushing up my skirt, inserting his frame between my weakening knees.

Parting me so the slit in my step-in might be found and dark curls exposed.

And I could not wrap my mind around the fact that I was allowing it.

Holding my eyes, his touch slowly moving up my inner thigh, he said, “That gentle kiss I promised. I’d like to give it to you now.”

“I won’t like it.” Not the way the woman did on screen. Never like that.

His fingertips reached my undergarment’s opening, pulling it wide to expose even more of me. “Then I’ll stop.”

One could say the first touch of his lips in that forbidden place was indeed chaste. Soft pressure at the apex of my sex, right where I tingled the most.

Pressing my head back into the couch cushions, I gasped. Hips rocking so I might know more, just like the woman on the screen had done.

And more, I was given.

I don’t know if his tongue was forked, but it was evil through and through as the demon sluiced through my juices to flick at my lower lips. To strum a delicious knot of pleasure above my hungry opening.

There was nothing shy or modest in how he *kissed* me. Nothing innocent. Nose, chin, mouth, tongue, even teeth played me like a song.

And I did scream, bucking and wild and someone else entirely, climaxing with shaking legs within minutes.

It was as if I had finally been exorcised of a demon.

Breathless as he redoubled his efforts and pierced me with a tongue I knew was black, fat, and far longer than any human tongue. Undulating that thing within me, his nose nudging the bead where all sensation centered, I screamed again.

And again.

And again.

I was *kissed* until the sun rose. Until my voice was gone and my senses were muddled by pleasure.

And then the man pulled back, licking his smiling lips with a tongue more dangerous than sin. Climbing over where I was spent, where I realized I had been brazenly clutching at my own breast and pinching the aching nipple.

He murmured, “Better than honey,” kissing me to share the flavor of what he dined on throughout an entire night.

I tasted nothing like honey, but I found his tongue in my mouth delicious. His weight on my body divine.

Nipping his way across my jaw, he whispered the ultimate temptation, “We could make love in the sunlight. Gentle and slow.”

Perhaps we could....

My final thought before exhaustion and an unnatural sense of relaxation took me away.

10

VLADISLOV

Laying her in her new bed, in this new country, in this fresh start, I knew my soul wouldn't wake until sunset. Not after the *progress* we had made… a dozen times or more.

She had not believed she would enjoy my tongue between her legs in her past life either. The first time had been quite a violent tussle. This time, all it required was some sensational media.

Bless the makers of softcore porn for women. I'd have them all changed so more movies of that nature might be produced and I might get the pleasure of eating pussy from dusk to daybreak again.

A vampire armada of smut makers! Ha!

Just wait until my queen viewed a real-life orgy. I bet she'd bob up and down my cock all night after furious blushing and five minutes of pretending not to look.

Was it too soon to throw her that style of party?

Yes.

I sighed, willing to press progress even if I couldn't have my orgy. It was not too soon to strip her out of those clothes and let her know the glory of soft sheets on bare skin. Which would get me in a bit of trouble when she woke, especially as I would be just as naked and pressed flush against her.

There was no helping my dripping erection, so that too she would experience and muse over.

How delicious her musings were.

What a pity I had not been able to read her thoughts in her past life. Had I been able to, I could have been far more cunning and much less violent with my jewel. She might have loved me even more.

I might not have had to threaten the life of the very baby whose delivery had drained her to the point of death. I might not have threatened to kill it if she had not made the oath that would bring her back to me.

A child I could not bear to look at as it grew. Who outlived all his brothers and took my throne when I wandered off to make the world bleed for leaving me soulless and desolate—the great, great, great, great, many more greats grandfather of Darius.

In whom, after a thousand years, I'd tried to make amends.

Considering Darius' head was now on a pike and my soul was afraid of the pleasure due her, I should have killed that baby after all—horrible thing that tore its way out of the only creature in existence worth anything.

I supposed my love's rebirth was a boon in the fact that she would remember none of this. And it would be thousands of years before she might gain the ability to pry into my thoughts and see what I'd done. By then she would be hopelessly tied to me, utterly in love. Devoted as I was to her.

Just lying near her made me ache.

I would give her physical pleasure for a thousand years and seek none for myself if only to please her. Though it might make my pants fit a bit oddly walking around with a constant erection. Perhaps codpieces might come back into style?

Nestling said erection between the warm buttocks of a sex-addled, drowsing daywalker, I covered us both with one wing. This too she would grow accustomed to, for I could not resist the need to do it.

The need.

Holding her in such a way fed me more than thoughts of fucking her. Though, there was no question I very much longed to plow her into oblivion. I could come all over her beautiful backside right now if I just let my mind wander into fun thoughts.

But waking up with dried semen on her back, already naked and in my arms, would absolutely make her mad. She might slap me.

I might like it.

And… it was too late. Like an untried boy, I had just spurt where I may or may not have been rocking myself against soft buttocks.

If I were to just… rub the come in, what was the harm in that?

Massages were very popular in this era. If she woke, I'd simply tell her I was trying to keep up with the times.

And still, she'd slap me.

It would be worth it.

Considering I was already hard again, I could keep this massage tactic up all night. Imagine how rested she would be when she woke. If I had a bath prepared, she would hop right to it in her modesty before really analyzing the situation.

Filling it with bubbles like the scene in the movie might even show her how adept I am in noticing what intrigues her.

Perhaps no bubbles, but a tub full of warm, immortal blood?

There were plenty of vampires in my prisons who were unworthy to pass her lips, but good as a blood bag to be tapped to luxuriate her skin. It would be a very vampire-y thing to do. Her first step into embracing her other half.

I'd be her servant, properly clothed with a toga around my hips, feeding her grapes and sips of blood straight from the vein while she soaked.

Three spurts of come on my sleeping wife's back was probably the limit I might get away with before the sheets turned crusty. Hand to my cock, pulling forth the greatest release of the night, I did my best to angle more of it at me than at the sweet globes of her pale ass.

I really was such a liar.

What man in his right mind would not come all over so plump an ass?

Absolutely sane, I lifted my wing enough to see the creamy globs dripping toward her more intimate area, salivating to lick her clean, and groaned.

Heaven was Hell, and in my arms slept the true ruler of the underworld. Tormenting me with her beauty, her goodness, her scrumptious tits and ass. I was Hades, and she was Persephone, except in the real tale, there was no Demeter to steal her away from me for half the seasons. And now death could not touch her.

She was mine!

Skin black and burning, talons lengthening as my hands grew and my body bulged with strength, I cupped her flesh and seared my seed into soft skin. A bit frenzied in the art of manipulating muscle into bliss.

Many hours had already passed, the tub of blood had been prepared at my mental bidding, and beautiful blue eyes opened, wide with shock to see that, no, I did not cradle her and have her covered in my wing. I knelt over her, massive wingspan possessively closing out the setting sun, my touch kneading her body as yet another throbbing erection dripped onto her belly.

Balls tight to my shaft, they churned to release, yet I ignored them to wish her good evening. "How did you rest, my love?"

Speechless from my attention, or maybe from the wide-eyed stare at my bobbing cock, Pearl failed to reply.

"There is no need to be frightened of your husband's body." The arm I had been stroking, I drew my kneading grip down her limb and brought her hand to hover over my erection. "You can touch me if you want to. Explore me and know you are safe. I will not have sex with you until you ask me to."

Had that been too similar to the line in yesterday's film?

There was something new in her at that moment. Terror, yes, but also bite. "And when you do, what happens then?"

That one stumped me. "I suppose it depends on what you're in the mood for next."

"Will you make me put my mouth on you like—" She swallowed, flushed skin going pale. Thoughts of Darius and his debauchery were in her mind, but it was the film she referred to. "—like the man in the movie did to his *wife*."

This, I could work with.

Flipping her over before she might scream or fight back, I put her in the exact position the actor had first fucked his captive. Draping my body over her back, I settled my wings to embrace us and took the lobe of her ear in my teeth. "He did this to her as well. Fucked her while her hands were chained to the headboard."

I did not penetrate, but I did let my organ smooth through her folds in a long, slow stroke I hoped would entice arousal and not screams.

"My love, is it not better to jump into the water and swim? Toeing the shore will drive you mad."

Shaking so hard I could hear her teeth chatter, Pearl stopped me in my tracks. "Don't."

But this was not the time for retreat. There was a reason I had conquered the known world time and again. I would conquer this too. "I'm asking for you to trust me."

And I scythed the long, aching length of my penis again between her folds. And again. As I cooed and stroked her, as my wings warmed her from her fear-inspired chill.

I mimicked the act of fucking without actually penetrating my darling one. Offering us both a taste of pleasure until she began to pant and the muscles I worked to caress all night began to relax. Her head to the mattress, her ass in the air. My breath at her ear, and my cock stroking her clit, I took my time. And in time, she took her pleasure.

But it would not be enough to send her to bliss.

If she wanted that, she'd have to ask.

And I could hump her gorgeous ass for all eternity. Suffer with her.

The sun rose, and though her hips had begun to squirm in an attempt to get the friction her body desperately needed for release, she didn't ask.

So I showed mercy.

Slinking down her body, taking her hips in hand, I brought her swollen sex to my mouth and let her experience the art of eating pussy from another angle. One that let me delve my tongue deep, tease her anus. Flatter her clit with praise.

Screaming my name, she came.

A thing she had not even dared the night before.

Progress indeed!

Progress enough that I crossed the threshold with questionable permission, while she was dazed and assumed the perfect position to end this standoff.

Cockhead to slit, I pressed in.

Knowing I was too big in my true form, I took astounding care and sealed our fates with the truth of the matter.

"You called for me." At the perfect shell of her ear, I growled like the animal I was.

And gained another inch.

Permission enough.

Battle won.

It took almost an hour, a great deal of caresses, incessant circles over her clit, and compliments in every language man had ever spoken before I was fully seated in my wife's cunt.

In which time she had come apart on my cock four times, unable to resist pushing back against my intrusion and impaling herself as her channel sucked at my meat and adapted.

My sword was sheathed in perfect, tight fire.

The beauty of her pussy stretched around me. Sound and pulsating. Wet and welcoming.

The very first time I had taken my wife in ages long past, I'd had to oil my cock to facilitate a struggling penetration. Now, she was wet for me. Now, I was home.

"I love you." I said it a thousand times or more, felt it where my soul had been returned to me.

I wept, rocking my hips to seek that perfect embrace over and over.

Exactly how I desired to spend the rest of eternity.

Yet ultimate bliss could not be held at bay forever. My darling, overwrought, screamed into her pillow, clenched down around my member in a series of rippling tugs, physically demanding seed as her orgasm blossomed.

As her eternal slave, I could do nothing but comply.

She drained me dry, my roar shaking the walls.

When it was over, when I carefully pulled out in smiling satisfaction to see the sticky cream flooding her contracting channel, I knew a child would be made before the year was out… and that she would love me for it.

11

PEARL

It was over…

Every part of me oversensitive to the point I would combust if he attempted to pleasure me further. Hand pressed between my legs, I turned my back to the beast and stared at the wall—the plaster now cracked from the monstrous howl that had set the building to quake.

"There is no need to hold my seed in, my soul." Settling at my back, draping my body in that wing, it snuggled me. "I can give you more any time you wish. Rest with me for a short while, then I have a surprise! The first of many."

I couldn't imagine what could possibly be more surprising than what had just taken place.

"I feel as if a feast is in order to celebrate! Oh, sweet wife, you have given me such a gift that I cannot even fathom how to adore you best."

Given him?

Wife?

Was I now more the wife he believed me to be because I had let him rut me? Because I had shamelessly shut my eyes to the monster on my back and abandoned all reason.

"I won't always be ugly to you. A pure heart like yours will learn to love me for who I am and not the shell I wear." He kissed my neck, lightly scraping his fangs on my flesh. "I know this, because I once was beautiful, and you didn't love me for my beauty as all other women did. It was my spirit that drew you. Even if I were to wear that form again, beauty would never earn you."

When his bite punched through delicate tissue, a great jaw holding my throat, it wasn't pain I felt.

Only a sip was taken.

"To drink from the throat of another immortal is only done between those who are excessively intimate. It's practically our only taboo." Licking at the twin wounds that were already closing, he hummed out a great contented breath. "My throat is yours."

"I don't want your throat." I don't know why I said it, or why my voice held such vindictiveness. But I felt a great need to hurt the beast. Or hurt myself.

Rolling me to my back so he might make me look at him—or perhaps he wanted to look at me, my body was planted between two massive arms. "Once upon a time, you wanted my throat. Held a knife to it on our wedding night, would have slit me ear to ear had you the talent for it. I've often wondered if it was your magic that made us what we became, our oath, or my will alone. But blood? It always comes back to blood."

And if I had that knife now?

Would I take the throat he bared?

Try to kill the monster who had pulled me from my grave, cared for me, clothed me, fed me, fucked me? Twice damned was I, meeting his gaze and hazarding a question. "Why did I try to slit your throat?"

"You didn't want to be queen, though you were born the jewel of the kingdom." The beast looked lost in memory. "Raised in seclusion, you'd never interacted with any man beyond our father. Who spoiled you to a fault and loved you more than our sisters. And it was not just for your great beauty. It was for your tenacity and will to have your way. The greatest queens never hunger for the duty. They must be tamed. When you tried to kill me, I'd never been more in love."

"That sounds sick." Truly sickening.

Careful of his talons, Vladislov cupped my cheek. "There is nothing sick in love. You found joy in freedom, in my body, in my obsession, and even in your duty."

Joy might not be the emotion I would equate with what had just happened. Unable to decide if I had tricked myself, or he had fooled me, or if I really was a whore willing to take the cock of a demon having been tempted with little more than a tickle between the legs.

What bothered me most was that if he had asked me, I would not have said yes.

"Which is precisely why I didn't ask. You called out my

name in need, and I gave you what you *needed.* It was an ask enough."

How he could play at words, and actions, and move me at his whim…

Laughing, the beast contradicted my concerns. "It's the other way around. I cannot think but for you. Watch your every minuscule movement, listen to your heartbeat, see you fed, clothed, cared for… bedded. I am your slave."

"Then I order you to leave me forever."

Laughter turned to so pained an expression my heart ached to see it.

He spilled a tear. "I would not go, because you are incapable of such cruelty."

"I'm sorry." Why I said it, or why I meant it, I could not even begin to contemplate.

Boxed in by his arms, arms that were muscular in ways no creature should be, solemn as the grave, Vladislov said, "I would make love to you again, face to face, before we bathe. I want you to see me when you feel beauty, and know that I see you."

My ardor had cooled, yet the seed between my legs was slippery enough for seeking fingers to play in when his knee moved to separate my thighs.

With an arch, my body refused the command of my thoughts. And though I fought to keep my legs closed, it did not take long for his weight to settle between them. The first thrust stole my breath, dragging over something inside me that drew out a shameless moan.

Just as he had commanded, I witnessed his pleasure as he

took my body. Eyes roving from bouncing breasts, to my parted lips. And where his eyes went, his mouth followed.

Tongue twisting with mine, fingers dancing over my breasts, I submitted as a wife submits to her husband. Locking my ankles at his back, taking all he would give me.

As Adam took Eve in the garden.

Hideous as he was, every bit of me burned. But not with shame as it should have. With passion when I was given what my corrupted body craved. My world turned to pure white when he sliced his throat and set it to my mouth.

I drank as he filled me, coming so violently that had he been human, I would have accidentally killed him.

In the panting aftermath, whatever surprise he had planned was forgotten. The night spent entwined while I came apart under beating wings, a snake-like tongue, and eyes full of adoration that moved me.

And frightened me in equal measure.

The sun rose, the sun set, over and over while I learned the ways of pleasure. It was not until I was straddling the beasts, riding at my pace while I sang out my release that I was shown mercy.

Exhaustion left me crumpled on his chest, sleep winning over even as I felt more of his seed pumping inside me.

I dreamed of Jesus in the desert and forty days of a dark winged angel trying to talk sense into his son.

12

VLADISLOV

The bloodbath was not a hit with my bride. And in all fairness to my intention, was unfair in itself. After all, I offered candlelight, flowers in abundance, snacks… a cake! But she would not put a toe in the tub.

Pearl even tried to yank her hand from where our fingers were entwined… as if I'd let her run off and possibly hurt herself in an unwarranted panic.

Human in form and lighthearted in tone, I attempted to smooth ruffled feathers. "The mass murder playing in such detail through you mind did not take place. Every drop was donated. All immortal, all happy to indulge their queen in a fun… let's call it… *tradition.*"

Which was not exactly dishonest. Those immortals drained for the event really were happy to be thrown a snack so I might plump my withered prisoners up again for future bath time fun. But the miniscule details were unimportant. "It's the perfect temperature, enhanced with essential oils, full of petals to slip against your skin, and the finest salts to soothe your aches. Best to get in now before it begins to curdle. Do you want our people to be sad to hear their gift was wasted?"

But she was not budging no matter how gentle my voice or touch.

The expression of horror on her face was not melting into gratitude.

I could work on that. Lips stretching in a smile that displayed the fangs Vampirekind was known for, I reached for a golden dome, sweeping it from a beautiful offering with a silly flourish. "I have chocolate for you. Parisian delicacies," the words sung as I tempted her with a bite of sweets.

Though her nostrils flared at the aroma of so much decadence, under her breath, she muttered, "This is sin."

My own muttering was far less tragic and far more eye-rollingly annoyed. "Wasting it might be."

Okay, so this was the third tub I had filled over the last few days of rigorously fucking my bride. But what had swirled down the drain was not wasted *exactly*. It was a practice run to make sure that *this* tub was perfect. Even the candlelight had been arranged just so to play off the quickly setting sun. A pretty stage, a room inviting my timid bride to embrace the heritage that had been denied her.

What point was there in hesitation? My Pearl just needed a little mental nudge. "Humans have bathed in milk for as long as I have walked this earth. Does milk not come from animals? Yes, it's generally used for sustenance, but it also softens the skin and is enjoyed as a luxury. You ingest immortal blood—" I gave her a roguish wink, growing hard just at the thought of it. "—and we both know I'm your favorite snack. The only difference here is perspective."

Opening her mouth as if to argue, like a true gentleman, I put a finger to her lips and saved her the trouble. "I'm right, of course. So in you go."

Where my touch traced her kiss-swollen lips, she frowned. "I wouldn't want to take a bath in milk either. I'd hardly had the funds to taste it before you woke me up from the nightmare." Visibly shuddering, my darling bride grimaced, because somewhere deep in her very scarred psyche, a bubble of awfulness I refused to pop grew. It grew, and it teased at the scars Darius had dug into her mind.

Everything that had been done, taken, rewritten, molded, concealed… it was in there. It clamored. Someday, it would make her a monster in need of checking. Which was why my gentle Pearl needed taming and self-acceptance.

I'd make her a God… and she might make the whole world pay for it.

Maybe the world deserved what they created—Vampire, human, Daywalker, and all the other monsters creeping along the earth's crust.

Pupils dilating, Pearl stared down at the warmed tub. "I can hear the screams."

Yes, she could. But they were her screams. Buried and in need of exorcism. Hand to my heart, I set my obsessive, complete, unbreakable love plain on my face. "On my honor, no contributor to your warm bath died."

There was really no point in bringing up the human livestock that had gone into fattening up the donating immortals… considering the unraveling mental state before me. Their blood was not technically in the tub, so it didn't matter. The effort, the two previously drained tubs, and the volume—a cool hundred humans had most likely been eaten. But they would have been eaten anyway. Just like cows were butchered in messy slaughterhouses en masse.

Pools of scintillating immortal blood, romantic moments of this nature, were not produced from mass hunting of monkeys on the streets. The humans involved had been taken from pens all over my worldwide domain. And not even the good bloodlines. Those fed to immortal prisoners were waste product. Hardly edible.

But again, that was neither here nor there. Overthinking wasn't going to get my bride into that tub. The racing echo of her heart, the ripples of her mind, the little twitches all over her body—nothing that night was going to get her into the tub.

I had misstepped.

I had conquered nations.

Therefore, I knew every mistake held the seed of an even better victory. "Pearl, I'm sorry."

"Why?" How confused she was. How disarmed. Horrified, dangerous, full of my strength and learning her own. The very essence of her trapped in the mind of a stunted seventy-year-old. An infant, considering our longevity.

A survivor whose fangs would grow back sharper than they had ever been before.

It wasn't her hesitation or the newness of the situation. It was a fundamental, lingering complaint. My Pearl was offended, yet she didn't comprehend why. My vicious bride reborn was angry, but not with me.

Even in that moment, her mind wrestled with the joy she found in our physical pleasure. The pain Darius had stripped from her. The pain he had left her with.

The endless slog of her life until, in a state of terror, she had finally found other beings like her.

The unfairness.

A bath of blood.

A cracked porcelain sink she had vomited crimson poison into after ripping the throat of Chadwick Parker on that snowy night in 1927. The unfairness of the world and the fact that a thing she regarded as the antithesis of the Christian God was the only creature to show her kindness.

Her mind screamed. Her face became that of stone.

The impassive visage of an angry queen.

"I won't go in your tub." What a voice she could wield when she dug it out.

What a woman.

She challenged me. Me? A creature of her worst nightmares. Her bridegroom. A bat of my eyelash and she would implode.

The things Darius had done to her were nothing compared to a true imagination.

There were vast, innumerable, disturbing, elegant reasons

I was feared the world over. Why I had earned so many monikers.

There were reasons I was also beloved. *The morning star*. The most beautiful creature to walk the earth.

The most hideous.

Running my fingertips through her tousled hair, my heart aching with love, I gave her truth. "I can have the building burned to the ground so your eyes might never lay upon this room again."

Waspish, she threw off my touch and crossed her arms under perfect breasts. Plumped, delicious skin I might never have my fill of was distracting beyond belief. But I kept my eyes on hers, even as she challenged, "You can't burn a building down because I don't like something in it!"

"Of course I can." Seriously, starting fires was really easy. The amount of cities I had sacked....

I mean, really. If mankind had any concept of the civilizations I had crushed into powder—metallurgy, plumbing, technology—the entirety of documented history would be upended.

But it all had come too soon when the rest of the world was still picking fleas from their hair.

And the best minds were welcome to join my family. To become my children, of a sort.

Da Vinci still painted hidden works when he was not unraveling astrophysics. The *human* lives that child of mine has suffered. Because living as a human is suffering. Especially to the brilliant.

"Vladislov"—had she just spoken my name?—"I

dreamed of your time in the desert. He warned you. You warned him. Neither father nor son listened."

Taking her chin in my hand, struggling to remain human in appearance when I was so deeply affected, I said, "The tub, Pearl. We can talk of my indiscretion while I was awaiting your rebirth later."

"Would he hate me?" And the question was bare to me—I could see it plain as moonlight. Would he hate her for what had been done to her?

"He will love you." Though it had to be said, "You may not love your Jesus in return. In fact, you may resent him. So much hinges on the legacy he never comprehended, and I warned the boy. The second coming will never be what humans have imagined. It won't be at all. He is unloved no matter how he represents himself through the ages. "Even now, he stands in the American Senate proffering love and change. Jewish, ethical, strongly beloved by a loud minority, threatened and quashed by a more powerful majority. No different than his early years."

"You said he was in Brazil?"

"Your daughter is getting married to the soldier who ripped your fangs from your skull tomorrow evening." My granddaughter, my stepdaughter—my weak yet stronger than many, oddly bound offspring. "She too is now free of Darius. Would you like to witness her find peace?"

So much regret passed through the mind before me. Flashes of how Pearl had seen humans hold and nurse their babies. How she had no memory of feeling kicks behind her ribs or suckling. How she had been ripped to shreds.

“As the tub is getting cold, might I suggest you offer the experience to a friend? We’ll go out to dinner. You find a place on the Yelp. Any city, and we can be there in a flash.”

“What would someone wear to a wedding these days? Pants?” How she despised trousers on women! It was endearingly adorable. But, those were tears gathering in her eyes.

Pearl had not yet accepted the facts. “You could show up naked if you wanted to. You’re my queen.”

The idea of a child was still spinning in her mind. Proving I was once again right for seeking to impregnate her for her own joy.

Wide, wet eyes met mine. “If I took the bath, would she like me more?”

This desire for acceptance was going to be a problem. One I had overcome with countless generations of offspring. “No.”

Pearl’s heart slowed. “I shouldn’t go.”

Tired of pretending the human form, my arms grew black as pitch. I displayed all of me. Every last, hideous bit.

Soothing my wife, claws delicate as the traced skin, I said, “She doesn’t know who you are. You will arrive as only my guest. She needs that now Later, she will need you.”

13

PEARL

I'd never attended a wedding, though I had seen some in films and read about them in the papers. Not that I had much basis for comparison, but it would seem vampire weddings were not much different than human ones at first glance. Formally dressed and greeting one another with elaborate displays of affection, guests chatted. Other guests avoided one another, offering their counterpart little more than an icy stare.

It reminded me of the Supper Club: the cliques, the grandeur. The affection and the cruelty.

Vladislov had seen me lavishly dressed. Blood-red so bright it seemed garish to my tastes. I stood out like a sore thumb in a gown fit for a queen. Enough jewels hung from my throat and dripped from my ears that the weight of them was uncomfortable.

The choker must have been ancient, the style odd and the

metal imperfect. It circled my throat, from collarbones to jaw. It pinched.

But how he had smiled to drape them around my neck, explaining, "Our kind does not expose the throat at public events. It's considered… uncultured. Though, if I might say so, the true motivation behind the collars is fear. The jewels are armor. The only bare throat you will see tonight is that of the bride and groom. If someone should expose themselves to you, do not drink."

No soul had done such a thing at Vladislov's party. "Why would someone do that?"

"Because you smell of sunshine, and all Vampires desire the use of a Daywalker. Stay by my side," he teased, "or one of the less wise might just try to snatch you away."

I was going to be sick. Already nervous to see the child I'd never known—one I had been warned would dislike me at first glance. One I was not to speak with, not on her day. After all, I had been reminded over and over that we had eternity to thaw the ice.

These instructions, given by a monster in the shape of a man, were not for Jade's benefit. They were for mine. Vladislov didn't want to see me hurt by what would be obvious and public rejection. I didn't need to read his mind to grasp that fact.

From the way he spoke as he decked me in jewels that could buy kingdoms, I also wondered if he cared for Jade at all.

As if to defend himself from my thoughts, his fingers stilled, and his eyes turned up to mine. "I find your daughter, my granddaughter… refreshing. Never forget that I gave her a kingdom, though she is difficult and looks too much like her father."

Which made me all the more nervous. Darius was my living nightmare.

A light peck landed on my lips. "She has your eyes, though the blue turned red when I gave her the throne. Look there and you will see yourself. She has your resilience and your strength. Darius was always a weakling in a strong body."

Red eyes? Why was I even going to this wedding?

"She's your daughter. She's getting married. You will regret it for eternity if you miss it out of unfounded shyness. Think in eons, Pearl. One day, you will be her friend. One day, she will be grateful you made the effort. That day will not be today. Again, do not speak to her."

"And her fiancé?" I remembered the pale-haired angel who'd torn out my fangs, broken my jaw, and dumped me at the foot of a despotic evil.

"Malcom knows that if he approaches, I will kill him. Which would ruin the wedding." He said it so lightly, as if so wild a declaration it were nothing at all.

"My daughter loves him. You told me he led you to where I…." I didn't have a name for that room or for what had happened in it. "I'm not so stupid that I don't understand why he—"

Echoing my earlier thoughts, Vladislov showed enough temper that his whole form twitched as if he fought to maintain it. "Ripped out your beautiful fangs, broke your jaw, and delivered you to Darius so he might play his games with you when you should have been immediately brought to me?"

I could already see the seams stretching, patting his chest as if to hold back the beast and its wings. "You'll rip your fine clothes if you don't take a deep breath."

My warning only earned me a poke on the forehead. "If you could only see the mess in here. I tolerate Malcom out of some misplaced fondness for Jade. I tolerate him, because he was loyal. But I can clearly see what he did to my wife. How terrified you were, the pain it caused. Why should I care if it was done in service?"

"You don't get to have an opinion about it. That's why. It was done to me." Had those words just come out of my mouth?

"Consider me chastened." And tamed. He went from smoking devil to playful puppy. Kissing my lips in little nips and calling me stunning as his fingers found my nipple through the daringly low cut bodice of my ridiculous dress. "Before we go, can I fuck you on the counter? In this dress, just like this? I want to know I'm leaking down your leg while peasants approach and fools think to negotiate."

It was less of a question and more of a prayer. Already, he'd begun bunching up my voluminous skirt, the edge of the dressing room's marble counter at my thighs. Moving faster than my eyes might register, he pulled himself from his trousers, uncaring that his pants fell to his ankles, and was in.

In me.

The pinching fetters of so many stones around my neck,

the initial cramp when something too big filled a place that seemed incessantly wet. I found bliss.

He fucked me. Right there as I clung and gasped.

Coming too soon, earning cruel laughter from an incessantly hard bull, I braced. Because there was always more.

So much so that we were late for the gathering. My hair, once beautiful, was a half-fallen mess. And yes, he was dripping down my leg.

Not yet recovered from the bending world that went from dressing room to riverside wedding, I stumbled. I clung.

I knew I was ridiculous.

Many approached my guardian.

"Husband," he whispered at my ear, giving it a lick despite the audience of immortals.

Languages were spoken that I didn't know. Addresses were made, even to me—polite, tolerant nods in many cases. Wide-mouthed grins in others.

Fangs were on full display, glittering in the moonlight.

Though when I forced a smile in reply, I saw how vampire eyes went straight to my stumped incisors. There were looks of pity, looks of disgust.

"The groom tore them out himself!" Vladislov chuckled, though the very tone of his laughter was menace.

Under my breath, I tried to stop him. "Vladislov!"

"She asked me not to kill him." My less than delightful companion eased nearer the latest supplicant. "But she never asked me to spare you. Leave."

A man I hardly noticed may as well have pissed himself, vanishing into the night as if he'd never been there.

Could this be more uncomfortable? "That wasn't funny."

"He looked at your throat." As if that was explanation enough.

Like a king approaching his throne, Vladislov entered the fray, literally dragging me into the masses. Tripping over my skirt, one arm flailed, and a spray of glowing, white flowers began to fall.

Caught before the crash by Maya. Who gave me a wink before a goddess in the flesh moved back into the crowd. I didn't have a chance to say thank you.

"I've known Maya for thousands of years. Believe me when I say, she is genuine, unforgiving, and willing to spend her time getting to know you. That is rare." With a pout on his lips, my face red and posture shrinking, I heard him add, "I suspect you will be fast friends and that I will be very jealous."

"Can you please stop? Just stop, Vlad!"

He didn't stop, but all around us did. It was as if time froze, the stillness of all in attendance. A mercenary indrawn breath to see what would happen next.

"For you, my bride, anything." Leaning down to press a kiss to my cheek, he added, "I'm sorry."

Everyone turned my way. A chilling unison of movement. A sea of people, of costume, of fanfare. Of years and years and years of life. This was not an event for the unimportant; even naïve as I was, I grasped that. And all of them were staring at me.

With a smile, Vladislov wrapped his arm around me and

addressed the mob. “My bride’s name is Pearl. Be respectful.”

Cocked heads, low spoken greetings, far too much interest.

But Vladislov was on to the next thing. Snapping his fingers for a tray of snacks to be delivered by a beautiful woman dressed like a sacrifice for the gods.

Smiling, eyes downcast, she displayed what had been prepared for the humans in attendance as she described the offerings. And that is when I realized there was a clear divide between immortal and mortal.

Some came on the arms of lovers. Most came to serve.

Every last one of them was stunning.

Such as this woman, her neck marked from bites. Her wrists, her arms. Her exposed thighs. “I am of Grecian stock. My line has been fostered by Ivan. O negative, if it suits your taste.”

Her plate of food was for the human pets, and her body was for the guests.

And she was happy. I had faced enough smiles serving ungrateful men and women to know the difference.

“Ah, Cassandra. Never could I forget you.” He popped a savory bit of deliciousness between my slack lips, taking up the beauty’s arm. “I will enjoy this.”

Chewing, cheeks puffed from too large a bite, I could not respond. Instead, I watched her moan when my lover pierced her glowing skin.

He sipped.

And I hated seeing it with every fiber of my flawed being.

Before I might stop the hiss, it came from my mouth. Automatic, utterly embarrassed, my hands covered my crimson lips. I knew mortification.

And I worked to justify all of it. Of course he ate. I ate. We all ate.

But I had never seen him partake.

Had I not refused the bath of immortal blood? Yet here I was acting like a monster.

And Vladislov drank deeper.

He drank until the poor girl swooned. Until I put my hand to his bicep and asked him to let her go.

Others came to cart her off, yet her pretty figure was soon replaced. Other immortals taking a sip of the next beauty offered as a snack to the guests.

There was no need to speak of how embarrassed, confused, horrified, enticed I was.

It was so much so that I took a glass of wine from a passing human's tray. He too was dressed as an offering and marked with the wounds of the vampire's trade.

Drinking too fast, I coughed, spilled red wine on a red dress… and knew I was a fool.

"You're charming when you're jealous."

My lip shook as I cut a glance to my right, to my tormentor. In that moment, I saw in him the window I had so desired, so needed, in my past. I saw something worth working for. And I had no idea what to make of myself or these feelings.

My thighs were already smeared in the watery aftermath of our passion. A daughter I did not remember and knew would hate me was soon to arrive. My hair was a mess, my throat itched under the collar, and I was—

Vladislov, snarled. “Why must that boy try me so?”

Boy? I looked up and saw an old man. Sporting a paunch and a threadbare sweater, regularness moved through perfection. Cut through it, more like. The sea parted.

“Erev tov, Father. This must be Pearl.”

14

PEARL

The old man smiled in the kind way I'd seen grandfathers smile at children. A calm gesture, a patient one that held wisdom and lacked… fangs. Because I could sense that he was like me, that the sharpness of what set us apart from both human and vampire was a burden. That he worked to embrace his nature yet deny his hunger.

That he understood me. That he felt compassion for a stranger.

Another Daywalker.

I wasn't alone. Such knowledge gave me a profound sense of joy and left me reeling. "You're like me!"

My companion scoffed. "He's nothing like you. The boy is an impudent pain in my ass."

Gesturing at the old man's informal clothing, rude, and clearly annoyed, Vladislov sneered. "What were you thinking arriving in such a state? As Darius was my offspring, and Jade his daughter, you are a clear blood relation. Yet you show up to your queen's wedding dressed like a beggar… wearing that face?"

A face lined by years yet still somehow fresh.

With a peacemaking nod, the stranger replied, "No insult was intended."

Vladislov ground his teeth, leaving the muscles in his jaw jumping. "Your throat is uncovered."

The old man sighed. "As my father is failing to make an introduction, allow me. My given name is Yeshua. It's a pleasure to meet you, Pearl." He held out a hand so I might shake it. The first being at the party aside from Vladislov who dared touch me.

I did not take his hand, not when I could feel how Vladislov seethed. Instead, I offered a polite, "Hello."

Vladislov did not move his body in front of me, but it was as if he intended to shield me all the same. "You were warned never to approach her without permission."

But it was as if the incensed monster at my side had never spoken. The old man's conversation was only for me. "He's written to me about you, countless emails detailing your history. I feel as if I know you."

What?

Outright exasperation was met with equal parts boredom when Vladislov countered, "Countless? You always were one for drama. There have been seventy-eight emails precisely. How many times must I lecture you on the importance of accuracy?"

Though I had denied the old man's hand, he placed his on my shoulder. "It wasn't done to invade your privacy. It was done to document a monumental occurrence. You see, Pearl, the pages recount your life and all the ways in which the consequences of my existence complicated it."

His hand was warm, not the brimstone touch of the beast who held me to his side, arm around my waist, and palm open on my belly. If Vladislov was fire, this man was sunlight.

If Vladislov was beautifully hideous, that old man was painstakingly ordinary.

And I was extremely confused. "I don't understand."

Did the man look embarrassed? It was so hard to tell when his gaze was so deep. "I've been told my father sends you a priest each day for a private mass and confession."

He used to.

I had not seen a holy man since Vladislov had first penetrated me, nor had I asked for one. In that moment, it dawned on me that I had forgotten. Where was my rosary? Had I forgotten to bring it to a wedding?

Before I fell from the knife edge of nerves into hysterics, Vladislov spoke softly at my ear. "Your rosary is in my pocket, my soul. You may have it in this moment if you wish."

What I wished was to know why the man before me seemed as if he felt grief at the mention of the beads I used to pray. Instead, I took a deep breath and focused on the fact that this was my daughter's wedding and I had already made enough mistakes. "What is an email?"

The old man shook off his gloom, responding with a kind smile. “An electronic letter, typed instead of written by hand. As my father refuses to communicate with me in any other way, we rarely exchange words unless they are in written form. He believes it to be a lesson on the power of truth in the written word over the spoken one. But if you could see the things he’s written, you’d understand that he lacks the ability to tell the truth in even the most basic of exchanges. Just because it’s been written down does not make it true. Read any newspaper these days and you’ll find it's just as easy to lie with the pen as it is with the tongue.”

With his free hand, Vladislov physically removed the old man’s touch from my shoulder. “You are not amusing me, child.”

For a brief moment, the old man glanced at my companion—an expression of weariness, of deep concern aging his face all the more. “Heaven knows it will be many ages before reconciliation between us is possible, especially after I tell her the truth. But it is good to see you.”

Dry laughter preceded Vladislov’s threat. “Son, I could end you with a thought. And I’m very *tempted*.”

As if they shared a private, dark joke, the old man chuckled. He chuckled as if he was not only fearless, but the more powerful between them. “I am the only thing you ever created that is good. You have no more power to end me than I have the power to end you.”

When I had been dragged into Darius’ Cathedral, the world moved around me as it did now. I knew the son Vladislov claimed to have fathered. I remembered the dreams where they fought in the desert. But that man was not this man. Just like the angel's form Vladislov had taken was not the monster I knew him to be.

Turning his face from his offspring, Vladislov looked down at me. "You're frightening her."

I did not return the glance. How could I? How could I look away from what might be standing before me? How could I reconcile an immediate and unintentional overflow of love and resentment? "Jesus?"

Brown eyes soft, voice like cool water on burnt skin, Vladislov's son said, "My father will work to convince you that there is no God. It will drive his every move to draw your love from Grace so he might drink it down himself. Do not listen to him. God is in all of us, even in him. God is the love we feel for one another and the forgiveness we strive to extend. Compassion, patience, acceptance, that is the face of God."

Lips came to my ear, but not those of the man speaking to me. They were the same lips that had been all over my body for days on end. "Do you see the flaw in his argument, my soul?" Vladislov stood taller, arm around me as he mocked his offspring. "Boy, it is true a priest was delivered every day to satisfy my bride's indoctrinated need to confess her sins and ask for repentance. You see as clearly as I that she is as innocent as any might be. What sins might she carry? Yet she weeps. Did you hear her prayers? Did the *Father* you prefer to me deliver her? No, son, that figment of your imagination did not. I did. Just as I delivered you."

The old man did not rise to the bait. Instead, he smiled at

me, gracious and calm. “It was a pleasure meeting you, Pearl. I hope, in time, we might get to know one another.”

Groaning as if this conversation taxed him down to his bones, Vladislov said, “You may stay. But change out of those rags and wear the face I gave you.”

It seemed a lighthearted exchange. “I will, Father, if you wear the face God gave you.”

The nightmare at my side smiled, his bone-cracking hold on me easing. “And this is where I reply that every face is my face. To which you will say ‘Exactly, and they all came from God.’ And we will go back and forth for eternity yet get nowhere. How many rocks must I roll away after you’ve been mauled by the very cattle you seek to *enlighten* before you come to see the world for what it is?”

“I see it clearly, and I worry for those who live in your earthly kingdom.” The old man’s attention turned to where I clung to Vladislov’s arm. “Though, if she really is your soul, there may be hope for all of us yet.”

Though he turned to leave, the old man was interrupted by a monster thoroughly up to no good. “One more thing, son. There has been some debate between sweet Pearl and I. Your accidental religion with its myriad rituals has sparked some confusion. So you are best to end the debate. Is she or is she not my wife?”

Everything in the old man’s expression seemed to say he had strong thoughts on the matter. “In the Jewish faith to which I was born and to which I adhere, the Zohar claims that a husband and wife are one soul, separated only through their descent to this world. When they are married, they are reunited again. You claim to be reunited. It would follow that she is your wife. No one who has seen my father and still became of one flesh with such a beast could be anything but wife."

I might have had wine spilt on my dress. My hair might have been embarrassingly mussed. I might have been uneducated and naive. But at no time in my years had I not recognized an insult. "Excuse me?"

Vladislov's fingers on my belly fluttered one by one, as if delighted. "She's offended, but she doesn't know why. How charming."

I was offended. I was baffled. And I was being discussed as if I were a sheep and they were wolf and shepherd. All because I could not find the words to ask what my brain clamored to know. Was this real? Was this some trick? Was I speaking with Jesus? How did he only know me from the thing called email? Why must I perpetually be the butt of some joke? Why had God forsaken me? Why had Darius been allowed to toy with me? Of all the saviors that might have come to save the sinner, why had it been Vladislov who carried me out of the dark?

As if he could see straight down to my soul, as if he could pick through the mess of my thoughts, the old man said, "God makes us what we are, tempers the great by terrible trials. Had your life been anything other than it was, I could not hope that you are indeed my father's soul. Which is why I fear that if you will not take him as your husband, this world will be doomed before all those living in it have a chance to find the peace of God."

First, there was a vicious chuckle. Then, Vladislov smacked his lips. He smacked his lips and then bent me back over his arm, thrusting his tongue into my mouth in a salacious kiss that stole my air. He even dared tear into my bodice to clutch a breast as if he intended to fuck me right there in the middle of the crowd. It wasn't until I was breathless from fighting and dared bite him that he drew back, laughing as if the world were wonderful and my flustered state truly divine.

Jesus was gone. The party moved around us as if nothing untoward had taken place.

And I? I looked back at a monster who mouthed the word "wife" before he pulled together my dress.

It was then I saw her. The bride dressed in white, who unlike the rest of the crowd seemed to be paying close attention to whatever had just passed. Our eyes met. Mine blue, hers glowing red.

She sneered.

And I loved her for it.

I loved her as if she'd always been mine.

15

PEARL

Over the course of my years, and especially of late, I imagined many things—about my future, about a world I longed for yet retreated from… about my unknown child. Thoughts of her unsettled me the most.

My baby could have been anything, grand or monstrous. One look at her might have cut out my heart for a multitude of reasons that made me unworthy of such a gift. Not once in my life had I ever considered that I'd birth a child. I was cursed. I was sickly. Yet I had. Not that I remembered it, or her, or why, or how, or anything. I'd even tried to, finding only a black hole in my thoughts. And that hole was far too easy to fall into and so much more difficult to climb free of.

Entire pieces of my brain had just been yanked out and filled up with sawdust.

The few memories of Darius I had were enough. Never

did I want to know the rest. But I burned with something deeper than anger, a constant pinprick behind my eyes.

An infant's creation, her time in my body, her birth had been torn out of my mind. A person I was entirely blind to, who I would have never known existed had Vladislov not told me she walked the earth, had no idea I was her mother.

A disturbing, worrying, guilt-inducing horror I'd have to answer to God for. At the feet of my Lord, I'd have to explain my misgivings and disgust. I'd have to confess that the first mention of her did not bring me joy. It brought me horror.

I'd have to ask forgiveness for the sin of bitterness-laced fascination. That I wasn't at her wedding for her benefit, but for purely selfish longing to know *who I was*.

A sick curiosity wrapped up in pretend obligation to a fully grown woman.

Yet, one look at the woman my baby had become… and every last pang of disgust and uncertainty blew from my skin like unsettled dust when a tomb was disturbed.

I grew lighter. I knew that somewhere stuck in the untouchable parts of my memory, I had felt that child move inside me and loved her.

Had her first cries been beautiful? Had she nursed from my breast after I delivered her into the world?

I bet her head had smelled divine.

What had she looked like as a baby?

"You want to know, so I will tell you this." Softly at my ear, a creature who could see into my darkness whispered, "True to form, he cut her out when your condition became inconvenient. Though you fought him despite your entrails spilling everywhere, Darius never allowed you the honor of holding her in your arms. Not after she'd drawn your attention away from him once too often. The squalling, naked, and bloody babe was delivered to the man Jade will wed tonight. You were never allowed to love her."

But I did love her. Right in that moment, I loved her as I have never loved anything. And it moved me to cuddle closer to the beast whispering ugly secrets in my ear—to lean on him as if there was nothing more natural than sharing the moment my heart felt whole for the first time in all my existence.

As a bride, my baby was a vision.

Perfect in every conceivable way in my eyes. Even the obvious evil of her.

That was how God had designed her, and God was flawless.

The arm around me grew all the more reassuring. "And if you follow that logic, then you must also concede that you are perfect. I'll even concede that this might be the only topic upon which your false God and I agree."

God loves his children just as they are. God is love. The immeasurable love I had for my child was the love God had for all things. Even Vladislov.

Even Darius.

Who had harmed my child by taking her from me.

A thought that led to a complicated resentment it was not the time to indulge in. My eyes, my devotion, were for one being only that night.

Jade, her limbs draped in exquisite white lace as she observed me in return.

I knew that high forehead, the more feminine lines of a jaw from my worst nightmares. The aristocratic nose. She was her father made female.

The vivid red of her lips oddly highlighted eyes that burned of hellfire.

There was nothing in that regal woman that had the look of me.

"You're wrong. Her eyes, my soul. They *were* the same shade as yours." Pulling me before his body so I might rest against his chest and enjoy a better view, Vladislov wrapped me tight in his embrace, causing the woman to cock a sculpted dark eyebrow. "Blue as the burning core of the hottest flame. When the day comes for you to know one another, she will find comfort in recognizing that part of herself in you."

I'd never thought much of my eyes, but I would every day from that night forward. I would look in the mirror and see this child, even if that was all of me she had.

"There are portraits of her from when she was younger. I will have one brought to you before sunrise." I could hear the smile in his voice. "You'll see much more of yourself, all the softness. She hides it now with her paint and sharp tongue, because she believed her humanity a weakness. But you are very much a part of her. As Jade grows in confidence as a queen, she will let go of the idea of being only part of herself and embrace the whole."

Watching me, Jade unconsciously touched elegant fingertips to a ruby encrusted contraption circling her throat. It was similar to mine in the sense that it covered from jaw to collarbone, but far less delicate than the collar around my neck.

Even from a distance, I could tell it made her uncomfortable. That it must chafe and be difficult to move in. Edges of it even appeared sharp, a constant scratch against delicate skin.

Leaning farther into my personal demon's warm embrace, I whispered, "You said her throat would be bare."

I felt him smell my hair, nuzzling into me intimately no matter who darted startled looks in our direction. Positively sentimental, he cooed, "Isn't it romantic? Malcom won't let her take it off, though it clings and annoys. He wants his love to know he's always there and she's always his."

I didn't like that one bit.

"She fights it, believes she hates it. But she's lying to herself. That girl needs the reminder as much as she needs his rule. Jade might be Queen of the Americas, but he is her custodian. And I swear to you, all life on the planet is safer for it. Your daughter is a right bitch when she's in a temper."

Hissing under my breath, I dared break the spell of observation and cut a glance back to the man who insulted my daughter. "Don't say that about her!"

Vladislov chuckled. "She has your fire too. I doubt you realize how fierce you can be. Not one in a billion would dare speak to me as you do. Not even Darius had the balls. That makes you better than him."

I had never been fierce a day in my life. Women were

intended to be meek. Which led to the oddest feeling that I had just been insulted.

Which, of course he knew. He even laughed. "You pretend to be meek, because that is what you believed was expected of you. But you've ripped out more than one throat in your lifetime—you just have to be pushed far enough to snap. You fought your tormentor for your baby. And you're here, in the midst of the most powerful of our kind, staring down a woman who dislikes your presence… because you are her mother and you have every right to do so."

I began to tune out Vladislov's latest soliloquy just as I would tune out my patrons when I walked from table to table offering cigarettes. In that moment, it didn't matter what he thought. All that mattered was my girl.

Who had caught herself touching the collar and pulled her hand away as if mildly embarrassed. Until a man with hair as bright as hers was dark approached and took her in his arms.

"Malcom. You can say his name."

She glowed, leaned into him, forgot about me entirely.

"Jade is an absolute fool for that boy."

Malcom. That boy. Very normal terms for the veritable angel who had beaten me against a brick wall all those years ago, breaking my jaw as he ripped out my fangs. I could still hear him laughing as I wept, that memory more real to me than the horror I imagined Jade's birth to be.

"Shhhh, don't tremble, Pearl." Warmth stroked over my arms, a deep male voice offering comfort. "He is forbidden from so much as glancing in your direction. And rightly concerned that I might change my mind about his continued existence."

My Jade so clearly adored him that should Vladislov dare to harm a pale hair on Malcom's head, I'd be very upset.

Vladislov didn't even try to conceal his irritation. "I know, which is what makes this so unfair to me. How am I supposed to relax when I really want to do unspeakable things but can't because it will upset you? Pity me."

"You're being ridiculous." And oddly cute with the whining. Whining that worked its magic and left me smirking instead of afraid.

Like an eager puppy, Vladislov curled around me. "I promise to behave if you'll give me one kiss."

One kiss, quickly given before he might try to distract me further or delve his hands back into my dress.

Even with the complete lunacy of the situation, it was as if a spark snapped when our mouths met. Chaste yet lingering. When it ended, Vladislov looked down at me, eyes glowing, a soft smile on his lip. "Now, shush. It's beginning."

My daughter and the man who had delivered to a demon for torment because I had broken an unknown law joined hands.

Beautiful side by side, Jade caught up in her husband's eyes. Even the fool I was could see plain as night that nothing existed to her in that moment but him.

If she loved him, so would I.

Behind me, Vladislov muttered, "Ugh, you're far too gracious."

"I forgive him." And it was really that simple.

Malcom, as if he heard our whisperings, let out a pent-up breath. I don't know why I sensed it, but I felt in that moment that he wanted to glance my way, just for a second. Just to acknowledge what seemed like a gift.

"It *was* a gift. His entire bloodline was at stake should you have refused. I had only granted him five years with Jade before the culling might begin. Now I'm in the mood to reconsider."

Lately, it had become simple to forget just who I was with. An ease had grown between us, even laughter. Passion that seemed to rewrite the very fabric I'd been cut from.

It would just slip my mind in tiny moments.

"Five years was generous and only granted because he led me to where Darius had hidden you away. Had I found the memory in his head, had he tried to hide it, an eternity in a tomb was only the beginning of what he might have suffered. But he came to me, he *knew* there was something vital in so small a memory. He knew, because Darius ripped out his heart, so Jade ripped out the heart of her father and put it in the chest of the man she loves. Darius lives in him in a significant way, so rethink your easy forgiveness in a sentimental moment."

"No. And you cannot tempt me from my decision either, demon."

"Fine." A brisk, irritated *fine*.

"And you will allow him to look at me, and speak to me."

From annoyance to amusement, a snap in temperament from one to the other that kept me on my toes and him *interesting*. "And here you thought to pretend you were meek."

16

VLADISLOV

My will poured over the gathered guests at the wedding party in such a way that Pearl was clueless as to my designs. I deigned who might hear us, who might so much as see her. Each glance she garnered was at my whim for a specific purpose. Whether it was to announce to other females with whom I had shared physical pleasure not to think to proposition me for more. Or to dash the hopes of those who clung to the idea that someday I might return their ardent affection. Or to ordain that this is your goddess and I am her slave. Or so males might know just what would become of them should they brush against her or think to tempt her from me.

And they would. That was the game amongst our kind. They didn't know I wore a plain face for a purpose. I didn't flaunt my riches. Why should I? Their riches were my riches.

The very blood in their veins, regardless of their sire, came from me.

I knew what I had created the first time I was tempted to set my vein to the mouth of a near-dead mortal. It was as if the world had unfolded before me. A scroll accounting family trees, impossibilities, eternity, joy, sorrow, fascination to end my loneliness and agitation at how difficult my children would be.

Those first vampires, my bright-eyed babies, were all dead.

I ended them, one by one, after they had left my flock and begun flocks of their own. Their purpose had been served—propagation. Their egos, titles, the worship of them in temples… it was too much and far too gaudy.

Never did I request temples to my name or call for minions to hear my gospel. Not that temples didn't exist. And it would be an outright lie to claim that several of my names were not called out in vain by those foolish enough to think I might give them power. But unlike my son and his faulty religion, I had been born a living god to my people and understood exactly the flaws with such a path.

Worship led to tragedies like my poor Pearl, her hammering heart, the way she clutched at the rosary I slipped into her fingers—one she didn't even realize she held.

I would be picking apart that knot in her life for eons. On the day when Pearl's eyes truly opened to the way of the world, she would be…

Inconsolable.

My poor darling. Maybe it was a kindness that my son

had filled her head with false ideals. The longer she held to some sort of faith, the more time she would have to see that all along it truly had been *I* fulfilling her needs.

Heart already breaking for her, I pressed a kiss to her hair. She really did smell of sunshine, of goodness. She smelled of all the things that had been torn away from me the day fate dared try to take my soul from me.

Humming in her hair, I confessed an open truth. "I love you."

No change came to her bearing, no stiffness. No fear in her scent.

Progress!

Tenderly swaying as if the pair of us moved to music that was ours and ours alone, I enjoyed this corner of my mind while the rest of me worked.

As I said, I exerted my will on all who stood in attendance.

I whispered in the minds of every last immortal. A cohesive symphony of soft, indomitable rule. A smattering could hear it, the thousand voices moving like mist over thought, or like daggers through resistance. Some could only feel it, taking comfort or distress.

This is mine.

Do not touch.

Look at her and envy.

Look at her and know she can unknowingly decide your fate with little more than a frown.

Look at her and love her.

Look at how I touch her, how I hold her. I would never touch you in such a way.

Look at how she trusts me, how she fits against my body because we are one.

Do you see her mouth? There was no need for paint. Her lips are red from my attention.

Do you smell her cunt? My seed even now drips down her thigh.

I will make her fat with life as she drinks down yours.

Never question me.

Offend her and it won't only be you I unravel thread by thread. I will eat your home, your children, your children's children. You will be erased from the world.

Weep if you wish, but I will never love you.

Prostrate at her feet. Offer your wrists.

Those who bleed the most shall gain my favor. Those who seek to deny my soul her due shall learn the true meaning of regret.

Yes, I had a flair for drama.

True, few in that myriad collection knew just what I *might* be to them.

Rumors of the winged-demon had begun to spread in private whispers between those I wished to suspect.

Those who did not deserve to know me? I plucked the thought straight from their puny brains.

Yet, it should be noted that when working with immortal minds, it takes something more than a soft spoken order to gain the attention of something that has already seen everything and found it wanting.

Those with the skill and the years whispered back to me, carrying on their current conversations as if we were not discussing the very fabric of their existence.

"No insult is intended toward your bride. What excellent taste you have. I've longed for a Daywalker of my own."

Then fuck a human and make your own.

"It's been ages, Vladislov. How do you fair?

Oh, I am well. I am well enough that the world might actually bloom for a space. Well, maybe after one more plague.

"Gifts will be sent."

Indeed they would be. The most honored of the flocks would be bled for my soul's breakfast. And it would be delivered, steaming hot, in jeweled cups. There would be gowns, art, trinkets, land, palaces, secrets....

And those who delivered most would have no true understanding of why they did as they did. Something deep within would niggle at them to produce, that their survival was on the line.

All of this would be kept from Pearl. Well, not the blood. She deserved to sample the fare. But all the chalices, all the wealth, would be tucked away. She would drink from the same crystal to which she had grown accustomed. Live in what she considered quite lavish circumstances, though they were far from what true depravity might offer.

The simple things made her soul sing all the louder.

Caskets of jewels? Those could wait and be playthings for our children. An entire museum of cups crafted just for her lips would be erected in some far off country. To amuse her, I'd take her there some day.

She would laugh to see it.

Gold, diamonds, silver… cups carved from meteors. I could already say for certain that she would still prefer the simple cut crystal.

But few would know such secrets.

Of course, there would be grand soirees in which she might hold a finer cup. But the guest list would be excruciatingly hand-selected. Maya could be trusted with such a task, should I be able to tempt her away from her immediate hunt of those who dared plunder her homelands for what humans considered ancient—such a laughable term—artworks of one of the most interesting and valuable cultures. Nok, they called it these days.

She'd been a wonder, born to a family of wonders.

Such a soft spot I had for wonders. Most of whom were wise enough to take the invitation in my less *structured* flock.

Ach, but Maya was also in love with a human man, which I pointedly ignored and equally found intriguing. She lived with him as a human.

"Work from home."

What a term, what a marvelous construct. Vampires anywhere smart enough to install the proper windows could play human. She had children!

Hid their nutritional *needs* in their food.

That would be an epic disaster the day she came clean that she was older than dirt, wanted in several countries for very grisly murders of art "collectors," and that they would not age past their prime.

The husband… would she change him?

Not that I cared. Really. I didn't. I even wondered if she did it all to amuse me. *That's how self-centered I am.* Am I not a wonder on my own?

She, who fought for the treasures of a people long lost, had seen me in my hideous glory thanks to Pearl's request I show her my true face. And Maya had wanted to know when she too might have such wings.

Adorable.

Unlike the stunning brunette of true Grecian stock daring to glare at me, and who I would unmake before sunrise. One pretty female I had turned thousands of years ago.

She'd had her time in the shadow of my interest.

And she knew better than to allow jealousy and dark thoughts of comparison between herself and my *true* bride. Apphia seethed, demanding her due for servicing me for so long to be thrown over for a skinny daywalker with a mind she could easily see was Swiss cheese.

That's how she thought of it! How *dare* she!

She even dared ask me if I had fallen into madness.

As I stood in the midst of the strongest I had created, as the most powerful of my kind fluttered and gathered like bees about their queen. As my dear bride laid her eyes upon her child for the first time and worked through the complications that arose from such a monumental occasion, I tore the jealous harlot's mind to ribbons.

But with subtlety. After all, this was a wedding, and it would be inappropriate to make a scene.

First, I took away her name, so that she would never recall it. A small thing that would lead to very amusing situations later. A thing she wouldn't notice, not while she was still arguing with me over the sacrifices she made for me. Not when she dared claim that she loved me in a way my Pearl could not.

Nothing, ever, would love me as my soul already did. Pearl wasn't aware of her connection yet, how woven together we'd already become. My son was right in claiming that any who saw my true face and willingly took me into their body in that state and survived the onslaught had to be my equal.

There was a reason I called her my soul. But Pearl was so much more.

If I was a demon, she was an angel.

Maybe in ten thousand years she'd have white, feathered wings and glow with the sunlight running through her veins. Instead of the imps she had imagined, our babies could be fat cherubs.

Wouldn't that be cute?

The creature in my arms spoke, her attention fixed on the couple preparing to link their immortality together. "Vlad, you're growling."

Fine. I was.

Wait? Had she just called me Vlad?

SHE HAD!

I was now Vlad!

A pet name. A term of endearment.

How my heart soared!

Fuck Apphia. Not literally. Eww. Never again.

So what if I had seen that girl's beauty while I awaited the return of my soul? Yes, I had taken the maiden from her family. Sure, we had eaten her parents once she'd woken to the night and made sport of her siblings until any remnant of her human line had ended so her vampire line might begin.

But Apphia had never borne me a child—all the seed sprayed meant for another and dumped because time was monotonous and pricks liked to leak into slits.

I owed her nothing. Not after the palaces, the notoriety, the power, and the distinction she held with our race. Foolish woman.

Who would I make the new queen of the European nations? Maya?

No.

Maya would laugh at the very idea. She was already a queen and needed no nations to prove that point.

Vacuums in power were extremely annoying. "You have no idea how hard it is to get anyone to do their job these days, my love. Really. Can I have another kiss? Please?"

Ah! I had made Pearl laugh. She found my angst amusing, did she? Well, that I could lay on thick. "One kiss, sweet soul. I promise to keep my hands out of your bodice. And yes, I know you are blushing and still embarrassed. But those tits. Come now, darling. They are perfect, and I am incapable of resisting."

She giggled even more. Giggled! Oh, I was so getting laid later. "If I kiss you again, will you please be quiet?"

"Yes." *No.*

Another quick slant of her lips upon mine, her neck craning to meet me.

I felt the erections rise from those males who found pleasure in females, all of whom I had called to look. Showing off my bride...

...was gauche.

But really. If they were not allowed to touch, they should at least suffer knowing why. Pearl was stunning. Her pulse beat at her throat as if she were human.

She exuded the scent of all things delectable, I could gobble her up.

I would have had she been born nearer to my turning.

Oh.

Well then.

Now I knew why she had taken so long to be reborn. I lacked any sort of self-control when it came to such a being. I would have killed her on accident and wept over her bones until the earth rotted.

And it would have rotted. That was how it worked.

All in me reflected, as it should. This was my kingdom.

And her new name? Pearl.

How had I not seen?

A bit of sand in the belly of an oyster. Rolled about. Made smooth. Made precious and glorious over ages.

I cackled, startling my bride. Head thrown back, I practically howled at the moon.

A pearl. *A Pearl.* The scratching bit of sand in the world—my realm's—belly. Because I refused to let her leave me and she had sworn on the life of her newly born monster to return. And here she was reborn and named and hilariously exact.

Nothing had ever been so hysterically deserved. Oh, fuck you, fates.

Now I could stand near so much deliciousness and not crunch her bones in my maw.

Enough pretending. With just a bit of effort, I could make others see whatever I wished. Fabric tore as my body expanded. Wings knocked into spectators who had no clue why they sidestepped or what had sent their hair flying back.

My precious Pearl liked me as I was.

So I *was*.

But only for her eyes.

Everyone else saw what I told them to see, including the couple preparing to speak their vows. No soul knew me but her.

She didn't even mind that I singed her dress.

Looking back and forth, her concern not for her skin that burned or the way I dug my claws in until just a touch of her blood scented the air, Pearl asked, "Why isn't anyone screaming?"

Of course she would be more concerned for strangers than herself.

"Because I am yours and they cannot see me. Because you love me and they don't." Spittle dripped from my fang, hissing when it landed on red silk.

One time, she rubbed her lips together, turning in my arms to look over the burning mess of my fine clothes. “I really want to watch my daughter get married. Can you please control yourself until it’s over?”

“Yes.” And that was truth. Every last winsome part of me settled. Physically, I formed around her, wings and all. I took her in my embrace, as I was, as she was.

The ceremony began.

17

VLADISLOV

How long had it been since I actually paid any attention to such tripe? Modern weddings. I must have attended several. After all, I knew the dress code and the expectations. But gatherings were a question of impression—of the mental variety in my case.

All talk in my head ceased.

My damned offspring's blood-born Daywalker child linked hands with a man whose easy breaths were the wedding gift of my wife. The mother of the bride.

My wife, who had borne that child in pain so excruciating that I would indeed scrap that memory from her mind, even if she hated me for it later. Never would Pearl see what had been done or know how much of her was lost that day.

My Pearl and that Pearl were not and never would be the same.

Jade had been granted what Darius had stolen from my soul. It glittered under her skin for those who knew how to look. The shimmer of a Pearl. It made her.

As strange as such a thing was to say, *it made her*.

Her mother's loss, the fight, the abundant will to save her child… the universe had passed that to Jade.

Who glowed.

Who was truly at peace so long as Malcom was near.

I knew exactly how she felt.

"I give myself to you while I take everything that you are." Spoken in Malcom's native tongue. Words I translated, in soft hues of speech so Pearl might know what took place.

She shivered under the burn of my wings.

"A world I lay at your feet."

Jade did not know the language in which her bridegroom spoke, but she knew every last promise made by the River Seine. Just as Pearl knew me and would soon recognize what we were.

"Eternity by my side. For eternity, I shall care for you."

Jade, as queen, would not return the vows before guests. That would be something done in private, out of the ears of the immortals she ruled. Still, she spilled tears of happiness.

Clear as night, I could see the dark things stuck inside her falling away like dead flies off a reborn corpse. Jade was made new.

"She looks so happy."

My darling one was desperate that her words sang true. So I let her see. I opened up just enough for her to see what I saw.

Jade was in bliss.

Malcom loved her as no man ever had loved, save I.

Weeping in joy, my bride made demands. "You can't ever hurt him. Never."

"As you wish."

Blubbering, extremely cute, and every bit the embarrassing mother at a wedding, Pearl added, "Men don't… they don't think of women as he thinks of her. He sees beyond her beauty or what she can do for him."

Black talon tracing her cheek, I said, "Come now. I love you even beyond the ways in which he loves her. And you know that."

"But *you* are not a man." As if that might make her not realize her slip.

The very slip that brought a frightening grin to my lips. Sharp teeth on display, I let a black forked tongue trace my lips. "You know I love you."

She wouldn't lie. She wasn't capable of it. That didn't mean she wasn't going to be shy. "I know you think you do."

Taking her chin, I turned her back to the spectacle. To Jade and Malcolm.

He offered his naked throat to his queen.

As she nuzzled in, he found the place where her collar split just enough, where fangs placed with infinite care could be snapped off by the prey, daring enough to try to drink from such a guarded throat.

He pierced her flesh delicately. She tore at his—an expected statement, considering their vastly different stations. And they fed.

The sucking sounds were suggestive to an extreme, inspiring the onlookers to begin their own feast, whether with lovers or upon those humans delivered as snacks.

One moment, the couple was feasting on one another. The next, Malcom manhandled his queen into his arms.

They vanished into the night.

After her daughter was gone, as Pearl processed, it was the first time I had ever heard regret in my bride's mind for her shortened fangs. Imagination full of her own potential wedding, she knew there was no skin she might break.

"I would slit my throat before every last one of my chattel. You could drink me to death." Every word sang through my being.

She turned in my arms yet kept her eyes on where the ribbons of my shirt still smoked. "Don't be silly."

The tip of my thumb delved into her mouth, the world blocked out so none might see or hear. Wings raised so even the sky had no access to my female, I pressed the pad of that thumb to her sad fang. "They will grow back. Until then, cut me to ribbons in any way you please."

Shy blue eyes went from cracked, fiery chest to my hideous face. "This has been the strangest night of my life."

All that, spoken around the digit that still teased at her slight fang. That pressed until my skin gave the flavor of her favorite treat.

Not that my delicate flower would suck me before the crowd.

Kidding. She was already licking at the droplet. The poor dear had absolutely no control once she had a taste of me.

Who would blame her? I was hideously delectable.

"I'm going to fuck you here. On this ground. Where everyone will see it," I told her as her pupils blew on the high of a God's blood. "And you will be angry with me for it later."

"No."

"But my hand is already up your skirt." And it was. A very human-looking hand attached to a very human-looking body. That had a human-looking cock that she already fingered, unaware that she was addicted.

Everyone fell into states of undress.

Pearl's first orgy.

I let her keep her ripped crimson dress, working myself in after her back hit the planks of the platform created for the wedding.

One thrust saw me deep in my bride's body before she might recognize the depravities I pulled her down to.

Blood-red satin singed and bundled to her waist, I thrust like a king might into a serving wench he favored. The girl was shocked. The girl's mind trying to catch up as things took place beyond her ken.

Pearl keened, cunt weeping about my human girth.

The cry was not for my tricks. It was for my falseness. This was not my cock. This was not my body. But I made a show for all to see. Her perfect tits bounced from the tears in her bodice I had prepared for just this moment.

At no time did she fight back. Instead, she tilted her hips so it might end all the sooner and she might die of shame in private.

Rough, because she needed rough as the moans, hisses, and screams of pain rose up on that platform, I took her chin and forced.

My Pearl liked to be forced.

A dark secret I had manipulated to my advantage. "We celebrate."

A tear escaped the corner of her eye.

"They have to see me this way, my soul. They have to watch me ride you as if I was one of them." I was so close to spilling, just to end this. "I will fuck you into the next century day and night, while you feed on me until I am sad skin on old bones. Cry harder. I will finish sooner. And they who do not know me will see and respect the claiming."

Not waiting for a reply, I caught a peaked, red nipple with the flick of the tongue and a trick of the teeth. And I made her writhe.

Dancing as the ripples and waves rocked her on my invasive, hideous human cock, I made the show one worth remembering.

Of course, I added in some flair my bride would have never abided.

I came. She gaped.

I had given her no climax even as her womb was assaulted with my spend.

Which drove doubt hard on the heels of a maiden's stained morality.

Resting my forehead against hers, I whispered, "This was for show in honor of a wedding. Expected. It's easier to rip off the band-aid."

Her teeth went to my throat, because my words offended her to such a degree. It was utter reflex. Cornered prey fighting back… as she had done so many times. Yet fangless, she could do nothing.

I could do everything.

I could see all the men who had used her in this way. Noted their faces, their names, and made easy decisions on how to shuck their descendants into feeding pens. Bending the rules, I also empowered her in those memories, ripping the inborn church guilt away from a creature doing nothing more than trying to defend itself and succeeding.

The flesh on my neck parted, because I willed it to do so, and black blood more delightful than sin drenched the tongue of an angry woman.

She drank me, that sad human cock inside her, until her belly poked out. Falling back and panting with fullness.

This moment, she would not understand for some time. But it was the price she had to pay to see Jade wed.

For standing with me as wife in public.

For my love.

"Did I hurt you?"

Glassy-eyed, she stared at the stars, utterly ignoring my presence.

"If I had made you like it, that would have been wrong." Why was I begging her to understand what had been on the agenda before time had been written? *"This is not me."*

Cerulean eyes moved from vacancy to daggers. "And that is what makes it so horrid."

My monstrous cock changed before the rest of me might

stop it. Groaning in discomfort from the stretch, my bride's hips wriggled to make room even as her body tried to remove me. "You refused the bath. You were ashamed of your breasts and how I enjoyed you. I knew public fucking would unnerve you, but your survival and acceptance require you to bend at least *once* to your heritage. I can make you forget this."

Not that I would.

Drunk on my blood, she struck out with the tiniest, cutest little moon-white claws. My cheek was torn to shreds.

Really.

Down to the teeth and gums.

Another dollop of come burst forth unexpectedly for us both.

This must have been what the idea of heaven had been formed of.

"Do it again," I begged. "Rip me to ribbons down to the bone."

"No." The weight of words she had never been able to speak in the past fell on me like boulders. "Get out of my body."

Hips snapping back, I pulled out the recrafted, human dick as if it had been burned with acid.

And then she vanished.

My bride left me there at her own daughter's wedding.

Shucking the fluids from my cock, I buttoned up the tatters of my demon-torn clothing, certain I was in more trouble than I anticipated. And that she should not tempt me with a chase.

Pearl had no idea how much I craved a hunt. But for the first time since the sky lost its stars at night thanks to the cities' ambient light, I felt a twinge of fear.

She could be anywhere. And precious as they were, despite the time required to craft them, Pearls were delicate.

18

PEARL

I should have known. This is where all men, *or monsters*, left things. With their seed inside me and my pride crushed. Yet this time, I had taken my innate foolishness past the pale. I had *appreciated* the monster. Not because he called me pretty or had given my pretty things. Because he had seemed to listen. I thought it was *me* he saw.

Not my tits.

Not my face.

Not the things I might do with my mouth or the way the place between my legs might sate him.

And though it had only been a blip of time, considering… considering the decades it had taken me to walk from California to the East Coast. It had been, what? A month? Maybe three?

Half a year?

Ten years?

Who could tell how time passed when most of it was spent lost in the huge black hole of my mind?

He had seemed so hideously kind. Ugly, grotesque in his mercy poured on my wounds. Care.

For a *thing* like me.

And ultimately, he had been no different from any other man who had pushed me down and thrust in.

No different than the demon who had kept me for a pet in a stone box. I was still a pet, just with better surroundings.

The rosary in my grip, I could feel the beads begin to crack from the force at which I fisted it. "I bet you're laughing at me, aren't you?"

Of course he was.

How could a crispy head on a pike do anything but?

In France, I had been standing in the deep of night. Now, moments later, I was dumped in a pile on the soft grass of a balmy garden at dusk. Back in Manhattan where I'd once been so sure all my dreams might come true. Where I'd had a window.

The sun set at my back, warming my skin, leaving my shadow stretching over the drooping eyelids of a grotesque familiarity.

It didn't matter if I was in France, or my golden city, or walking dusty roads, or begging strangers for scraps. I had been born in hell.

I had never left hell.

And hell would never leave me.

I, the damned, whose slit ached with unsatiated need, sloppy with spend. A backward body buzzing with irritation at having not reached climax while totally unaroused by the horror before me.

Darius.

The pike jammed into the stump of his neck was layered with what seemed to be an endlessly dripping crust. The head *juicy*, despite its scabbed and hideous burns.

What should have been shrunken from the rigors of the sun and starvation still possessed form. Cheekbones, sharp but identifiable. Burnt hair leaning toward the deepest brown. Lips.

I knew the sting of those lips.

The sun fully set, drooping eyelids twitched.

"Yes. You *are* laughing."

So loud it almost felt as if my ears bled.

"I know this place." Turning, humidity leaving torn, red silk to stick to my skin, I took in the jutting stone edifice that seemed to erupt from the ground itself. A cathedral. A cloister. A monastery. A place where screams had seeped into the stone.

My screams so small in the cacophony.

I was *home*.

How I knew that—considering not once before that night could I recall my eyes setting upon the outside of the terrifying warren—was utterly beyond me. But I knew. This was where I had rotted. This was where I had begged God to redeem me.

This was where I had sold my soul.

There was very little I could pull on from my memory, but I remembered the abject pain, how it was twisted up inside me as if it were pleasure, and how the little of me left splintered and let evil in just to make it stop.

Lying in my own blood and shit, I had begged. *I had begged.*

The ground had shaken.

Darius had left me.

And here he must have been since. Head on a pike in a garden outside his usurped kingdom now controlled by the child we'd created.

While I wandered a room, frightened and alone.

While I uncovered the secrets of my tomb. A Coney Island funhouse of horrors written in my own hand. Beautiful things too. Paintings, jewels, indecent nightwear. Tiny forgotten flecks of blood on the stone.

In that room, before I had extinguished the last candle, I found myself.

And found that I was nothing of worth.

Forgotten.

There would never be salvation. So I had sang the same songs I had heard mothers sing to their young as I journeyed from place to place.

And I had dreamed of nothing.

Yet still sang.

Though my bones were brittle and my mind was rotted into mush, I heard another pick up the fading tune.

Hideous life dripped down a withered, resisting throat.

That first hacking cough, trying to expel not only the music but succor.

I fought each part of me as it came slowly back to life. I could not take a single further second of *myself.*

All of it had been....

I knew the bible back and forth, and no scripture burned into what was left of my mind might assuage whatever I was. My very life was a cancer on the world, one that grew roots into it as I'd desiccated.

The little hairs from those roots, I still felt them tugging me into the ground. Or maybe they were tugging me *back* into the ground.

I had no idea how I had even appeared in this place, in a heap of skirts and weeping. One moment, I looked into the eyes of a monster I had mistakenly trusted. The next, those fuzzy roots—those spreading incessant roots—snapped me back where they had grown.

Home.

That is what I had longed for.

And this.

THIS!!

This godforsaken ground was my home.

Darius rotting on a stick. But alive and hungry—the eyes in his ragged head glowing as he drank me down under the rot of drooping lids.

What was left of him was famished.

Slack jawed head twitching.

Even so, Darius began to heal before my eyes as if such a state could be made beautiful. His eyes, those terrible eyes, looking right at me as if to say that, *yes, he laughed.*

Not that he didn't also beg.

"Come to me, treasure."

Damaged as he was, despite blaring, continuous pain, the demon was dangerous.

And so familiar in the way he picked at my thoughts, indelicately scratching at each memory he fingered through.

I should have gone screaming into the night.

I should have done anything other than meet his eyes and *feel*.

All my pain.

ALL MY PAIN.

Wrapped in a pretty bow of desecration and disappointment.

That thing on the stick hated Vlad. Burned with the blackest bubbling oil of greasy animosity.

I might have hated Vladislov in that moment too, but I hated Darius far more. "I enjoyed lying with him in a way you could never inspire me to enjoy you."

What was I saying? Never had I heard that level of spite in my voice. That dark seed only grew, expanding in my chest until I felt my sad fangs attempt to descend only to ache with the inability to be little more than nubs.

As if that sorry head thought to console me, it whispered in my mind, *"Dear treasure."*

"I'm not your treasure."

"Always. None, but I care for you. Think of what you are now because of me and the sacrifices I made in your name."

Soft grass under my bare feet. Where had my shoes gone? Lost when Vlad pushed me to the planks. Fallen off when I popped out of thin air a few feet too high above the ground and thudded into the earth like a bird shot out of the sky.

Dress torn, wrinkled, sodden, stinking of what had made me seek *home*. Ugly inside and out. So many gemstones around my throat that it ached. Breath confined, heart racing, I stood as I was. As who I was.

A broken thing.

"Your lips, Pearl. Put them to mine."

"No." Resolute, that filthy word twisted my tongue into the most unfeminine of replies.

I had been designed to be meek. Otherwise, God would not love me. I had allowed males to do horrible things to me in the name of subservience.

And in that moment, held by the heat of blood-red eyes, I swore to myself that it would never happen again. "This sight comforts me, knowing you are trapped on a stick in *my* sun, boiling at midday and begging for scraps at midnight."

"*Come, pet.*" That fiddling in my thoughts, that itch. *"Embrace me. I can save you from them."*

Not that I had not noticed the growing shadows once the sun was no longer a concern, the Cathedral's inhabitants began to gather and whisper, edging nearer where I stood in a breathtaking garden.

The denizens of the Cathedral had seen me. No sun lingered to keep them away. And I was unwelcome.

Openly threatened yet perfectly stalked.

They wished for me to run.

They thirsted for a chase.

Yet still I stood hissing to the head of my personal demon

as it oozed feted matter down the pike. Damn the whispering shadows back to their hell! I had words to say to this beast.

"You tore my baby out of my body!"

And it had words to say to me as well, the tone having skirted from seduction to cruel laughter. *"More than one."*

Bile in the back of my throat, visibly swallowing, I felt the distortion and the fact. "You're lying."

If thoughts could smile, Darius was grinning like he'd eaten my babies for sport. *"I can take you to them. How they cry for their mommy."*

The mental flash of the monster tearing at the flesh of a newborn was jammed into my brain like a hot poker. Darius sucking their marrow as if it were fine wine.

Yet, it didn't *feel* real.

Nor did the flashes of children flung into the night to defend themselves against the monsters alone.

He had the power to plant lies like seeds. To water those lies with the victim's doubt.

And still it was his head on the pike and not mine.

And terrible as those memories were, *I laughed.*

I had been that beaten child. Those monsters had already devoured me. It was my bones bashed into uneven brick and mortar in an unforgiving world that needed to feed.

It was a parlor trick of using my past, changing the hue, and pretending it was another.

I laughed harder.

Choking back a giggle once my mind flooded with images of a little boy who looked every bit mine—same features, same tenacity. But his blue eyes held none of my fear as he fought. His were the sea in a storm.

Refusal to submit.

And I knew as I saw him that no matter what the monster tried to show me, the little boy was real.

It was almost as if I could feel his little ghostly fingers curl around mine. The perfect greeting of a sweet child to a discombobulated stranger.

It was too real to bear.

"Mommy," the memory called out, as if we had known one another. There was the lie. Not the voice. No, that voice was very real. It was the word.

Mommy.

He did not know me. Just as Jade did not know me. Just as I had never known my mother.

"You will give me my son!"

"For a kiss."

No. Though the argument was personal, more had come to bear witness. The undead, hissing threats yet failing to come closer. As if there were an unseen line in the garden no toe might cross.

Lingering, circling, they called out obscenities. Clicked their tongues as if to draw my attention away. Others only cocked their heads as if this were the most entertaining display they had seen in ages.

More laughter.

But the unhinged sound was mine. I was laughing at *them*.

They were afraid of a head on a stick! The irony being

that... so was I. I was petrified of a skull with sorry flesh hanging from its twitching muscles. One that could not touch me in any way that mattered.

One I was extremely tempted to simply… eat.

He was already inside my mind, why not just digest what was left? I could imagine the crunch of bone in a powerful maw. Even though the sound of those screams had been more beautiful than any the sun might inflict on the most terrible demon of hell.

Red eyes I remembered held mine as I said it. "I hate you."

I don't think I had ever said that to another being in my life.

But it was freeing! "I do, Darius. Not once did I love you. I might not remember, but I know I fought your desires."

And I had never fought Vladislov, not in that way. Not even on the planks when I'd let him have his show at my expense. No, I just ran, because I could not bear to look at him when he seemed so giddy.

And I would deal with him later.

What a thought. I would deal with the king of monsters, and I already knew he would kneel to me, perhaps even cry, but never learn.

In a very strange, comforting way, I could even accept that.

But first… Darius.

Lip curled, I stood just as I had seen my haughty daughter stand, snarling, "You'll be nothing but a display in a garden, scratching at the minds of those who wander too near in the same way mice scratch at the walls. You're a pathetic infestation, Darius."

"Kiss me, my treasure."

Oh, I'd kiss him all right. I'd eat his face right down to the bone!

Tongue already tracing the sharper edges of my teeth, I took a step closer, caught by a voice at my ear. "Pearl, this is no place for you."

What?

Who on earth would dare come between me and the finest, most pure moment of rage.

True hatred sang in me as if it had always been there, would always be there, and would give me all the comfort I lacked since my first breath.

What was love when hate might empower? What was love but a figment of the imagination?

Hate was far more real. It was palpable.

I could be whole!

A figure stepped into my periphery. "Look at me. One look and you'll understand why hate will never devour love no matter how hard it tries. Compassion triumphs over cruelty. Self-respect feeds while self-indulgence diminishes. Pearl. I'm right here."

A man, brown-skinned and beautiful in a way tranquil seas were beautiful. Eyes as hypnotic as waving barley in a soft breeze. Voice… his voice was water to quench an endless thirst. He offered a kind smile, even as he said, "This particular demon knows you in ways you cannot imagine. Look at your hands. Already, you're pulling Darius free of his prison. He's luring you into his whims, feeding your hatred."

What?

Oh God….

My outstretched hands *were* sticky with rotting ooze, both palms flush to the torn ribbons of throat that needed to be worked free. I had already pulled the snapping head a good three inches higher, fighting the crusting matter that had glued him in place.

I was touching the vilest of creatures, his crispy skin cracking against my touch, his teeth bared as if once I pulled him to my bosom, he'd feast.

While I thought I was making a feast of him.

Desperate, the monstrosity screamed vileness into my mind as I yanked my touch away, and a sickening sound followed the head sinking down the pole until the tip hit the inside of his skull.

Its face was a frenzy of twitching, brains scrambling, healing, scrambling, healing. Just like me, there was a hole. A pike, taking parts away.

And in that, I took pleasure.

Even as I gagged.

The effort it took to break my gaze from the boiling crimson of a half-rotted head was almost unbearable.

As if it might make me clean, I scrubbed my hands on the silk of my skirt, the red growing grisly with the bits of unspeakable things. The stain on the outside matching the stain on the inside as that *thing* screamed for me to return.

Darius had been so close to freedom, in the arms of a

daywalker who could move through space on an accidental whim. Who had fallen into his dream by teasing me with the angelic face of a dirty, suffering boy.

My boy.

Just like my girl, Jade.

"He has my son."

"He has nothing," the man said. "He's a head on a pike. One tormented knowing his heart beats in the chest of a good man."

Ignoring the ring of suddenly silent vampires—beautiful dead things that toed a line they could not cross—I faced the intruder.

And knew him.

Which was not comforting.

Arms folded under my breasts, further concealing my modesty from roving eyes, I saw the face he refused to offer on display at the wedding. And I found little gratitude considering all the years I called out for help and had been ignored.

"What do you think?" He was ignoring my narrowed eyes and heaving breath. "They fear their fallen king so much they cannot even step forward to snatch up two vulnerable daywalkers."

"You are not vulnerable." And he should not pretend as such.

Where brown eyes had dragged over the crowd, many vampires scampered back as though burned. They came back to rest on me. And gave me no pain.

Outstretching a hand, he said, "I'm not afraid of him."

"I am." That was not a hand I would take.

"I know. That's how darkness worms in. Evil feeds on fear yet is slain by love." The answer was easy, even offered with a kind smile.

"And God is real. And the world should vibrate with forgiveness. And my children were taken from my body. And the only lover I've ever accepted used me as a prop to stage a show. And I am alone. And you hide your face." My lip shook, fresh tears falling as I struggled to say, "And your teachings were false."

"So much of what I tried to share was twisted, even by those who claimed to follow me. I said one thing, and they claimed another long after I walked away from the tomb. Believe me when I tell you that the truth is devoured. It has to claw its way out of the belly of the beast. It has to fight what it is being replaced with. And, in doing so, is altered." He looked pained. Endlessly sad. "I had been warned."

I knew. I had dreamed of those forty days and forty nights in the desert. "So what do we do?"

"I had been warned," he clarified. "But that didn't mean I was wrong to disagree. I still do. You have lived miracles. You have seen God work in such amazing ways."

Hysteric giggling preceded. "I have lived miracles?"

My faith was a joke. Jesus was insane.

Looking side to side as if taking in the artwork of the landscape, the man said, "I have not been in this garden before. I imagine it must be quite beautiful in the sun."

Not that it was relevant, but it would be. There were fountains and flowers and little streams about, a façade to hide the ugliness of what lingered all over the grounds. "I didn't mean to come here."

"But here you came all the same. You cried out for home and slipped from one place to another. What does that say about you that *home* is at the feet of that thing?"

Ugly truth. I'd had enough ugliness for one night. "It says that I am—"

"Confused," Jesus, still holding out a hand to me, interceded. "Young. That's all you are. Please, I need you to take another step away from the demon."

"Why?"

"Because you are cutting into your wrist and you don't even feel the pain. All it would take is a few drops of you to worm his way deeper, and he possessed you long enough." His eyes pointed down to where my hanging fingers suddenly felt warm and icy all at once. "Don't you think?"

I was bleeding all over the grass, and not just a few drops. My nails had rounded into sharp little moonlight-white talons, and I had dug one in enough that bits of my torn muscle fibers were hanging from the corner of a claw. "Jesus!"

Tripping over my feet, that red dress, my panic, I put far more than a few steps between the head and my body—feeling a strain, almost to the point of a snap, between my mind and the mind of the monster who still played with me.

"This isn't funny!" No scream ever would be loud enough to trumpet that. Arm mending, my blood soaking into the dirt, and I was once again the laughing stock.

Those soft eyes turned toward the head, a frown turning a

compassionate countenance into one of sadness. “But still, he laughs.”

A grotesque cackle I could suddenly hear clear as a bell in my head. I could feel it on my skin. The papery dryness of a mummy possessing my body, and it tore my mind to shreds.

Hands to my ears, I screamed, “How can you stand it?”

“God is with me.” It was then I noticed the threadbare cassock. A pauper’s clothing, similar to what he wore as the old man at the wedding.

My dress was all the more garish beside it. “God has never been with me.”

“Has he not? The tree branch that broke so you could be free of the noose? The snowfall after you’d been harmed by the lecher, a dust of pure white covering your tracks so you might find your way home to safety?”

I’d had enough of men of God, of the complete lunacy around me. “Then why was I hung by a priest? Why was I raped for walking home from work?”

It was as if I finally asked the right question. The man gave a breath of relief. “So that we could have this moment in a lovely garden, enjoying the view.”

19

PEARL

Interlaced so tightly around in my grip that my fingers began to swell, the rosary grew red with my dripping blood. Cracked beads, a bent cross, the man depicted suffering upon it standing before me with his hand still outstretched.

A stranger to me, nothing like the vision I had clung to. As if he understood, as if he had witnessed this *revelation* more times than he could count, he crooked his fingers.

I filled them.

I filled that open palm with the lie of religion, abandoning my rosary and my blood-soaked utter stupidity in those waiting fingers.

Bead by bead, the string I used to say my prayers pooled in his palm. Red, damaged, but still beautiful. He let me look for as long as I could bear. And then, as if reading his mind, he closed his palm and tucked the last vestment of my flagging faith away.

"How can you stand living with the lie?"

He didn't seem to mind that my blood smeared his hand and clothing. Offering an elbow as if to suggest we might take a stroll through nightmares, he said, "I tell everyone the truth. No one listens. So I speak as this man or that man. I speak as I always have. I call for compassion. But my father's world is so unbalanced. It only reflects what he's become. *There are the good parts*. There are the entertaining parts. There are the parts that love his son and his creations. And then there is the famished monster. Who eats, and eats, and kills. Who devours everything in his path all while searching for *you*."

The only thing I had anchoring me to this world, the one thing that had pulled me from the crypt, I knew was too good to be true and too ugly to be anything but beautiful in my eyes. "I'm not his wife or his soul. I can barely keep up with his chaos. I wasn't his sister or his queen in a past life. I was a waitress desperate to stay in the sun, who was afraid he would realize I needed him, that he did not need me, and that he will never really love me, considering what I am."

Gesturing toward the path, he led me away from the head and past the scattering undead, saying, "Who are you to say what you are and what you are not?"

Excuse me? I was myself talking to a pretend demigod. Acknowledging that should have split me in half, but Darius had already done the rending. "I am *me*!"

That. That made Jesus smile. "A girl who dreamed of a

window so she might sleep safely in the sun. A kind heart who wanted nothing more than to find a home."

"Your father can read my thoughts, you're doing the same. That does not mean you know me." Why were all these men so insufferable? Why was he leading me through a throng of hissing vampires who scurried away as if they might be burned by the very sunlight we discussed?

"I can't read your thoughts. What I know is because Vladislov has written to me of you. The detail in his letters… he is *deeply* in love. A phenomenon I never imagined I might witness, though he had told me stories of his lost wife."

My heart had been broken so many times. I had trusted adults. I had fought to please employers. I had wandered and begged God to lead me to someone, anyone who might take away what made me wrong. And where had God led me? To an alley where Malcom had ripped my fangs from my skull. But he had not been able to remove my cravings.

Where had God been in that? Where had God been while Darius had done things I could not recall? Lip shaking in a way I hated, eyes prickling, I dared to ask, "And all my prayers?"

Where my arm was tucked into his, he patted me gently. "God heard them."

No, he had not. And nor had this man. "But I prayed in your name. I prayed to your holy mother."

"And that was foolish. Where in the scant, centuries-old catalogued recordings of my teachings did I ever say that prayers should be made to me or to my mother? Would that not be idolatry?"

I had been raised on scripture. The words had been beaten into my back. "The New Testament—"

"Is a blend of megalomaniacs seeking worship and false prophets using my teachings to gain notoriety. Have you witnessed the vagaries of Twitter? It's the same phenomenon yet more pathetic. Weak souls driven to share their every vapid thought. Their sick fragility seeking validation. Cults flourish. So much filth is spread with the intent to do harm and gain a high in the process. No different than the men and women shouting as I bore my cross. You've seen it in your own life, felt the hurled stones hit your body. Everyone has their cross to bear. You have a tomb and a hole in your memories."

"And a daughter who despised the sight of me. And a son you are trying to distract me from. Men think we don't know what you're doing. Women know. So stop wasting my time and tell me what Vlad had written of this boy in his letters." How much angrier should I be?

We turned at a cherry tree, following a path made misty from the damp lingering in the air. No undead approached. Instead, they still scattered as if there were a clear circle about us they were unable to traverse.

"Why aren't they hurting us?" A valid question, considering I could smell their intent on the breeze. Another valid question was why Vladislov had not come. Making me doubt him all the more. If he loved me, he would have come for me.

"Because I am not afraid of them," Jesus said, as if that explained everything.

The small pebbles lining the path under my feet squished when I dug in my heels. “I didn’t mean to come here. Considering that all my life what I dreamed of most was to be in your presence, I’m finding now that I don’t like you very much.” Whatever he really was. “I want my boy, and I will leave.”

My escort’s footfalls ceased. “And when I tell you there is no son?”

“Then I’ll call you a liar.” My mind had been played with enough that I was beginning to see where the fingerprints led. In Darius’ effective seduction, the boy he showed me *was real*. Alive now. *AND HE WAS MINE.*

Vladislov’s son, a figure a huge portion of the world’s population believed was their savior, said, “What you saw is feral, unnamed, and dangerous. It isn’t a son, it’s a burden.”

Why mince words? “Because Darius made him that way!”

Jesus agreed, eyes full of pity, “Because Darius made him that way.”

“You will give me my boy, or by God I will end you. You who I prayed to all my life and who could hear nothing because you are only a man.” And men were fools who lied and tricked to get their way. “Your cassock doesn’t change that.”

“I’m glad you are beginning to recognize what you see. The cassock is only fabric with the intention to denote station. It’s not real. I hung on a cross as long as you hung from a tree. My father, wings and all, rolled back the stone to set me free once he figured I’d learned a lesson. Stories came and grew wildly out of proportion, just as they will about you to Vampirekind, soul of Vladislov. You won't be able to stop it, though you will decry the tales time and again. You will be powerless over your own retelling. The wife of a God. The mother of a queen. The keeper of an untamed demon child."

His complaints or comparisons, I didn't care. I cared about his roundabout point. "You are not as different from your father as you might imagine. You're younger, prettier, but just as crazy."

His smile—I could see what was in that smile now. The smile of my fallen lord was full of secrets. "Your son will need a name."

"Jasper. That will be his name." Drawing my arm from the elbow of my companion, I faced him head-on. "Tell me what you want for him."

He took up the arm I yanked away, leading me toward a better-lighted path bursting with night blooming flowers and the scent of life. "Acknowledge that you are my father's wife, nothing more."

Torn red silk splattered with crusted guck, rotting matter, grass stains, and the acrid stink of fear-induced sweat. One tit hanging free. I was anything but a bride. "You want me to lie."

He shook his head, long hair waving in a way that was far too familiar. "I want you to admit what all of us who have seen you already know. My father isn't here, so grasp this moment in which I keep him away. The acknowledgment can be between us. Torment *him* for all eternity as he seeks out your favor. He deserves nothing less. But right here, in this garden, you and I will come to an understanding. Take him as your husband, and you'll save more than just the boy."

Fine. I'd trade the only currency I had if that boy would be laid in my arms. Vladislov could have my body and a troth. He would have taken both anyway. "He's my husband."

"Are you his soul?" The question was breathless.

"No." *Yes*.

Relief fell from the lips of a man I never wanted to see again—a man I wanted to get to know, whose knee I wanted to cry on—who was no different than his father.

And it seemed their agenda was not much different either. Though from where I stood, both of them were blind to that truth.

The family squabbles that would happen over the table would be interesting.

Jade and Malcom would watch them bicker, and I wondered if they would see it too.

Leaning forward to whisper atrocities in my ear, Jesus told me where my son was tucked away. Why he was there. How many I would have to kill to get him.

I didn't scream. Not then. What would the point be? I didn't rage at God for the unfairness of what had been done to a child. I simply nodded and turned away from *the son of God.*

And entered the Cathedral.

The path before me, it was as if I had walked it a thousand times. Those who dared come near a mother seeking her child I killed with surprising ease.

And I drank.

And they ran screaming when the carnage in my wake was discovered.

Vladislov had made me strong. God had designed me to be deadly. Darius had wrung the goodness from me. And I had agreed to be wife to the Demon who controlled the world.

Glassy-eyed humans in pens, deep under the rot of the twisted church. Hundreds, thousands in the catacombs. They didn't speak at the sight of my blood-soaked body as I passed by. They didn't ask for help.

Their minds were mush, their state hardly above that of an animal.

Though I could have, I didn't help them. I wasn't there for them. I didn't even acknowledge them.

My mind was filled with the glowing beauty of a towheaded child that had his own pen, his own rags, his own snarling rage.

I tore the bars of his door right from the stone, bent metal… as if it were a simple task.

Scooping up a wild beast who tore into my throat in his hunger, I grew complete.

I sang as I rocked him, until the drowsy thing had a full belly and I had a sleeping child in my arms. His head lolling against my shoulder, I carried him away from his suffering. I bore him out of the desecrated Cathedral straight out into the world.

My son.

He smelled of poison ivy, of birch, of blood, and of fire.

The sun rose as he indelicately snored. And he nuzzled against his mother, a stranger who wanted him.

Vladislov did find me in time, resting on a park bench, curled around my boy.

A boy he looked upon as if he saw through the pretty, filthy shell. Smiling, honest, Satan held out his arms to take the burden from me. I allowed it.

Cradling the still sleeping little one, he waltzed slowly around, humming a few bars. Our eyes met, my husband asking, “Can we keep him?”

Forever. “Yes.”

“What bliss!”

20

VLADISLOV

The boy lying fast asleep upon the bed was an angel. Well, at least angelic in appearance. I couldn't even blame Pearl for falling in love with him at first *sight*.

Parted lips and apple cheeks smeared with dried blood, on an utterly cherubic face. He smelled of my wife, the same wife seated beside him as she continuously petted his matted, pale hair. I don't think the little thing had ever been bathed, not that I had any intention of poking around in his wee brain until greater topics had been sorted.

"Pearl, my darling, beloved wife, I'm angry with you."

Her hand stilled, just as filthy as the boy lying atop a pricy silk coverlet. It hovered, the tips of her claws unable to fully retract with her young near and a very real threat looming beside them.

"Don't think I can't see how you seethe, trying to hide it because the fate of the boy matters more to you than your pride. And I know why you're angry too. I can see that as well." Stooping down so my lips might brush her ear, I growled, "I can see right through you."

She didn't have an answer for that. How could she after the night she'd lived?

My Pearl may have refused the perfectly wonderful bath of blood I'd prepared with love, but she had bathed in plenty of blood on her own.

Drenched. I found her sitting in a human park in broad daylight looking like an extra from a horror flick. Rocking a small child in her arms, too taken with him to notice the looks she was garnering from the locals.

True to human form, no one approached what looked like a wild-eyed vagrant to offer help. Police were not summoned. Strangers walking dogs gave her a wide berth, their snapping little spaniels pulling at the leash to sniff at the bloody woman.

Anyone could have hunted and ended her, caught as she was in her distraction.

And they might have, considering the enemies she'd made in one night of bloodlust. Except I was watching over her. Giving her time to settle down and enjoy the feel of sunlight and the weight of her sleeping child in her arms.

"Running from me out of temper was unwise. I'd rather you strike me before—"

That was all the permission she needed, her upper body turning so she might lay open palm full-force upon my cheek.

I'm not sure who was more surprised. That even stung!

Where was I supposed to go with this? "Okay... that's a start."

"Don't you *ever* do that to me again!" Hackles raised, she stood from the bed, put herself physically between my body and the sleeping child as she railed. "You can't claim to love me and do something like that!"

My bride was too young to grasp that I did it *because* I loved her. "You could not have attended the wedding and failed to participate in the aftermath. It's expected to fuck in celebration, and rejection would have been a slight on the couple."

Arms crossed under her bosom, her free breast pushed up so invitingly it took all my will not to glance downward and lick my lips.

She hissed, "You could have warned me."

"You wouldn't have gone. And then you would have regretted missing what has thus far been the most important moment in Jade's life." Yes, I was highhanded. *I know that*. But I was also right.

My soul was in a state—an agitated, furious, angry state. The same tenor of state that had unraveled into a rather beautiful massacre. And yes, I had already heard *all about it*. It was all vampires could talk about, the story growing outlandishly garish.

The amount of complaints I had received. Yikes!

As if Pearl might have actually ripped a head from some old fart's shoulders. Please.

She didn't rip it off completely. She had delicately separated the majority of the throat, but her sweet little claws had not cut through the spinal cord. I'd seen the corpse as I had directed the cleanup.

Excellent work, I must say. Totally worth pissing her off, if that was the response I might get.

No one was going to fuck with my wife now.

Not when the vampire she had "dismembered" was so damn ancient he might as well have farted dust. The undead were terrified of the glowing angel.

I'd added in that last tidbit—glowing with sunlight that burned all who dared approach.

Dramatic stories were far more fun when they were peppered with a touch more flavor. I mean, how many times had a total stranger walked into a hive and just torn through the locals, draining them dry as if they were human cattle?

I heard all about how they had run screaming from the *avenging angel*. What a lark!

Considering a mass murder was not enough, the tale was far more outlandish. She had approached Darius and dared confront the maniac for his crimes.

A Daywalker reeking of my come.

As anyone who was actually important would have been at the wedding, who cared if Pearl had been a bit overzealous as she fed?

Her first real hunt!

What a success. And she got a prize.

A cute one that at first blush seemed perfectly innocent. At second glance just might be the antichrist incarnate.

"I have lived too long to see you risk yourself out of anger. And let's not pretend you won't be angry with me again. You were born angry. Just as I was born to rule you."

"No." Squaring her shoulders, Pearl unknowingly took on the mantle of a queen. Of my Goddess. "You were born to see in me a thing you want but will never completely have."

Oh no…

I was growing brave, and she could see it, and she was already growing angrier.

Pinching my pointed ear as if I were a child, she dragged me from the room in which our little boy dreamed of rivers of blood.

And I let her.

She really had no idea the effect she had on me. If I just brushed the tip of my cock on her blood-soaked skirt, I was going to spurt.

Already, I was angling my hips, the urge ruined when she snarled, "Don't you dare."

But we were in our bedroom now. The bed was right there! And she looked absolutely delicious, and I wanted to fuck her, and *she admitted she was my wife*. "Please?"

That set her to screaming, Pearl threatening to leave me forever if I ever did something so horrible again.

I asked her to define horrible… and she struck me again.

Really hard!

Which made me really hard. Achingly hard.

My throbbing excitement leaked a string of pearly fluid that dangled from the tip, making her all the more enraged.

So, I got down on my knees. “You can’t be mad at me for seeing you like this and wanting to fuck you. You look glorious, my love!”

“I’m covered in dried blood *and other things*, in a torn, ugly dress, and I smell.” Every word was shrill, Pearl tearing at her tangled hair in frustration.

“Exactly! *So pretty*! And please, darling, lower your voice before you wake up our son.”

Those were not the right words, the woman on the verge of further violence. “He’s *my* son. *Mine*!”

Ah, ah. I had been very careful with my word choice when I approached my angry woman in the park. “You said *we* could keep him. That makes him mine too. Also, you love me and want me to be happy. Don’t try to deny it. You told Yeshua as much. Don’t pretend you didn’t. And don’t gape at me like a fish when you know I can read the memory as if I was standing right there beside you.” Palm to my heart, my entire being lit up in joy. “You even claimed to be my wife.”

Her face was turning red, and not in embarrassment.

Holding up my hands, I softened my approach. “I know. He’s tricky in the way he gets what he wants. He said you never had to *tell me*. He suggested that you could torment me by withholding the statement. And you will!” I smiled, the last vestments of my human mask fading and the real me on full display for her to enjoy. “You *will* torment me. But… you know just as well as he does that I can see all the beauty of your thoughts. So don’t be mad at me or cross with him.” My smile stretched, the hideousness of my mouth and all the sharp teeth on display. “Get it? Cross?”

"That is not...." But the corner of her mouth twitched.

Oh, but it was. "It is funny, my soul."

I was myself before her, all charred skin and crackling fire. Massive, winged, ugly, pure. Taking her dirty fingers, I brought them to my lips for a kiss. "I'm sorry. Really, I am. I have not felt fear in so long that when you disappeared last night...." What really was there to say? "I love you. I know you're angry. But you are only angry, truly angry, because you love me and it scares you."

Pearl worked to collect herself in her storm of feelings, letting out a deep breath as she snatched back her fingers and pressed her palms to her face. One moment passed, then another. Her breath slowed, her heart rate normalized. She peeked through her fingers and looked at me as if to say *what am I going to do with you?*

She was going to love me. Already, it throbbed in her chest right beside the annoyance. And it frightened her to no end.

But I reveled in both.

She was so stiff, and I was so much larger. So I let my wings hover around her slight form as if they might embrace her. "Pearl, do you want to talk about the Cathedral?"

"No."

"Should we discuss Darius?" She had withstood far more than my son had given her credit for. That pussy was unable to know her like I did. Pearl *would* have eaten Darius' face down to the bone. Though I am glad she didn't. He probably tasted terrible.

Voice smaller, she answered, "I'd rather not."

It was like pulling teeth sometimes with this woman, but I loved every moment of it. "Okay. Then let me bridge the gap you have failed to address. Why haven't you asked me if I knew about the boy?"

Lips turning down in a frown, eyes flagging, my soul went from queen to grieving mother. "If you had known, you would have offered him to me in exchange for exactly what your son demanded."

She was so right. I which is why I had offered the boy when I really wanted to get my way and make her a bit less angry about the wedding thing. Though I had not anticipated Yeshua would act after only having seen my bride a single time. Though it would be a lie to deny I was grateful he had.

My worrisome boy wasn't usually so spontaneous. Which meant he was also desperate.

What Pearl really should really have been asking was, *how did my son know about the boy?*

God had not whispered that secret in his ear. I had. Tucked it right in his memories so the desperate bugger might have an opportunity to get what he wanted most.

For me to be laden with a soul.

And now I was. One who'd acknowledged she was my wife.

The part of me the fates had finally returned.

"Please tell me you love me, Pearl."

She wanted to say it badly, because she was infinitely good. She craved the moment she might divulge that there was more to her than confusion and sorrow. But she didn't have the conviction—

"I love you." Her voice had been small, her eyes on the floor when it slipped over her lips.

My jaw might have hit the floor. She admitted it! The wife I swept up and began waltzing around the room as my wings broke everything in their path said it.

And the pair of us were laughing.

This was *real*.

"I don't deserve you." I never would. EVER.

Laughing, she agreed, "You don't."

Swallowing her words, I kissed her so hard I knew my teeth tore at her lips. And I drank of my bride. I lapped at her closing wounds. I *ravaged*.

What I had done to her at the wedding had been calculating and boring. What I did to her then? Poets would write songs about it.

That dress, no matter how she gasped or bled at my onslaught, was demolished. Her filthy skin, scoured clean by my tongue. In no way had she been ready to see the true starvation I endured or how it had to be quenched.

Had she not grown so fierce, she would have been terrified.

Each breast, those perfect, delicious tits, were worshiped. Wide, burning palms pressing them into her body, kneading the flesh, claw teasing the nipple so it might be sucked.

She screamed no. She screamed yes. She screamed for more.

She even screamed my name.

Right as I held up the monstrosity of my cock and lined it up where she was wet, aching, and owed. I told her I was going to fuck her for three days straight and offer no succor.

Not to my wife. Not to my queen. Not to the other half of me, the better half. The half that commanded such action by raising her hips and hissing when my hand went about her throat.

Milking my cock on that first thrust, she came.

She came, weeping with the joy of release.

And I fucked her.

No woman had ever been fucked the way my Pearl was fucked through those days, through those nights. Blood pouring from where I had slit my throat, I fed the monster who strangled my cock for more.

Deceitfully slight thing that she was, she worked to drain me dry in all ways.

I hurt her.

She hurt me.

I pleasured the Goddess.

She fed me the torment that made my sac draw tight.

That first time I came, the ground shook. The second time, bits of Paris began to crumble.

Soothing me with a soft touch, even as she rocked her hips over my exhausted form, Pearl asked me to leave the city in peace.

The words alone drew another bubbling of seed from my body, my thumb rolling her clit as I expanded almost to the point her pretty body might not take.

Weeping, she found another climax, sucking my offering deep.

And I knew, that was the one that would plant a baby that would grow in her womb.

A baby in which she would find joy.

EPILOGUE

VLADISLOV

"Why doesn't Mommy ever play with us?"

Because Mommy had been fucked senseless and was too tired to even feel when I carded my fingers through her hair. A pretty dark, waving lock I lifted off her pale cheek less than an hour before so sun might fall on her face as she slept.

Precious Pearl, always the napper, sleepy darling lass that she was.

"Mommy's body is busy growing your sister." Winking at the little hunter at my side, I said, "You've seen how big her belly is. She'd fall right over if she tried to run."

The kid laughed.

And adored me.

The feeling was mutual. So much so that my other son had shown up more than he was welcome, the jealous sot.

"I'm going to catch her something good to eat." And get all her kisses for it, no doubt.

Since she'd shorn him, washed him, taught him to speak, he was her world. *But I was her God.* Worshiped in the sun and in the moonlight.

Often, I had wept on her breast because the sensation of so true a love overtook me. I was her slave.

Which was why we now lived here, in the jungle, on an island where the world might let us enjoy what we were. Away from cities that quaked when my moods were free to roam. Away from Cathedrals she had a drive to purge.

And for sport, all the vampiric houses who wanted to survive my wife's reign dropped immortal treats into the jungle for our boy to snack on.

Down to his bones, that kid was a killer. Even I, the perfect predator, had not needed to teach Jasper how to stalk.

And Mommy didn't need to know that her occasional sip of morning blood had come from a screaming vampire her cute progeny had caught and dragged home especially for her.

He relished the screams, and he drained them into a teacup. Because it had to be fresh for Mommy.

Silver platter and all, Jasper would carry it in with a smile. "Pretty Mommy, look what I brought."

Pretty Mommy would glow.

On her silk sheets. In the palace I ordered built for her. Where live-in staff treated my erection as a castle.

Yes, that was a penis joke.

There were *civilized* parties. There was passion. There was a garden tended by the only human on the grounds. One strictly off-limits to our son. Not that he had not tried a time or two.

Jasper was a real devil.

And Pearl knew it… and loved him anyway.

He brought her trinkets, sneaking out of his room while we slept. Amputated fingers, juicy leg bones… three times he tried to impress her with severed heads.

Which even I did not know how he found.

Because, once again, we lived on an island where there was none but us and those I knew were delivered.

Jasper, my beautiful, sweet, angelic boy, was a world ender.

One time, I cracked a joke that he was the antichrist.

Pearl refused to speak to me for almost a week.

She loved and she knew, fawning over her begotten monster as if the human jawbone he dug up that afternoon were a treasure.

I mean, *I made it a treasure* when I had it dipped in gold and set with diamonds.

I don't think a more elated boy might have existed in the world when he saw it. When he presented it to his mommy.

Who kissed him for it and playfully put it on her head like a crown.

Unlike our son, I knew she cried after I'd taken the kid for a stroll.

I knew she fretted.

I knew that was why Yeshua sat at our table and smirked

at me at least once a month. That was why Pearl asked him to be her tutor so she might no longer be ignorant.

My son, *my obnoxious son*, agreed.

She bloomed under his tutelage.

She still didn't like him.

Who would? Her Jesus was a sanctimonious pain in the ass who refused to let a topic go, strangling the argument until there was nothing left but a carcass. He dumped way more dead things at my wife's feet than the boy she had taken from the pens.

The night Jesus dared offer her his wrist for dinner, I almost killed him. And that was not in the hypothetical sense.

He and I battled for a week, bouncing from landscape to landscape. We rent, we purged, we fought like the truly elemental things we were.

Until I heard my wife weeping from hundreds of thousands of miles away.

Hand around the throat of the *messiah*, I dropped him to the cracked dust and flapped my wings.

Jesus laughed, careless of the blood that dripped from his mouth. "You deserve everything that is coming to you."

Instantaneously, I found myself home, where women of my wife's acquaintance had gathered to cheer her out of the gloom that continued to upend civilization. Our son, Jasper, rested at her feet, his beautiful head on her knee—behaving himself in a way I had never witnessed.

Kicking free of his mother's embrace, he shot up… the babe stalking me as if I might serve as dinner. Fist in my face, he hissed. His first hiss. "Never leave her this way again."

His first hiss.

How could I not love this boy?

Eyes wet with unshed tears, Pearl looked up at me and welcomed me home. Proud as the queen she had grown to be.

What need had I of pride? Before the gathering of women there, I fell to my knees at her feet. Tired, focused, sorry. I prostrated where all those of rank in my presence would share the tale of the devil who loved an angel.

The angel who drank me down like wine after forgiveness was lavished on my form.

Dreaming of murder down the hall, Jasper smiled in his sleep. Diabolically entertaining, those dreams held my attention. I reveled in them.

Once, I even made the mistake of telling Pearl the best parts of our son's intentions.

The world would burn.

Terrified, she clung to me and begged that I might help him change.

Creatures didn't change, but I promised her I'd try.

That was the first night she felt our baby kick.

In one moment, her attention was on the vagrant. In the next, it was swallowed up by our baby.

Jasper was twice as enamored with what grew in Mommy's belly and fully in *love*.

Obsessed.

The ground shook, our *son* up to his normal tricks when he didn't get his way should she brush his incessant prodding off. He practically tore down our house when the fetus didn't respond to his songs.

"This is mine!" he would shout.

"She's not yours." Lips service I offered to appease his mother. Because I knew just as Pearl feared that *he truly believed she was his*.

"Mommy, eat more. She's hungry." Jasper would rub that burgeoning belly. "Oh, and so pretty! We will be the best of friends. Her favorite color will be orange, and she will slurp down liver just like I do."

Jasper was not allowed to be present at the birth, the scamp unable to contain his excitement and far too distracting to the mother working to deliver. It was only the two of us while our son sulked in the jungle.

I was the first to see or touch our daughter, Pearl exhausted yet smiling when I set the babe on her breast.

Strength. Endurance. Intention.

The little girl was her mother incarnate.

As if he knew the moment his sister had taken her first breath, Jasper appeared and asked to hold her, the babe covered in vernix, mucus, and blood. His arms outstretched as if the only thing that might quench his endless appetite was soon to be delivered. Pearl made him wait, as the baby was learning to suckle.

The boy might have sacked an entire community in his temper, but his mother called him forward when his tantrum grew outlandish. She let him lay a single touch on her head.

A babe he longed would be his *best friend*.

And I knew what coursed through his veins. I had suffered the same.

Kissing my soul, I knew joy with my wife at the beauty of our child. Jasper named the babe—Beryl.

And dared call her his.

Pearl didn't tolerate it, chastising our son. "She isn't yours. She belongs to herself."

His soul, the mirror of mine, begged. "You're wrong, Mommy."

Our pretty phenomenon, Jasper... an amazing child. A true devil.

Who coveted, who hunted, and whom I found more than once standing over the cradle of my daughter, stroking her cheek and speaking of battles fought long before they were born.

Five times he threatened to kill me if I dared deny him his due.

So I did what had to be done.

I cast Jasper out to wander, removing all memory of him from Pearl's mind so she might enjoy her daughter without the constant worry over her son—a deadly son who had been born to run wild and was growing all the more manic caged by an island too small to satiate his whims.

I told him this, honest when I dropped him at the doorstep of the Cathedral.

He might have only been a boy, but he had the memories of a man. Until he grew into his body and learned to control his urges, he was not to be permitted near his mother or his sister.

After all, eternity was a long time. What might a few dozen years mean in the scheme of things?

Jasper didn't wail. He didn't cling to me. Instead, he made an oath.

To bring the world down in flames if his soul was not returned to him. Tussling his hair, I was so proud, knowing exactly how he felt, and glad I hadn't had my Pearl in those hungry centuries where I wreaked havoc.

The kid would do well getting it out of his system. Then he might return to the flock, where he would find it was not his sister he was drawn to. It was the possibility for what might have been in her. Whoever he had lost and been reborn to find would not be delivered so easily.

He'd have to search for her. Suffer for her. Learn to control himself so as not to frighten her with his greatness.

And when he saw her, he'd know.

There was no need for him to project what he saw in Mommy and Daddy.

He'd know.

The boy nodded, threw a rude gesture my way, and told me he would get even with me for this, before turning his back and climbing the steps of his new home.

I believed him.

That would be fun!

"I'll come visit tomorrow! Be a good boy!"

Heaven help the woman he fell in love with.

Chuckling, I returned to my wife, smiling to find her in such peace. Babe in arms, she danced around our room, humming in the sunshine, all the constant niggling worry over her beautiful boy lifted away.

An indulgent smile paired with beautifully sparkling blue eyes. “Welcome home.”

Kissing the top of Pearl’s head, I brushed the back of a claw down the smiling cheek of my sweet little girl. And all was right in the world.

Thank you for reading THE RELIC.
I hope you enjoyed this decadent box set and the twisted tales within.

ADDISON CAIN

USA TODAY bestselling author and Amazon Top 25 bestselling author, Addison Cain's dark romance and smoldering paranormal suspense will leave you breathless. Obsessed antiheroes, heroines who stand fierce, heart-wrenching forbidden love, and a hint of violence in a kiss awaits.

Visit her website: addisoncain.com

Sign up for her newsletter.

Join Addison Cain's Fan Group.

amazon.com/Addison-Cain/e/B01E1LKWMY
bookbub.com/authors/addison-cain
goodreads.com/AddisonCain
facebook.com/AddisonlCain

ALSO BY ADDISON CAIN

Don't miss these exciting titles by Addison Cain!

Smoldering Standalones:

Swallow it Down

Strangeways

The Golden Line

Thirst

A Night by my Fire

The Alpha's Claim Series:

Born to be Bound

Born To Be Broken

Reborn

Stolen

Corrupted

Wren's Song Series:

Branded

Silenced

The Irdesi Empire Series:

Sigil

Sovereign

Cradle of Darkness Series:

Catacombs

Cathedral

The Relic

A Trick of the Light Duet:

A Taste of Shine

A Shot in the Dark

Historical Romance:

Dark Side of the Sun

Twisted Tales:

The White Queen

Immaculate

Omnibuses:

Shepherd (Alpha's Claim, Books 1-3)

A Court of Poison